SYNCING FORWARD

Syncing Forward
By W. Lawrence

Syncing Forward by W. Lawrence

Copyright © 2014 by W. Lawrence

All rights reserved. No part of this publication may be reproduced, stored in a retrieval system, or transmitted, in any form or by any means, electronic, mechanical, photocopying, recording or otherwise, without the prior permission of the publishers.

First printing

Published by W. Lawrence

Book cover design by Lasse Perälä

All characters and events in this book are a work of fiction. Any resemblance to actual events or persons, living or dead, is purely coincidental.

Print Book
ISBN-13: 978-0-9904861-0-7

Printed in the United States of America

http://syncingforward.com

This book is dedicated to my daughters.
I pray that you never have to grow up in the world I have written.

"The saddest aspect of life right now is that science gathers knowledge faster than society gathers wisdom."
—Isaac Asimov

— Part 1 —

One Bad Decision

Syncing Forward

Chapter 1

November 1, 2021

A video camera and three chairs occupied the otherwise empty office. I was partial to vacant rooms—they unsettled the guilty. No windows in my interviewing room. No tables on which to rest a drink. No motivational pictures sporting the virtues of teamwork to distract my subjects. I wanted nothing between me and the person who would step into that room. My office down the hall lay buried in a morass of thumb drives, paper files, empty crumpled remains of take-out lunches, and pictures of my family teetering on my cluttered desk. My interview room—my inner sanctum—became a veritable focus of purity for my career compared with my otherwise untidy workspace.

Dr. Rajesh Jotwani was our first subject of the day—one of seven employees at Innovo Pharmaceutical who had managed to steal more than two million dollars in assets as well as engage in highly unusual activity in the company's labs. I convinced my director that my choice to interview him first was based solely on how easily I reckoned he would roll over on the other six employees from my company. But truth be told, I wanted to get this one done and over with. You see, my pending interview of Rajesh happened to be a necessary refresher course in making friends at work.

In any sort of asset-protection position such as mine, your friend one day could be your thief the next. I went out of my way to distance myself from employees socially, but Rajesh ended up being so dang likeable that I couldn't help but hit it off with him. A dad like me, we enjoyed the same television shows, had the same sense of humor. And then he had to get himself mixed up in the largest, most scrutinized case I had ever worked on. This case wasn't just big, it was prison-time big for even the smaller players. Lord, I wished I hadn't known Rajesh at all.

The electronic lock chimed as my counterpart, David Tsai, stepped into the room and held open the door. Rajesh walked in next, looking completely out of his element. Forty-five years old with dark freckled skin, my friend was built so thin that he'd have to stand up twice to cast a shadow. He was a Pakistani Hindu who fled to the US in 2018 when the Pakistan-India conflict erupted. Rajesh became widowed during the religious slayings that broke out in Punjab and barely escaped with his young son, Arjan. A memory of my daughters laughing and playing with Arjan at his latest birthday party bubbled up to the surface. I popped it, trying to distance myself emotionally from the interview that would destroy his career.

"Dr. Jotwani, thank you for making the time to meet with me this morning." I greeted him formally with a handshake that he firmly returned.

"I'm the *doctor* today? How very official, Martin." Rajesh moved to give me a man-hug. However, my stiffened arm prevented him from closing with me. His expression transformed from comfortable familiarity to concerned confusion; Rajesh must have been thinking I had a backache or sunburn for not wanting to embrace. All the while I was preparing myself to crush him.

"Well, I'd be lying if I said you were here for a social call. I'm conducting a security investigation as directed by our corporate office. Please sit, Doctor." I watched Rajesh's friendly face melt away, revealing his worry hidden underneath. He uneasily settled into the chair that I placed directly in the middle of the room.

"Martin, I don't understand. Is this a joke?"

I shook my head. "I'd be a liar if I said it was."

His eyes flashed a split second of fear when my partner David Tsai closed the door and turned on the tripod-mounted video camera. Dave came off as an unassuming man—average height and terribly ordinary-looking. However, stories I had told Rajesh in the past of my

Syncing Forward

previous investigations must have come to mind; he knew that when we interviewed in pairs, the subject had reason to worry.

I picked armless chairs for subjects to sit in for a reason. No walls or cabinets or ledges to lean against. With nothing to rest his arms or feet upon, his limbs would fall somewhere, and wherever they landed, they would tell me more than the words he would utter. It is glibly peddled that human communication is 80 percent nonverbal, but the average person has no idea how true that is. Our words are vastly eclipsed by our facial expressions, body posture, hand gestures, foot positions, pulse rates, flushing, blushing, pupil dilations, tone inflections, and dozens of other tells. My friend Rajesh was about to find that out the hard way. My *friend*. Could I call him that anymore?

I sat four feet across from Rajesh, and Dave sat to my left nearest the camera as I began the interview. "It is currently zero-seven-hundred hours on November first, 2021. Senior Investigator Martin James, employee ID number 564882, conducting an interview at the Innovo Pharmaceutical campus in Paramus, New Jersey."

"Also present is Senior Investigator David Tsai on special assignment from the Innovo Pharmaceutical plant in San Francisco. Employee ID number 600101." We had prearranged that I would be the point man for the interviews, and while Dave had risen through our security department as the golden child, he was smart enough to recognize I interviewed stronger than he did.

Since we weren't law enforcement, our interviews in many respects had to be more effective than a police officer's. We couldn't force our employees to speak with us, only inform them that they risked their employment if they didn't. If a guilty person wanted to walk, the most we could do was terminate them and call the cops, but even then it meant proving our case before an arrest could take place. Soliciting a confession made everyone's job easier.

I continued. "Doctor, please state your name and employee ID number for the record."

"Dr. Rajesh Jotwani. Employee number 640197."

W Lawrence

"Your position here at Innovo Pharmaceutical?"

"I am a senior researcher for the Pharmacokinetic Department. Martin, can you tell me what this is about?" His eyes were darting between David and me.

"How long have you been in working in that position?"

Rajesh grew irritable in a hurry. "Martin, you know perfectly well I have been here for three years."

Dave interrupted. "Doctor. These questions are standard protocol for a security interview. If you can't get through these basic questions, it makes us wonder why you are so nervous."

Dave made several notes with the stylus on his computer pad, tapping the end of it in irritation. The black sheep son of Chinese nationals, David applied for citizenship to the United States around 2019 after the Chinese-Taiwanese Reunification. Dark straight hair cropped short, average height and on the thin side, always wearing a typical gray suit and bland tie, Dave would have been easy to lose in a crowd in Beijing or in his adopted home of San Francisco. Ten years my junior and single, and having only been with the company for five years, he had become legendary regarding his attention to detail. But I quickly found his patience lacking when it came to interviews, and when he broke into my questioning, I could hear the frustration in his voice.

Now, in the law enforcement world, police have all sorts of leverage they can put on a subject to get them to confess. Arrest powers, lying, prosecutorial bargaining—not to mention additional less-savory methods—all helped coax confessions from individuals. In the private sector, however, we were at a bit of a disadvantage when it came to soliciting the truth. Interrogations—or, as we called them in the private sector, "accusatory interviews"—were by their very nature a combative environment. Even honest people became hostile when asked a pointed question.

"Are you sure you did a proper pill count?"

"When you verify the box tally, do you log it every time?"

Syncing Forward

"Do you know Miguel Reyes outside of work?"

"How long have you been taking your prescription for back pain?"

Of course we had one major advantage in a corporation—one solitary statement that virtually everyone dreaded to hear:

"While your cooperation is voluntary, failure to answer my questions could result in your suspension or termination . . ."

With unemployment at over 12 percent, most people would sit through at least an hour of unpleasant questions with their job hanging by a thread, regardless of whether or not they were guilty. The difference was, innocent people had done nothing wrong, so their conduct came off natural and fluid. Guilty people, on the other hand, wanted to prove their lack of involvement in anything unsavory, and so their conduct in the interview became an act, a bluff, a sham. They wanted to appear ignorant of the very things they had been involved in, and would try all manner of behaviors to pretend to be who they weren't. So the game would begin.

I put up my hand to refocus our subject's attention on me. "Doctor, policy states your employment is contingent upon cooperating with the security department. Would you please answer our questions?"

He did. With his work visa potentially at risk, what choice did he have? Rajesh responded to every one of our questions with thoughtful, perturbed precision. It smacked of Interviewing 101, and to a person unfamiliar with the process, it could be unnerving. We knew all his answers from his personnel file, but that wasn't the point of asking. The questions were there to establish a baseline for him during the interview from which we could judge later responses that we may not be able to verify. I ran through a litany of questions: what were his old phone numbers, when had he applied for his visa, had he ever been arrested, what were the names of his colleagues, where had he been educated.

Set the tone—check. Establish a baseline—check. Develop a rapport— Well, that was the easy part, since Rajesh and I knew each other well to begin with. There was no putting off the meaty questions. I began questioning him about unauthorized tests he had run, equipment he had requested that vanished before it reached Innovo's labs, late hours he had worked with no reported research conducted or logged.

With each innuendo and veiled accusation, Rajesh Jotwani shrank further back into his chair. His knees drew together, and his hands were folded tightly on his lap as if he were protecting his groin. Men often assumed this position when they felt threatened, so I knew my questions were getting to him. A half hour later Rajesh's dark skin had transformed to a raspberry-chocolate color, and his thin mustache stretched when he pulled his lips tight.

"Why would I take hundreds of thousands of dollars in equipment?" His voice became raised but pitchy, and the timing of his gestures was off. Rajesh postured and deflected. Behind the veil of anger hung legitimate fear, and he distanced himself from his own actions—but it wasn't working. "I have unlimited access to these analyzers. Why would I not simply use them here? I could easily sign off on reports, change the test counts, and you would be none the wiser."

I reached into my briefcase, grabbed the file I had been slaving away at for three months, and tossed it to the ground between us. The slap of the heavy paper file reverberated in the room, and the doctor jumped a little from the sound. "You mean those reports? You mean the reagent inventory supply requests? You mean the fuel cell depletion reports? You mean that stack with your name on it? You must think I'm dumber than a day-old pig."

"This is preposterous, Martin!" he declared, but his breathing grew heavy, and he was clearly caught off guard that we had done so much homework. His Indian accent had grown thicker as the interview progressed, but his flawless English never degraded. "You are falsely accusing me of wrongdoing—"

I cut him off. "What? You betray my trust and tell me I am falsely accusing you? Dr. Jotwani, you didn't think I would do my homework before bringing you into this room? I already know you've been working with some of my security officers. I already know about Margaret Finch and Gan Jiāng and the other doctors . . ."

With every snippet of information I dropped, I watched Rajesh Jotwani slowly come apart. I wouldn't give him everything, but I had to make him believe I could know just about anything. The frustrating aspect of all this was I didn't really know the whole truth anyway. Sure, we figured out the missing equipment and the unauthorized tests. Sure, we managed to tie in several other employees. But there were so many questions that remained unanswered, questions my director, Gavin Thomason, wanted answers to.

The doctor was correct in saying it made no sense to steal any of these assets; they had no black-market value, and no legitimate laboratory would buy highly sensitive serialized equipment from anyone other than the manufacturer. The materials they were working with were expensive, but none of it was rated toxic or dangerous. And the tests? This was no case of industrial espionage in which a competitor would try to steal our research. Rajesh and the other scientists were *doing* research, but on what, we had no clue.

Rajesh's posture began to fail, his face drew down, his objections softened. I could see the stress lines in his throat when I brought up the missing analyzers. Some part of this forty-four-year-old man remained resolute, still stubbornly protecting one name I wanted to hear.

"Well, *Mister* James"—he emphasized the honorific in retaliation for me ignoring our previous relationship—"you seem to have all the answers. Why do you need me here?"

"Innovo Pharmaceutical—our company— still respects its employees enough to get their side of the story. Maybe if you were to finally 'fess up and admit your part in all this, we could come to some agreement on how to proceed." It killed me inside that I had to feed him this load of crap. Innovo could have cared less about Rajesh the moment I discovered his dubious activities. They wanted the analyzers back; they wanted the mysterious research he was doing. And when we wrapped this case up, there would be little anyone could do to save Rajesh from civil and criminal prosecution, or even deportation.

"Why would I admit to such a thing?" he asked innocently, but we had clearly beaten him down. His eyes were shifting back and forth, and he looked as if he might bolt. I had to get him to admit something. Even though I knew he lied, anyone watching the video would see a man denying everything. And his question was one I didn't have an answer for.

"Maybe you did it for money? Revenge on the company? Maybe you're working with a competitor? Maybe just to see if you could do it?" When presented with a list like that, usually a subject would respond to something with a hint of body language. There were only so many motivators for lying, and I had tried all the common ones, but Rajesh Jotwani showed no indicators. When he didn't respond to those, I tried something out of the box. "Maybe because you think you're justified?"

That's when his pupils dilated and his eyes shone in surprise for a fraction of a second. So, Rajesh felt justified in his actions.

Now, all people exhibit seven basic facial expressions: surprise, contempt, sadness, and so on. These expressions are the same for everybody, from Vietnamese executives to Peruvian laborers to New Guinean natives. Stranger still is that human beings will frequently flash these expressions before their brain has a chance to tell their face that the joke they are listening to isn't appropriate and they shouldn't laugh, or that they shouldn't appear frustrated while the camera is rolling, or that their lie was discovered and they shouldn't act surprised. These expressions told me a lot about how people truly felt when they were doing their best to hide something.

The picture of the man I knew from my investigation started to knit together with the picture of my friend I had known for three years. Rajesh Jotwani came off as a highly ethical man. We spoke about concepts of right and wrong frequently, and I knew the honest way he raised his son reflected his personal values. It was the reason I was so surprised, and so disappointed, when I found him stealing from our company. But it seemed Rajesh had a strong motivator, something that allowed him to rationalize violating his own convictions.

Frequently he spoke of attending symposiums and conferences related to science and ethics. When he brought up the topic with me, I found it all very highbrow and out of my area of expertise; after all, I worked as an investigator, not a scientist. I enjoyed debating the best soccer players or the merits of first-time-offender programs. His involvement had to be related to his ethics concerns, but I didn't know how.

"Rajesh—" I caught myself and corrected. "Dr. Jotwani, is there something Innovo is involved in that you feel is unethical in some way?"

He looked away and shook his head. "No. It's nothing like that."

That came out as an unintentional confession, although I doubted my friend knew he'd made it. There wasn't enough for an arrest or even disciplinary action from our company, but there was an opening I stood ready to exploit. "Well, if it's *nothing like that*, what is it like then?"

Rajesh looked at David and then back to me. He said, "Martin, do you remember us having lunch in the cafeteria many months back? I was talking about the IEEE conference I went to?"

"Vaguely. Remind me again."

"We spoke of some of the new genetically modified foods hitting the market. Do you remember that?"

I racked my brain. "Kinda. Although, I have to be honest—I wasn't exactly keeping pace with you that day."

"I asked if you considered that we may have taken our technology past our understanding. You see, we are building a world in which most people don't appreciate the technology we use, and the people who develop it are not even asking why we need to improve upon it."

Dave tried to bring the odd comments back around to the thefts at our company. "Does that include Innovo research?"

"Of course it does, but that doesn't matter, don't you see? This isn't about Innovo!" Dr. Jotwani exploded. "It's about what is the right thing to do!"

"And what is that? What is the right thing to do?" David asked.

Rajesh shifted his terrified gaze back at me. "Martin, please. Don't do this. I can't protect you."

It didn't sound like a threat, but it rubbed me as menacing nonetheless. Dave wrote with his stylus on his tablet, a message from him to me that appeared on my tablet instantly. We used this simple app—silent communication—so that we could exchange anything of interest without speaking. In his choppy printing the message read "WTH does that mean?"

I wrote back, "I dunno," and underscored my words.

Rajesh stared at the door now. Would he bolt? Did he just want our conversation to end? I had never seen my friend like this; in fact, rarely I saw any interviewee act in this manner. His face looked like the face of the female dockworker I helped last year whose ex-husband stalked her at work.

"Dr. Jotwani," I said, pressing, "tell us what is going on. What do you mean you can't protect us? If this is part of some organized crime—"

"No."

"—or gang activity—"

"No."

"—then you've got to tell us."

David slipped his question in between Rajesh and me talking over each other. "Is this related to Doctor Bruchmuller's research?"

Rajesh stopped breathing and looked right at David for a long while, his mouth slightly open as if the words had stalled on his tongue.

Syncing Forward

This was the moment of contemplation when a subject made his final decision to confess or deny.

When he finally spoke, he enunciated very carefully. "Please, Martin. I'm asking one last time as your friend. Let it go. You don't understand."

The interview fizzled out, and we were left with nothing. Nothing except Rajesh wordlessly implicating Dr. Dieterich Bruchmuller.

Chapter 2

We escorted Rajesh Jotwani to an office we called the holding room and put a security officer outside the door. I had three such rooms, all used to keep employees separated during investigations. The way things were going, we might need them all. Denial after denial—I knew Rajesh, and he wasn't some streetwise thug stealing pain meds off our dock. Something or someone had scared him.

Dave ran his hand across his hair nervously, looking at the case files on his tablet as he paced. "That sounded like a threat in there. Didn't it sound like a threat to you?"

"Yeah," I answered flatly.

"I thought you said you could crack him?"

"I did crack him, I just didn't break him. Something big is holding Rajesh back from telling the truth, Dave. He's legitimately concerned."

"*He's* concerned?" He thumped his chest with his palm. "*I'm* concerned! We have to tell Gavin Thomason about this."

"Tell him what? That we can't finish the interviews because we *think* we *might* have been threatened? You know what he's going to say." Truthfully, my motivation wasn't related to my director at all. A Texas-sized bonus rode on solving this case, but Innovo didn't pay big bonuses to their security personnel for half-baked investigations and almost-admissions. They wanted the whole pie.

Dave took a deep breath. "Okay, Martin, let's take him at his word for a moment. If it's not organized crime and it's not gang related, then the only option left is—"

"Don't say it!" I warned.

"—terrorism," he finished.

Growing up, terrorist attacks were atrocities that took place in other countries, but 9/11 changed all that. And as I grew up and had

Syncing Forward

two kids of my own, the frequency of attacks in the United States grew and grew, with the last four years being the worst. Bombings, slayings, shootings, kidnappings. They were so common in 2021 that if we were to memorialize the day of each attack, we would be mourning three months out of the year. But nobody suspected our seven suspects were involved in terrorism in any way. Not me. Not our director. Nobody. Nobody except David Tsai.

"Dang it, Dave, we've been over this before."

"Then let's run through the list again. I don't feel like getting this one wrong, Martin."

I sighed, frustrated. "Fine. But we don't have a lot of time." Dave pulled up the data file issued by the Department of Homeland Security and started rattling off every active terrorist group on the list. "Okay, let's start from the top, shall we? Islamic Brotherhood?"

"Nope," I responded. "Dr. Kamani is Muslim, but two of our subjects are Hindu, and Albert Vies is a Mormon. You can cut out all the Islamic fundamentalist groups while you're at it."

"Well, that eliminates five different IF groups operating stateside. Uh, next on the list is Texan Separatists."

"We're not in Texas or a bordering state. Next."

"Cemanahuaca Conquistadores?"

"They don't trust non-Hispanics, and we're way out of their zone. Next."

"American National Socialists?"

"They don't trust nonwhites. Next."

"Black Panthers?"

"Come on, Dave. Do you see any black people on the suspect list? Next!"

"Hey, I'm just reading down the list, Martin. Don't be an ass! Moving on . . . New Mexican Drug Cartel?"

"Our guys didn't steal any schedule-two narcs. And they had plenty of access. They're out. Next."

"Heartland Isolationists?"

"Never operate east of the Mississippi. Next."

"Students for a Democratic Society?"

"God no. A bunch of mental midgets—I don't even know why they're on that list. Next."

"Tea Partiers?"

"They don't steal from corporations. They're antigovernment. And do you see my paranoid brother Jacob here? Next."

"Occupiers."

"Maybe on stealing the equipment. Definitely not on the lab research. Next!"

"Animal Liberation Front?"

"Normally I would say yes. But what about Dr. Bruchmuller? Bruchmuller and Kamani were definitely doing animal testing in the PK lab. If we're right about him orchestrating everything, then that eliminates ALF as suspects."

We polished off the terrorism watch list, and I felt the stiffness in my neck tightening up further. I snuck a look at the camera feed from the holding room on my tablet. The view looked down at Rajesh Jotwani's thinning hair as he fidgeted in his chair. Of course, he wasn't the only one fidgeting. Dave looked ready to crawl out of his skin.

"Who are these people?" he asked himself aloud.

That was the question we had been asking for months. Seven individuals from entirely different backgrounds in different departments all working in concert, and the only thing they had in common happened to be their employment at our company. Six of them had been identified as either stealing equipment or making unauthorized use of our facilities. The seventh was the director of the pharmacokinetic laboratory, Dr. Bruchmuller.

Syncing Forward

Dave poked at the list. "You know this terrorist watch list is far from comprehensive."

"I think you're freaking out over nothing," I told him.

He turned and faced me. "Damn it, Martin, something is wrong! Can't you feel it? He threatened you in there, and you're fine with that?"

"Why are you so taking him so seriously?"

"Why are you so quick to dismiss him?"

I knew how concerned Dave felt. I could feel it myself—a pang in my gut that told me the puzzle was much bigger than any of us expected. And he knew I shared his concerns, despite my stubbornness in ignoring them. But what was I going to tell my colleague? That I didn't want to lose my shot at the bonus money for completing the investigation? That my wife's car needed a new radiator, and my water heater barely worked? That we had credit card bills that were going up and not down? That my elder daughter, Amara, was on the verge of getting kicked out of school, and we needed the money to send her to private school? Yeah, that wasn't going to go over well.

The disagreement lingered in the air until David broke the silence and pulled up some very familiar video on his tablet. "Well, whenever we bring Bruchmuller in, we're going to have to bring up the rat experiments he was involved in." He tossed the tablet on my lap, and I barely caught it. The captured video my coworker referred to was barely worth mentioning, but it remained one of the few data points we had for Bruchmuller. I grunted in agreement while massaging the tension out of my forehead.

As much as I didn't want to admit it, Rajesh Jotwani's warning was still fresh in my mind. I couldn't help but wonder what we were missing, and the best way I knew how to find answers was to ask. I had Dave prep the camera in the interview room for Bruchmuller while I went and checked on Rajesh in the holding office.

I brought him a cup of tea and gave him an opportunity to revise his statement. Rajesh declined. "How long do I have to wait here?" Truth was he could walk out anytime he wanted—we had no arrest powers. The police would never detain him without us making a case, and that took time. I didn't disclose that tidbit though.

Dang, this was awkward. Rajesh's son sat in school, expecting his dad to pick him up in a few hours, ignorant that a caseworker from the state would be his ride to a new home. But as much as I hated watching my friend's life destroyed, I couldn't let this go even if I wanted to. I answered, "It won't be long,"

I only had seven security officers on duty, and two of them were involved in the thefts, maybe more. I wasn't naive enough to think we had netted everybody—I knew there was a possibility of other accomplices. I had pulled one of my new hires—Jim Reynolds—from his training schedule and posted him in front of the holding room's door. The one thing I could count on was him being wholly unconnected to the thefts. He was green, but it didn't take much talent to stand in front of a door.

We were about to call Bruchmuller for his interview, when my cell phone rang. The Franklin Elementary School vice principal's face appeared in the four-inch screen with a look that spelled trouble. "Hello, Mr. James, sorry to trouble you at work again . . ."

"Hello, Mrs. Pagliotta. I'm in the middle—" I stopped, seeing her unease. "It's . . . it's okay. What did Amara do this time?" I set my phone next to my tablet, and the video phone connection automatically transferred the woman's image from one device to the other. The video seemed to highlight the gray in her roots and the stress lines around her mouth as she picked her words carefully.

"Well, Amara had another episode in class today," she began. Episode? I couldn't stand the doublespeak and just wished she would say what had really happened. "Some boys were roughhousing, and they knocked her tablet over. There is a little crack in the display, but it's working fine. However, Amara isn't coping well. She said some rather unkind things to Mrs. Bloom and then went into a crying fit. She's up here in the nurse's office so she won't continue to disrupt the class. We tried calling your wife, but it went straight to voice mail. Did you want to talk with Amara?"

At my nod, she put me on hold. The school's logo replaced her head in the center of my screen as I waited to talk with my child. I sighed, frustrated that my wife hadn't answered her blasted phone—she knew today was going to be a rough one for me. Amara was nine years old and well past her peers academically. She had skipped a grade and was pulling straight A's in classrooms filled with kids a year older than she. She was taking online courses to keep herself challenged. But Amara was beyond difficult to deal with.

The tablet's screen lit up again, this time showing me the nurse's office and the back of Amara's head. Her wild dark curly hair draped down around her face, hiding her mixed Hispanic features from me. I heard a woman's voice saying something about the phone, and Amara screamed, "I don't care!"

"Amara. Amara. Amara!" She stopped protesting and froze. I lowered my tone. "Amara, please, look at me."

She turned toward the screen and snapped, "What?"

"Kiddo. You need to relax. It's okay. Mrs. Pagliotta told me what happened. We can fix your computer. It's no big d—"

"I hate this class, and I hate this school! They're a bunch of stupid jerks getting taught by a stupider teacher!" The rant went on and on about how two boys were fighting and knocked over her desk and everything on it, but then her teacher sent *her* to the office. It took a little coaxing, but Amara admitted that when the boys weren't punished, Amara called Mrs. Bloom "a pathetic loser," which landed her in trouble.

"Look what they did, Daddy!" She held up her tablet to the camera and pointed at the crack in the display. It couldn't have been bigger than her fingernail, but she rubbed it as if it were a wound on her body.

David walked into my office and caught my eye. "Bruchmuller's ready and waiting," he whispered. I held up two fingers, and he ducked out and closed the door.

I turned my attention back to my daughter. "Amara, listen, sweetheart. You know I love you so much, but you can't go off half-cocked with your teachers. I know you're mad at those boys for breaking your computer, and they probably should be punished. With that said, you need to get yourself together and apologize to Mrs. Bloom."

She kept rubbing the crack obsessively as if trying to scrub it away. "Can't I just go home? I want to go home. Please, Daddy, I don't want to go back in there."

"Honey, I can't pick you up. I've got a big case going on. You've got to deal with this."

"Please . . ."

"Listen, I've got to go back to work. I love you, kid."

Her voice turned soft and defeated. "Daddy, the nurse said I wouldn't be so upset if I took this medicine they give to kids. I don't want it, though."

I steamed. They had been bullying us to get Amara on meds for a year now. "Don't take anything they give you. I'll deal with the nurse."

"Daddy, is there something wrong with me?" Amara whimpered.

Did she know how close she was to being kicked out of school? Did she know that even her own mother wanted to medicate her? Did she know that her mother and I fought tooth and nail with each other about sending her to counseling? I despised the fact that I couldn't be there to give her a hug, to console her.

"No, sweetheart. Absolutely not." I kissed my fingertips and touched them to the screen. "The only thing wrong with you is that you are too smart for your own good."

Syncing Forward

"I love you, Daddy." A smile crept to my daughter's face. "I'll *try* to apologize."

I transferred back to the vice principal. It took some convincing, but she agreed to defer any punishment for my kid until we had a chance to meet. Again.

Mrs. Pagliotta warned me once again. "I need to inform you that continued infractions from Amara could end up in her expulsion."

"I'm sorry, ma'am. I will deal with her." I was desperate to take a parting shot before I hung up. "Tell your damned nurse to stop pushing drugs on my kid," I wanted to yell. Mrs. Pagliotta had to be the last school official on my side, though. The snarky comment would have to wait. "Thanks again for keeping me in the loop."

I pressed my lips together and hit the Disconnect button.

Dave barged into my office again. "Okay, are we doing this or not?"

"Sorry." I stood up. "That was an important call."

"More important than this case?"

"Lay off, Dave. It was Amara. Again." I sighed.

He raised an eyebrow, but he knew enough about the arguments Miranda and I were having regarding Amara not to say a word. I grabbed the files and my tablet and walked down the hallway to the interview room, peeking in on Rajesh as I went. My friend sat alone at the tiny desk still, hands folded in front of him. He looked up at me briefly before lowering his gaze back to his fidgeting thumbs. Closing the door, I nodded at Jim Reynolds. "Alert us if there are any issues." It was time to get answers.

I opened the door to my interviewing room. Dr. Dieterich Lenhart Bruchmuller sat across from my seat, his white lab coat draped down around the interview chair. His sun-spotted hands were folded comfortably on his lap and his posture excellent, no doubt from years as a German military officer in the Bundeswehr. The doctor smiled broadly when I entered the room, but his insincerity escaped through his eyes. Before my butt sank into my chair, I knew that Dieterich was anything but happy to be in the room with me.

The doctor and I had never spoken before. It was typically only an employee's wrongdoing that would cause his career to overlap with mine. Rajesh Jotwani was the exception and Bruchmuller was the rule.

"Dr. Bruchmuller, thank you for making the time to meet with me this morning." I greeted him with a handshake that he confidently returned.

"Thank you, Mr. James, although I was a bit surprised to find myself called up here. We have quite a few issues down in the lab that require my attendance."

I hid a smirk. I'd bet he was a bit surprised. We had done a very quiet job poking around, and Rajesh's interview was the first time we had spoken to anyone directly. Bruchmuller's chin turned up and purpose was solid. His English came across crisp, even though he carried a thick Germanic accent.

"Well, no doubt the message you received from our director, Mr. Thomason, indicated that this is a serious matter and clarified the need for your full cooperation. Besides, I'm sure your technicians are more than capable of being out from under your wing for an hour or two."

Dave turned on the camera while Bruchmuller's eyes tracked my partner from the tripod to the empty chair. I watched his body stiffen a smidge. As Dave picked up his tablet, I went through our typical preamble: date, time, location. "For the record, please state your name."

"Doctor Dieterich Lenhart Bruchmuller."

"Your position here at Innovo Pharmaceutical?"

"I'm the North American director of the pharmacokinetic laboratory."

"How long have you been working in that position?"

"Eight years in PK. And sixteen years for the company."

Syncing Forward

His smile melted fast, and I wanted to poke at him to test his irritability. "And where did you work prior to Innovo Pharmaceutical, Mr. Bruchmuller?"

His eyes flashed. "It's *Doctor* Bruchmuller, and surely you didn't call me all the way up here to confirm my résumé?"

Unreasonable resistance at the beginning of an interview meant a person was guilty 63 percent of the time. I ran through a litany of questions: his old phone numbers, when he applied for dual citizenship, had he ever been arrested, where he was educated, the names of his colleagues. In the middle of a list of names I dropped "Dr. Jotwani" and spotted a full half-second pause before Bruchmuller said that he and Rajesh attended symposiums together.

"What type of symposiums have the two of you attended?"

"I can't imagine how this is relevant to any investigation you would be conducting, Mr. James."

My partner broke into the interview. "These symposiums, Doctor. Would you say that they are highly political?" The question shocked me. I knew where Dave wanted to go with that line of questioning, but even if right about the terrorism angle —which he wasn't—it was too soon to bring it up. Motivation was the last thing we needed from this man; the first thing was a confession.

If Bruchmuller had been looking at me, he might have picked up on my anger. Instead he answered, "The presentations and discussions revolve primarily around ethics. Politics is merely an extension of a people's ethical views, wouldn't you agree?"

I redirected the question to family to help develop our rapport. "And you have one grandson, correct?"

As I anticipated, he looked surprised by the question and softened slightly. "Yes. Yes I do. He is seven."

"Ah, seven," I couldn't help but grin. "It's a good age."

"Then you have children of your own, Mr. James?"

"No," I lied, "no kids. I just have nieces and nephews around that age." Truth was my younger daughter Bella was seven and my treasure—my sweet, huggable girl. *Yes, Doctor, let's swap pictures of kids while you're writing out your confession letter and waiting for the authorities.* A good interview rapport didn't mean he needed to know about my personal life.

"Ah, that's a shame." He shook his head. "But perhaps for the best. This is a difficult world for children to grow up in. Things seem to be falling apart. Murders, riots, corruption . . ."

"Theft," I added.

"Yes, theft too. People stealing, living off the scraps from a decaying society. People are becoming desperate, driven to make difficult choices. It scares me to think of what my grandson might be forced to face as the world spirals into disorder."

"There's no 'might' about it. We all have to play the hand we're dealt," I responded.

He said nothing.

The battery of questions we had prearranged went easily enough. Questions constructed with the intent of committing Bruchmuller to a specific set of answers so that if he answered differently later, we could accuse him of lying and set him off-balance. So the doctor continued with his answers, and we continued with our questions until Dave put up his hand.

Dave glanced at his tablet. "Dr. Bruchmuller, we will need to take a small break. Will you excuse us, please?"

Hiding my consternation from the doctor was important, but I was unsure of how well I performed. The two of us left him behind with the camera still running. From experience I knew the room was soundproof from both directions, and I snapped at Dave as soon as the door shut. "What the hell is going on?"

He didn't wait for me, just strode briskly down the hall. "Dr. Jotwani just walked out."

"I thought you were watching him on the camera!"

Syncing Forward

"I was watching him! I watched him get up and walk out."

"Why didn't Jim stop him?"

"I don't know."

I followed him, both of us at a trot. We discovered the holding room empty and nothing left of Rajesh except sweaty marks on the desk where his hands had been folded. Our security officer had gone missing too.

I called Jim on his cell, and he picked up right away, "Yes, Mr. James. What can I do for you?"

"Jim, where the hell are you? You're supposed to be watching our subject."

He stopped and thought before he answered, "Uh, Mister James, didn't you tell me to go back to my training schedule?"

"Who told you that? I never did."

"Al did. He took over my post outside the office."

"Al told you? Jim! I asked *you* to be on that post, not Al." Albert Vies had worked for me for six years. A bulky man in his fifties with fading, stretched tattoos along his neck. The only interesting quality about Al was he made the list as one of the seven employees we were investigating. We knew he had helped load at least one of the stolen analyzers onto a cargo van and had falsified the manifest, to boot, but Jim Reynolds couldn't have known. I made a motion to Dave to go back and make sure Bruchmuller wasn't flying the coop too.

"Jim, do me a favor. Tell nobody what you are doing. I want you to go to the front gate and see if Dr. Jotwani has left. If he tries to leave, call me."

"Go there now?"

"Jim, I want you there three minutes ago. Move." I hung up and rubbed my face hard with both hands, to try to erase the anger from my expression. I still had a job to do, and good interviewing meant an outstanding poker face. As I rounded the corner, I found

Dave standing by the door; Bruchmuller still sat waiting for us, thank God.

One of us had to finish the interview with Bruchmuller solo. The other had to track down Albert Vies and Rajesh Jotwani, and that meant scouring three million square feet of laboratories, warehouses, administrative offices, and manufacturing stations spread out over the vast Innovo Pharmaceutical campus—the equivalent of searching more than fifty football fields.

I summed up our situation. "We can't involve the other guards, and Jim Reynolds is about as useful as a back pocket on a T-shirt."

"I told you we needed another investigator to run the interviews," Dave reminded me.

Yeah, and split the bonus even more? This case had me getting used to ignoring my inner voice. "Can you go to the main entrance?"

"Yeah. I'll check the cameras from the front gate. It's the only way off the campus, so if they try to leave, I can try to talk them out of it, or call the police if they give me a hard time. Keep your tablet on, and I'll message you if anything comes up. You okay running the interview solo?"

I hesitated. I wasn't sure why, but I did. Interviews were second nature for me, but something about this particular investigation stank, and I couldn't get over the feeling that I failed to see the bigger picture.

"Hey, I'm fine with calling the cops right now," Dave offered.

"Nah, I'll be fine. I've done plenty of solo interviews. You go."

Dave trotted off. I took several deep breaths to steady myself and then sauntered back into the interview room. The doctor's arm turned as if he had pocketed something, and his eyes were large in surprise.

"Dr. Bruchmuller, were you just using your phone?"

"No, not at all."

"Are you sure?"

"Are you accusing me of lying?"

Syncing Forward

The break in our dialogue felt like a chess game. Did I force the phone issue? He might have sent a crucial message off to one of the conspirators, in which case I could exploit the information. Then again, he might have simply checked what time it was, in which case I looked desperate for information. I decided to double back to the phone later.

Bruchmuller looked at the empty chair next to mine. "Should we wait for Mr. Tsai to return before we continue?"

I hadn't lived in the South for many years, but I could still lay it on thick if I wanted to. I gave the good doctor a half-cocked Southern smile and cracked, "Nah, I like to put my feet up." I didn't want to tell him Dave was looking for Bruchmuller's fleeing accomplices. Thinking about all that was just going to ruin my concentration, and I had to trust my partner could do the job.

He chuckled lightly and then gestured at my camera. "Well, let us continue then."

Almost ten minutes of direct questions went by in which Bruchmuller outright lied. He was good, I had to admit. If not for Rajesh's interview earlier, I might have had doubts, but knowing Bruchmuller lied allowed me to see through his deceit, and each lie taught me more about his dominant pantomimes.

He stared at my corporate badge that dangled from its lanyard around my neck, half-listening to my questions. "Tell me, Mr. James, what does the *H* stand for?"

I blinked. "Come again?"

"On your badge, your name reads 'Martin H. James.' What does the *H* stand for?"

He must have been trying to derail me. "Dr. Bruchmuller, I don't see the relevance of my middle name to this interview. What is important is your answer as to why you signed off on a dozen reports that you knew to be either falsified or incorrect."

"Is it Harold? Hamilton? Hancock, perhaps?"

W Lawrence

I pulled my chair forward, drawing closer to his personal space. "Dr. Bruchmuller, are you refusing to answer me? I hope you realize that not answering my questions is considered a failure to cooperate, which can lead to disciplinary action by Innovo." I intended to get him back on track, but the truth of the matter was I could not understand his game. A normal person would not go on such a befuddling tangent during an interview.

"My apologies, Mr. James. I'm willing to cooperate, of course. It is just that my curiosity often gets the best of me. You see, I spent a great deal of my younger years studying onomastics—names and their origins and meanings. Sometimes a name is just a fancy of creative parents, but other times names tell me a great deal about a person. Your first name, Martin, for instance, is derived from Mars, the god of war. A man who relishes conflict—"

"Doctor, you should be less concerned with my name and more concerned with my title. I am a senior investigator for this corporation, and your stonewalling me is going to accomplish nothing. I'm giving you an opportunity to tell me your side of the story, but if you aren't interested, I am sure the authorities will be fascinated with what's been going on here."

"So you haven't contacted the authorities?" He raised a lone eyebrow. The question had been posed by other employees in the past, but there was something about how he asked it that seemed awry. The tone of his voice, the calculating stare—a little voice inside told me to end the interview right then and there.

I ignored it.

I didn't want to explain that the authorities would be more inclined to press criminal charges with Bruchmuller's confession in hand. "No, I have not contacted the authorities. That's not how we operate. Innovo has a policy of discussing these matters first with employees. Even when there has been some sort of wrongdoing, we'd prefer to avoid the bad press. It hurts the price of our stock, you see."

It was partially true that the company liked to avoid high-profile cases getting out to the public, but that didn't change the fact that we pressed charges in virtually all our cases. I reasoned that if Bruchmuller felt he could walk away from the table without being arrested, he might be inclined to speak the truth. It was a standard direction we took with subjects, and I habitually used the same line in most of my interviews.

"That's very comforting," he said slowly.

My tablet buzzed lightly, and I snuck a peek at the message from Dave.

Can't find Jotwani or Vies. Didn't pass gate so have to be on campus.

I held my thumbs above the pad to text a message back, when worse news came across.

All of our subjects are missing. Word must be out. Checking vid now. Crap crap crap!

The pause in the interview lasted longer than it should have, and I turned my attention back on the one man we actually could keep tabs on. "Dr. Bruchmuller, how often do you review the DL-12 quality reports from your department?"

"It is standard protocol for all directors to review their DL-12s daily."

"I know the standard protocol. I asked you how often *you* review them."

"Daily," he grumbled. He was lying again. I knew that most directors fell short on this requirement. *Yeah, keep lying, Doc. Keep digging your hole deeper.*

"And how often do you check the PK lab's asset report?"

"Monthly, as required. Surely you don't think I had anything to do with the losses of equipment! It was I who notified your security director that there was equipment missing in the first place."

"Yes you did report the losses, *after* your department failed an audit. One could say that you filed the reports because you were required to."

He was aggravated now, and it didn't take a trained interviewer to know it. "I don't like what you are insinuating, Mr. James. How would I take a seventy-five-pound optiprobe out of this facility, let alone why?"

"One man couldn't do that, I agree. Something like that would require help. A lot of help."

"Does Director Thomason know you are accusing a senior researcher of the company of stealing?"

Posturing. Seventy-one percent of respondents who use their position or stature to guard themselves are guilty.

I inched my chair slightly forward again, bringing it to the edge of his comfort zone. "Director Thomason is fully briefed on this case and has complete confidence in our investigation."

"I don't like where you are taking this, Mr. James."

"I'd like to see your phone, if you don't mind, Doctor."

"I think I do mind. I don't see how it is relevant."

Another message caused my tablet to vibrate in my palms. Dave, no doubt, but I dared not answer him. This pivotal part of the interview required focus, and I needed Bruchmuller to confess to something . . . anything. He needed to think that I knew more than I truly did. I stared straight ahead, doing my best to maintain a confident demeanor.

"How well do you know Albert Vies, Doctor?"

"I want to speak with my attorney," Bruchmuller said pointedly, his gaze fixed hard upon me.

The words were the final blow in a losing bout. I was required by company policy to end the interview when an employee asked for a lawyer. Even though he was guilty as sin, even though he remained the only subject who hadn't vanished on us.

At that point I should have let it go, but I didn't. It might have been my pride that took over, driving me to single-handedly solve the case. It might have been the fantastic company bonus that sat at the

Syncing Forward

end of the rainbow or the stacking bills at home or just the frustration of coming so far and falling short. Whatever it was, I believed if I could push him only a tiny bit more, I could convince him to confess. One question more . . .

"Tell me about the rat."

It was as benign a statement as could be uttered, and yet it was as if I had driven an adrenaline needle into his heart. He stared at me with a look that I had only seen a handful of times in my life, and I knew at that moment I had made a grave error.

One second. Two seconds. Three seconds. Four. My subject went from immobile to a blur of movement so fast that I didn't have time to react. Bruchmuller might have been nearly twenty years my senior, but he jumped out of the interview chair like a leopard and closed the few feet between us in a blink. I started to get up, but he pushed me back down into my seat. The momentum drove my body weight onto the back legs of the chair, and I tipped backward. Dieterich reached down and grabbed my ankles as my legs went up, accelerating my movement, flipping me flat on my back, and rapping my skull against the hard floor.

I rolled off the chair and onto my hands and knees, my rear end to the man assaulting me. Looking back, I managed to make out the looming figure of Dr. Bruchmuller as he solidly kicked me in the groin. I landed facedown on the cool tile. My guts ached, and I balled up in a fetal position, my hands shielding my crotch as my eyes instinctively shut. When they opened, I made out Bruchmuller as he grabbed the camera tripod, gripped it tightly in both hands, and swung it down hard at me. The camera mount caught me squarely on the side of the head. A second blow struck me as I spiraled into darkness.

Chapter 3

My own words still echoed in my ears: *"Tell me about the rat."* Five words followed by the crunching of the camera shell as my assailant smashed it into my skull. Even though I hadn't been in a fight since I was a kid, I had never expected to get so thoroughly beaten down— not to mention by a man who was close to retirement age. Things like that didn't happen at work. I was supposed to be the one in charge, the one controlling the interview, and yet I hadn't even had time to stand up.

I tried opening my eyes and met with half-success. My right eye was either swollen shut or caked with blood or both. As my left eye came into focus, I noted the ceilings were low and the walls were windowless. I was still seeing stars but could make out the conduit running along the walls with an occasional solitary line branching upward and into the concrete. But even in pitch blackness, I would still know where I was from the musty smell and the echoing rush of water from the pipes.

I was in an alcove off of one of the many tunnels that ran under the campus. The tunnels beneath Innovo Pharmaceutical were clearly labeled to keep employees from getting turned around, so I glanced around to find an alphanumeric painted on the wall. I could barely make out the yellow number 7, but the letter indicating which building was above me was just out of sight. How long I had been out or how I got there was a mystery.

My mouth was gagged, and I could taste the bleach on the fabric as it pressed against my tongue. When I reached up to grab the gag, I was met with resistance across my abdomen and wrists. I fell back on a thin pillow and took notice of the leather straps across my chest and around my wrists. Kicking my legs out, I heard the straps around my ankles strain against the rails on either side of me. Somebody had secured me to a gurney and left me in the shadows underground. I moved to unfasten the belts, but there was no reaching more than a couple inches.

Lights flickered to life down the hall as the motion sensor picked up movement. Footfalls. Many of them. A group of four people rounded the corner, the tone of their conversation urgent and argumentative. When they got within eyeshot, they stopped and huddled. Rajesh Jotwani stood on the right, talking with a broad-backed man who looked like he wore a guard uniform. A third person, perhaps a female, stood behind the security officer; were it not for his bulk, I would have been able to see her face clearly. I guessed it was Albert Vies, although I couldn't see his tattoos or his face. The fourth, Dieterich Bruchmuller, stood sideways across from Rajesh. My stomach churned, and I found myself paralyzed with uncertainty. Holding my breath, I closed my left eye slightly, hoping they didn't know I was awake.

A fifth person, another man, joined them from the opposite direction. I could see his face more clearly than the others, but that didn't mean much given the combination of the dark and my battered eye. He towered over the others, his head as bald as an eagle.

"They're gone, on the road. It's just us." His voice was unfamiliar. There were more than two thousand employees and vendors on the campus though, so it was possible I had never met the man. I had a decent view of his chest, and he wore no company ID.

"How much time do we have?" the female asked.

"I called in the threat four minutes ago," the security officer answered—it was definitely Albert Vies. "They should be sounding the alarm any second now."

Called what in? A threat? A fire? The haze of unconsciousness was lifting, only to reveal more confusion.

"We need to get Martin out of here," Rajesh Jotwani whispered.

"We don't have time for this, Dr. Jotwani!" the unknown man hissed. "We've already risked too much bringing your friend down *here*. Now you want to move him up to the surface?"

"Oh Jesus Christ, we're not doing this!" Albert banged his hand against the conduit running over his head.

"Rajesh, why should we?" the female voice whispered. She had an Indian accent, and I recognized her from the molecular biology lab, although her name escaped me. One thing I did know was that she wasn't on our list of subjects. Damn it! How much had I gotten wrong?

"Because," Rajesh responded with a direct tone, "I don't want to kill Martin, and we cannot leave him."

"But you promised—"

"I don't care what I have promised. This man has done nothing to deserve death."

"Quite forgiving for a man who was just interrogated by our guest here," Dieterich injected.

The security officer raised his voice. "And for somebody who spilled his guts about us."

"I told them nothing!" Rajesh yelled back.

Just then the fire alarm sounded through the tunnels, and the red directional lights moved along the floor and ceiling to indicate the closest exit. A chorus of alerts from their respective cell phones joined the alarm ringing in the corridor—a standard feature to alert all employees of a potentially dangerous event.

The woman spoke sharply above the din of the alarm. "It is only a matter of time before our escape is blocked. What do you propose we do with this man?"

"We can take him with us," Rajesh suggested. "Drop him off someplace along the way."

"No," Dieterich said flatly. "If we take him, he is going all the way with us."

"You can't be serious," Albert Vies hissed.

Syncing Forward

"I can't be? We have no idea how much he knows, but he knows about the rat. Either we leave him here or he comes to the crypts. We'll take him hostage and release him later after conducting our own interrogation. Besides, we are running out of precious time to debate the matter. So, Dr. Jotwani, will you please assist me?"

"This is insanity!" Vies complained. "We have no room for him!"

Rajesh stepped forward. "Leaving him here is the same as killing him. I have room for him at our crypt. My wife's spot."

Doctor Bruchmuller put up his hands to stop the bickering. "The decision is made. We can't have him waking up along the way. We're treating him here and now."

My head pulsed with pain. Why had they taken me down to the tunnels to begin with? Did Bruchmuller bring me down here or Rajesh? Or both? Talk of being a hostage, not to mention being treated and being placed in a crypt meant for Rajesh's late wife, had my brain spinning. The smart thing to do was sit tight, but I wasn't thinking smart. I didn't know what the hell was wrong with these people, but I couldn't just lie there doing nothing.

I pulled hard against the restraints, not understanding how strong they were or caring how much noise it made. I needed to get away, to run, to get help. My futile attempt to get away only alerted them of my consciousness.

"Ah, you're awake, Mr. James." Bruchmuller strode the distance between us and patted me firmly on the leg, which caused me to reflexively pull at the leather straps. "We were just debating what to do with you."

He stole a glance over his shoulder to look at my security officer, whose face remained in the shadows. Turning back to me, his smile slowly dissolved. "I must say, we have anticipated a number of contingencies, but your investigation has pushed our timeline up. Had you meddled in our affairs a bit earlier, you might have ruined everything."

He turned his attention to a metal push rack up against the wall. He moved his hands through a leather case atop it, unloading its contents onto the tray with a quick precision that smacked of routine. I could see needles. Lots of needles. The other four were still arguing in a huddle, but the noise from the alarm made it impossible to know exactly what they were saying. The male stranger made a rather vocal suggestion that they should kill me, and I started hyperventilating into the bleached gag.

A cell phone rang, and Vies picked up quickly. "Yeah . . . yeah . . . okay, we're moving out. Thanks." He hung up and stepped toward where I lay restrained. I could see his face clearly now, even though he avoided making eye contact with me.

"Doctor, we need to get to the crypts. DHS are here and looking for us, *now*. If they catch us, we're all screwed."

"Just another few minutes," Dieterich Bruchmuller said evenly, lifting an extremely large syringe and tapping the air bubbles to the tip.

"Jesus, Dieterich!" Vies hissed. "Are you insane? Just leave him here! We are going to get caught, and the cell they put us in will be deep and dark. Whatever you think you are doing, it isn't worth it. *He isn't worth it.*" Albert pointed at me, but got his face right up in Bruchmuller's. Even as my life hung in the balance, I found myself wondering what the crypts were and why they needed to get there.

"Go then! The two of you get the van ready. Dr. Jotwani and I will finish up here. We'll be done soon enough." Bruchmuller prepared a second large syringe, and then a third, and then a fourth. "Go!"

I struggled, screaming into my gag as Vies and the female lab tech walked past me, staring at me with shameful, fearful eyes as they went. The male stranger looked down at me, dark-brown eyes hidden beneath a pair of thick glasses, curly brown hair. He frowned in disgust as he passed. Disgusted with me? With Bruchmuller? With himself? I didn't know.

When their footfalls were softened by distance, Bruchmuller turned to me one last time. He delicately held a large syringe, and behind him lay three more just like it. A fifth smaller syringe was laid out as well, and panic started to set in when I finally realized Bruchmuller was about to inject me with all of them. I looked back and forth between Rajesh and the syringe, pleading with my eyes for my friend to save me from my confines, screaming into the gag incoherently.

Fear spun into unblemished terror as I convulsed against the restraints. What the hell was wrong with this man? How had I misjudged the situation so badly? What was that silvery liquid in the syringe? I screamed as loudly as the infernal gag would allow and flailed my head back and forth.

"Shhhh," Bruchmuller said, shaking his head lightly. "It will all be over soon enough. Now hold still, or this very large needle will break off in your body, and I trust you will not like that at all."

All I could think about was how Miranda and I had been fighting and how the last thing she'd heard out of my mouth was that she wasn't being a good mother because she let the kids walk all over her. The last memory Bella would have of me would be me yelling at her to get to bed or I'd throw her stuffed animal away. What a mouth I'd had on me these last few weeks. I hadn't been the man I wanted to be, and definitely not the man I wanted my family to remember.

One powerful shift would be all I would need to escape. Every bit of strength I had I focused into a single motion, swinging my arm upward and rotating my body with it, torquing against the restraints with my arm. The strap pulled taut, and the shock of my movement went deep into my shoulder. All of my might amounted to zero change in my compromised position—I felt no hulk-like endowment of superhuman strength as I fantasized would happen. I was still secured to the blasted gurney.

"Hold him, Doctor!" Dieterich Bruchmuller commanded, Rajesh complying by pinning my shoulders down. The director gripped my forearm in his thick fingers and leaned all of his weight on me to pin me in place. With his free hand, he shoved the needle into the crook of my arm and pressed the plunger down. I felt the sting of the needle and the rush of the chilled liquid as it entered my body. And then the needle pulled out as fast as it had plunged in.

My captor grabbed the second needle and walked around to my other arm. I screamed again but dared not move, staring into Dr. Jotwani's fearful eyes. The second injection squeezed in, and Bruchmuller started to reach for the third. This needle he drove into the meat of my right quadriceps, piercing my slacks and sending a shock through my leg. It hurt like hell, and my leg instinctively kicked up against the leather strap.

Rajesh consoled me. "I'm sorry we didn't go through the effort of prepping you, Martin, but time is of the essence. Normally we would just let the system dose you, but there is no telling what you might do to the equipment." The man I had shared many lunches with assumed my knowledge of their plans was far more extensive than it really was. Of course he did. I had spent an hour convincing him I knew everything, trying unsuccessfully to get him to give up his secrets. Oh, he gave them up now, though. He continued, "I'll make sure they don't hurt—"

"Hold him!" Bruchmuller bellowed, his voice making Jotwani jump. "He's moving around too much, and if this needle snaps, we won't have enough of the injection to prep him. Harder!"

Bruchmuller put an exclamation point on his sentence by stabbing downward. The fourth needle found its purchase in my left leg with an identical reaction. The two injections caused my upper legs to throb as the large volume of liquid wormed its way through my muscle cells.

His wrinkled hand reached for the fifth and final syringe, when his cell phone rang. The director touched the Bluetooth on his ear and responded with a simple, "Go ahead." There was a short gap, and then he responded, "I'm just about done. Excellent; we'll meet you topside."

Dr. Bruchmuller lifted the last syringe and cleared the tip. "I wish I had time to explain," he said, "but I suppose we'll have to discuss your participation at a later date. Perhaps I will see you in the new age, Martin H. James."

Syncing Forward

Nobody knew where I was. Nobody was coming to help me. The interview room wasn't networked with the CCTV system so the guards couldn't snoop on investigations that weren't their business. Dave probably had no idea I had been attacked, no idea I had been taken. I was totally screwed.

The needle hovered inches from my arm, when the sound of a half-dozen boots trampling down the corridor made the pair of doctors look up. I lifted my head and could see flashlight beams bouncing about the walls and floor. The motion sensors had turned on the lights above the group coming our way, casting a fluorescent halo in our direction. Bruchmuller dropped the syringe on the sheet between my legs, and my two remaining kidnappers rolled the gurney opposite the approaching group, breaking into a run.

I yelled into the gag, redoubling my efforts to be heard, a renewed hope that I might be rescued. Bruchmuller's ID bounced on the lanyard, flapping about until some rhythmic pattern flung it high up to slap him in the chin. Sweat rolled down Jotwani's forehead. I tried to look behind them to see who followed us, but the doctors' lab coats bellowed out like superhero capes.

What had they stuck in me? Was it something to knock me out? Something experimental? Was that tingling sensation in my arms and legs from the injections or just from being tied down? They turned the cart sharply and took me from one panicked thought to another. I instinctively grabbed the metal rails on the sides to stabilize myself. It was a bad move—as the cart turned the corner, it slammed into the wall. My cry for help became a yowl of pain; my fingertips pulsed as if I had gotten them caught in a car door. They were sprinting again. Running, pushing, driving us to some unknown location.

My body rolled in the opposite direction as the doctors turned us down another corridor. I just let the restraints hold me in place this time. As my body lurched to one side, the fifth syringe rolled underneath my leg and against the side railing. I managed to read the designator on the wall: "Q 10–12." We were on the way to the shipping and supply building. I had no idea who chased after us, but I prayed that whoever they were, they would hurry. I didn't know what these madmen had injected me with. I felt no pain except from the needles themselves. Dizziness turned my stomach, but that could have been from the blows to the head or the cart moving around. Not knowing what the hell they had done to me was the worst part of it all.

They pushed me straight for a long stretch, and the motion sensors barely kept up with us as the corridor lit up with each stride the doctors took. I recognized the layout of the tunnel—we were definitely heading for the Q building.

"Freeze!" the distant voice bellowed.

Had David Tsai come back and found me missing? He must have found the room empty, the camera broken, the chairs overturned. That had to be it! Everything happened so quickly, but my captors had no intention of freezing.

Bruchmuller pulled down a set of supply shelves as he ran, blocking the tunnel behind us. Their pace had slowed, but only because the tunnel inclined upward, and they were exerting more effort in rolling me up to the elevators at the top of the ramp. As the gurney moved along the incline, the fifth syringe struck the floor. Out of the corner of my eye, I watched Jotwani grope for the tumbling needle, but it was too late. Without both his hands on the handles, the gurney swung left and the rear swivel wheel crushed the syringe underneath, streaking the mysterious liquid across the floor.

Bruchmuller looked down and froze for a moment before letting go of the gurney and running up the ramp. "Come, Doctor! We must leave him now!"

"No!" Rajesh cried. "No, no, no! We need the last injection!" The man's face was a mixture of frustration, fear, and panic, but he had little time to dwell upon the matter. The authorities were closing in, and options for the renegade director and senior researcher were dwindling.

"There's nothing we can do! Now go!" Bruchmuller wasted no time in abandoning his colleague and doubling back, bounding up the

Syncing Forward

emergency exit steps toward the bottom of the ramp. Rajesh wheeled me to level ground, where two sets of freight elevators and a standard passenger elevator waited. He pressed every button, and the smaller elevator opened immediately. I prayed that my rescuers would get to me in time, but the doors opening made me doubt I was going to get the help I needed.

Rajesh shoved my cart past the sliding doors until the end slammed into the elevator wall. I heard him curse in Hindi, but I didn't realize why until I looked up. The gurney didn't fit—it stuck a full foot out of the lift. He pushed me in and out, in and out, trying to angle the gurney to fit, but the clock had just run out on the pursuit.

"Don't move!" a low voice boomed. I caught a glimpse of a man in a suit with three uniformed officers to either side of him. Four Glocks aimed at Rajesh. They looked like they were aimed at me too, and I shook my head frantically, hoping they wouldn't shoot.

The doctor looked down on me, cast with a sad visage. "I'm sorry, Martin." He gripped the cart's handrails and shoved me out of the elevator and back down the ramp, causing the cart to shoot down toward the armed men. I caught one final glimpse of Dr. Rajesh Jotwani before the elevator doors closed. Even in the face of imminent capture, his expression was one of utter embarrassment.

My cart accelerated down the ramp and spun toward the armed men, who tried to stop me. The momentum was too much to overcome, and the gurney slammed against the railing next to the fire exit, jarring me hard in the straps and blocking the stairwell leading to the supply building above us. The man in the dark suit dodged left and ran for one of the freight elevators in pursuit of Rajesh Jotwani. They managed to push me out of the way, and two uniformed officers disappeared up the steps. The remaining officer pulled the gag out of my mouth and puffed out, "Sir, are you okay? Are you hurt?"

The words caught in my throat. While I tried to respond, the officer looked at my ID card and called over his walkie-talkie, "We have Martin James. Repeat, we have Martin James. Targets took steps and elevator from underneath Building, uh, Building—"

"Q," I sputtered. "Building Q. Supply building."

"Q Building, the supply building," the officer echoed, nodding thanks as he did. More radio chatter crackled as others chimed in on the status of the chase. Something big had to be happening above ground.

"I've been injected," I croaked. "Dr. Bruchmuller . . . he did something to me. Maybe poisoned me. I need to get to a hospital!"

"I'm going to get you out of here. Don't worry. Here we go." The officer left me restrained as he pushed me back up the incline. We had to wait for the second freight elevator to arrive, but once inside he unfastened the leather straps and tried to call in for assistance over the radio. The frenzied chatter kept him from getting a message through. He pulled his cell phone out and called somebody, presumably from his own department.

"Yeah, it's Jackson. I've got Martin James, and we'll need immediate medical attention . . . We're at the Q Building . . . supplies . . . right. He's got a major gash to the head and maybe damage to the eye. He's been injected with an unknown drug. No, no info . . . confirmed . . . moving topside."

"Thank you." I sighed in relief at being rescued. I had the incredible desire to jump out of the cart and start chasing after Bruchmuller, to repay him for getting one over on me. I swung my legs over the edge, and Officer Jackson stopped me and pushed my legs back on. "Whoa, you stay up there, tough guy. Can't chance you getting injured on my watch."

I acquiesced and lay back on my elbows. The lift doors opened with a clunky sound to the unpainted grayness of the dock area. Officer Jackson rolled me over the bumpy lip of the freight elevator and hesitated, pushing me left and then right. I pointed toward the last overhead door, and the police officer trotted over to the corner. He pressed the green button, and the winches began coiling the chains, lifting the door that led to a vehicle ramp.

Syncing Forward

Daylight flooded the dock area and caused us both to squint while our pupils adjusted. He was already in motion, getting behind me and pushing the gurney along the vehicle ramp. "Hold on," the police officer told me as we accelerated down to the trailer lot. The swivel wheels vibrated so hard that I thought the whole dang thing was going to come apart and send me sprawling on the ground.

Fortunately we leveled off and then moved toward an ambulance with flashing lights that was on an intercept course to us. Behind it, the concealed red-and-blue lights of an unmarked police car flashed rapidly. Innovo's Paramus campus lay out over several acres: nineteen buildings with unimaginative names like H Building and Q Building were arranged roughly in alphabetical order from front to back. We were in the far back of the property where supply trucks were sent so as not to be an eyesore to any guests who might be visiting the prettier parts of the campus up front.

Off to the left of me, between the Q and L buildings, two more men in suits were running across our manicured lawns with pistols drawn, chasing after a speeding cargo van marked with the Innovo logo. They were more than a hundred meters away, but I could hear one of them yelling into his radio. Firemen and other police officers clustered off in the distance—many others. Dozens of white lab coats dotted the horizon as they fled the C Building. The mammoth cement rectangle dwarfed all the others around it both in its ordinary design and its unusual size.

This was the main research facility, the center of Innovo Pharmaceutical and the place where Bruchmuller and the others conducted most of their research—known and unknown. Four stories high and incorporating eight hundred thousand square feet of space, it was Innovo's largest facility and contained more than a thousand researchers, lab technicians, specialists, molecular engineers, animal handlers, and administrators on any given day. It ran twenty-four hours a day, seven days a week, and it never shut down. Not for Christmas, not for New Year's Day, not ever. But now technicians and doctors streamed out of the building like ants out of a nest.

"Martin James," a man in a striped shirt and gray slacks said, "I need to ask you some questions as we go. I'm Agent Franciscus." He flashed DHS credentials at me that I barely got to view before a heavy woman in a white uniform shoved him out of the way, intent on shining a small flashlight in my eyes.

"Go? Go where?" I asked. "What the hell is going on?" They were loading me from the gurney to the ambulance rack, the paramedics securing my chest, hips, and legs in place with Velcro straps. I panicked a bit, the tight restraints reminiscent of what my captors had done to me. My fingers rubbed over one of the spots where the needle pierced me. No coursing pain, no dizziness—nothing but a mystery that made its way through four holes in my body. Four, not five.

"Mr. James, stay focused. We don't have a lot of time. Did Dr. Bruchmuller mention anything about a bomb?"

Bomb? The word both shocked me and brought focus to the conversation the group had in the tunnels. "No, but one of the others might have. Albert Vies. He's one of my security officers. He said something about calling in a threat. Is it credible? Have they—"

"Martin!" Franciscus snapped. "Look at me. We're already running a general evacuation. The other investigator, David Something-or-other, is assisting us. Now, did anybody say anything about an explosive device?"

"No!" I bit back. "Nothing specifically about a bomb or anything like that."

"Did they make any demands?"

"No."

"What did he tell you?"

"About what?"

"Didn't you interview Dr. Bruchmuller? David said you were interviewing him."

I rolled my eyes. "Yes, I interviewed him for a half hour. He told me a lot of things! You gotta be more specific." They weren't making any sense. Or maybe they were? I was still disoriented from the blur of action around me and the blows to my head.

The dark-haired agent climbed into the ambulance and helped the second paramedic pull me in. The whole rack snapped as the wheels folded underneath. The woman slammed the doors shut and ran around to the driver's seat. She called information in, but I couldn't make out anything over the cross-chatter in the back. The male paramedic barked orders, moving my arms out of the way as he hooked me to an ECG and blood pressure monitor. The agent's face showed growing agitation at being interrupted repeatedly as the ambulance spun into motion.

We sped down the oval road toward the front of the campus. Franciscus tried to stay calm, but it was clear he was shaken just as much as I was. "Tell me about the building! About where he might want to set explosives."

Explosives? He was serious about this. But for them to get bombs into the building would mean getting around our security checks at the front gate, in the Q Building, our regular guard patrols. They couldn't have . . .

"I told you he didn't mention anything about that. I was questioning him about misappropriating some analyzers and running unauthorized tests. That's when he bashed my head in with my camera—"

"Where was most of his research done?"

"C Building. The main structure in—"

"Got it." He touched his earpiece and flipped something on his waistband. I couldn't tell if it was a cell phone or a radio, but he was right into the conversation. "Yeah, Franciscus here. James confirms the C Building as the most likely location for the IED."

I stared at him, wide-eyed. "Are you kidding? I didn't confirm anything! I just said that's where he did the research! There can't be any bombs here. They called this in to create a panic so they can get aw—"

W Lawrence

Without warning, a massive explosion shook the ambulance, and less than a second later the emergency vehicle we all sat in was struck by something big enough to crush the rear quarter, smashing the outside of the van inward and sending medical supplies flying. The male paramedic and the agent ricocheted around the inside, smashing into the equipment and each other before collapsing to the floor next to my rack. They had strapped me in place, but I grabbed the edge of the bed anyway.

Agent Franciscus and the paramedic blurted out a string of expletives as they were tossed about like beanbags. The back door whipped open, and the left door ripped from the hinges as it was struck by a large chunk of concrete; it went by so fast that my eye could barely register what it was.

The ambulance teetered to one side, and my stomach lurched as I prepared to tip over. Thank God the van bounced back on all four tires. Another shock wave hit the ambulance, but this was either smaller than the first or further away. I couldn't be sure. All I knew was that when the shocks finally settled, the back of the vehicle pointed directly at the C Building—or rather, where the C Building once stood.

The monolithic lab building was crumbling, teetering, collapsing in every direction. Black smoke filled the sky, rising from the center of the ruins. Two-meter sections of concrete were scattered in every direction along with glass and flaming debris. There had been bombs. Bombs in *my* buildings. How had I missed this?

Off in the distance another explosion went off, and then another, and then another. I saw somebody run past screaming, but I couldn't hear him. Instead, all I heard was a sharp ringing in my ears and the thumping of one detonation after another. Blasts of gray dust pierced the sky while tiny forms scratched for safety on their hands and knees. The driver got out and shuffled to the back, stuffing herself into the already cramped quarters. She checked on the DHS agent and then the other paramedic. Both nodded their heads as she turned her focus to me. The woman was asking me something. What was she asking?

Syncing Forward

Her words came through as she shouted them at me. "Are you okay?" She put her hand on my chest in a reassuring manner.

I didn't answer. The buildings were gone. I saw another cloud of flame go up and realized it had to be my office. All my files were destroyed. Had I backed up my files? The paramedic rubbed her knuckle on my sternum in a most unpleasant way.

"Are you okay?" she repeated.

I locked eyes with her and finally answered, "Uh, yeah, I'm fine. I'm fine. I think."

The woman climbed back into the driver's seat, called for everyone to hold on, and floored the ambulance. Despite gripping the gurney's handlebars, the two men struggled to keep their heads level. Another shock wave hit; we exchanged frightened glances, unable to know if the building we would pass next would explode and send a two-ton chunk of concrete colliding with the vehicle.

The wheels screeched as we rounded a corner and successfully pulled to the front of the Innovo Pharmaceutical campus. The ambulance came to an abrupt halt. Within seconds I was being pulled from the back and into the middle of a crowd of emergency vehicles.

Everything between the front gate and the A Building had been set up as an evacuation point for emergencies. This was our main office in North America and was a stunning piece of beauty, even with fires raging in the ruins behind it and smoke filling the air. I looked up at the inverted ziggurat, the sun gleaming off the slanting windows, the ledge-jutting offices, the asymmetrical architecture. The edifice tapered outward in sharp angles, accented in crystal buttresses. It leaned over the trimmed bushes and walkways, imposing its beauty on the amassing evacuated employees even in the face of danger.

Hundreds of Innovo employees huddled in the designated evacuation locations in front of the A Building, with more streaming in by the second. A pair of fire engines, three ambulances, and half a dozen police vehicles sat in our midst, all with their lights flashing and spinning. But even the evacuation point was being evacuated, police yelling for everyone to get further away from the building.

The female paramedic pulled me over to the rear doors of another ambulance and started to load me into the back, when one of the EMTs stopped her. "Hey, what do you think you're doing?"

"Taking this patient to Bergen County Hospital," she barked.

He thumbed the ambulance I was just pulled from. "What's wrong with your ride?"

She eyed him with disdain. "The flippin' door ripped off when a chunk of that building hit us. He's a priority one, so move over, Bert."

Halfway into the new ambulance, a familiar face appeared. "Martin! You're alive!" David Tsai jogging over to the back doors, a data pad in hand. He swung it over to his left hand, climbed into the back with me, and gave me a one-armed hug.

"Barely. I got owned pretty hard by the doctor." I gingerly touched the swelling around my eye.

"Holy crap! Listen. You're headed for the hospital. Here's a data pad. Call Miranda. She's called me a half-dozen times, but I didn't pick up. I didn't know what to say since we had no idea if you were, you know . . . okay."

"Thanks." My mind tripped over itself as I tried to sort through everything that happened. The explosions had momentarily chased my bigger problem from my mind, but it came back in force now. The needles, penetrating my arms and legs, leaving God only knew what behind coursing through me. "I'm in trouble, Dave. Bruchmuller injected me with something. With what, I don't know."

"You're kidding. Are you feeling okay?"

"Not great, but I don't know if that's from the injection or Bruchmuller using me like a whack-a-mole."

"Why did he attack you?"

"I mentioned the rat—nothing offensive, nothing provocative—and the man pounced on me like a bobcat on a baby."

Syncing Forward

Dave scrunched his brow. "The rat? Why would that, of all things, send him over the edge?"

Before we ever interviewed a soul, we'd watched dozens of hours of video. While watching one of our suspects on the CCTV system, Bruchmuller walked into the lab and dropped off a cage with a dead rat. No big deal. Innovo had plenty of animal experiments going on. But this particular cage was picked up by Bruchmuller forty-eight hours later, then moved to another lab, then picked up by Bruchmuller again. No animal experiments were recorded on his activity log. Was it an oddity for a director to be carting around a dead rat for no apparent reason? Sure. But there was nothing illegal about it.

"Beats the hell outta me. Literally."

"Listen, we'll talk—"

Another explosion went off in the neighborhood of the J Building, and yet another closer by. Everyone ducked for cover, and even in the relative safety of the ambulance I found myself flinching. Several employees screamed while firemen and local police gathered them to the lawn in front of the campus.

Dave climbed out and stood by the ambulance doors, grabbing his phone as he went. "David Tsai here . . . no, not yet . . . I'm still waiting to get head counts. Two more explosions . . . They found Martin, so that's good news, but . . . yeah . . . okay, let me find out." He hung up.

"Is everybody out?" I called out.

"We have no idea. Listen, I need to roll. Go get patched up. We'll talk later." Dave started to walk away, when the A Building detonated.

The crown jewel of the campus came apart beginning at the center of the structure and working its way out in a wave. Glass shattered and flew like tiny missiles across the sky. The employees ducked and fell to the grass, covering themselves and each other for protection as a sonic wave from the explosion made a skeleton of the once-magnificent office building. Furniture joined the debris as powerful blasts propelled ergonomically friendly chairs, LED computer screens, pens, and files from the ruined building. Dave took shelter behind a squad car next to a handful of police officers as a length of rebar sailed through the sky and lodged itself through the roof's siren.

Shrieks erupted as the employees panicked and ran from the evac sites. The male paramedic who had been seeing to me pulled the doors shut from the inside, and his female counterpart leaped into the driver's seat. Agent Franciscus ran around the front bumper and jumped into the passenger side. His door wasn't even closed before our driver peeled out from the parking lot and onto the main road. Sirens wailing, lights flashing, the ambulance sped toward the hospital.

As we left the destruction of Innovo Pharmaceutical behind, my mind kept wandering to the fantastic wreckage that had been made of my company. I lay there, tortured by the questions, not knowing who was alive, who was injured, or if we could have prevented the attack.

Dave's words of caution haunted me: *"I think these thefts are related to terrorism."*

I should have supported him, trusted his instincts, spoken up when our director asked for my opinion. Had we listened to him and gotten DHS involved, maybe they would have investigated, uncovered the bombs on our campus. Countless millions of dollars in lost research data and materials. An unknown number of employees unaccounted for. I almost killed myself, leaving behind my wife, my daughters. Maybe I could have stopped it all. Instead, I was worried about my water heater, a nice vacation, a fat bonus padding my bank account.

I rubbed my thighs where the needles had been shoved. They had planned to give me five injections, but only four had made their way into my body. The final syringe had been lost and destroyed. But what did that mean to me? Was it some catalyst to trigger the other four? Was I better off with or without it? When he left me underground at Innovo, Rajesh appeared worried, and that fact alarmed me

Syncing Forward

more than anything. The questions battered me about as the ambulance screamed forward. Until they got me to the hospital, there was no way to know now if the last injection would have been a blessing or a curse.

Chapter 4

The hospital swarmed with activity as injured from Innovo Pharmaceutical packed the ambulance bay. Patients were quickly triaged and thrown into the already overstuffed waiting room. My coworkers were stacking up by the dozens—bruised, bleeding, unconscious. I feared that the drug Bruchmuller had stuck in my body—whatever it was—would take its toll before a doctor could ever get a chance to look at me.

I watched Emily Devereux, an elderly executive secretary from A Building, get rushed past the crowd on a blood-soaked gurney. The EMTs pushed everyone to the side while Emily was left holding her thigh, wailing and crying, her wounds wrapped in crimson. A young intern from Norway fought against the Velcro straps on his gurney, screaming in a language that nobody around him understood. They didn't need to—a large shard of reinforcing glass stuck out of his eye socket. The ice-blue broken glass was wrapped heavily in bandages and secured to his skull.

I felt the same as I had down in the Innovo corridors. My head throbbed and my ribs ached, although the nausea had abated some. On top of it all, my heart pounded with guilt as each new victim entered the hospital. Agent Franciscus exchanged angry words with the admittance clerk, throwing his authority around to get me seen before some of the other priority patients, but the strong-arming and badge-flashing wasn't having nearly the impact he hoped. I heard catchphrases like "national security" and "homeland security director," but the unshaven clerk refused to budge.

"The man's been injected with an unknown chemical. It could be killing him right now while you're sitting on your fat ass! How is that not a priority?"

"We'll have somebody check his vitals every thirty minutes, but right now we have patients with more severe injuries. Now can I get back to my job?"

Syncing Forward

Picking up the tablet Dave lent me, I dialed the house and connected in a near-instant as Miranda immediately came to view on the screen. Her brown skin was flushed, and her dark eyes shone with worry. My wife was an attractive woman who had a secret affair with cleaning—her long curly hair was pinned up in an oversized clip, and she wore her "scrubbing shirt." She cleaned houses part-time, I think because she ran out of rooms to clean in ours. The destruction of Innovo had probably interrupted her wiping down our shower because there was a spray cleanser across her lap. I did my best to muster a reassuring voice and preempt her concern. "Honey, I'm fine—"

"*Dios mio!* What happened to you? Your face! *Qué pasó? Hay una*—"

"Miranda, Miranda, sweetie, Wife, shhhhhh! Just—just stop for a second!" She continued on in Spanglish as I struggled to get her to be quiet long enough to listen.

"Honey, I'm fine. I got cut over my eye, and it looks worse than it is. I'm at Bergen County Hospital, and there are a lot of people hurt way worse than me."

"What happened to your eye?"

"I told you, my eye is fine. It's just a nasty gash along my eyebrow."

"Was David hurt? I sent him messages looking for you, but he never responded."

"No, he's as fine as frog fur. He passed your messages on to me." I glanced over at the doorway through which Agent Franciscus had disappeared, then turned my attention back to Miranda. "What are they saying on the news?"

"They are saying on TV that it is another Islamic Fundamentalist attack. Nobody has come forward to claim responsibility though." She looked straight ahead, watching the news. She grabbed the control pad in front of her and manipulated the controls, most likely sending my image to the corner of the screen so that she could see the news as a full image.

"Eh, they are saying something about a group called something 'tareer' might be responsible. . ." My wife looked scared. I could easily pull up the information myself, and I wasn't expecting her to research it for me, although the task seemed to be focusing her away from her worries about me and more on the bigger picture.

I put on my best smile and got Miranda's attention by waving at her. She quickly swapped the picture-in-picture and refocused on me. "Hey, baby, listen. I've been knocked around but I'm not dying, and I've got all my parts. I need to go, okay?"

"Wait, before you go . . . the school is doing an emergency dismissal, and the girls are already on a bus on the way home. What do you think we should tell them?"

I grimaced. Something like this could send Bella and Amara into a spin, but then again, they probably already knew it was my company that had gotten attacked. Each time a terrorist attack happened it was standard protocol for schools to send kids home, and each time it happened the girls would ask me if I was safe. Of course I told them I was—I had believed my own reassurances that a pharmaceutical company would never be a viable terrorist target.

"They're going to wonder if I'm okay. Tell them the truth. Tell them you spoke with me and that Daddy is hurt but not badly. You can call me when they get home, and once they see me they should be fine. I think that's the best way to handle it."

"I'm worried about how Bella is going to react looking at your eye—it looks bad. But Amara is going to want to come see you. I'll bring them to the hospital."

I grimaced. "We better talk first before you come up. It's bad here. A lot of injuries, things the kids won't want to see. Besides, there's some stuff going on."

Miranda paused, and curiosity crossed her face. "What's wrong, Martin?"

How was I to tell my wife that I had been beaten, kidnapped, and unwillingly injected with an unknown drug? Or that I was clueless

Syncing Forward

as to what the drug Bruchmuller had put in me even did, if anything at all? That with a single question I had set in motion events that brought chaos to my company and career? That the hospital was filled with bleeding bodies that would give the girls nightmares? How could I have known?

"I can't talk about it right now. But I'll call you in a bit, okay? Don't bring the girls. Yet."

"Okay. I love you. I'm so happy you're alive, Martin."

"Te amo," I whispered, kissing my fingers and then touching the screen.

"Te amo. Call me." She pressed Disconnect, and my pad screen went to a pale-blue background.

I let myself dwell on those parting words for a moment. My grandma on my father's side was a wise old Creole who told me, "A good marriage grows stronger in the sufferin'." Miranda and I had been fighting for weeks over how to handle Amara's problems, but all that seemed to wash away in the face of tragedy. *Te amo.* Yup.

The waiting room was packed solid with bloody bandages and splinted legs. Juan Kinley, one of the Innovo tech support specialists, lay next to me half-conscious with his rib cage bloody and bandaged. Two men in bluish scrubs jogged over and grabbed his cart, then wheeled him past the security doors to awaiting doctors. It drove me nuts not knowing what strange concoction pumped through my blood, but it was hard to justify being seen first when I felt fine and Juan looked like he was on the verge of death.

I pulled up my personal messages and found about twenty new texts. It was obvious that the attack on Innovo Pharmaceutical had made national news.

From my brother Jacob in Tucson: *Hey call me—your co on news. Worried.*

From Miranda: *Honey please call me emergency.*

From Miranda: *Martin call me please I'm scared.*

W Lawrence

From my sister-in-law, Marisol: *call Miranda—she's worried. Us too.*

From my old buddy Ali in California: *Hey a pharma company in NJ blew up, is that your office?*

Everyone and their mother had heard the news. I found messages from Dave that gave me an eerie glimpse into what had happened after Bruchmuller attacked me. The text messages from Dave came one after another:

Martin, how are things going in there?

No luck on Dr. Jotwani or Al. Not on any video anywhere. Could be in the tunnels?

Reminder to tell Thomason we need cams installed down there. How interview going?

Where you? Intervw room trshd. Better not be screwin w me.

Calling police. Call me asap if ok.

There was an alert memorandum sent twenty minutes after Dave's last message:

~~~INNOVO ALERT MEMORANDUM~~~

THIS IS NOT A TEST.

THREAT OF IMPROVISED EXPLOSIVE DEVICE AT INNOVO/PARAMUS NJ CAMPUS.

LEAVE YOUR POST IMMEDIATELY AND PROCEED TO THE NEAREST ASSEMBLY POINT.

Syncing Forward

Down in the tunnels, Albert Vies had told the other conspirators that he had called the threat in. Once the security desk got the information, the alert memo was automatically sent to every phone, tablet, and workstation in every building. I wondered what went through everyone's mind when they got that message.

I scrolled downward and clicked Dave's last message.

Martin, where the hell are you? There is a bomb threat. You need to get out of the building.

So many messages followed after that from coworkers and friends and family—I could have spent an hour going through them all. I powered down to save my battery, when I heard a buzzing like a hornet's nest outside the hospital's waiting room windows. I craned my neck to see media cameras held high above the heads of reporters trying to capture any images they could sell, vultures waiting to pounce on the next biggest story.

It took two blasted hours for them to finally admit me. Two hours while I fielded calls from both the office and the family. Two hours wondering if I had been injected with a poison or a cancer-causing agent or God only knew what. The bar-code reader scanned my National Health Services card and my gurney tag number, and only after an administrator confirmed my biodata was I granted admission beyond the waiting room.

The emergency room doctor talked fast, and I found myself nodding and signing release electronic forms before I was off to another room. Vial after vial of blood was drawn from my arm. Confounded doctors prodded me for descriptions of the unknown medication Bruchmuller had injected me with, walking away with as much information as I had to give them, which was absolutely none.

Franciscus's partner, Agent Guirres, joined him in the urgent-care room and greeted me professionally, although underneath there was something brewing; his brow was squared and his gaze fixed and hard. Franciscus asked me how well I knew Bruchmuller. I could have sworn from his tone he thought I was somehow involved.

"And you're sure that was the first time you spoke with Dieterich Bruchmuller? You never even spoke to him in the hallways? That's hard to believe."

"Not really. Do you have any idea how many people Innovo employs at the Paramus campus alone?" I shook my head, worried about how many fewer employees we would have when all was said and done.

Guirres stood back, watching me silently. He was assessing me the same way I would a suspect. Two doctors approached and told the agent he needed to leave while I was treated. While they spoke, Agent Franciscus leaned in close and spoke low. "Mr. James, it is really important that you do two things: tell us everything you know, and tell nobody else. You know how complicated this could get for you, right?"

I wanted to swear at him. It was the second time I had been threatened in the same day. Homeland Security could detain me for seven days under the 2019 Priority Domestic Protection Act for any reason. And if they really wanted to flex, I'm sure they could trump up a justification under the National Defense Authorization Act to hold me indefinitely. It had happened to hundreds of people in the last several years, and I didn't want to be one of them.

"Yes sir." I gave him a tiny nod. Inside I was seething over being bullied, but I couldn't let adolescent pride get the better of me. I had a family counting on me, and the last thing they needed was me screwing the pooch on this one.

Thankfully, the doctors banished both agents from the room while they checked on the face wound that cut deeply into my skin. I breathed a sigh of relief when one doctor told me my eyeball hadn't been damaged, but the truth was my tension level had been ratcheted up a notch by DHS pushing on me.

". . . and you should be able to see fine once the swelling goes down," the doctor reassured me.

Syncing Forward

"Huh? Oh, sure. Good," I replied, but my distraction wasn't lost on my caretakers.

"Are you with me here, Martin?"

"Yeah. I'm just dandy."

He wasn't buying it. "We're going to send you for an RMRI. With the blows you took, there is a good chance of a concussion."

I put up a few protests about feeling fine even though my head was swimming. I don't like tight spaces, and having my whole body shoved in that machine would not be my favorite part of the day.

Inside the machine, I breathed deeply and clenched my eyes shut as I failed to imagine my favorite country song. The volume in that contraption was off the scales, like the back ass of a bowling alley. Thankfully the RMRI lived up to its name: Rapid Magnetic Resonating Imaging. I was out in a few minutes and free to go back to fixating on DHS's accusatory words.

Between prods from nurses, I caught clips of news on my data pad. Multiple reports were in that IF—Islamic Fundamentalists—were involved. Hizb'ut Tahrir, or the Islamic Liberation Front, had denied involvement, but the news reporter theorized this was perhaps another splinter group. ILF had been blamed for more than twenty terrorist attacks in the US over the last several years. But after the day's events, I knew that any attempt to blame the terrorist attack on IF was undeniably false. It smelled of a desperate fabrication on the part of the media, or maybe a terrorist group falsely trying to take credit. Or a cover-up.

Sounds of tragedy played out from beyond the hospital curtain that had been drawn around me. Whispered conversations that had me doubting and regretting my actions. Again.

"The doctors did everything they could to revive your husband . . ."

"Your daughter didn't suffer . . ."

"She's not expected to wake up . . ."

W Lawrence

"Your brother's injuries were too extensive..."

"The breathing apparatus is the only thing keeping your father alive..."

If I had listened to Dave, or followed my instincts, or stopped the interview when Bruchmuller asked for an attorney, maybe none of this would have happened. Maybe Rajesh and Dr. Bruchmuller and all of their cohorts would simply have vanished. I kept telling myself it wasn't my fault to the sound of weeping families. Their voices blended and softened, and in relative solitude, my fatigue managed to swallow both my helplessness and guilt.

Syncing Forward

Chapter 5

I awoke to my three ladies, who had taken up station around me. Miranda sat in the chair at the foot of the hospital bed, her eyes closed and the corners of her mouth pulled down by worry. Eyes closed, she slowly stroked a head of brown hair belonging to my seven-year-old daughter; the lighter shade of her locks gave away Bella's Caucasian half more so than her sister. My little baby had buried her sobs in her mother's lap as she clung to Miranda's pant leg. Amara had fallen asleep leaning against the wall, her fluffy brown jacket rolled into a ball to act as a makeshift pillow. Her dark curls had wrapped around her face and stuck to her cheek with the help of some perspiration and drool from the corner of her mouth. A glance at the muted television up on the wall showed the time as 8:43 p.m.

"Hey, family," I said, smiling as I came to. Bella perked up immediately to reveal rosy cheeks slick with tears. "Hey, Baby Bella, what are you crying for?"

Miranda opened her eyes with a start as Bella screamed with elation, rushing forward and doing her best to give me a hug. "Daddy! I love you! I thought you were going to die!"

I chuckled. "No, sweetie. I'm fine. I'm hurt, but not nearly as bad as that time you fell down the basement steps. Remember how we had to take you to the emergency room too?"

Miranda stood and bent over me, gently letting her kiss linger on my lips before she pressed her cheek to mine and sighed. Amara woke up quietly and stretched like a cat, not really sure what the commotion was. When she noticed I awoke, she ran to my bedside and hugged my arm in silence.

Behind them in the doorway, Agent Guirres was talking into his Bluetooth and glancing into the room like a hyena, waiting for me to be conscious and alone.

Miranda caught me up on what had happened at the school, the battery of phone calls, and the nightmare of getting in to visit me. She mentioned that somebody in the hallway had flashed a badge and asked her why she was visiting me, pestering her with one question after another until a nurse rescued her and escorted her and the kids to my room. According to the nurse, the agents were making quite a business of harassing everybody who came to visit. One man had been arrested because he got belligerent with them.

"He just wanted to see his wife. The police threw him on the ground and put handcuffs on him." Miranda ran her hand through my hair. "Martin, what's happening?"

I glanced over at Franciscus, who stood in the doorway now. He subtly shook his head. I looked back to Miranda. "I wish I knew. They're just doing their job, honey. Somebody blew up most of Innovo. If I were them, I'd be cautious too." Franciscus gave me a tiny nod and disappeared from view, no doubt waiting just within earshot.

Miranda didn't notice the exchange. "Well, David isn't hurt, thank God. He called to make sure we had heard from you. He mentioned there were still a lot of people unaccounted for, though. Oh, how awful, Martin!" She stifled a cry as the kids looked back and forth between us, unsure if they should be encouraging or sympathetic.

Amara looked like she wanted to say something, so I patted her hand. "Hey, big kid," I said with a smile. "What's on your mind?"

Amara held my hand comfortingly. "I was just wondering if you needed me to bring any of your favorite things to the hospital. You know, like a book or something."

She was such a good kid—I grinned. "Yeah, you could bring my Zacks book from my nightstand next time you come. Thanks, sweetie."

Then the girls gave their account of the frightful day: the call at school, watching the news, all the video calls at the house. My children each processed the tragedy so differently, a distinction that only exemplified how polar opposite they were. They had the same

Syncing Forward

parents, the same extended family, the same genetic material, lived in the same home and went to the same schools, and yet a stranger would never guess that Amara and Bella were sisters. It was the grand enigma of child rearing, I suppose. Bella talked about how scared she was, how sad she felt, how happy she grew when she found out I was okay. Amara gave a detailed chronology of events, including what she had managed to absorb from the television. She wasn't an unfeeling child; she simply had a difficult time expressing how she felt. When Amara finally let loose, there was no telling what she might do.

One of the nurses came by twenty minutes later, poking her head in just enough to inform us that visiting hours were over soon.

"Thank you." Miranda nodded and politely smiled. Turning to Bella, she asked, "Do you have to go to the bathroom?"

"Uh-huh." Bella reached for my wife's hand, and the two disappeared down the hallway.

I gently held my older daughter's hand and looked at her. Lowering my voice, I said, "Hey, big kid, I wanted us to talk with your ma and sis gone."

Amara shrugged and sat down. "Sure. What's up, Daddy?"

"It's about school."

"Oh yeah. I was wondering when you were going to say something. Did you tell Mommy?"

"No, I've been a tad busy." I grinned wryly. "Besides, I think if we talk this out, you might be able to avoid your mother's wrath."

My nine-year-old sneered. "I suppose that would be preferable. For the record, I apologized to Mrs. Bloom even though she didn't deserve it."

Miranda and I knew that the day Amara realized she was smarter than both of us, we were utterly screwed. "Oh, kiddo, you're a good girl for saying you're sorry. The apology isn't the big issue, by the way. Well, it is important, but it isn't what I wanted to talk to you about. My concern is over why you had to apologize in the first place."

"I didn't say any 'inappropriate' words, if that's what you mean." Amara bobbled her head as she did air quotes with her fingers. "I called Mrs. Bloom obtuse and a liar, *which she is*."

"No. Tell me why you were flipping out in the classroom."

Amara looked down and started biting her thumbnail. "I don't know. I just did. Brian and Rafael broke my tablet and the teacher sided with them, which is ridiculous. Then she tried to tell me that tablets get broken at school all the time, but they don't and she knows it. I can't stand her; I wish I could get a new teacher."

"Sweetie, it isn't the tablet. It's your reaction to disappointment. You do this all the time. Sometimes life doesn't go the way you want it to. Sometimes there are circumstances beyond your control. If it's important enough, sure, you fight for it. Even then, though, sometimes you need to just let it go." She was such a smart kid, but this concept seemed so lost on her. I hoped to God she would get it soon.

"How do you tell the difference?" she asked. "You know, how do you figure out when you should give up on something or fight for it?"

I paused while I considered how to answer. "I reckon you just have to make a judgment call, kiddo. As you get older, it will get easier. I hope it does, anyway. It's like that girl last year who refused to be your friend. She didn't like you, she didn't want to talk to you, but you got it under your brainpan that she had to like you. So what happened?"

"She pushed me. And that hurt too! I fell into the lockers, and it gave me a bruise on my tailbone." Amara sniffled, trying to keep her nose from running. "I don't know why she was like that."

"She just *was*, kid. There are people out there you are never going to change. There are circumstances you are never going to change. It's just life. You need to learn to accept that, okay?"

"I can't, though, don't you understand?" Amara's eyes got glassy, and I could tell she was unsuccessfully trying not to cry. "Daddy, you think there's something wrong with me too, don't you?"

"Why would you say that?"

Syncing Forward

"The way you're looking at me. It's the way Mommy looks at me. And the teachers."

My heart sank as I pulled her close to me and rubbed the top of her head. "Listen to me real good, okay? You want to know what I think? I think I love you just the way you are. We all wrestle with certain things in life, and that's okay. You're my big girl, and God made you the way you are because he knows best. And who am I to argue with the Big Guy?"

Amara chuckled and gave me a big hug, a few tears sneaking their way out and hiding in my hospital pajamas. "Thanks, Daddy. I love you so much!"

"I love you too, kid. You're my first—my big girl."

Miranda returned with Bella in her arms, my baby's eyes closed and barely awake, drooping like a wax figure from fatigue. "She hit the wall," my wife said quietly.

"What did she do? Pee herself to sleep?" I whispered.

Amara stifled her chuckles while Bella waved her bitty hand disapprovingly at her sister, groaning something unintelligible. While I didn't want to be alone, I knew visiting hours were over and the kids were done. Miranda couldn't even lean over to kiss me without my baby girl toppling out of her arms. Instead, she blew me a kiss, mouthed *"te amo,"* and nudged Amara from the room. A nurse was right behind them, making sure they left the facility.

The smell of my wife's perfume and my girls' sweat hung in the air. It reminded me of the blanket we kept on our living room sofa, for some reason—it made me long for home, to lean back on the sofa with the girls snuggled up under my arms and Miranda's legs draped over my lap, the four of us under this worn-out tan blanket watching a movie in the dark with a bowl of popcorn on a Friday night.

Agent Guirres was there in the doorway, staring at me. He couldn't have been there for very long, seconds maybe, but his gaze reminded me of a gargoyle, fixed permanently as he looked down at me. I jumped.

W Lawrence

"Holy crap—you startled me! What the hell are you staring at me for, Hoss?"

"Comfortable, Mr. James?" he asked.

"Not anymore." I reached for the control pad attached to my bed and let my finger hover over the nurse call button.

"Get some rest, Mr. James. We're going to have a lot of questions for you tomorrow." He walked away, leaving me alone with my chest thumping.

Syncing Forward

Chapter 6

Eleven o'clock at night, and a nurse came to check my IV drip and my blood pressure. The TV droned on and newscasters were chattering away, comparing the threat of Islamic Fundamentalists against that posed by other domestic terrorism groups. The rip of the Velcro band coming off my arm signaled that the systolic and diastolic numbers had been recorded and I was now free to speak. The nurse was an old-timer, easily in his seventies, bald as a baby and sporting sun spots that disappeared under his scrubs.

"How am I doing?" I asked him.

"Well, your blood pressure is a little low, but that isn't a bad thing." He spoke quickly, as if he needed to get out of there in a hurry.

"First good news I've gotten all day. My doctor has been after me to get my blood pressure down for two years."

"Well, I'll update him on your e-chart. Maybe he'll give you a lollipop when you go in for your next checkup."

"Anybody figure out what I might have been injected with?" I asked.

He looked at the information that scrolled down the length of the large Rx data slate. These were brand-new data pads that a lot of hospitals were putting into place. Larger than the average data pad the public had been using for years, they linked your e-chart, which contained all your health records, with the hospital database. "Eh, I don't see any notations. My guess is your file will update in the morning. The system is running slow again."

I thanked him as he turned off my television and returned the remote control to its holster on the bed. Once alone, I grabbed the tablet and dialed up the house. A quick voice authorization and my call went through, the scrambled image on the video clarifying into a shot of our living room covered in dim light. Miranda had answered on the TV camera, and I noticed in amusement that the kids were both passed out, each one using my wife's thighs for a pillow. Blankets draped over their sleeping bodies, so it was difficult to tell which protruding foot belonged to whom. Only the different shades of their protruding locks gave away who was on which side, but the three of them took up the entirety of the sofa.

"Hey, honey," I said in low tones. "How are y'all?"

"Much better after seeing you. All of us," Miranda said softly back. The two of us caught up in whispers—Miranda had two sleeping children pinning her down on the sofa, whereas I hoped to keep our conversation away from any prying ears outside my door. "We watched some movies and ate dinner in the living room. I'm keeping them out of school tomorrow."

I nodded. "Good idea. So how are you planning on getting off the couch?"

She giggled as quietly as she could. "I don't know. The girls have me trapped here. I might be spending the night with them both."

I hesitated, uncomfortable with broaching the subject, but spoke up finally as I understood I could do very little without my wife's help. "Miranda, tomorrow morning I need you to call the Life Assistance line from Employment Benefits. We have a legal insurance account, and we may need to use it."

"Okay," she responded slowly, "but can you tell me why?"

"It may be nothing, but I don't know exactly if DHS has my best interests in mind. Call them first thing in the morning and arrange for an attorney to be assigned to me. Tell them I'm in the Intensive Care Unit at Bergen County and that I'd like a personal visit."

"Martin, you're worrying me."

"Don't be worried. I'm just being safe, that's all."

A little hand popped out of the tan blanket on Miranda's left, and I heard Bella's sleepy voice. Her face was barely peeking from underneath the covers, and I saw a sliver of her precious little face. "I love you, Dada . . ."

Syncing Forward

My heart melted. "I love you too, kid. Get some sleep." Bella turned over and disappeared under the throw once more, her wavy hair swirling out. Our conversation would have to wait till tomorrow. To be honest, I was thankful Miranda didn't ask me to elaborate further. Smiling at her, I blew her a kiss through the camera and mouthed that I loved her. She returned the air kiss, and the screen went black. I tucked it under my pillow and went into a deep sleep.

"Good morning, Mr. James." A new face, a young pretty nurse with a braided ponytail, woke me up.

"What time is it?" I groaned.

"It's only a little after seven a.m." She reviewed my e-chart as I reached under my pillow to find my tablet missing. The nurse took it off her cart and handed it to me. "I placed it in your locker after you fell asleep."

"Thank you, ma'am." I checked my work mail and was surprised that there was no e-mail from anyone in my chain of command, no message from our legal department. Somebody should have reached out to me by now.

I sent a message to Dave: *Call me with an update, please.* No response—not that I should have expected one so quickly. He must have been going crazy working with police, setting up an alpha site, getting battered with a thousand phone calls, trying to organize the fragments of our company.

The nurse was on the way out when she turned and asked, "Mr. James, is there anything I can get you before I go?"

"Do they know what I was injected with yet?"

She shook her head. "Nobody has said anything to me. Can I get you some ice chips?"

"I'd really like something to eat. What can I have?"

"We're not sure what we can feed you yet. I'll have to check with Dr. Prasad."

"Why are you worried about what I can eat?"

I got no answer.

"May I speak with the doctor, miss?" I asked, my mood grim.

"I believe he'll be in shortly."

"Thanks."

She scurried out of the room. The door had barely shut before a police officer opened it again, this time for an older man carrying an Rx tablet. The doctor's smooth dark skin stretched across large cheekbones, and a series of burn scars ran along his neck and cheek.

"Good morning, Mr. James," he said. "How are you feeling today?" His hands maneuvered a chilly stethoscope under my hospital garb and onto my chest.

"Fine. Rested. Why is everyone in a hurry?"

"No hurry. Given the circumstances, things are pretty slow around here. My name is Dr. Prasad. I'm up here from Langley helping out DHS on this case." The doctor was clearly of Indian descent, but his accent told me he had probably been raised in Alabama or perhaps my home state of Louisiana. If he was from Langley—CIA headquarters—it was almost a certainty he was American-born. "So tell me, Mr. James. Do you have any symptoms, pain, dizziness, discomfort?"

"My ribs still bug me where I was kicked and my head hurts, but not nearly as bad as I thought it would. I'm still dizzy from last night. Everything seems just a bit off."

He smiled. "Well, you haven't eaten breakfast yet, so let's start you off with that and see if it helps."

"You have no idea how happy that makes me feel. I desperately want some bacon."

The older man chuckled as his forefinger zipped expertly over the tablet.

"Dr. Prasad, can you tell me anything about what I was injected with? I keep asking the nurses, but nobody seems to know anything. I'm not sure whether I should be relieved or concerned."

Syncing Forward

He stifled himself for a moment, as if evaluating what he could or could not say. "I can tell you we are trying to analyze your blood as best we can, but whatever was injected into you was quickly absorbed into your blood and tissue. It's proving to be quite difficult to isolate, to be honest."

Sixty percent of the time, people are lying when they utter the phrase "to be honest." The doctor was telling me the truth this time, however. I was certain of it.

"Do you know if I can go home today?" I asked, changing the subject.

"I think that depends on the gentlemen on the other side of the door. There are two agents who are waiting to speak with you, but before you ask, I don't know why. I am just here to assess your health and figure out what was done to you." Dr. Prasad's fingers slid effortlessly across the data slate as he performed some type of analysis on my condition.

"Can you at least tell me what's wrong with me?"

He glanced over the slate briefly before going back to reading, talking as he went. "Well, it appears you have a mild traumatic brain injury, commonly called a concussion. We'll take a more thorough scan after breakfast to see how you've improved. Your ribs are bruised badly, but no broken bones."

He pulled out a penlight and flashed it into my right eye. "The eye is looking remarkably better than it did when you came in. I don't see anything wrong here, although you'll probably have a nasty scar when the stitches fall out. They did a good job of sewing you up, but the gash was pretty significant. Your blood pressure is a little lower than I would like, but that could easily be from shock. It certainly isn't lethal. With all that said, I really can't think of a good reason to keep you here. Although, given the circumstances, I would be more comfortable running more tests to be sure."

Maybe the purpose of the fifth vial was some sort of activating agent? I should have been relieved, but instead, my concern grew. It made no sense for the four other syringes to be some type of sedative. It had to be something else.

The concussion was worrisome, but Prasad's lack of information was worse. Dragging the IV stand with me, I visited the bathroom and then took a look in the mirror. The doctor was right—my face was decorated with a shiner the likes of which I hadn't seen since living in Chicago. The intern who put in the stitches had done a phenomenal job, though—nice tight loops cinched the wound tight. I figured the scar wouldn't be too bad. Unfortunately, my head throbbed from the change to a vertical position, and it seemed lying down was the best move.

Stepping out of the bathroom, my attention was drawn to the door opening and a freshly shaved and showered Franciscus and Guirres. Dr. Prasad had left while I was relieving myself. "Mr. James, how are you feeling?" Guirres asked.

I shuffled along in my hospital booties, returning to the bed. "Good, thanks for asking."

"So, are you ready to come and answer some questions for us on the record?"

"What about my breakfast?" I wasn't being difficult; I really was hungry. I wanted protein. Salty bacon and sunny-side-up eggs with toast. Even the hospital food version of breakfast would have sufficed.

"Don't worry about that. We won't be long."

I spread my arms out wide to display my paper hospital gown. "Do you think I can put on some clothes? Or do I need to have my cheeks sticking out the back for this on-the-record interview?"

Guirres put his hand up. "We'll bring you a fresh set of clothes."

What I really wanted was an attorney. But a fresh set of clothes would have to do for now.

Syncing Forward

Two hours later, DHS had me in an interrogation, and my stomach was grumbling. The hospital scrubs they gave me rode halfway up my calves and were made even more ridiculous-looking with the hospital booties on my feet. For some unknown reason the air conditioning was running in November, and I shivered in the padded wheelchair. I stared across the table, flustered as their questions came rapid-fire.

Franciscus brushed his fingers through his short wiry mustache. "So this unidentified man you saw with the Innovo employees—where do you think he came from? We've been over the video from your CCTV system, and there isn't anybody who meets that description."

"Maybe he came in on one of the cargo vans in the back?" I offered.

"What are the inspection procedures for Innovo on incoming freight? How often do you sweep the access tunnels? Who sets the scheduling for the security officers?"

"Just slow down, okay?" I snapped. My head ached.

Franciscus snarled, "Stop telling me to slow down. What's your problem? Are you hiding something? You need more time to think about the answers?"

"Give me a break. The doc you guys brought in from Langley diagnosed me with a concussion. My eyes are bugging me, I haven't had anything to eat since last night, I've got a headache, and I'm going commando in thin cotton scrubs while sitting in an ice-cold room. You don't exactly have me at my best."

Guirres interrupted before his partner could retort. "Martin," he said slowly, "tell us again about the other two people. What did this security officer say when you were in the lab?"

"I told you we weren't in a lab. We were in the access tunnels."

"You sure about that?"

"Yes, for the third time, I am sure."

"So what did this security officer say down when you were down in the tunnels?"

"His name is Albert Vies. He was on our suspect list as being involved in stealing medical equipment from Innovo Pharmaceutical. He and Doctor Bruchmuller were arguing about leaving before the cops showed up. The two of them seemed to know each other really well—"

"Is this before or after you allegedly were injected?" Franciscus butted in.

"Allegedly?" I snapped. Rolling up my sleeve, I showed him the bruises from Bruchmuller holding my arm down, along with the distinctive dark color in the crook of my arm where a needle had penetrated my vein. "What do you call this black-and-blue mark, genius? Body paint? Jesus, no wonder you guys can't stop the terrorist attacks in this country."

"Screw you!" Franciscus stood up. This wasn't posturing—the agent glared at me with an expression that reminded me of Bruchmuller's before he attacked. This time, however, hunger had me borderline combative.

There was a bitty bit of me that was whispering in my ear that I should stop flapping my gums, but Franciscus had me so riled up that I kept pushing. "No! Screw you, Hoss! You've got guys killing my employees, and you sit there calling me a liar? Does *special* agent mean you take a short bus to work?"

Franciscus sat up quick, kicking his chair back with his boot. The feet screeched across the unwaxed floor before colliding with the wall. He came around the table just as Guirres grabbed his wrist and held him fast.

I shot him a nasty look. "Wow! I must have touched a nerve there. Did you get a bad review or something?"

Our growing belligerence toward each other showed no sign of easing up, and one of my comments touched him either personally or professionally. There was no telling which as Franciscus pointed at me. "Don't talk to me like you've got it goin' on. Who do you think you are, Rent-a-Cop? Can't make it with the big boys, so you get a cushy job and think you—"

Guirres slammed his hand down on the table and startled us both. "Stop it! Both of you!" Unlike his partner's, Guirres's response was not genuine anger—it was posturing. His hand slamming on the table didn't coincide with his vocal command, a sure sign that his actions were deliberate and thoughtful. It was clear what they were doing. He sent the red-faced Franciscus out of the room, the finishing touches on the good cop–bad cop routine.

"So you were saying?" Guirres asked calmly.

"I was saying," I echoed, "Vies said something peculiar after arguing with Jotwani. I was still hazy from the attack, but I am pretty sure he said they needed to get to the crypts."

"Crypts? You're sure you didn't hear him wrong?"

"No, I told you I'm not sure. Crits. Crips. Cribs. I'm pretty sure they said *crypts*. It might have been short for another word too, but I don't know."

"So crypt? Like at a cemetery?"

"I don't know—maybe."

"Why would they be going to a crypt?" The skin between Guirres' eyebrows creased vertically as he bit at a loose tag of skin on his lower lip.

"Don't have the faintest. Do you know what they were talking about?"

Guirres didn't answer me, and from the look on his face he didn't have to. Franciscus reentered the room with a sense of urgency. In his hand was a stapled paper printout that he flapped in his hands. "We've got to get him upstairs. Ahora."

"What's that?" Guirres asked.

"Prasad's prelim report," he answered nervously, "but that's not why they need him back. The other investigator—Tsai—he found something."

I decided to break into the abrupt exchange. "Did he figure out what Bruchmuller injected me with?"

"I dunno, man," Franciscus answered.

Guirres pressed his partner. "Well, what did he find?"

Agent Franciscus shrugged, flapping his hands. "I don't know, man. It's—it's something weird. You gotta come see."

Guirres grabbed the handles of the wheelchair, and soon we were racing down the hospital hallway. Everything around me was slightly blurry, and I wondered if the concussion was worse than the doctor had thought. A nurse met us at the elevator doors, and we rode up three floors while the agents conversed in Spanish.

I had poked at the language in high school, and being married to a Mexican woman meant I needed to speak Spanish just to survive an argument with my wife. But Guirres and Franciscus were Puerto Rican, and the dialects differed enough to throw me off. Plus, Puerto Ricans are rapid-fire conversationalists—practically Olympian in how many words a minute they can convey. Add the fact that my nausea was kicking in, and their conversation was near impossible to follow. One thing Franciscus murmured I did catch, though: *"La rata está vivo."* The rat is alive.

I had no clue what that meant yet, but my heart raced in anticipation. We went up two floors and worked our way into the intensive care unit. As we walked past a small cluttered office, I caught a glimpse of David Tsai through the doorway, talking with a man with a shoulder holster. There was no telling what they were doing, as I lost sight of them and was wheeled into a new room. Machines with lights and displays and cords that terminated in sticky pads filled most of the space.

A male nurse joined the female nurse, and the pair helped me into a new bed and began applying the adhesive squares to my chest,

Syncing Forward

head, and arms with proficient speed. His blue scrubs smelled like some type of antiseptic, like a cross between a dentist's office and a janitor's closet.

"Is everything okay?" I asked nervously.

She wouldn't look at me, instead replying, "The doctor will be in shortly."

While I didn't care for her evading the question, she wasn't lying. Dr. Prasad trotted in with Dave, the man with the gun holster, and the two DHS agents. Dave's eyes were sunken and strained like those of an insomniac two days into his energy drinks.

"Mr. James, how are you feeling?" Prasad asked, but the way he spoke made me think he was in a hurry.

"Well, being that you've wired me up like a Christmas tree, I'm feeling downright uncomfortable. What the hell is going on?" My stomach was doing gymnastics, and it felt good to vent a little steam.

"Mr. James." Prasad prodded at me and shone a light in my eyes. "Are you able to see and hear okay? Have you noticed any changes?"

"I'm a little dizzy, and things are a bit blurry from time to time. But that could be the concussion, right?" I looked at Dave, who ran his bottom lip nervously along his teeth while gripping his data pad. "Buddy, tell me you've got some good news on that tablet you're strangling."

Dave looked at the man with the holster, who gave him a tiny nod before he stepped forward. "Well, I don't know what kind of news I have for you other than I think I found out what Dr. Bruchmuller injected you with. I couldn't retrieve the video of either interview we conducted—they hadn't been loaded off-site yet. But I did go back to the archives, which were backed up at the corporate office. It didn't make sense that out of everything we were asking about, Bruchmuller would go ballistic over the dead rat. So I watched the video we had of the rat cage, and that's when I noticed . . ."

He stopped, as if he didn't want to say what he saw. I rolled my finger in the air to get him to explain faster.

"I don't know how to say this, Martin, but the rat wasn't dead. It was alive, just moving really, really slow. Remember that camera shot in which he put the rat up on the shelf right in front of the camera? We were pissed off about not being able to see the rest of the laboratory all that well? We missed it—it was right in front of our faces. I zoomed through the video at about thirty times normal speed to skip to the lab's next work shift, when I noticed the rat breathing. The damn thing was breathing, but slowly. The legs moved too, but in slow motion. There was no way to notice it without watching it on high-speed playback. Look."

Why this was important to me I still hadn't put together, but I trusted my friend enough to know he wouldn't be wasting our time.

Dave handed me the tablet, and I confirmed the video ran at thirty times normal speed. The human eye can't really track details past ten times normal speed, and anything past fifteen times normal playback meant the software was skipping frames. We almost never used the ultrafast modes unless we wanted to skip forward to a specific time of day. In this case, however, I could see the chest of the rat rising and falling slowly. I could see its furry little mouth opening and closing. I could see its nose wriggling on the tip of its snout, its tail sliding about on the cage floor, and its little rat claws scraping against the metal surface. All of this occurred at a snail's pace.

I looked at Dr. Prasad. "So they were making slow-motion rats in our lab? I don't understand—do you know what is going on or not?"

"No," he answered with painful honesty, "none of us do. But here's what I do know. Your blood pressure has been steadily dropping despite experiencing stressers like the interview DHS conducted. Your body temperature is dropping. Your pupils are dilating slower than normal. You were complaining to the agents that they were talking too fast, and you've been describing your vision as blurry. As strange as it may sound, I believe this drug you were injected with slows the human body down considerably, and it does so on a subcellular level. I've never heard of such a drug before, and it doesn't match anything Innovo Pharmaceutical research disclosed to us.

"Despite the fact that we can't isolate the drug from any blood or tissue samples, we're moving forward with the theory that these rogue doctors developed a drug that slows down cellular activity and—for whatever reason—they injected you with that drug."

His voice sounded faster than normal. All of theirs were. They didn't have the high-pitched fast-forward quality you might expect to hear when things speed up, but they sounded muffled, like I was listening to their words through a blanket. I rubbed my blurring eyes as the room seemed to pitch to a five-degree angle—just slightly off-kilter. The moment reminded me of a time from my youth when I'd had an inner ear infection. We were living in the hurricane shelters in Texas, and I remember stumbling around the house, bumping into walls and doors. Now, even though I was strung to the hospital bed with a dozen electrodes, I just knew that one step would have me toppling.

"Daddy!" Bella's cute little voice pierced the air as she rushed past the doctor and nurses and everyone else in the room with blind enthusiasm. Seven years old and oblivious to everything except wanting her father. It was only when she grabbed my arms and got close that she realized my body was drizzled with wires. "Daddy, what is all this stuff?"

Miranda and Amara followed with a hospital worker in tow. Franciscus snapped at the worker that my family needed to leave, and the next few seconds were a buzz of everyone talking over each other.

"—they can't be in here right now."

"Martin, are you okay?"

"—isn't the best time—"

"—going on with my husband?"

"—not going to tell you again to get them out of—"

"Nurse, check those connections to make sure it is reading right—"

"—let go of my daughter!"

Nurses and a new doctor quick-stepped past my family and the agents. One woman was talking to another so rapidly I couldn't even make out what she was saying. The world turned about fifteen degrees sideways, and instinctively my hand reached for the railing. The air felt hot as nausea swelled, and I took a deep breath to keep from dry heaving.

Bella yanked on my fingers. "Daddy, can you take me to the vending machines?"

Amara snapped at her little sister. "Stupid, how is he going to take you anywhere! He's in a bed!"

"Ma'am, we're going to need you and your children to step out—" Agent Franciscus raised his voice.

I closed my eyes to gain my composure. They were moving and walking and talking as if I were watching a surveillance video through my own eyes.

"Hi, Daddy, how are you hey you look funny are you playing around Daddy stop playing around Momma Momma Daddy is acting weird!"

Bella's sentences were all blended together, and before I could respond she was being pulled from the room by my wife. I blinked hard and flapped my eyelids to keep them from stinging and—hopefully—to clear my head. I tried yawning to pop my ears, thinking perhaps they were clogged. A second later Dave stood by the bedside, shaking my arm.

"Martin Martin are you okay can you hear me what's wrong Buddy you're not looking so hot can you please just say—" Dave was talking as if on fast-forward, his words riding one upon another.

"Slow down," I started to say, trying to cut through their rapid speech and the concern on their faces. "I feel very strange—"

The nurse cut me off. My voice sounded raspy in my own head, and low-toned.

Syncing Forward

"Martin why are you talking so slow do you understand what I am saying?"

"Yeah, but you can't talk so fast—"

"I need you to tell me what you're feeling right now."

I tried to get a word in edgewise. "I'm trying to answer, if you would let me—"

Amara had been standing in the doorway, watching the chaos from a distance after being yanked into the hallway by somebody on the staff. She ran back into the room with the hospital worker chasing after her. "Daddy why are you talking like that are you fooling around you're fooling right come on Daddy tell the truth you are playing right you are pretending right Daddy?"

"No, sweetie, I'm not. I don't—" I couldn't even finish one sentence as the girls kept talking over me. The woman grabbed Amara with both hands and pulled her kicking and screaming from the room, her face flushed with anger as they rapidly sank backward toward the hallway. "Let go of my kid!" I tried to yell, but the command stalled in my throat and sputtered out like a whisper.

"Leavehimaloneleavehimalonenowstopit!"

"We'vegottotransporthimtothelabrightnow . . ."

"Wherearewemovinghimto?"

"Ma'amyouneedtocalmdownandtakeyourchildrenoutofhr—"

The room became a swirl of battered sentences strung together and overlapping. The doctors and nurses took the foreground, asking me questions, never waiting long enough for me to answer. For split seconds I could catch the movement behind them. Miranda was holding onto Amara now, dragging her from view. The hospital worker was bent over the crying face of Bella.

"Belladon'tworryyourfatherisgoingtobefinethesemenarehearto helphimit'sokayit'sokaydon'tbescaredcomeonlet'sgowithyourmomands isterokay?"

". . . thereisnosignofastrokewe'veplacedacalltoLangleyyes . . ."

79

W Lawrence

"... sealoffthisareafromvisitors ..."

"... goingtoneedtotransporthim ..."

Life turned sideways as they wheeled my gurney from the room and raced to the rooftop. Tears were building in my eyes again. I had to resign myself to quick glimpses of the world as I shut my lids and peeked from behind them when something caught my ear or moved me enough to rouse my curiosity.

By the time they got me into the medivac helicopter, I finally understood what Bruchmuller had injected me with. Those four syringes were the culmination of what these doctors had been researching. The world wasn't speeding up; I was slowing down.

I had become the rat.

Syncing Forward

Chapter 7

What was typically a deafening experience of rotors chopping through the air vibrated with a quiet hum. My teary eyes made it difficult to see details, but I could tell there were four others on the helicopter, all men. All the normal feelings you would normally sense when flying were present, including the flutters in my stomach as we took off and bumped around. The takeoff and leveling took a matter of minutes for me. And the descent—that felt like a freefall that had me grasping at the rails for dear life.

Conversation was difficult to make out now, their accelerating speech a slur to my stifled ears. ". . . Whewelanneettahitotheforfloancontdocsopa . . ."

Their movements were a blur, hand movements—so typical in conversation—spellbindingly swift. When the medivac landed, I had to close my eyes again for fear that the disoriented movements would make me sick to my stomach. I hoped that they were taking my feelings into consideration, that they were moving me as slowly as possible, but there was no way to be sure. From years of experience watching a CCTV system, I knew that at fifteen times normal speed, you could sneeze watching a surveillance recording and miss a grown man in a bright orange jacket walking down twenty feet of hallway. What was happening to me seemed to be on the cusp of that rate and maybe even increasing.

Not that my perception was identical to watching video. Surveillance cameras take pictures and string them together, like a piece of film. How often those pictures are taken depends on the quality of the camera and the recording device, frame rate, and how much memory your system has. My eyes were calculating movement about me as if I were watching an air show. The closer somebody drew to me, the faster he moved. Faces became featureless distortions. Legs seemed to merge into a hazy triangular shape as people walked by. Arms seemed to belong to conductors as they directed symphonies at high speed. And with my eyes tearing up worse than the worst allergy attack, making sense of the goings on around me became damn near maddening.

Within a few minutes, all motion had stopped, and I was sequestered in a fluorescent-lit room as quiet as Christmas morning. Somebody had rolled me slightly onto my side, and I could make out an IV hooked up to my arm. Somebody buckled a single strap loosely across my belly, presumably to keep me from falling out of bed. While my eyes were closed, I heard a man's voice near to my ear. "Martjamcayoheame."

By the time I opened my eyes, he was gone. Perhaps it was my imagination, but surely somebody had been there. I hoped so. A doctor. A friend. A government official. A stranger asking me questions. Anyone to talk to would have been comforting.

The lights went out, and I plunged into darkness. So there I lay, desperate for answers. There was a clink across the room, like what you might hear if the neighbor two doors down dropped a pipe on his driveway. Unable to stand for fear that I would fall, oblivious to where I had been taken or who had me, I curled into a ball and waited.

If I slept, it was a catnap at best—like dozing off in a car, only to be roused by the tires hitting a rumble strip. From behind my eyelids I could tell the lights had come on, and I cracked one eye open to witness a team of doctors and nurses spinning around me. Within seconds they were gone. I got the distinct impression I had changed rooms, but it was hard to be sure. The lights in the room were dim, and a computer screen sat near me with an old-fashioned corded mouse on a table that hung over the bed. The screen had words on it in large typeset, but I couldn't keep my eyes open long enough to read it.

MARTIN JAMES, WE KNOW—

That was all I managed to make out. When I shut my eyelids, they felt like sandpaper against my corneas. I didn't dare open them for longer for fear that I might do long-term damage. The stitched cut on my face still ached, and I reached up to feel the stitches. My arm felt

Syncing Forward

like it had been wrapped in cement, and I found it easier to simply slide it along the bed to my face. My fingers made contact with the ridge-like stitches—my present from Bruchmuller's attack—but still my skin felt asleep.

Even with my eyes closed, I could tell the lights had been put out again. The computer screen too. The moments ticked by without a sound or a touch or a change.

The dark hated me. It deprived me of what little sensation I had. It filled me with more mystery than I cared for. I returned the hatred, desperate for answers, cursing my custodians for leaving me here wondering what was to come—quietly, of course, since nothing but a hiss escaped my mouth.

I worried about my wife. She was out there, probably asking questions that nobody would answer. She still didn't know what had transpired at Innovo, and my opportunity to explain had vanished. I didn't know who had me, but they were clearly from the government. Would they tell her I was sick? Contagious? Maybe they would tell her I had died. That thought preyed upon my imagination as I pictured my children crying for me and my not being able to be there. Not being able to console them or tell them I was alive.

I hoped that Dave would tell Miranda what I had shared with him. God, if Dave didn't share my plight with somebody else, I would be at the complete mercy of Homeland Security.

The quiet disturbed me to the core. No air-conditioning units humming, no cars driving by. Some side effect made the loud noises muffled and the quiet noises vanish. I could hear the beating of my heart, the sound of my dry tongue scraping against my teeth. My stomach growls echoed up through my body. Quiet had been something of a premium in my life, with kids and cell phones and cars and whatnot, but the lack of noise was awful, and the sounds of my innards gurgling was unsettling, to say the least. I had read once about an anechoic chamber in Minnesota that was so quiet, a person sitting within would go insane after forty-five minutes. I had no idea how

83

many minutes passed for me, but I boxed my own ears just to hear something.

The lights flashed, and I felt as if I had swallowed a piece of hard candy whole. The insides of my cheeks were so dry. I peeked with my left eye to see a tube coming out of my mouth, but in the time it took me to close my eyes, the pain in my throat disappeared and the lights winked out.

The lights came on again. I strained to open my eyes just long enough to see the room transformed. More equipment had been wheeled in, more instrumentation for studying my condition. Or perhaps they had relocated me to another room? It was possible. Thank God there was a sound now. An air-conditioning unit? A fan? I didn't know, and the sound was faint, but I tried concentrating on that one sound, begging for it to be louder.

They hadn't moved the computer, and the same message from before remained on the screen.

MARTIN JAMES, WE KNOW YOU ARE ALIVE—

Two people were in the room with me, and this time they managed to stand still long enough for me to recognize that they were both men wearing white lab coats. Four hands were on my head, holding it fast, positioning it so that my chin cocked forward and my nose slightly pointed to the ceiling. I felt them pull my eyes open, and after several iterations pieced together that they were placing eyedrops in my eyes for me.

It was beginning to make sense now. Every time you blink, you wash your eyes with fresh tears, allowing you to see properly. But I reckoned that if my body moved real slowly, even blinking would be a very slow process, and my body was probably making tears much more slowly as well. Thank God they had figured this out.

Now my vision had become less painful, clearing up with the regular attention of the gentlemen in the room and washed with artificial tears, returning to an almost-clear view. Blinking reminded me of driving in a heavy storm and trying to make out the road in those

Syncing Forward

moments when the wipers pushed the water out of the way. I could see the men coming and going often, always coming back and holding my eyes open and applying drops to them.

They clearly wanted me to read the message they had left for me, and they placed my hand on the computer mouse. My arm felt as weighty as if my daughter Bella were hanging off of it, playing the carry-the-sloth game; her legs and hands would be hooked around my forearm while I'd carry her about the house giggling.

MARTIN JAMES, WE KNOW YOU ARE ALIVE AND CONSCIOUS.

YOU ARE IN THE WALTER REED MEDICAL CENTER.

YOUR FAMILY IS FINE. THEY KNOW WHERE YOU ARE.

WE ARE UNSURE ABOUT WHAT YOU CAN SEE OR HEAR OR DO.

WE ARE WORKING TO IMPROVE YOUR CONDITION.

<MORE>

I noticed the little arrow hovering just to the left of the word *more*, and I manipulated the mouse to click it. The screen went blank, and more words came up.

WE NEED INFORMATION ABOUT YOUR CONDITION.

ARE YOU IN PAIN? <YES> <NO>

I clicked *no* and moved on. The eyedrops kept coming.

ARE YOU THIRSTY OR HUNGRY?

I clicked *no* again, although after that question I quickly became mindful that my mouth felt dry and my stomach felt hollow. The mental image of a cheeseburger popped into my head, and I cursed them for reminding me that I hadn't eaten for hours. Well, what I thought were hours.

DO YOU UNDERSTAND THAT YOU ARE MOVING SLOWLY COMPARED TO THE REST OF US?

Yes.

DO YOU HAVE ANY ALLERGIES NOT LISTED ON YOUR MEDICAL E-CHART?

No.

The screen wiped clean and was replaced with more questions.

ARE YOU TIRED?

No.

ARE YOU HOT OR COLD?

Thankfully, they gave me a *fine* option. I clicked it.

DO YOU KNOW WHAT DATE IT IS?

I snarled at the stupidity of such a question. Why not tell me the date? I answered *no* and moved on. The next paragraph caught me off guard. In the time it had taken to answer those few questions, I had lost count of the dozens of times the attendants put eyedrops in for me. How slow was I going?

YOUR ATTORNEY HAS REQUESTED THAT WE ASK FOR YOUR PERMISSION BEFORE PROCEEDING WITH MEDICAL TREATMENT. YOU HAVE BEEN EXPOSED TO SOMETHING THAT WE DO NOT

Syncing Forward

FULLY UNDERSTAND. WE HAVE EVERY INTENTION OF IMPROVING YOUR CONDITION, BUT SOME OPTIONS MAY COME WITH A FAIRLY HIGH LEVEL OF RISK. CAN YOUR WIFE MIRANDA JAMES MAKE DECISIONS FOR YOU?

Miranda had hassled me a million times over the need to get a Power of Attorney form drawn up in case of a medical emergency. I had put it off for years. Now I was getting a crash course in why preparation was so important.

I answered *yes*.

MIRANDA JAMES WOULD LIKE TO KNOW WHAT LEVEL OF RISK YOU WANT TO TAKE.

The question preceded the numbers 1, 2, 3, 4, and 5, with the word *highest* next to the 5. I paused and thought about it. I had no idea what was wrong with me, and my wife was trying to gauge her decisions based on a single number. What should I do? If the people here had an antidote, I surely would have received it by now. It was impossible to know what my wife knew, and I was in no position to ask questions. The last thing I wanted was to be a test subject, but then again, I couldn't stomach the idea of remaining like this. Without taking extreme risks, I wanted them to do everything they could. Answering with a middle of the road 3 was going to provide no help whatsoever. Hopefully Miranda and whatever attorney she got us would read between the lines of my answer. My single-digit answer.

I pressed 4.

The next screen filled me with hope.

MESSAGE FROM MIRANDA: I LOVE YOU. DON'T WORRY. I'VE GOT THE KIDS. WE MISS YOU.

MESSAGE FROM BELLA: DADDY, I MISS YOU SO MUCH COME HOME SOON.

MESSAGE FROM AMARA: I PRAY EVERY NIGHT, DADDY. I LOVE YOU SO MUCH.

The messages were short, much like the rest of the messages from the hospital. If they had no idea how slowly I perceived the world, they had probably told the girls to write something brief. It didn't matter. The fact that they knew I was okay was enough to get me through this trial.

One last message came across the screen.

WE WILL BEGIN TRIALS SOON MARTIN JAMES. YOU ARE IN GOOD HANDS HERE. REMAIN HOPEFUL.

I barely had time to read it before they took the screen away and moved me about. With drops no longer being fed into my eyes, my vision went back to blurry glimpses stolen through barely opened slits. I believed I went through some type of scanning device, but the trip was so fast I couldn't make it out. That scanner became a regular visit for me over the next half hour.

Half hour? *What was I thinking?* What was a half hour to me? How long had I been here? Hours, days? If I moved at one-tenth the speed of a normal person, a few hours would work out to over a day, and I had no true sense of when I'd gotten here or how long I'd been sitting in perfect darkness.

Dozens of times they brought me into the scanner room, and I wondered why they didn't just leave me in the blasted thing. Even with my eyes closed, the lights from the machine would still strobe viciously. I scrunched my face to try to block the sensation, but each time my reaction fell just a bit behind the event. Then—as if by magic—a pair of dark-lens goggles appeared on the bridge of my nose. I looked out through my right eye and managed to figure out I was in an RMRI, like at the hospital.

After a few minutes passed—from my perspective at least—somebody ripped the goggles from my head, and I found myself back

Syncing Forward

in the room where I started. The men were back, holding my head and dousing my eyes with some type of spray gun. It looked like the mist from the nozzle of a hose, and it made seeing even more difficult overall. A new machine that looked like a tube on the end of an adjustable arm was aimed directly at my head. Just beyond my perception, the technicians must have fitted me with a headset as well. The pressure of the earpieces barely tickled my senses before I heard a voice.

The computer mouse appeared again along with the screen. Two words, *yes* and *no,* were set at the bottom.

"Marnamsayunusanis . . ." The sounds came so fast I barely had a chance to recognize them as speech. Did they expect me to answer the message on the screen? It might have been them asking if I understood, but I couldn't be sure. Guessing seemed like a bad idea. I started a mental count, and after I hit twenty seconds, the message came again.

"Martinjamescanyouunderstandthis?" While the question was intelligible this time, the words still came rapidly, like a radio disclaimer for an auto dealer advertisement.

I clicked *yes.*

Immediately new words were feeding into my earpieces. "Arethewordsyouarehearingtoofastortooslow?"

Three new options appeared on the screen, and I chose the one that said *too fast.*

"Aaaaaaaarrrrrreeeee tthhheeeeeee wooooooooooorrrdddss yoooooooooouuuuuu arrrrrrrrrrrrrrre heeeeeeeeeeearrr—"

I clicked *too slow.*

We went through several tries before I finally was able to answer *good.*

"Martin James, we are trying to calibrate this voice to the speed at which you are able to perceive. We are estimating based on your pulse and eye movements as you read these messages. Do you understand?"

W Lawrence

Yes.

"We will be treating you soon to counteract the effects of the drugs you were exposed to at Innovo. Relax. We are taking care of you. There may be some slight discomfort."

The words barely registered before I arched my back and launched my arms out to the side in agony. A sharp pain shot down my left arm, and my chest felt as if I had fallen into a trash compactor.

A heart attack? Dear God! Was I having a heart attack? There were restraints on my legs and arms where there'd been none just a moment before, and my body pressed against them. Strapped to a gurney and injected with an unknown drug: the situation was all-too-fresh in my mind, and I wondered if Bruchmuller was the one who had me here. Maybe I wasn't in Walter Reed Medical at all. Had Bruchmuller been able to orchestrate my kidnapping once again?

The sharp, stabbing sensation subsided quickly and unexpectedly. I opened my eyes for a split second and found the room stale and quiet. The doctors or technicians or whoever they were moved with a blur just as before; only, now their movements were within my perception. I took some relief at the notion that I was speeding back up, that my senses were returning to normal.

The first thing I noticed was the ample number of wires stuck to my chest and head, each one running to a set of machines on either side of me. Joining them was an intravenous line in each of my arms. The spaghetti-like ensemble rounded out with a clear and uncomfortable tube running into my nostrils.

"Cayonersndmemisrjames?" an Asian woman in her forties or fifties asked me, her triangular face close to mine.

I tried to speak but found my voice a hiss in my own ears. I had no idea what it sounded like to the lady in front of me. She tried to hold still as I spoke, but her slight movements made me dizzy nonetheless. It looked as if she was holding a spray bottle near my mouth, and I felt a slightly oily wetness on the insides of my cheeks and on my lips, enough to make me swallow. The same dryness that tortured my eyes had affected my mouth and throat as well.

When I opened my mouth for just a moment, how much time had really passed? It felt like I'd gulped down a dang hedgehog, but the second swallow felt better than the first.

The woman sat down in a chair alongside my bed, reading a tablet and occasionally looking up at me. Everyone else had cleared the room. Her movements were still quite fast, but well within my ability to make out what she was doing—probably two times normal speed or less. It seemed like a long while in which I sat there awake, getting accustomed to catching up with the rest of the world. I had to blink a lot, but at least my eyes weren't drying out like before. The tension I'd been carrying bled off noticeably as I dared to believe the nightmare was ending.

Feeling some discomfort below the waist, I peeked under the thin blanket and traced a catheter line that disappeared beneath the hospital gown and into what looked like an adult diaper. I don't know if I had actually relieved myself at any point during this ordeal, but the catheter had to be either a precaution or a response to me making a mess. I also felt some discomfort in my stomach, something I had never felt before—almost like bruising.

I tried to speak again and found myself pleasantly surprised to hear my own voice, raspy as it was. "So, Doctor," I began. "Are you monitoring me?"

"With this?" She held up the tablet. "No, I'm reading the new Veronica Swells book. What can I say? I'm a sucker for trashy romance."

"I'm not familiar with her," I croaked. I ran my tongue along the inside of my cheeks, the unpleasant aftertaste of whatever she'd sprayed in my mouth still prevalent.

"I didn't think you would be." She grinned, standing up and discarding the pad carelessly on an instrument cart. She shone a small light in my eyes, moving it about. "Don't worry—there's nothing wrong with your eye beyond the bruising you had before. Just checking your tracking and dilation . . . so, Martin, tell me how you are feeling."

"Hungry," I answered. "And nauseous. And my stomach feels achy. Not the best combination, I suppose."

"We had to remove the food from your small intestine. No easy way about it."

My lips furled in disgust. Rather than dwell on how they managed to extract my last meal, I turned my attention to the only company I had. "Who are you, if you don't mind me asking?"

She grabbed a semicircular metal tray and set it on my lap. "I'm Dr. Gonzales, one of the twenty-six specialists who have been taking care of you."

"Gonzales?" I questioned. Clearly she hailed from the Pacific Rim, from her angled eyes to her slight but noticeable accent. She wore heavy makeup, probably to cover the pockmarks that managed to show from underneath her foundation.

"It's my husband's name. Come now, Martin—you're in an interracial marriage. You sound so closed-minded."

"Ah, that makes sense. Sorry. I wasn't being closed-minded, just confused . . ." I stammered through my excuses and decided to simply let it go. "Well, thanks for patching me up, Dr. Gonzales."

"It's okay. I get that all the time; I actually enjoy putting people on the spot." Gonzales let out a short, mischievous laugh that, if we were in a bar or at a party, would be considered friendly and encouraging. In this clinical setting, it was oddly out of place.

She pulled the chair over and knelt on it, poking away at a medical pad that she pulled from the bottom of my bed. "Don't get too excited, Martin. We're not out of the woods yet. Now that you can interact with us, I need some information from you about—"

"Did I have a heart attack?" I interrupted. The question just blurted out of me.

Syncing Forward

"You did go into cardiac arrest, but not because of any arterial blockages. Your body didn't handle the treatment we gave you nearly as well as we had hoped. Your heart's electrical impulses were confused, and the result was you died."

"Died?" I stared at her, wide-eyed.

"Dead as a desert. If you were anywhere else in the world, they would have dumped you in a body bag. Bad for you wherever you woke up. We managed to revive you after five hours and thirty-three minutes. We're not certain if it's a world record, but it's up there."

As I sat there stunned into silence, Gonzales took the opportunity to take control of the dialogue. "Listen, Martin. I know you have a lot of questions, and I'll answer all of them, but I need to get mine in first in case you relapse into your previous state."

The thought hadn't occurred to me. I didn't like the idea that my return to normalcy might be temporary at all, but I figured it was time to cooperate, not question. "Yes ma'am. Ask away."

"Since we're on the topic, how painful was the cardiac arrest for you?"

"On a scale of one to ten? A ten. It was short but bad. I actually thought you were trying to kill me."

"No, we're definitely not trying to kill you." Dr. Gonzales pulled up a prewritten list on her Rx slate and began chugging away. The questions were mostly about how I felt, how I perceived things, what I recalled, how clear things were to me. The Q&A session was interrupted as I dry heaved a couple of times over the aluminum dish on my lap, but the doctor went right back to reading off the list, typing in my responses as we went.

"So the lights were bugging you for the entire time or just the beginning?" she asked me.

"At first they were bugging me, and then when you guys were scanning me in that big oval contraption. After the goggles were put on me, I didn't notice any light changes at all." I dry heaved again.

93

W Lawrence

Doctor Gonzales shriveled up her nose slightly at the sound of me trying to upchuck food that wasn't there. "Sorry about the nausea. There isn't much we can do about it." Underneath the cart was a small rag that she used to dab a stringy line of spittle that landed on my chin.

"Problems you experienced in there? Perception? Clearly the eyes and mouth were an issue that we were slow to pick up on. No pun intended. Anything else, though?"

"Yes. The sound. I mean the lack of sound. It was awful."

"We figured you couldn't hear too well. Your eardrums wouldn't vibrate slowly enough for your brain to interpret the sound, so the slower you went, the quieter it must have gotten."

I told her about the humming sound and how it was the only thing keeping me from losing my mind. She made a little note on the pad, sighed, then said, "So here is the big question. How long have you been here at Walter Reed?"

"Uh, shouldn't you be answering that question?" Being sarcastic wasn't my intent, but it came out that way.

"Martin, you know what I mean. *From your perspective,* how long have you been here?"

"It's hard to say. Maybe twelve hours? Sixteen hours? Hell, it could be a whole day. I wish I could give you a better answer, but to call the experience disorienting would be an understatement."

"Care to take a guess?"

"Well, I was guessing that things were moving around ten to fifteen times their normal speed. Hard to say, but I reckon fifteen days."

Doctor Gonzales seemed to be sizing me up, calculating how I would react. "Martin, you have to understand that what is happening to you should be medically impossible. This is all very new to us, and we've failed in our attempt to reverse engineer this compound that has been completely absorbed into your system. What we've been able to do at this point is convince your cells to move much faster than they should. You were in a state we are referring to as chemopreservation. That's a fancy way of saying your body functions have been slowed on a cellular level. With the—"

"How long?" I pressed. Doctors usually gave a lot of information ahead of time when the news was bad, and the longer she went on, the worse I knew her answer was going to be.

"Four months and four days," she said flatly.

My tongue tried to make a word but instead just flopped about silently in my mouth. I shook my head and managed to make noise, "That's not possible."

"That's what all of us said, and yet here you are. It's March 5, 2022, Martin." She showed me the date on the tablet, as if her words wouldn't be convincing enough. She was probably right.

I took a deep breath and let it out. Stunned. Four months was a long time. The pulse meter began beating faster; even though the volume was low, we both knew my heart was racing. It was nearly springtime. I had missed Thanksgiving. I had missed Christmas with the girls. I had missed our family's New Year's Eve celebration. I had missed Miranda's birthday. Winter had come and gone, and I hadn't shoveled an ounce of snow or felt the sting of New Jersey's February cold.

Okay, missing those last two wasn't exactly breaking my heart, but even winter had its special moments. Building snowmen with my daughters, watching football with the guys, that crisp smell in the air that you never quite experienced living in the South. There were so many questions I had wanted to ask, but all of them evaporated save for one.

"Can I see my family?" I asked, choking up as I did. "Please? I'd like to see my family now."

"I'll see what I can do. We didn't tell them we were performing the procedure for fear that it would give them a false sense of optimism," Dr. Gonzales responded quietly.

"I guess you didn't tell them when they visited me?"

W Lawrence

Her eyes turned down along with the corners of her mouth, "Sorry, Martin, but your family hasn't been here. This is a restricted area of the hospital. Nobody is allowed for visits." She stood and walked from the room, leaving me alone to stare at a white door in a white wall.

Four months.

An older white man in blue-and-gray scrubs took Dr. Gonzales's place and kept me talking while he pressed buttons and read his tablet. In complete contradiction to my time in chemopreservation, the next few minutes seemed to drag. I sat there waiting for answers. Waiting for company. Waiting for Miranda to wake me from this unpleasantness. Waiting for God to pluck me from these circumstances. I would have been happy to learn that I was hallucinating.

The man in the scrubs walked away to the corner and fiddled with a computer. The silence was marred only by the soft dings and whirls of the instrument panels that surrounded me.

Chapter 8

A knock jolted me from my somber reflection. A few seconds later, the door opened, and a familiar face came into view. It was not the face I expected or wanted to see. Agent Franciscus sheepishly inched into the room with Dr. Gonzales right behind him. The two were followed by a woman in a white lab coat whom I might have seen in my incapacitated state. She was easy on the eyes, and her smile was warm as she patted my leg.

"How are you feeling, Martin?" she asked me familiarly.

"Well, come to think of it, my eye is sore right here." I touched the stitches on my brow. "Hey, if I've been here for four months, why haven't these stitches come out?"

She leaned in and looked at my face closely with a small flashlight. "These are actually the third set of stitches we've put in you. The first set were the dissolving type, but your skin didn't heal nearly as fast as we would have liked. I'm guessing your skin-healing properties are very much like the rest of you—slow."

I grinned wryly at the woman's ribbing, but had nothing to come back with. "I guess that makes sense."

"Glad to see you awake, Martin."

I thanked her before she turned away to upload her Rx slate with the instrumentation in the room. I cocked my head to the side to look at Franciscus, who was waiting patiently by my bedside. "So, what brings you here?" I couldn't make myself sound happy about his presence.

"Hey, Mr. James, I just wanted to peek in on you. I was in DC giving depositions when they called me and told me they were going to try to wake you." His speech had completely changed from the accusatory tone I had experienced back in the Bergen County Hospital. It was almost remorseful.

"So what can I do for you? Are you here to arrest me or just interrogate me again?" Four months might have passed for him, but my agitation remained fresh.

Franciscus didn't bite. He just pulled up a stool and sat down next to me. "Nah, nothing like that. We actually need your help."

There sat an awkward stillness between the two of us that nobody in the room interrupted. They were busy chattering about vitals and levels and numbers, and as much as all that interested me, I could neither understand them nor ignore the DHS agent in front of me. Breaking down, I finally asked him, "What could I possibly do to help you? I've been stuck here for four months."

"We've had some setbacks, hit some dead ends." He cleared his throat before moving on, "Just so you know, we've been digging into what's left of your investigation files. Dieterich Bruchmuller's recorded interview was partially lost in the explosion, along with some files that didn't fully upload to your company's cloud backup, but for the most part we've been impressed with what we found. You did some good work."

"I don't know what to say. I appreciate the compliment, and the fact that that you came and got me. Who knows what would have happened if you hadn't?" I simply fell into the reconciliatory direction of the conversation. It was strange to consider myself lucky that Dieterich Bruchmuller had kidnapped me and stolen four months of my life.

"Any word on what was in that fifth vial?"

He simply shook his head.

"What happened to Dr. Bruchmuller? Were you able to catch him?"

Franciscus glanced toward Dr. Gonzales, who briefly looked up, caught listening to our conversation. He cracked his neck to the left and right and nudged his stool closer. "Hey, I don't know how to tell you this, but—"

"He got away, didn't he?" I probed.

Syncing Forward

"Mr. James, Dieterich Bruchmuller was killed. Albert Vies, Rajesh Jotwani, and Sandy Vangdamas are all dead too."

I swallowed hard. Rajesh, my friend, my suspect, my kidnapper, my defender. "How did Rajesh die?"

"Fleeing the scene. Struck by a tractor trailer on Interstate 287 when their vehicle flipped."

"And Doctor Bruchmuller?"

"Shot and killed."

"What about the other suspects we had at Innovo? Did David Tsai give you that information?"

"We got all that by subpoena. Dr. Feingold swallowed a bullet in a standoff with NYPD nine hours after the Innovo bombing. All the others from your list are currently missing."

I shook my head. "Agent, I wish I could offer you something, but I poured my life into that case. I spent months collecting all that data, blowing off other cases, ignoring my wife and kids. Everything I know is in those files you subpoenaed."

"Not everything. You told us in the hospital there was another man there. Somebody you didn't recognize. If I showed you some pictures, do you think you could identify him? I know it's been a while, but we were hoping that events would still be fresh in your mind, given your circumstances."

I peered over his shoulder, hoping Dr. Gonzales would give me some word on my family. She met my gaze and held up one finger. "We're trying to reach your wife, Martin. Hang tight."

"Come on, Mr. James. We're trying to help you. Take a look at these faces." Agent Franciscus handed me a tablet with three faces side by side and arrows pointing to the left and right.

I looked over at Dr. Gonzales again. She was busy directing the younger woman in some activity. Turning my attention back to the agent, I sighed. "Listen, can't we do this some other time? I'm really worried about my family. They haven't seen me in four months."

"Mr. James, just look at the faces for a few minutes. We think—"

I cut him off. "I barely got a look at the guy. Can't you follow up with the other suspects?"

"There's nobody left to investigate!" He spread his arms wide in exasperation. "Bank accounts cleared. Relatives vanished. Computers sanitized. These people, they're like ghosts. We've got nada. The men on this lineup all have expertise in explosives—any one of them could have helped construct the bombs set at Innovo." The tablet was extended to me once again.

I shook my head and hesitantly took the tablet with the faces on it. I swiped through a few dozen of them and could tell these were a mishmash of "most wanted" and former arrests. The counter at the bottom read 37 of 351, and that told me everything I needed to know. "The man you're looking for? He's not going to be in here."

"Why would you say that?"

"Because every single one of the men and women involved had no criminal background, nothing that would make them stand out. If that was the case for those seven, why would this eighth man be any different? You're looking for the wrong type of suspect."

His brow furrowed as he hesitantly took the tablet back. "Fine, Mr. James. Let's go back to the man you saw. When we interviewed you at the hospital, you mentioned that this unknown male was"—Franciscus pulled out a small tablet of paper from his pocket—"white, forty to forty-five years old, medium build, bald, wearing a suit and tie. Anything else? Height range? Tattoos? Did he wear glasses? Anything at all would help."

My kidnapping might have taken place four months ago, but to me it was as fresh as the cut on my face. "No glasses, no facial hair, no tattoos that I could see, but he was head to toe in a suit, so even a neck tat could have been hidden. He was tall, I can tell you that."

The agent did not look impressed. "Not that I'm doubting you, but weren't you strapped to a gurney? Maybe he just looked tall?"

Syncing Forward

I shook my head. "No, he was definitely tall. The man could hunt geese with a rake. They were all in a group together. Bruchmuller was, what, six one? Six two? This guy was taller than him by enough for me to notice. I'd say at least six foot four."

Franciscus bobbed his head from side to side. "Huh. Somebody that tall is going to stick out in a pool of suspects, but it isn't much. There has to be more you remember."

While talking with the agent, I became increasingly aware of an increased tension in the air. Two older white men walked in, and—while they gave me brief, courteous smiles—they were clearly discussing an important matter with the younger woman and Dr. Gonzales. Even though it was unsurprising to be the topic of conversation, I didn't have a good feeling about how everyone acted. They were congregated around the instruments, pointing and scowling and whispering in hushed tones. Any person on the street could look at their faces and read what they were feeling: concern, frustration, disappointment.

I finally made eye contact with the Asian woman as she glanced over her at me. I raised my voice a bit. "Doc, what's going on?"

Dr. Gonzales finished making her notations on the Rx slate and then turned her attention to me. "Martin, I've got Jamie from our staff getting your family on video. As soon as we can reach them, you will have as much time as you want to speak to them. You may want to prepare them for another long wait."

"I don't understand. Earlier you said 'if' I relapse. Now it sounds like you're saying it's a certainty." My heart started racing faster at the prospect that I wasn't fixed. Franciscus stepped back and made room for the others, who had begun circling me like bees.

A young white man with spiky yellow-and-green hair slammed the door open and came running across the room. He held a large lap pad, and I could see my wife and kids moving on the screen.

"Jamie, is that thing muted?" Dr. Gonzales asked him.

"Uhhh"—he looked at the screen to confirm the settings—"uh, yeah. Muted and video off. They already know he's awake, but that's it."

The doctor tapped me hard on the hand to get my attention. "Martin, listen to me, okay? We had hoped that the treatment we gave you would shock your system into normalcy, but our readouts right now indicate that you are already slipping back into a chemopreservative state. I don't know how much time you have to talk. It might be hours or minutes.

"You need to understand something, though. We believe the treatment caused you to go into cardiac arrest because you hadn't reached equilibrium. In other words, you didn't slow down to the lowest rate that this mystery medication intended for your body. We're afraid that if we try to bring you back to normalcy again before you reach that state, we could kill you."

I looked about, trying to see my family on the lap pad, not understanding why she was wasting my time. "Can't we talk about this afterward? Please?"

"No, Martin. You need to know now. This drug you were injected with has a target speed that your body is intended for. You haven't reached it, we have no idea how slow it really is, and we have no idea when we will be able to bring you back to normal. We are guessing right now, but it could be two or more years."

Two *years*? Was this woman out of her mind? "This is not happening . . ." I murmured, staring at the faded stretched tattoo on her wrist. It must have been a pretty one twenty years ago.

"Yes, Martin, it *is* happening. Martin . . . Martin!"

She flicked me hard on my knuckle, the pain causing me to flinch away from her. The doctor glared at me with her piercing black eyes. "Martin, are you paying attention? You're not dreaming. You're not hallucinating. This is *real*. You need to compose yourself and figure out what you want to say. This whole thing may be difficult on you, but it is going to be a hell of a lot worse on your family. Now tell me you understand. Say it—tell me you understand!"

She flicked me on the fleshy part of hand between my index and thumb. I yanked my hand away, stopping short of backhanding the wretch. Doctor Gonzales's features softened, and it dawned on me she wasn't trying to hurt me. Her expression was one of sadness. "Martin," she repeated, "please tell me you understand what's happening."

I wanted to deny it all, but she wouldn't let me. The unpalatable words stuck in my throat. "My— My— My family is not going to see me for a long time."

"That's right," she confirmed. "But they *are* going to see you. Do you understand me? Martin, we're going to find a way to fix you. Now let's hurry and get you cleaned up."

She grabbed a washcloth, wet it at the sink, and wiped down my face with gentle swabs. The female technician pulled the oxygen tubes from my nostrils and did her best to groom my unkempt light-brown hair. I had no idea what it looked like, but after four months it must have been a bird's nest. The technician with the crazy hairdo checked my vitals on a screen that sat just out of sight. Strangers all of them, yet they were the closest thing I had to friends for the moment— nameless friends for a sliver of time. And how long that moment would last was anyone's guess.

They placed the lap tablet in my hands with the quiet images of my girls talking to each other, waiting patiently to see me after so many months. Miranda was telling them to behave; I didn't need the sound on to know that. My wife had obviously been out in the rain prior to the call coming in from the hospital. Her black locks dangled in her eyes—her soft hands pushed them up and out of her face only to have them drop back into her eyes all wet and messy. She looked a radiant sight.

Amara looked dead serious, checking the time on her phone several times, probably asking what was taking so long, unaware that her father was doing everything he could to keep from losing his mind.

Her face was longer, her features more pronounced. What a difference four months made! I swore she was a miniature Miranda in the making. Any parent who has been away from his kids for even a week knows that children grow up too quickly. Bella was no exception. My baby Bella's hair was so long! What else had I missed? What special moments had I been cheated out of?

I took a deep breath and glanced at Dr. Gonzales. She nodded to me, grabbed my cheeks, and shoved her fingers upward to force a smile into my face. Nodding with reassurance, I turned back to the pad and opened the line. "Hi, pretty ladies!"

I got my harmony of greetings, and then they all started talking at the same time. I caught barely a complete sentence as they chattered in excitement. I put up my hand, and they eventually calmed down. "Miranda, how is everything?"

"We're doing fine. The girls really miss you. I really miss you. They haven't told us much, but we've been trying to get permission to come and see you in Washington. They say you are in the Walter Reed Medical Center. Is that true?"

"I think so. They've been doing a good job of taking care of me. I'll make sure that you can come down and visit me." I glared over at the scientists who were huddled together as they watched my drama unfold. With the kids listening, though, changing the subject seemed the best course of action.

"Amara, Bella—how was Christmas? What did Santa Claus bring you?"

The two fought for who was going to speak first before Amara acquiesced to her sister's whining. "I got a Baby-Learn-to-Walk and a new sweater from Grandma, but I got it snagged on a screw on the fence, and it ripped the sleeve and came undone, and Mommy is still angry with me."

"It was a knit sweater, and there was no fixing it," Miranda clarified.

Syncing Forward

"It's okay, sweetie. I am sure Grandma will be able to get you a new one." I asked Amara again about her gifts, and she hesitantly responded.

"Mom and Grandma and Grandpa all pitched in and got me a Tumi game console." She kept looking over at her mother as if to make sure it was okay to tell me. She added defensively, "But it was the only big thing I got for Christmas, honest!"

I had told Miranda a dozen times that those things were way too expensive, but it seemed that in my absence things had gotten a little lax around the house. This wasn't the time to bring up any of that, so I reassured Amara that she was a really good girl and deserved it.

We chatted some more about what the girls had done in my absence. Amara was a regional finalist for the spelling bee and had joined a jujitsu class. I was shocked to hear that, since my big girl had always been a princess and cried when her little sister pushed her. Amara spoke fondly of her dojo and the fact that she was only one of two girls in the whole class, and she liked feeling like she could stand up against the boys—especially given how dainty she was. In the midst of the conversation, Miranda hinted at the class being a good outlet for Amara to focus her frustrations.

Bella had quit her dance class back in December and decided to hold off from any extracurricular activity. That was a surprising change as well, since Bella loved dancing. The kid would spin and spin all day long, leaping about the house, inventing clumsy ballets and stories to entertain us. Don't get me wrong; my youngest was not an undiscovered talent and would not be going to Julliard anytime soon. She simply loved dancing, or at least had loved it until recently.

Bella broke slowly into a frown as we spoke, and I tried to speak more cheerily to counter her gloomy mood. "Hey, Baby Bella, what's with the frowny face?"

"Daddy," she said with a quivering lip, "why are you still in the hospital? When are you coming home?"

I swallowed hard. The reality crashed in harder than I'd known it could. *God, I don't want to do this. Please, don't make me do this. Please don't make me tell my children they aren't going to see me for two years. Make it all a dream. Please make this a nightmare. I'm sorry for anything I've done to tick you off, please, God! Please!*

My prayers went unanswered. "Sweetie, Daddy is still getting better, but it is going to take longer than they expected. You know how Daddy has been going really slow? Well, they are able to make me speed up to keep up with you, but not just yet. They're still working on it."

A tear dripped down her cheek, followed by another. "Does that mean you are going to be slow again?"

Gonzales had told me to be strong, but it was proving a lot harder than I imagined. "For a little while, sweetie. Yes, Daddy is going to be slow again. But just remember that I am still alive and still breathing, and I can read notes and even see pictures, so it's kinda like Daddy is just on a long trip, okay?"

Bella was lost to sorrow, burying her face in her mother's lap, gripping Miranda's leg and sobbing.

"Did the doctors say how long, Martin?" Miranda stared ahead at the screen, understanding of my doomed condition just beginning to dawn on her.

"They don't know, hon," I fibbed, unable to tell her the news. Not right now, not in front of the kids. "It might be shorter than this time or longer, but they don't know."

"Daddy, I want to come see you. Can we come see you today?" Amara's eyes were tearing up as well, but she was still keeping it together for the time being.

I looked at Dr. Gonzales, who glanced at her pad and then—looking up at me—sadly shook her head.

"Amara, I would like nothing more than to see you, but I don't think we'll have enough time before things start to get very blurry for me. New Jersey is at least five hours away from DC, and I think I'm down to minutes here." I touched the screen, and Amara stepped off

Syncing Forward

the sofa and touched fingers with me. The picture was distorted and the experience cold. That was as close as I was going to get to my children.

Bella jumped from her mother's lap and ran off-screen. I asked Amara to be a good big sister and take care of her younger sister while I was away. "I love you, Dad. I'm going to go get Bella. I'll be right back. Don't switch off yet, okay?"

"Okay, big girl. I'll talk to your mom while you take care of your sister."

Amara was out of the room when Miranda finally spoke. Her hand was on her cheek. "Martin, what's going on? The hospital called us on the way home and told us you were awake. We rushed home in the storm, and the girls were expecting to hear you were coming home. What happened?"

"I'm not exactly sure myself. The doctors here seem competent enough. The problem is they don't really know how to fix me. To be honest, I don't even know what you know or where to start."

Miranda told me how Homeland Security had briefed her. She had been told that a terrorist at Innovo Pharmaceutical injected me with a drug that slowed my body down to a fraction of what everyone else experienced, and that it was a matter of national security. The bastards had threatened to have her arrested if she let out a peep, so Miranda was left with the difficult task of muzzling our children. She managed to direct their efforts toward making pictures and writing notes, of which only a few managed to get sent to me. I sensed these attempts to stay in touch were going to be more important than ever.

"I'm sorry I'm not going to make it home," I mumbled.

Miranda shook her head disbelievingly. "You make it sound like you know that's going to happen."

"I don't know anything other than what the doctors tell me. They say I'm already slowing down. I can feel it too, so they must be reading my body right. I will try to write to you and the kids, but it is going to take me a while to get messages out. Things are very strange for me, very confusing. I'll do my best, though."

"Martin, the attorney bills are adding up. Dulaney & Singh gave us three different attorneys, and now they're saying the insurance isn't paying them anymore, so we owe them six thousand dollars. Innovo sent disability checks, but they aren't enough to pay for everything. And I haven't even opened the hospital bills. We won't have anything left in our savings account after April. I'm so scared, Martin! My mom and dad have no money to help out."

I hadn't even thought about money. "Call Miguel and Alex; see if they can loan us some cash. Call Jacob too. Between your brothers and mine, we might be able to get by till May."

"And what do I do with the next month's bills? Martin, if you are out for another four months, we might lose the house!"

She was either talking faster or I was slowing down—probably both. I wanted to take this time to tell my wife that I missed her, that I needed her. Instead I was managing our checkbook from hundreds of miles away as my own personal clock spun down to near inactivity. The bad news was the last thing she needed, but I couldn't sidestep it.

"Miranda, I won't be back in four months. The doctors are saying it will be closer to two years. I didn't want to upset the kids more than they already were, but it's going to be a long time."

Miranda started crying. "Martin . . . I don't know what to do. The girls, the house, the bills . . . and I don't even know when you are going to be back . . ."

"Shhhh . . . let me think . . ." My mind reeled. Every second that passed for me meant two were flying by for everyone else, and each moment was a step in the wrong direction. There were few options and none of them good. "Here's what I need you to do: cut the attorney. Just get rid of them. Don't pay the legal bill."

"But they said that—"

Syncing Forward

"It doesn't matter what they said or how important they are. Call David Tsai and have him reach out to my director, Gavin Thomason. Tell them everything."

One of the older doctors interrupted me. "Mr. James, she can't do that."

"The hell she can't," I snapped at him. Turning back to the screen, I spoke as evenly as I could manage. "Get Thomason in the loop. If we're lucky, we can get some legal support from the company. I just hope they'll help us out."

The doctor stepped closer and tried to take the electronic tablet away. He probably could have done it if he really tried. "Your wife cannot tell anyone about your condition. This is a classified matter."

I snapped. "Screw your classified matter! Screw this hospital! And screw you! I'm not going to sit in this stupid bed for two stinking years just to come back to my family living in an alleyway box! I'm not your lab rat, you son of a bitch!"

"Martin, wait!" Miranda tried to get me to stop shouting, but I was livid. By the time I turned back to the screen, it was too late. Bella and Amara were both in the picture listening to everything I said.

"Two years?" Bella wailed. "Daddy, no! You can't be gone for two years. Come home, Daddy! Please!"

"Baby Bella, I can't. They need to be able to make sure I'm okay. They need to make sure Daddy is okay and give me medicine to make me better . . ."

"Dad, can'tyoujustcomehome?" Amara spoke up. "Please, wewantyouherewithus. I'lltakegoodcareofyou!"

The chemopreservation was kicking into full gear. My condition was decelerating at a slower rate than before, but the voices were dulling, movements were blurring.

My poor kids. I had to get my final words out. When you only have seconds left before you are separated from the ones you love, what do you say? A memory of one of my best friends popped into my mind, of me watching uncomfortably from a distance as Barry said

109

good-bye to his wife and young son at the airport before going off to war. I spoke the same words, simultaneously praying that my fate would be better than his. When he came back, I held his boy's hand as his casket was lowered into the ground.

"Write me. Send me pictures. You're in my heart." My voice started to hiss once more; the air in my lungs passing weakly across my vocal cords, barely vibrating them. "Love you."

"MartinIloveyoubestrongyou'retheloveofmylifewe'llbewaitingforyou..."

"DaddyIllprayforyoueverydayIpromise..."

Bella screamed.

My eyes were burning again. The doctors swarmed me, and the lap tablet was yanked from my fingers. The adhesive electrodes were pummeling me about the head. Goggles followed, yanked down over my eyes. My nostrils were invaded by clear plastic tubes. Somebody snapped my head to the side, and before my eyes the familiar screen appeared. Gonzales typed for a split second before her message flashed for me to read.

WE'LL GET YOU HOME, MARTIN. I DON'T KNOW HOW BUT WE WILL.

She touched my face in what was meant to be an act of consolation, but the nerve endings in my cheek scarcely registered her touch before it was gone. I barely read the eleven words before the equipment was moved again and life accelerated past me. Whirling. Spinning. Distorting. Streaking. And then the lights went out.

My world dipped into blackness as I sat alone, trembling through the seasons.

Syncing Forward

— **Part 2** —

I, Rat

Chapter 9

Solitary confinement was the only comparison I could draw to my condition. It was beyond quiet; a silence enveloped me such that even the ringing in my ears was absent. Breathing felt artificial and my chest felt tight, as if the muscles between my ribs were fatigued.

I tried to keep my mind off the peculiar sensations and pressed down on the mouse; the large screen in front of me filled with thumbnails of digital pictures. This was much better than the letters from my family given to me a couple hours ago. Or was it a couple weeks ago?

Goggles sprayed tears directly into my eyes, keeping my vision relatively clear. Of course the goggles were foggy, but even so I could process the images faster, understand more, and feel closer to the ladies in my life. Don't get me wrong—the words my wife and children had sent were heartfelt and kept me connected personally, but my heart ached in isolation, and my eyes were starved for a vision of Bella, Amara, and Miranda. To see them meant they were safe and well and put my soul at somewhat at ease. Each image became a colorful change from the mundane, windowless room, and I found myself struggling between racing through the captured memories and dwelling on the fine details. How long I actually gazed upon each picture, I do not know. I clicked the top left thumbnail and watched my loved ones spring up on the screen.

My older brother Jacob holding up Bella in a bathing suit in our backyard as Amara sprayed her with the hose. Summertime had obviously come, and was hoping my side of the family knew I was incapacitated. The girls seemed to be having fun too. That stung, knowing I wasn't there. God only knew I didn't want them miserable, but I felt jealous I wasn't there to make those memories with them.

Miranda asleep on the sofa with no makeup on, colored rubber bands covering her face and sweater. The kids must have taken that picture while she napped on some lazy Saturday morning.

Syncing Forward

Bella in an arm cast, frowning. The pink glossy cast swirled around her forearm with vents exposing her skin below; it was so different from the tight itchy casts I'd worn when I was growing up. I had heard about these new casts but never seen one personally. Across the bottom of the picture was writing in glitter: *"Bella vs. Tree . . . Tree wins!"*

Amara blowing out birthday candles. I counted ten candles and realized the picture had been taken on November 15, 2022. The image stamped my temporal captivity at eleven months and counting. My big kid's birthday looked festive on the surface, but there were no friends in the picture, and the cake looked small. Sometimes we had a separate party for family, and I hoped Amara had gotten a chance to spend some time with friends too.

Miranda, Bella, and Amara in front of our church with Father Buchanan. Miranda was smiling . . . from the cheeks down. Her eyes told a different story. Maybe it was just the lighting, but she looked tired. Her eyebrows were pulled together, and it was obvious she was saddened about something. The girls' demeanors were about the same. Bella wore a strange-looking knit cap, and Amara wasn't even looking at the camera. Something off to her left must have caught her attention. Icicles hung from the awning near the main doors.

Bella showing off a short hairdo. The weight of her hair no longer pulled her loose curls down, and instead her hair bounced up and outward, making her look like a vintage American Girl doll. She looked so grown-up in the picture, with a wide grin and two teeth missing.

A picture of our basement submerged in a foot of water. Miranda stood there with wet boxes and papers bobbing around her shins, looking miserable. Her mouth stood wide open, and I could just imagine her telling one of the girls to put the camera down and come help. The bottom of the picture said "Hurricane Edna." Our house was way too far inland for hurricane damage, but flooding was another topic entirely. I didn't understand why the sump pump hadn't kept the water out.

A picture of a street underwater with water up against houses. It didn't look familiar until I looked carefully at two flagpoles in the yards of adjacent houses, and I suddenly knew where the picture had been taken. It was Fulcrum Street, a low point near Pompton Plains. We had friends who lived on that street, and while I couldn't see their house in the picture, I knew they must have been hit hard.

Amara in a martial arts outfit. A green belt wrapped around her waist, and she held another girl up midair, her opponent a mere projectile. Amara's hair was pulled back in pigtails, but one of the thick bundles of black hair had snaked up and obscured her eyes in the picture. In my imagination I could see her dark eyes ablaze with determination. It was an awesome picture, and a vision of my normally timid daughter I had never expected to see. The other girl didn't look happy.

A close-up of Bella holding a stuffed teddy bear—Jingles—that we'd bought her when she was five. Letting go of that stuffed animal was beyond impossible, and it went everywhere with her, except school . . . sometimes. Bella's face was a big frown as she gripped her brown bear. Electronically finger-painted underneath was one sentence that got me choked up all over again: "I miss you a lot today."

I continued to click through the seemingly endless set of pictures, each one filling me with a jumble of emotions ranging from jealousy to amusement to isolation. The next click brought a face I hadn't expected to see in the jumble of pictures of my family.

David Tsai, dressed in a light-blue suit, sat on the edge of a desk in an office unfamiliar to me. His arms were folded. The picture struck me as peculiar, so I took some extra time to look about. It appeared to be a windowless room and on the smallish side, to boot. The desk was equipped with the standard items you would expect, minus actual work. The nameplate was barely readable through my tinted goggles, but I managed to get a clearer view by cocking my head slightly upward. In capital letters it read, "MARTIN JAMES, INVESTIGATOR."

That desk had my name on it, yet I was sure I had never set foot in that office. Either the concussion had done a number on my memory or that was a new office. I reasoned with myself that with

Syncing Forward

Dave there, it was obviously a newish picture. Could it be the new building? Were they expecting me back? Or perhaps they knew of some cure for my near-frozen state? While that seemed unlikely, my cohorts at Innovo Pharmaceutical were clearly involved in providing for us. Even if that small gesture only meant I had a job at the end of this ordeal, then I would be happy. But with the money issues piling up at home, it was possible Miranda had solicited their help. Extra money, waived attorney fees, who knew?

On the wall beyond the computer screen hung a rare spectacle: an analog clock. The minute hand swung around its face; had it been a propeller, it might have lifted the clock right off the wall. I just kept track of the hour hand, which was pointed at the five. I set my fingers on the keyboard and began typing a message, WHY OFFICE. I looked up at the hour hand—twelve. Seven hours to type two words.

The response came back instantly.

DAVID: YOU ARE ON THE COMPANY PAYROLL. YOUR FAMILY IS GETTING YOUR PAYCHECKS. INNOVO IS TAKING CARE OF YOU.

Payroll meant steady money, and I sighed in relief knowing that Miranda wasn't scrounging. The clock read eight o'clock. A third of a day had passed while I read a stinking tweet. I looked off to the corner of the room, where a rack of medical equipment sat. Occasionally I found my eye drawn to the metal fixture. Because of the strange effect my slowing had on my vision, the shelf constantly undulated with movement as items were shuffled, used, and replaced. My contemplations went back to the picture of my mystery office as I stared at the streaks of movement that were the Walter Reed medical staff.

My family pictures were replaced by another series of pictures from DHS. More suspect photos for me to help identify the mysterious man from Innovo. After reviewing hundreds of pictures I wasn't even sure what the man's face looked like anymore, but I kept up with the search. If DHS was still looking for this man, it meant there might be a chance to find him, to find an antidote for whatever they had injected me with. Behind the worries and anger and frustration and glumness, I still had a lingering question: Why did Bruchmuller and the others develop this drug at all? What could possibly be gained from it?

MARTIN, CAN YOU READ THIS?

Yes.

WE HAVE ANOTHER SURPRISE FOR YOU.

What happened next was a bittersweet reminder of my once-normal world. I was whisked away to what I could perceive only as a large cushioned sofa. Moments later a blur of figures swept into the room and enveloped me in their warmth. As the figures settled into the sofa with me, the exceptional quality of this surprise dawned on me. I was there with my wife and kids, who seemed to be doing their best to remain motionless.

Bella lay across my lap while Amara tucked herself under my left arm, resting her head upon my chest. Miranda slid under my right and held my hand. I felt the pressure of their bodies against my body, the warmth of their skin on my skin. Looking into their faces unsettled me because movement blurred their features to smooth, alien-like visages. Bella was the only one who seemed to get it, sitting very still and trying not to make any changes at all. Her face was angelic, her eyes closed, her curly hair lying shorter than I remember it but still long enough to drape over half her face. I brushed it out of the way, and a smile appeared for a split second.

And then it was over. A blur of motion. Other people entered the room. Discussion ensued that would never be comprehensible to me; my inner ear was not attenuated to vibrate enough to register such sound as speech to my brain. I felt dizzy as they placed me back in my room, surrounded by cold machines and distortions of doctors. Miranda and my daughters had stayed for roughly nine hours, while the experience for me lasted perhaps eight seconds.

Syncing Forward

We returned to the room, to the soft sofa and a repeat of my family nuzzling into me. It had to be a weekend, two days to spend with me. I was ready this time to take advantage of the few moments we had, and I leaned in to smell my wife's hair, gripping both girls' hands as I did. I took a deep breath and swore I could make out the aroma of some sort of fruity shampoo. I turned to Bella when I felt her moving and then realized they were all moving. Moving away. Gone.

I blinked and was back in my hospital bed. The girls left some personal notes on my computer screen that were quickly replaced with new ones, and new ones after that. Several of them I missed because they flashed by so quickly or because the goggles were fogging up. I got the distinct impression I was slowing down even further.

I reached for the keyboard and typed out SLOWNG DWN MORE, hoping they would keep the messages up for longer than they had; I didn't know why they couldn't just leave them up until I closed them out on my own.

New images showed up, not of family but of suspects provided by our beloved Department of Homeland Security with a message underneath in bold letters:

MR. JAMES, PLEASE LOOK AT THESE PICTURES AND SEE IF ANY OF THESE INDIVIDUALS RESEMBLE THE UNIDENTIFIED SUSPECT FROM THE INNOVO BOMBING.

There was no option to decline their request, no place to type a message, no way to toggle back to my family's e-mails. Just pictures of unfamiliar faces.

I scrolled through each set of three, choosing an option that simply read *next*. This one had eyes too close together. That one's nose was too small. Forehead too long, ears too small, wrong cheekbones. One face looked close so I checked it off as a maybe. I really did want to help DHS on this, and God only knew what a lead on the case might do for me. Heck, I didn't even understand why Jotwani had thought this was a humane option in the first place.

I sent a message off to Franciscus.

JST 1 ON THS. MIGHT B HM BUT NOT SURE. N E THING FRM U?

The response popped up.

THE NAME OF THE GROUP IS MILLENNIAL. DOES THAT MEAN ANYTHING TO YOU?

I wrote NO.

HOW ABOUT SOMETHING CALLED SINGULARITY?

That word did sound familiar, but where I had read it I couldn't say. An article? A movie title? On television? A conversation? That's what it was—a conversation with Rajesh Jotwani. One of the myriad topics Rajesh had managed to beat me over the head with during our lunch breaks. I racked my brain to recall what singularity was. It was something bad, I was pretty sure of that. Or at least Rajesh thought it was bad. Hell, the guy was a chemist by trade; he took great delight in scaring the crap out of me with tales of flesh-eating viruses and infective proteins and anything else that might ruin my meal. But singularity . . .

RAJESH SD SOMTHNG BOUT IT BUT I CANT REMMBR WAT. SRRY.

It dawned on me that it could have been anyone typing to me, but for some reason I pictured Franciscus handling the messages.

MILLENNIAL IS CLAIMING RESPONSIBILITY FOR THE INNOVO BOMBING AS WELL AS THREE UNCREDITED ACTS OF TERRORISM.

Syncing Forward

A window opened up on the side of the screen, giving me an option to switch to seeing some pictures the doctors made available to me. I didn't like the idea of leaving the terrorism thing dangling, and I wondered what Dave Tsai and the rest of my company were doing to cooperate. But one click on the pictures had me distracted like a puppy in a spring field.

The pic was presumably here at Walter Reed, of my wife kissing me on the corner of my mouth as I lay in the hospital bed. She looked gorgeous with her perfect lips pursed against my face. Miranda's skin was a beautiful chestnut color compared to my pastiness. This was also my first time seeing the bizarre things they had hooked up to me. The goggles made me look like I was about to dive into a pool—which would not have been a good idea, being that I was wired heavier than an entertainment system. You could barely tell it was me in the picture. I didn't even know she had kissed me. I never felt it or perceived that she was visiting.

For those interacting with me, my response must have been painfully slow. For me, it was think fast or lose the moment. I banged out a quick message: TEL MIR BEL AM I LUV U DON'T GIV UP ME.

Words appeared again that turned me into a blubbering fool.

AMARA: DADDY I WON'T GIVE UP EVER. THANKSGIVING. I PLACED 2ND IN THE GIRLS MMA TOURNEY. STRAIGHT A'S STILL.

BELLA: YOU'RE THE BEST DAD IN THE WHOLE WORLD. THE ONLY THING I WANT FOR CHRISTMAS IS YOU HOME.

MIRANDA: I'M TRYING TO BRING YOU HOME, HUSBAND. FOR BETTER OR WORSE, RIGHT? THE NEW HOUSE IS BEING BUILT. HOPEFULLY YOU'LL SEE IT BY SPRINGTIME.

I wrote back, Y NEW HOUS? EVRYTHNG—

Before I could finish typing, my wife anticipated the rest of the question.

DON'T WORRY, MARTIN. WE'VE GOT PEOPLE TAKING CARE OF US.

WHO? I asked.

INNOVO.

The details weren't there, but perhaps Miranda had reason to be short. If attorneys were involved that would make sense. My hope grew stronger that things were going to improve.

I typed, WHAT DATE IS IT?

More strangers' faces for me to identify popped up, more notes from my family, but it became obvious that any reference to how much time had passed had been not so carefully removed. Sentences in my daughters' letters dangled. Miranda's words were cryptic as well. They couldn't hide the passage of time from the pictures I received, however. Miranda looked very much the same, minus the changing hairstyles. But you can't hide a month of change in a child's face, and Amara and Bella were growing up in a matter of minutes. Their hair growing, their bodies lengthening. I kept looking at the images, trying to get a fix on what grade they were in. One shot of Amara doing homework had a textbook with the word *Grade* printed on it, but the number associated with it had been pixelated.

I decided to be more to the point.

WHY ARE YOU HIDING THE DATE FROM ME?

The response didn't answer my question.

MARTIN, YOU HAVE NOT REACHED EQUILIBRIUM YET. WE ARE WORKING ON A STABLE AGENT TO ADMINISTER WHEN YOUR SYSTEM IS READY.

Syncing Forward

A split second later the message came across.

WE ARE ADMINISTERING ANESTHESIA. CLICK HERE IF YOU UNDERSTAND.

I clicked on the button, but it reset and remained on the screen, only slightly off-center. I moved the pointer and clicked again, finding it difficult to concentrate on centering the button. I was fixing to just toss the mouse aside in frustration, but somehow it seemed heavier than it had been just a moment ago. I made a third go of clicking the button, missed it the third time, and soon found I couldn't even hold on to the mouse, let alone keep my eyes open.

Eyes closed felt better anyway.

Chapter 10

Normally dreams occur in a matter of minutes or even seconds. We've all had those dreams that seemed to last for adventurous weeks, but the reality is your mind processes that information in a tiny fraction of the time. And in your dreams, the parts usually flow together in such a way that your unconscious mind makes sense of it all, even if the dream seemed like nonsense when you wake. Sure, the dream where you are getting a speeding ticket and are forced to wear Jell-O molds on your elbows sounds ridiculous, but while you're asleep, it is run-of-the-mill.

My dreams while under the influence of Bruchmuller's drug were disjointed in such a way that they confounded my understanding even while I slept. Places, faces, conversations from my past came together in a way that defied any understanding. Images in my mind were haphazardly spliced together as well, almost as if my brain were trying to process years of wakefulness all at once. But like most dreams, I felt as if I were awake, so I stood fearfully in the midst of a convergence of memories and make-believe, not understanding my place among them. Bruchmuller was there, standing over me with a syringe that looked like a two-foot cake decorator filled with blue frosting.

"Hold very still, Mr. James . . ."

The dream vanished like a pheasant in the underbrush. My lids popped open, and my eyes were immediately misted with a cool saline solution. I blinked a few times and realized I was wearing goggles that pressed down on the bridge of my nose and didn't seem to fit well against my skull. The dang thing was fogged up from the misting contraption.

Was I still moving slowly, or was I living at a normal speed? I reckoned the latter. I could smell fresh paint, and the sound of female voices hit my ears in a most welcome way. I could also hear an air conditioner humming softly. Its mechanical sound was . . . normal, and

Syncing Forward

a far cry from the muffled sounds I'd experienced when slowed to a crawl.

I yanked the goggles off and let my eyes adjust to the light streaming in from a bay window that spanned at least ten feet across. Outside, the ground dipped and rolled gently till it met a flat cornfield that extended far to my left and out of sight. To the right, a small country road bisected the field and led onward toward the horizon and several small homes.

My body moved in the swivel chair I was sitting in, and I took the opportunity to turn around and find out where I was. Wood paneling and glass sconces marked this place as very old. Glancing about, I noticed the back of the room housed corner-to-corner bookshelves with volumes upon volumes of hardbacks sealing up any last bit of empty space. Next to me, streamlined medical instrumentation hung on a rack, beeping quietly; its presence incongruous to the dated mid-twentieth-century appearance of the large room. This was no doctor office, government facility, or even an Innovo building. This was our new home.

Miranda stepped timidly from the doorway on the opposite side, a worried smile and distressing eyes gracing her face as she picked anxiously at her fingernail. Her curly hair was pulled back in a ponytail that tickled a white collared dress. The midsection was pulled tight, accentuating her top, and flared at the bottom. I dared not mention it aloud, but my wife had gained weight—twenty pounds, perhaps more. She had heavy bags under her eyes that she had done her best to conceal with makeup. Miranda had chosen to wear a lipstick that was classically dark red. It accentuated her already perfect lips and marked her troubled smile even more. I thought she was the prettiest thing I'd ever seen.

"Hi, Martin," she said with a quivering voice.

"Hello, beautiful wife," I rasped while holding up my arms for a hug. My throat was dry as a bone, and my compliment sounded more like a witch or a creature from horror film than the loving husband I was trying to be.

Miranda didn't seem to care. My wife's footsteps began small but quickly turned into a run as she crossed the room and embraced me firmly, almost knocking the chair over and ripping a half-dozen electrodes from my arm and head. Her smooth skin was covered in goose bumps and raised the little hairs on her arms. It dawned on me that the room was quite chilly; maybe as low as the fifties or sixties. That they had set the thermostat so low may have been in response to my chemically altered state; with my body working so slowly, it seemed logical that my body temperature and comfort level would be lower.

"I missed you so much." She sighed in my ear. "Thank God you're back!" After a long minute, she leaned over and grabbed a cup with ice water and a straw and put it to my lips. I began to gulp it down when she admonished me, "No, no, no! *Despacio!* Slow sips. Just wet your throat. Swallow slowly."

I gulped it anyway. Feeling that perfectly clear water washing over my throat and down into my belly was a welcomed sensation, like candy to my hungry nerve endings. She took the cup away and set it back on the small table. Facing me again, she delicately put her hands on my face and pressed her forehead to mine. Gently, she kissed me on the lips, and I cherished every instant of my wife's contact, even the waxy residue of her lipstick. When she pulled her head back, she chuckled and wiped the red excess from the surface of my lips with her thumb.

I reached out again and hugged her until the intravenous needle in my arm ached. "Aren't you a sight for sore eyes."

"Oh, stop. I look terrible," she replied weepily.

"Are you kidding? You're gorgeous."

"You're still so suave, aren't you?"

"Well, for me it's only been less than a day. You don't expect moves like mine to disappear overnight." I tried to be funny, but Miranda focused on the first of those two sentences.

"Hours?" She sounded almost hurt. "I thought months would have passed for you. Maybe weeks, but hours?"

Syncing Forward

"Yeah, maybe nine hours or more— I don't really know. But I'm here now. Why? What's the date?"

Miranda slowly, uncomfortably untangled herself from my arms and stood. "Martin, the girls . . ." She hesitated. She then called out loudly to the next room, her eyes firmly fixed on me. "Amara? Bella? Come in and say hi to your father."

"Amara?" I asked. I had to ask. The girl walking through the door was a different person. "Hey, big kid, come over here and give me a hug."

Amara awkwardly shuffled her feet with her gaze intently fixed on me, wringing her hands as she went. Had it not been for her lighter mixed skin, I might have confused my older daughter with my niece Genevieve. Amara was taller by more than a foot since the last time I saw her in real time. Her face had thinned out, and her cheekbones were more defined. My nine-year-old daughter was nine no longer.

My elder child's uneasy gait brought her to my side, where she embraced my arm lightly and kissed me on the cheek. Amara's plastered-on smile smelled of a kid who had practiced a line in a play over and over again but was performing for the first time in front of an audience. She went to speak, but the words caught in her throat, and her sweet little mouth bent down as her cheeks dripped with tears. She bent at the neck and rested her head on my chest, her body shaking from her sobs.

"Hey, hey! It's okay!" I held her tightly. "Amara, shhhh! It's okay, big kid." Her weight fell on me as I did my best to console her. My own eyes were wet while I squeezed her. My poor girl must have been a wreck with me gone. We were buddies, with Amara following me everywhere I went and doing everything I did. She would listen to me for hours about interviews, and my wife always accused me of turning Amara into a Mini Me. I was her one ally in altercations at school and with other kids. How had she handled life without me?

Miranda came up from behind, wrapped her arms around my neck, and slipped her cheek next to mine, kissing me over and over. I peeked between them for any sign of a third set of arms, but Bella remained elusive.

It took a while for the group hug to untangle, but I didn't mind. I could smell their hair and feel their warmth and was even glad in a way I could hear the cries. Amara withdrew a bit, choosing to hold my hand still while wiping her face with the palms of her hands. "I knew I was going to be a mess today," she grumbled. "Sorry, Daddy. I'm sure the last thing you want to see is me bawling my eyes out."

She sounded so mature. I clasped her hand gently. "Bawl away, kid. You don't apologize to me for anything."

"How do you feel?" she asked tentatively.

Her voice was so much lower than when I'd seen her at Bergen County Hospital, not at all the sound of the child I knew. The contrast was so stark that I ignored her question. "You are so grown-up! You look like a little lady. I don't remember seeing pictures of you looking like this. How old are you now? What grade are you in?"

"I'm thirteen and a half."

I swallowed hard. *Four years.* I had been away for four years. Twice as long as Dr. Gonzales had predicted. I stayed focused on my daughter, not wanting to deal with the loss of years. There would be time to sit and feel sad, overwhelmed, bitter. But not now.

Amara continued. "I just finished the eighth grade even though I passed the skip-level exams for the ninth grade. Then again, *Mom* keeps reminding me that we don't go to our old school anymore."

"What's that on your wrist?" I inquired. Wrapped around my daughter's wrist was a black band with a circular piece of plastic on each side. The number kept rolling between my ears: four years.

"Oh, it's just for school. They use it to measure our stress levels, but I set it off so much that I tweaked the sensor so it doesn't work right. Now I can pitch a fit anytime I want." Amara giggled through her sniffles.

Miranda rolled her eyes and stopped short of admonishing Amara. Instead, she sat on a cushioned ottoman near us and explained,

Syncing Forward

"Martin, Innovo moved us here to Beacon, Pennsylvania. We had to make some adjustments, but I think the girls are getting along better now."

Amara rolled her eyes. I asked her, "What? You don't like it here?"

She answered, *"Ahi nomás,"* which translated as "it 's okay," but really meant she was bored out of her mind. I asked Miranda why on earth the company would insist that we move out to the middle of nowhere. It seemed like they wanted me to come back to work, so why put one of their investigators far from any facility? The South Carolina facility seemed like a good idea. Warmer, closer to my old stomping grounds.

"The company doesn't want you working right now," Miranda told me.

"Why?" I asked, but Miranda walked toward the door, calling for Bella softly. There was no sign of my younger daughter.

I turned back to Amara. "So you want to be in high school, do you? Aren't you a little young?"

"I don't care. *Me enfada.* The teachers are dumb here—dumber than New Jersey. I could skip a week of school and score perfectly on everything. It's that bad."

"Well, I'm sorry you aren't challenged enough. Maybe we can find you some online courses to take?"

"I'm already taking two: one on biology and the second on networking." Her face lit up a smidge at the talk of her extracurricular activities. She began to explain how her mother had let her do most of the computer networking hookups in the house, and how she even got to work with the technicians when they had hooked up all the monitors that constantly transmitted information from the sensors to the computers.

Miranda was still talking to an unseen visitor who chose to remain outside the room. She stepped back toward Amara and me,

127

encouraging Bella, who still hid beyond the entryway. "He's not frozen anymore. Come on, it's okay."

I looked at Miranda as she raised her eyebrows and leaned her head forward, encouraging me to get involved. Still seated in the chair, I called out, "Baby Bella? Bella, is that you? It's your daddy, sweetie. I'm all better now. Come in here, baby. I want to see your pretty face."

A set of fingers wrapped around the trim of the doorway, and a single dark-brown eye peered out of the hallway and across the room at me. The face looked up at Miranda and then back at me with her mother's encouragement. After a few seconds, eleven-year-old Bella emerged. Her hair was tied back in pigtails, but there was no mistaking her for a little girl anymore—my younger daughter was a fifth-grader. But why hide? It killed me to think she didn't want to see me. I scanned her face as if I was performing an interview and struggled to read any one emotion. Fear, anger, happiness, sadness; they all registered in some capacity.

"Nobody calls me 'Baby Bella' anymore," Bella said finally. Her mom gave her a nudge to come into the room, and my younger daughter resisted it. Her hand went up and swatted at her mother. "Stop it, Mom!"

"Bella, *ijule*! What has gotten into you?" Miranda hissed. "Your father is finally home and with us and all better."

My daughter's eyes were getting foggy, and I could see her fighting to remain in control. After a tense moment, she ran back the way she came and out of the room. To have Bella flee from my presence as if I was some monster broke my heart.

"What's going on?" I asked my wife.

"I don't know," Miranda answered.

"Big surprise there." Amara's tone was sarcastic. Miranda stood gawking at the nasty comment while our elder child elaborated. "She's creeped out. Bella told me that Dad scares her, that it was like having a dead body in the house."

"Well, why didn't she tell me that?" Miranda asked.

Syncing Forward

"Because you've been acting like a bitch, that's why!" Amara stormed out of the room, shoving her mother as she went.

Under normal circumstances, one of the kids talking to their mother like that warranted getting busted on their rear end right then and there. Not that Amara would have ever used the word *bitch* when she was nine years old, but even taking that kind of tone with one of us would mean swift repercussions. This time I didn't correct her. I don't know why I let the child walk out without saying anything. Perhaps it was because I was still becoming accustomed to how different Amara looked and acted. She had grown up from the child I knew four years ago, and in some respects, I was getting my fatherly land legs back after being lost at sea for so long.

Miranda crossed her arms and walked back to my side; a single tear escaped her eye and ran down to the tip of her nose. "That's just great . . ." she mumbled. She grabbed my hand, and I clutched her delicate fingers in a supportive fashion.

"I still don't understand, honey. Bella came to visit me at the hospital, and I looked exactly the same. Given some of the pictures I saw, I think I look a heck of a lot better."

"I don't understand it either. She's been weird since Innovo brought you home. I swear it wasn't two weeks ago that she was acting even crazier than Amara about you waking up."

"Is there anything else going on that might have set her off?"

Miranda thought. "She had her first period three days ago."

"Uh . . . what?" That was something I hadn't been prepared to hear about, and I gave my wife a double take to make sure she wasn't pulling my leg. She wasn't.

She patted my knee and kissed me on the cheek. "Sorry, Martin. You're coming back to a house with three full-fledged crazy women."

I let out a long sigh. "Well, that was unexpected. Has Amara been talking to you so disrespectfully the whole time I was away?"

My wife put up her hand and stomped across the room. "Oh, I'm ready to ship your older daughter off to a boarding school. *Qué linde, mi diablo*! She's been awful!"

I shook my head. "That bad, huh? What has she been doing wrong?"

"Calling me a bitch, telling me she hates me, slamming the door in my face. Is that enough for you?"

I winced. "Sorry you had to deal with that on your own, honey. Any problems with her compulsions? Nail biting, stuff like that?"

"Take a look," Miranda offered, reaching over and grabbing the tablet that acted as a universal remote for the house. A beautiful television as thin as a magazine descended from the ceiling and lit up. Miranda poked the controller, and it dawned on me she was looking on a home network; the whole darned thing was hooked up beautifully. Miranda clicked on a file labeled AMARA SCHOOL HISTORY. Tucked away among her school files was a folder labeled MILLENNIAL. Within seconds we were looking at article after article about the Innovo bombing, about Millennial, about their attacks both before and after the explosion that leveled my company's New Jersey campus.

A few more clicks and I was looking at a timeline that mapped out the progress of the terrorist group Millennial from its start as an academic group in the aught years to the attack at Innovo in 2021. The group made brief statements about how they were trying to save humanity. Sounded like a typical terrorist organization to me, spouting tolerance with one hand while blowing up innocent people with the other. Another flick of Miranda's finger across the tablet screen and a host of articles and blogs and opinions about cryogenics and scientific publications on chemopreservation filled the screen. There were hundreds of them, and when I thought we had reached the end of my daughter's collection, Miranda showed me four more files filled with information just like the first one.

"And that doesn't include what's in her room. Books, medical journals, writings that she couldn't possibly understand. It's all she does; she just reads and surfs the Internet for information, corresponds with the doctors at Innovo and with the Walter Reed doctors. Most of them stopped responding to her questions or just send her a quick e-mail saying thanks. Dr. Gonzales still humors her, but their correspondence doesn't amount to much."

I hoped that Miranda was exaggerating, that Amara actually had some life outside of her obsessive research. "Maybe this is her way of coping?"

"This is her compulsive behavior," Miranda corrected. "She has it in her mind that she is going to cure you. That she is going to come up with the treatment for this—this—this condition of yours. Damn, after four years I still don't if I should call it a disease or a condition or an illness . . ." *Curse* seemed the most appropriate, but I didn't bother to offer it as a descriptor. Miranda had gone back to her rant about Amara, so I sat and listened. "Sure, Amara made it seem like she dropped most of her OCD habits when we started her on her medication, but it turns out she's been funneling all of her efforts into one big obsession: you. She couldn't accept that . . ."

"Couldn't accept what?" I asked.

Miranda swallowed her sorrow. "She couldn't accept that her father might not be coming back."

Standing up, my wife dabbed her face with a tissue and told me she was going to try to get the girls calmed down. My mind was still reeling from the flood of information—Amara taking meds against my wishes, her obsessive behavior, how Miranda seemed so at odds with both girls.

As she left the room to corral the kids, I thought, "*I hope you're burning in hell, Dr. Bruchmuller.*" The disappointment of my family reunion made me hate that man even more. The date on the flat screen highlighted the time stolen from me: June 23, 2026.

131

Chapter 11

A pair of male voices came from the direction Miranda had disappeared in, and two middle-aged men in khakis and golf shirts walked in minutes after her exit. Up until that moment, I had thought it was simply my family in the house. Hanging off their left shoulders, they each carried designer backpacks that Wall Street traders frequently wore in New York City. Both had a pleasant demeanor that smelled of corporate life.

"Martin," the first man said casually, "sorry to interrupt, but we need a few moments of your time. I'm Jerry Kiakowski from Innovo. This is Lenny Chari. You probably don't recognize us, but we've been taking care of you since you left Walter Reed. We're also part of the research team that helped come up with the Dambra 44 antidote."

"The whatcha 44?" I asked, reaching out as I shook both men's hands.

"Dambra 44. It's a trial number combined with the name of a compound, nothing fancy. It's the antidote we've developed that has brought you up to speed, no pun intended." Lenny sat down next to me and started pulling electrodes off my head and body. I winced when he accidentally caught my nipple with a sharp edge of his fingernail, eliciting a short apology. Jerry looked at readings on a data pad and compared them against the instrumentation from which I was being disconnected.

"Martin, you may not remember, but we met several years back at the Paramus facility." Jerry sat down on the table edge and carefully pulled the IV from my arm. It was as sore as hell from hugging Amara and Miranda, but I sucked it up.

"I'm sorry, I don't recall. What was the occasion?"

Syncing Forward

"A presentation in New Jersey my department was attending. The fire alarm went off, and you came up and told us it was a system glitch."

A lightbulb went on in my head as the incident came to mind. "Ah, yes. I remember now. Although truth be told, we had three temp employees who pulled the fire alarm and were trying to take off with a bunch of pills they found in the storage room."

"Pain meds?" he asked.

"Not really. Diuretic pills I had mislabeled and left for them to steal."

He chuckled. "That's pretty funny. Well, we figured something else was going on, but nobody was talking, so we dropped the subject."

"Glad to know everyone was tight-lipped. We try to keep it that way." Inwardly, I winced. I hadn't been in a position to keep anything any way for four years.

Lenny reached up the pajama pants they had me dressed in and tried to remove the catheter I'd been wearing. I yelped a little. "Whoa there!" I told him I didn't swing that way, but Lenny assured me I'd be more comfortable with it out. I wiggled around uncomfortably at his touch while I stared down at the bald spot in the middle of his salt-and-pepper hair.

"You're looking stable," he began, "but to be on the safe side, we'll want to monitor you throughout the week."

"Not that I'm not glad to have all those sticky bits gone," I responded curiously, "but if you need to monitor me, why are you taking all these monitoring electrode thingies off me?"

"Because we want you to get up and walk and spend time with your family, Martin. You can't do that from a chair." Standing up, Jerry patted me on the back. "We'll equip you with a bracelet that will remotely send your basic vitals to us. Twice a day we're going to draw your blood and analyze it in the guesthouse in the back. We've got it set up as a mini lab, but if this treatment worked as well as we are hoping, we'll be clearing it out within two months. You're family has been very accommodating, and we don't want to intrude any more than we have to. You are also going to get sporadic injections, depending on what we find."

"Wow." I was stunned. Things were working out.

"You seem shocked, Martin," Jerry said. "What were you expecting?"

I shrugged. "I don't really know. Not this. Don't get me wrong, I'm happy. Just unexpectedly so." Truth was, I'd half-expected to be turned into some guinea pig in the bottom of a secret lab or start growing a third arm out of my back.

"You look like you have some questions, Martin. Go ahead."

"I guess I'm a little anxious, since the last time I was told I was probably going to be okay, everything went south in a hurry. I mean, how do you know I'm not going to just go back to being slow again? It feels like the football is going to get yanked away again."

Lenny explained how they had been able to remove a small amount of my pancreatic tissue and then test the Dambra 44 antidote. It had remained stable for thirty days. I asked what happened after that, but I didn't quite understand the answer.

"Why am I here? I mean, what's the deal with the house? Shouldn't I be in a hospital or something?"

"Ah, yeah. That's a disclosure complication. It's only been four years, Martin, and attorneys still run the world. They made a decision to keep you out of the public eye. There's more to it than that, but you'll want to talk to Jason Sewell from the legal team."

I nodded, not entirely satisfied with the answer.

"Martin, relax. We're very confident in your treatment. Now, there is a lot of work to do still. For one, we need to get you up and walking around. Thankfully, your muscles have showed no signs of atrophying. It seems that muscle degradation is inhibited by this mysterious drug you've been injected with. But just the same, we would be more comfortable with you exercising." He clamped a smooth

Syncing Forward

bracelet tightly around my wrist; a cold plate of metal was held in place by an elastic band with a wire concealed within its coil.

I grinned. "So what you're saying is you want me to get off my ass?"

"Yeah, something like that."

"Jerry, before I go face my family, I have a very important question."

"Go for it."

"When can I have a cheeseburger and beer?"

"Let's get you walking first, okay, Martin?"

I was wobbly at first, but walking came much quicker than I anticipated. I had some mild dizziness and nausea, but nothing like I'd felt before. It was as if I had slept for fourteen hours after an all-nighter poker game, and my body craved wakefulness. My muscles were tight, and I took some time to lean against the wall and stretch my calves. It turned out Jerry and Lenny both held doctorates and had been working for Innovo for more than fifteen years. As veterans of the company, both had left their families to live with mine until I was physiologically patched up.

I stole some more water from the glass, and Jerry left to find my wife. Lenny stood by, his hands outstretched to catch me in the event that I fell. He explained that my condition had been classified as top secret by the Department of Homeland Security and considered to be classified by our company as well. Nobody beyond my immediate family, choice Innovo employees, and a handful of government officials knew what had happened to me. It all seemed rather extreme, but the government insisted upon it and had made it a condition in exchange for Innovo taking point on the research.

"And now," Lenny went on, "Innovo is being sued by the state of New Jersey for failing to disclose all happenings in Paramus."

"Why would they care?" I asked him.

"Open Society Law Act. All corporations need to disclose the health status of their employees," Lenny explained.

"I'm surprised the Department of Homeland Security wouldn't squash that. You said I'm a top-secret topic?"

"You still are. New Jersey is suing the federal government too. It's a very strange situation."

I heard my wife coming down the hall, and I straightened myself up for her. She saw me standing and lit up immediately. It looked like the smile Miranda gave me when we first met. She took me by the arm and gave me a tour of my new home. The kitchen smelled of fresh onions and spices and had been cleaned from top to bottom. The darned thing looked like it was from a home-improvement website. Moving on, I found the hallway decorated with large family photos. I was in most of them, although those were older, and none of them had been taken at the hospital in Washington, DC. The living room had some of our old furniture, but a significant amount of new pieces.

"Miranda, how did we afford all this?"

"You are still getting your salary, and we received a big moving package from Innovo. I was concerned at first, but Felix—our personal attorney—checked it all out. Almost everything here belongs to us."

"What doesn't belong to us?"

She frowned. "You don't."

I cocked my head. "Come again?"

"I don't know if you are going to be happy about this, Martin, but I had to sign over power of attorney for you to Innovo. We really didn't have much of a choice. I missed a mortgage payment trying to keep up with the attorney fees and medical bills. I was afraid the bank would take the house. So I did what you said and called David Tsai. He called your director, Gavin Thomason, and it went from there."

Miranda explained that I was in the charge of Innovo Pharmaceutical, Incorporated, and that they made all decisions for me financially, physically, and professionally. It was a strange feeling to

Syncing Forward

know I was owned and operated by my company. And yet somehow I was still employed by them?

We walked around the living room, which didn't have a masculine touch between its four walls. Perhaps as an act of optimism, Miranda had decorated a tiny den for me in dark wood. It sat opposite the kitchen. The den held some knickknacks of mine on the desk, but past that it sat empty.

The finished basement was half–game room and half-gym. Miranda told me that Amara had personally decorated the gym, cringing at the Asian dojo designs and paper walls. I personally thought it looked pretty cool, which drew a comment about the apple not falling too far from the tree. I had taken judo in junior high and was pretty decent at it too, although the hurricane that swallowed my childhood home ended all that. Over the course of decades, my love of the sport had been reduced to watching matches on the sports channel with Amara and feeling tough. The thought of Bruchmuller's attack on me suddenly became that much more humiliating.

Next, we headed upstairs. I could hear Amara and Bella talking, and then one of them said, "He's coming!" I couldn't tell who said it, but five seconds later Amara appeared at the top of the steps.

"Dad! You look great!" Amara said.

"Thanks, kid. But how do I really look?"

Grinning, Amara revised her compliment. "Eh, not so great. You should get washed up—you haven't had a shower in four years."

"I know for a fact that somebody was scrubbing me down at least once a month, you brat." I laughed but then changed the subject. "Sweetie, how is Bella? Is she ready to see me?"

"I think so. She lost it a little, but she finally stopped crying. *Tá en su cuarto.*" Amara whispered to me as I ascended to the top of the steps, "Be sure to ask her about how she painted the walls. She's very proud of it."

Amara's maturity startled me—she sounded so grown-up. No signs of anxiety, no obsessive-compulsive behavior. Obviously her

137

tongue was still as sharp as a razor, but I wasn't about to admonish her then and there for swearing at her mom. I gave her a kiss on the forehead and whispered back, "Thank you, big kid."

Miranda and Amara stayed back as I staggered down the hallway. I peered in each doorway, noting the impressive size of the house. A guestroom with a queen-sized bed overloaded with throw pillows. A closed door to Amara's room, with a holographic sign of a finger pointing straight at me and bold letters that read *"Prohibida la Entrada!"* The upstairs bathroom shining with chrome and dotted with little purple flowers on white towels.

The last room on the right was clearly Bella's. The walls were streaked with yellow and pink, blue and green. Paint had been rolled on in uneven strokes, using different-sized rollers with no visible pattern. A low mirrored dresser decorated in gewgaws was pressed against the wall with clothes escaping the half-opened drawers. In the center of the full-sized bed, Bella sat cross-legged holding a framed picture. It was a picture of Bella and me laughing after a water balloon fight in the backyard. It stung me knowing the most recent picture my daughter had of us together was from the summer before Bruchmuller attacked me.

I knocked on the open door and invited myself in when she didn't bother looking up. I parked myself on the end of the bed and cleared my throat. Bella lifted her head and tried smiling through her frowny-face.

"Hi, Dad," she said. "Sorry I ran away. I guess I kinda freaked."

"It's okay," I reassured her. "This is scary for everybody. I barely recognized you and your sister. You both look so grown-up."

"You missed my birthdays."

"I know. I didn't mean to, honestly. But I'm here now . . ." Reaching across the comforter, my hand met Bella's and locked with hers. She lifted her chin some more and stared at me with a quivering bottom lip. I pulled her tight to me and squeezed my baby girl so hard

Syncing Forward

I thought I might break her. She clutched me in her thin arms as hard as she could and blubbered worse than her sister.

"Don't leave us again. I'd kill myself if you froze up again."

I was only a part-time Catholic, but certain subjects were solid lines that never got crossed for me; suicide was one of them. Bella probably didn't mean what she said, but I couldn't help but respond, "Bella, don't you ever say that again. I mean it. I never want to hear you say that again. Nothing is worth killing yourself over, especially me. Suicide means you can never see any of your family and friends in heaven. It's the worst thing you can ever do."

"Dad, I wasn't being serious—"

But I couldn't stop. "Listen, you and you sister and your mom are the most precious things in the world to me, but even in the worst of circumstances, I'd never take my own life out of sadness. You have a lifetime of experiences ahead of you, good and bad. If you learn nothing else from me, I want you to know this: you must live your life right to the end. Do the best you can in everything. And be there for me when I am old and gray and fat."

She wiped her snot on her sleeve and smiled. "Well, you're already getting a little chubby."

"Hey, you brat! I haven't eaten in four years. I'm on the best diet in the world. I'll lose my belly in no time."

She giggled over her tears, and we hugged some more.

"I missed you so much!" I managed to say. Inside I was thanking God for bringing me back to my family. Maybe it was time to be a full-time Catholic. I felt my heart flutter from the conflux of sentiments, when our touching moment was interrupted by an unremitting chime from my bracelet. I jumped up, electrified. Jerry Kiakowski bolted up the steps and burst through the doorway, a data tablet almost slipping from his sweaty fingers as he stumbled into Bella's room.

"Martin, are you okay?" he said with a gasp.

Bella shrieked as the doctor practically fell into her room.

"No!" I yelled at him. "You scared the crap out of us! What the hell is wrong with you?"

"Sorry, sorry." He put his hand up. "Your vitals moved out of the safety parameters we set for your bracelet, and it set off all our alarms. But . . . uh . . . but now that I look at them, it just looks like you're just . . . emotional . . . and that's what set it off. I think we might have made the settings on the bracelet a bit too sensitive."

I didn't know whether to laugh or ping that tablet off his forehead. "You think?"

Syncing Forward

Chapter 12

The girls allotted me twenty minutes to take a hot shower, which made my skin burst with goose bumps—a side effect of not having any tactile stimulation for so long, I reckoned. The hot beads of water contrasted with the lack of sensation I'd felt for all that time, and I wondered how long it would take for this ultrasensitivity to wear off. It wasn't unpleasant, just strange. Miranda and the girls chatted me up the entire time from the other side of the opaque shower door, leaving me alone only long enough to dry off and dress. I learned of the legal issues that circled around me, details about the house, gossip in the small town we now lived in, family business. My head spun.

Lunch was closely monitored by the men. Ever since I had begun slowing down, the doctors had fed me intravenously: basically sugar. People stuck in the hospital for long periods of time were able to get along just fine. But nothing beats real food.

My first taste of "real food" was a light spinach salad and a glass of water. Disappointment was an understatement, but Lenny warned me meat and dairy were strictly forbidden and explained that vegetables were the most alkaline food I could ingest at this point. I recall mumbling something inappropriate about where he could shove the salad, but I ultimately conceded to eating it. I watched jealously as my family and the doctors downed homemade pork tamales and black beans, and Miranda sympathetically told me she was just as let down that I couldn't eat the dinner she had prepared. I highly doubted it—I wanted food.

As I jealously eyeballed Lenny scarfing down my wife's cooking, his words escaped while he chewed. "Miranda, your cooking never ceases to amaze me. My wife gets jealous every time you make a meal for us."

Miranda smiled graciously, but she didn't hide her displeasure very well. Something was up. Lenny kept talking, and Miranda kept being silent. The kids took over the table conversation for a spell, and

W Lawrence

I got filled in on which classes were boring, which boys were cute, how cold this past winter had been. I learned that our new house sat on top of the hill that overlooked the sleepy Pennsylvania town, and rumors still flew about the woman and her daughters who lived there. It made life hard on the girls; both had ended up having to lie about where I was in the family picture. The cover story for the family was that I traveled extensively with Innovo.

A chime sounded sweetly from the flat screen in the kitchen, and the video call ID showed GOV WASHINGT DC. Miranda looked at me, and her mood soured even further. She shushed the kids and pointed at the screen. "That's a call for you, Martin."

It kept chiming. I stood up and realized I didn't know what to do. "Uh, how do I answer this?"

"I'll do it!" both girls blurted out, and they both made a run for the screen in a fight to show me how to use the monitor controls. Amara beat her little sister and answered the call. "Hello, how can I help you?" A Department of Homeland Security shield showed on the screen, but the voice was familiar enough. "This is Darren Franciscus calling for Martin James, please."

I thanked both Amara and Bella for helping out, but Bella's irritation turned into a spat. "Why did *you* get to show him?"

"Fine, you can show him how to do everything in the house first, and then I'll just correct everything you got wrong," Amara shot back. Miranda yelled at them in Spanish, and the dynamic duo were ushered out of the kitchen.

"Hello, Agent Franciscus, this is Miranda," she said. "I'm going to transfer the call to the den so Martin can talk with you privately."

"Thank you, Mrs. James," I heard him reply before she pressed the screen. She touched a symbol that popped up, and the screen went black.

I shuffled off to the den, fumbling about for where the light switch was hidden. I finally found it, plopped into the office chair, and looked at the computer monitor that was lit up with a single yellow circle in the bottom right corner. One touch and it opened up a view screen to Agent Franciscus's face. He was sporting a goatee that was trimmed short and close to the edges of his mouth.

"Welcome back to the land of the living, Mr. James," the DHS investigator said.

"Thanks," I replied awkwardly. "You grew a beard."

"Yeah, after I got divorced two years back I grew it out. My ex-wife was always bitching about it being too scratchy, so now that she's gone the beard is back." Franciscus cleared his throat awkwardly. He gestured to the right side of his face. "Your face is still bruised up pretty bad. Or is that something new?"

"The drug that Millennial injected me with slows down everything, including my healing, unfortunately. So this is the longest running shiner on record."

"Pretty strange."

"Yup."

The somewhat awkward pause in the conversation afforded him an opportunity to get down to business.

"Listen, I know you are just coming back to us, but I've been directed to run something past you. We uncovered some information about eighteen months back, but you were unavailable. It's the best lead we've had on the tall man. Do you recognize the name Bernard Rendell?"

"No, not at all."

"How about this face? Does this person look familiar?"

The video conference was minimized on the screen, and the image of a white male with sandy blond hair and a pronounced jaw took its place. Just his upper torso shone, but I could tell he was a big fella just the same. The image was surrounded by a blue-and-yellow border, with the Innovo symbol in the bottom left corner. It was a company ID with an expiration date of May 31, 2019. "Bernard G. Rendell 810223" was printed on the side.

143

"Son of a gun," I murmured. This was him. This was the man in the tunnels with Rajesh and Dr. Bruchmuller and the others. The one person who had huddled in the tunnels beneath Innovo whom I hadn't recognized—but I knew him now. Stupid me for letting something like hair (or a lack thereof) throw me off.

"I know this man, and I remember his name now. He transferred in from the Carolinas about two years ago—" I stopped and corrected myself. "I mean six years ago. He was a shipping manager, supposedly ticked off a couple guys because he got the promotion and the local fellas didn't. Real nice guy. Had the shipping center running like a clock till he was diagnosed with cancer. I remember they were taking up a collection for him, and I felt like a jerk since I didn't have any money on me."

Franciscus nodded. "Well, being that he tried to blow you up, maybe you shouldn't beat yourself up too much."

He had a good point. Here I was feeling sorry for the guy who was ready to bury me in a hundred tons of concrete. "How did you track him down?"

Franciscus fidgeted a bit. "Driver's license records. I figured he had to be an employee. Took me forever since he was on extended leave and not on your regular company roll. Anyway, once I cross-referenced your company database with New Jersey DMV we got six hits: five men and one woman who were six foot three or over. Two are African American and two had strong alibis."

"I gotta tell you, Agent," I started, "he doesn't strike me as the terrorist type. Not that I've had a lot of experience with terrorists—"

"Well, given your buddy Rajesh Jotwani, I'd say you've had more experience than you think."

It was a good point. Poor Rajesh. I was still bitter over his involvement in destroying Innovo's research center and angrier over the fact that he had betrayed me, but he was my friend and a father. "Not that it's my business, but what happened to Rajesh's son? Arjan?"

Syncing Forward

"Not sure. State officials took him, but I never saw the kid." Franciscus cleared his throat, "But we are off-topic. Let's get back to Rendell. He's still at large, but where a man of this height vanishes to for years at a time I have no idea. What kind of dealing did you have with him?"

Virtually none. I explained that I'd conversed with him occasionally to pull a couple of his employees in for interviews, but beyond a "how's it going?" here and a "I'm gonna take your dirtbag clerk for an interview and he ain't coming back" there, we didn't interact.

Franciscus asked me questions about who Rendell associated with, where he hung out, what type of access he had, and if he seemed to know the other suspects—all questions I'm sure he already had answers for from people who knew the man much better. I apologized, but my contribution to this investigation seemed to be coming to a close.

"Do you have anything for me?" I asked. "I mean, what's the deal with the crypts these Millennial folk were talking about? And why inject me? And why this drug? What were they trying to accomplish? If they wanted to kidnap me, wouldn't it have been easier to inject me with some type of knockout drug?"

"We have no idea. There've been several other attacks Millennial has taken credit for and a handful more that they haven't. The only thing they have in common is that their targets are mostly technology based. Laboratories, chemical plants, a hospital research wing. They even killed a grad student who was interning with a robotics firm."

"Jesus."

"Did they say anything? Make demands?"

He shook his head. "No demands. But here's what they sent out to our offices."

The video screen showed an e-mail with redacted addresses in the heading. In large letters, the statement read:

W Lawrence

> WE ARE RESPONSIBLE FOR STOPPING THIS ATTEMPT TO ACHIEVE SINGULARITY. WE ARE MILLENNIAL. WE ARE ETERNAL. WE ARE WATCHING.

I rubbed the bruised side of my face and grew mildly perturbed at the fact that it hadn't healed in four years. Franciscus was about to sign off from the video conference, when I let out a "wait!" and held up my hand.

"One last thing, Agent. Maybe it's nothing, maybe it's something, but Bernard Rendell had cancer. So did Albert Vies's wife. Dr. Kamani was suffering from some blood disorder, although the name escapes me."

Agent Franciscus shrugged. "So what are you thinking?"

I tapped the desk in front of the video monitor. "Maybe this drug they injected me with is a way of storing people. I mean, what if these Millennial folk were preserving themselves in order to put off their symptoms? Or to wait for a cure?"

Franciscus scratched his beard roughly. "Like those crazy dudes who freeze their heads so that aliens will find them and reattach them to cloned bodies? Shit like that? I saw a documentary on it once. Those people are nuts, you know."

"Yeah, but think about it. These Millennial terrorists . . . they have a real drug. It didn't freeze me, but I might as well have been frozen. Look at my face—the bruise is still there. What if it held off cancer too? Not a cure, just a vacation from it. A second chance."

Agent Franciscus wasn't looking at me. He was scrolling through some files on his screen, nodding and mumbling quietly. "It's not everybody, but you are right about the disease thing. You might have figured out an important component to this case, Mr. James."

I felt vindicated as I signed off, and Franciscus had renewed his interest in the case. It felt good to contribute, to get back into the swing of things. The chase of the investigation made my blood pump

Syncing Forward

the way it used to when I hunted whitetails with my brother Jacob—that lingering low-level excitement that exhausts you when you come back from lurking about in the woods all day.

But it was more than that. I felt like I had redeemed myself from missing so many clues, for allowing the Innovo campus to be utterly destroyed, for the deaths of my coworkers at Innovo.

I wanted to keep on redeeming myself until this thing was solved.

Chapter 13

I wanted to call Gavin Thomason and see when I could come back to work. I wanted to call Dave Tsai and find out how the investigation had wrapped up. I was desperate to find out if I could get back to work. That one conversation with Franciscus made me realize how much I loved my job, piecing together a puzzle. Even if I wasn't working for DHS, at least I was helping them. But a blood test and physical from Lenny left me with marching orders that trumped my want list: Rest. Relaxation. Definitively, undeniably, no stress whatsoever. He told me to enjoy myself and pointed out that the company was paying me to sit and relax. One look at my kids convinced me that he was right. I needed to take advantage of the time I had to make up for the time we'd lost.

Bella told me all about the blond-haired bully boy on her bus who sounded more like a kid with a crush than anything else. She showed me a book of notes she had written that never got sent to me. Bella's light-brown hair fell around her in a mess as we looked at videos she had taken of the zoo and her flower garden in the back and her weeklong trip to my brother-in-law's house. Staring into their faces, I could see my younger children underneath, taking in how some aspects of their personalities had not changed at all while other aspects had changed entirely.

Amara showed me videos of her martial arts tournaments and then proceeded to challenge me. I would have loved to scrap it up with my thirteen-year-old in the basement, but Lenny Chari strongly suggested I not. She offered to do a demonstration on the doctor, who was foolish enough to say yes. Lenny wasn't a big guy, but he outweighed Amara by close to eighty pounds. Yet she tossed him over her like a rag doll, softening his fall at the last second by holding his weight on the downward turn. The man looked shaken and a bit humiliated, but he was a good sport about the whole thing. Still, it was the last demonstration. We went back to talking about Amara's trophies while

Syncing Forward

I beamed with pride. Every father wants to know that his daughters can take care of themselves in a physical confrontation.

It was time for the treadmill and a stress test while covered in electrodes. I was only seven minutes in when Lenny pressed the red button and Jerry scrambled over the data fed out by the computer tablet. His eyes bounced along whatever he was reading while he quickly compared the numbers with some unknown values from his head.

"What's up, Doc?" I asked.

"Uh, we're okay," Jerry stammered. "Yeah, uh, we're fine. We just think maybe some rest would be better for you."

Miranda stood in the doorway with her arms folded tightly along her belly. I tried to assuage her by repeating what Lenny had said. Miranda nodded silently and forced a thin, polite smile. She looked worried, and that made me worried.

We decided to take a walk out along the property. Dang if Pennsylvania in June wasn't the best smell in the world. It was such a good feeling to be free from a hospital bed and moving about outside while holding my wife's hand—even if she seemed as sad as could be. She explained to me how our family and friends had been told I suffered from wounds from the explosion at Innovo and that I had been in a coma for the last several years. Her family, my family—nobody knew. Miranda not only hated lying but rarely managed to get away with it; those two aspects were probably well intertwined. Who knew what everyone really thought?

The rectangular cornfields carved out below us contrasted with the rolling hills that bordered the valley, yet none of it seemed out of place. Farms always seemed so naturally placed, the crops bringing both food and a handsomeness to the land. Unlike the suburbs or the cities, people weren't living on top of each other. Neighbors were people you drove to see. "The only thing that makes it even possible is being out here," she said. "At least in the middle of nowhere, there isn't anyone to trip you up on your lies."

W Lawrence

My family represented varying levels of difficulty in hiding the truth. My father had been gone for years, and my mother and me . . . well, we didn't talk so much anymore. Not at all. My brother, Jacob, however, had climbed the walls when it came to the coma story. He had insisted on coming to see me, getting a second opinion. DHS threatened to pull me out of the Pennsylvania house if the matter wasn't contained, so Innovo went to great lengths to make me look like just a regular coma patient. How, I have no idea, but they even arranged for my faux convalescence when Jacob insisted on coming up to see me. The cover story expanded to include the house as a payoff to my family as part of an ongoing lawsuit.

That seemed to quiet Jacob for a time, but the lie created a rift between him and my wife. Miranda couldn't tell him the truth, and Jacob always felt as if she was hiding something. Contact with our family was not allowed until I was deemed "stable" for at least a month. It was an irritating position to be in, and one I planned to rectify as soon as I could reach this attorney of ours. Miranda wasn't so keen to push the matter, however, which I didn't understand.

Thirst got the better of me, so we walked back into the house. "You've been complaining about living this lie," I pointed out. "I don't understand the kickback here."

The kids stampeded into the living room with armfuls of memories, and Miranda stepped away from the conversation with a passing kiss. For the life of me I wasn't sure what was happening with my wife, but it was impossible to engage her with the kids about. So I dove into the memories and soaked up all the hugs and kisses I could get while keeping one eye on Miranda for clues as to why she was so distant. We spent the next several hours in a morass of report cards and stories, tears and fits of laughter, videos and news headlines.

"First Astronauts Arrive at Mars-One"

"Pakistan and India Declare Ceasefire"

"Marburg Virus Claims Thousandth Victim in Berlin"

Syncing Forward

"Fisler Genecom Scientists Create Superbabies"

"PRC Denies Guangdong Nuclear Site Meltdown"

"Texas Governor Pushes Neighbors for Separation"

"Freedom Tower Bombing Thwarted, Sixteen Arrested"

"Human Cloning Colony Announced by Moscow"

"Chinese Protesters Push for Reform"

"Cubs Win World Series 4–3"

"Dow Dips Below 12,000 for Second Time This Year, Investors Clamor"

My in-laws and brother had recorded multiple videos of themselves that were purportedly played for me while I was "comatose" to spur me to consciousness. They could have played these videos hundreds of times while I was slowed down and I would have seen them as a flash of light . . . maybe. Still, seeing their faces was a joyful experience even though the videos were recorded under false pretenses. Amara and Bella narrated every last detail of the video playback.

Blood test. Tissue sample from my mouth. A stress test that involved walking instead of running. Then it was dinnertime, but the delightful smells of Miranda's cooking were absent. The meal was a near repeat of lunch, with the exception of a "special" shake that tasted more like grass than anything else. The ladies ate sparingly in front of me, and Bella picked cautiously at the salad her mother put in front of her.

The evening eclipsed into the late hours, and the girls' eyes drooped. It was ultimately time for them to head off to bed, and Jerry came in to demand that I get some sleep. I shooed them away and told them I would go to sleep soon. With the kids ensconced in their beds and the duo of doctors in the guesthouse, it was finally Miranda and me alone in the living room. I tried holding her hand warmly, but she slipped it away slowly, giving me a consolation pat before breaking contact.

"So . . ." I let the word linger.

"I think you should get some sleep." She started to get off the sofa, when I grabbed her hand and pulled her back to a sitting position.

"So." I held her hand warmly but firmly. "Tell me what's on your mind. It feels like you're upset with me."

Miranda gazed into my eyes for a while before speaking. When she did, I was surprised by what she had to say. "Well, Martin, I am upset with you."

"Okay, why?"

"I don't know why. I just am."

"That isn't exactly true—"

"Damn it! Don't interview me like I'm some thief! I didn't like it when you used to do it, and I still don't like it!"

"Miranda, give me a break and just tell me what's going on!" I raised my voice but quickly softened my tone, not sure if the girls could hear us. "Honey, please, just say what's on your mind."

"Fine. I hate the fact that you are fine and perfect and have only had to lose days or maybe even just hours of your life while we've spent four years suffering through this nightmare." My wife was tearing up, but her antagonism clearly shone through.

I felt myself stiffening in response. "So you think I should be suffering more?"

"No! But you're like some transient father who disappears for a decade, comes walking in on his kid's thirteenth birthday, and expects everyone just to accept you as you are."

"How is any of this my fault?"

"Did I say it was your fault?"

Syncing Forward

"No, but you make it sound like I planned it all this way."

"Martin, you don't understand. This house, the money—it's all a bandage. I've been fighting to keep this family together and barely able to take care of anything. I have no family out here. No friends. Lying to everyone I know about your condition. Lying to Mami and Papi! *Mis hermanos*. Your brother. Bella is impossible. Amara is worse than ever—"

"Jesus, Miranda, what kid would deal with this problem well? And if you haven't noticed, I am back. I am alive and here and wanting my wife back, and you're mad at me for that!"

Her arms went out wide. "For how long, Martin? How long do we get you back for? A day? A month? The doctors can't guarantee you'll recover."

I shook my head. "No, you're wrong. They told me specifically that they felt confident in the treatment I received."

"Oh, did they now? And you know how many treatments you received that they 'felt confident' about that did *nothing*? They didn't tell you about the dozens of medications and implants and treatments they tried that failed miserably? They don't call it Dambra *forty-four* because they like the number. So sorry if I don't share your excitement over Jerry and Lenny's stirring speech."

I looked down at my lap and fidgeted with my own fingers. What words could I say to put my wife's heart at ease? I didn't dare debate her, nor did I even want to question how hard it had been—how hard it still was. Miranda was going through what many soldiers' wives went through: raising a family on her own, managing a household, trying to have a life she could call hers. But the worst thing for a soldier's wife had to be not knowing what might happen to her husband. Would he die tragically early, or come home fine, or perhaps return with a handicap? There were no assurances in the life of a soldier's wife, and Miranda had experienced everything they might go through.

And yet somehow her life was even more stressful. I got that. There was no support group for husbands injected with mysterious substances by crazed terrorist scientists. My sweet wife had been going through this ordeal for four years truly alone. Dr. Gonzales's words rang in my ears from back in Washington, DC, when she warned me that my family would suffer far worse than I would. She was right.

Miranda wiped her nose with a new tissue when I leaned over and squeezed her.

"I'm so scared, Martin! I just want to keep you home like this, and I'm afraid—"

"Don't be. You had to go through a lot, and don't think I'm unappreciative. But I'm not going anywhere. I'm home to stay."

Miranda and I held each other for a long time before we finally unlocked our arms. Our cheeks slid slowly against each other, our lips brushing softly. At first awkward, our lips touched pensively until they finally remembered our marital relationship. The kiss was followed by another and another. Miranda silently stood up and guided me by hand to our bedroom on the first floor. The four-poster bed was lovely dark wood that—unlike the bed in our old house—matched the furniture around it. Curtains carefully coordinated with the borders along the wall signaled that Miranda had spent a long time designing and working on this room, unlike our New Jersey house, where we had bought whatever was on sale from an online store. This was everything she had always wanted in a master bedroom, and from the tone of her voice earlier in the day I could tell she was proud of how it had come out.

The bed was turned down and the air scented with a cinnamon candle; my wife knew I loved cinnamon and must have lit it during the course of the evening when she wasn't angry with me. Smoothly we sank onto the bed, embracing as a husband and wife were meant to, touching, holding, grasping. I could feel her heat against my skin, and for those brief moments we were completely oblivious to the torment time had put upon us. Despite the days and years we had been separated, my wife and I were finally together.

Syncing Forward

Miranda's kisses fell upon me faster and faster, along my neck and ear and cheek and mouth. Her hands moved so quickly I had trouble perceiving their movements at first. The bracelet alarm was going off, but it sounded like a Doppler effect, its pitch dropping and the sounds becoming increasingly muffled, as if the alarm were rushing down a country road and off into the distance. My wife stopped and stared at me for the briefest of moments before she spoke hurriedly.

"Martin are you okay please Martin Martin no no no not again notagain . . ."

I saw her grab for a tablet on the nightstand, and she called for the doctors to hurry to the bedroom. Lenny and Jerry stormed into the bedroom in a blur of motion with instrumentation in their hands, asking me questions I was too slow to answer. Even if I could, my hazy eyes and subdued ears were fixed on my poor wife, who sat on the edge of the bed rocking back and forth, pulling at her hair. All I managed to make out was her fading repetitions.

"Ican'tdothisanymoreIcan'tdothisanymoreIcan'tdothisanymoreIcan'tdothisanymore . . ."

Chapter 14

My "sitting room," as the girls referred to the living room, was equipped with photovoltaic glass that darkened and lightened automatically with the sun. The tech made life much easier for me as I gazed out the box window to rest my eyes from the pictures and messages that bombarded me on a regular basis. The farmland beneath our property was tilled and plants grew, and I could see huge swaths of land tilled in a matter of seconds. The glass would lighten and the night sky would shine down upon the world, disturbed only by my glowing display. Eleven seconds later and night would vanish and be exchanged for a precisely shaded day.

I'M TRYING AGAIN, DAD. HANG ON.

After about ten seconds, Bella's voice came through the audio buds in my ear. "Hi, Dad. Can you hear me okay?"

Her voice was pitchy but discernible, enough for me to recognize it this time.

YES, I responded with a key press.

My slowing was not a smooth process, and the rate at which my body decelerated varied enough each day to make matching audio speeds difficult to accomplish. The voice modulator had to be constantly recalibrated so that I could understand what funneled to my ears. The emotional connection a voice can achieve as compared to written words was never clearer to me than while I was sitting there. It wasn't only technology that made connecting difficult, however, but the fact that as the years passed, Bella's voice matured. Any tone of a child's voice vanished, and it ate me up inside to have that taken away so quickly.

The interface was far superior to what I'd had at Walter Reed. It amazed me how fast the technology advanced in what was, for me, a few hours. I looked about the sitting room of our Pennsylvania home and watched the blur of Amara and Bella coming and going, doing

Syncing Forward

their homework, watching TV, the doctors making their typical rounds. No Miranda, though—not that I could see.

Touch was a sensation in short supply. Bella made a habit of coming and sitting with me once each week for three hours at a time. She became quite adept at sitting perfectly still with her hand in mine or her head on my lap. I could feel her soft hair in my hand or the warmth of her cheek on my fingers. Sometimes I swore I smelled her freshly shampooed hair, although I could easily have imagined it. My little angel did her best to be affectionate and supportive, but despite her best efforts, the hours she spent registered as less than a few seconds to me. The consolation was that every week to her was only two-and-a-half minutes to me, so I didn't have to wait long for her company again.

For now, anyway. The ratio by which I perceived the passing of time constantly changed, calculated by my pulse rate, blood pressure, and pupil dilations: for now, one minute for me worked out to about two-and-a-half actual days. The Dambra 44 antidote had failed just like the synthetic catecholamine tried by the government; the fact that it had a fancier name was of little consolation. Dambra 44 had managed to mitigate my deceleration, however, so my slowing this time was much more gradual.

A mere conversation ago, the ratio had been around 1:500 seconds. The doctors didn't dare try to bring me back again until I was stabilized, and that meant waiting until my body reached the speed the Millennial drug had intended for me to operate at. If that number was consistent with the first two times, it meant I needed to reach a ratio of about 1:4,000. At that rate, an hour for me would equate to roughly five months for the outside world. A calculus problem lay buried in there somewhere to determine how much time would pass before I could be brought back, but that was for people far smarter than me to figure out.

I didn't say a word, but panic set in as I looked at the electronic readout on the wall. I was fast approaching the year 2028. Another two years gone, and this go-around was taking longer to bottom out.

Headlines scrolled up the screen for me to read.

"Mars-One Colony Mourns Two as Four More Arrive"

"Happy Birthday Song Officially Becomes Public Domain"

"First Networked Human Twins Present at Symposium"

"Extinct South China Tiger Back Thanks to Geneticists in Hong Kong"

"Los Angeles under Martial Law—Riots hit Thirtieth Week"

"Russia Attacks Afghanistan on Fiftieth Anniversary of Original Invasion"

"Sino-Russian Moon Base Construction Begins"

"Vatican Destroyed in Aerial Bombardment"

"Iranian Military Tightens Grip on Eastern Iraqi Provinces, Oil Fields"

What about Millennial? There was no word from Agent Franciscus, no word from DHS at all. My inquiries were answered with "I don't knows." I tried to get to the bottom of things, but the doctors were asking me questions and the kids were keeping me occupied. You can't dominate a conversation when you're a statue. The log of my messages sat on the left side of the screen while information from news headlines scrolled by on the right side. I put up a message.

MIRANDA IS EVERYTHING OKAY?

There was no response. Instead, there came a series of acuity tests and then a trip to the laboratory. I passed out and then came back around while sitting in the living room. Amara spoke to me through

Syncing Forward

the calibrated message. "That wasn't good, Dad. That treatment almost killed you."

Almost killed me? How long was I out for? The panic I felt before kicked into fourth gear when I looked up at the wall display and read October 15, 2030: nearly eight years since I was injected by Bruchmuller. I was going to have to start calling that day something else... Innovo Destruction Day. Injection Day. Become a Statue Day. God, I was losing it. I felt my hands shaking and wondered how that would look to my wife or my daughters. I balled them into fists to try to bleed off the tension, but it wasn't helping.

The latest bout of news flooded in, and the headlines were scrolling off the screen faster than I could read them. I typed a message to SLOW DOWN, which allowed me to grab a helping of information.

"Euro No More—Currency Dives!"

"Global Markets Tumble on Euro News"

"Riots Engulf La Forteresse de Bercy, Paris"

"Spain's Emergency Vote; Leaving European Union"

"Greece Parliament now 1/3 National Socialist Party"

"Bombs Rock Rome, Milan; IF Take Credit"

Bella's grown-up voice buzzed in my ears while I read. "Uncle Jacob sent us cactus candy from Tucson and a bunch of pictures of our cousins. We're uploading them to your folder. His new wife is pretty, and she seemed nice on the video chat. She's pregnant already. I wish you could talk to him. Hey, by the time you are done listening to this, she might give birth!"

SMARTASS, I typed back. Bella's joking around about my condition seemed like a healthy response, but I couldn't muster the energy to kid her back.

I was glad to hear Jacob had remarried. Fiona, his first wife, had gotten hooked on a nasty drug called synth after their twins were born. One night she overdosed and slit her own throat in bed while standing over my sleeping brother. It messed him up big-time, and the twins went into foster care for a long while. He asked us to take care of them—which we did for a few months—but packing six people into our dinky New Jersey house was unwieldy at best. Once school started, they went back to Arizona and ended up in a reasonably nice foster home. Jacob was furious with me, however, blaming me for my niece and nephew being "handed over to the state." Early in 2020 he had managed to get them back and start anew. My brother and I reconciled, but there was still a thin layer of resentment. Bella uploaded a couple of pictures to my computer of him and an attractive blonde captioned "Lily."

I frowned at the sight of the calendar—even being lost in thought cost me weeks of my life. I focused my attention on the news screen on the right as it continued pumping out headlines. Bella and Amara regularly fed me information, sometimes once a week or sometimes several times a day. To my eyes, these glimpses of the world scrolled up the screen as quick as a clever retweet. There would often be a note or a little "A" or "B" next to each headline. Amara was inclined to give me a more global perspective on the news, while Bella sent me enjoyable things like World Cup winners or bizarre articles about robotic spying squirrels.

I KNOW YOU WLD TEL ME BUT PLZ SAY CURE COMNG??? I rattled on the keys.

Amara sent me a voice mail. "Daddy, we're trying. Going to have to put you under again soon, though. We love you so much. I wish you were there for graduation."

The picture she sent over wasn't her high school graduation—the dark robes she wore held the double-tied cord of a *summa cum laude* college graduate. If my heart could have broken any more, it would have at that sight. She was a woman; my older daughter a college graduate. Another stolen moment that forced a frown and made my

Syncing Forward

chest tighten. No, this mysterious drug didn't dull heartache now, did it?

"Milk $11 Per Gallon, Public Sours"
—B—*Don't worry, Dad, we've got food!*

"US Dollar Dumped in Early Trading"

"Inflation Uncontrollable"

"Interest on National Debt Now a Quarter of Spending"

"Mortgage Rates Climb to 23% Average"
—A—*Mortgage paid up, not sure if u knew.*

The world was falling apart, oblivious to my desires as much as I was to its struggles. Wars and failing economies, riots and coups, bitter winters and extended droughts—all manner of hardship was falling upon my country and my family while I remained apart. Miranda's oldest brother got into trouble at work and lost his job. Her dad was out on disability because of an injury to his hand. The wealth bestowed by my corporation's gift of a salary and a home were the only solace I had—somehow the secrets locked away inside me were worth the expenditures to Innovo Pharmaceutical.

The monitor showed my heartbeat ratio at 1:3,913. I was so close, I just needed to slow down a little more. I tried one of those damn yoga breathing techniques Rajesh had taught me years ago, and the number jumped to 3,960. Then 3,988. I was so close.

Amara spoke to me through the earbuds. "They administered an anesthesia a few weeks ago, Daddy. You should feel it soon. You should be back to normal when you wake up."

The dimming of the world began with my sinking eyelids. I felt my chair recline and realized Bella had snuggled up next to me, falling asleep in a set of pink frumpy pajamas with an afghan wrapped around her legs. I couldn't help but remember Bella at seven years old, wedging herself between Miranda and me after watching too many scary movies, wiggling around in bed so much that our sleep was a fitful one. Now she was a teenager and as still as a mountain lake. But for those precious seconds, I was holding my Baby Bella.

    I closed my eyes and let that single thought carry me to black.

— **Part 3** —

Unraveling

Chapter 15

I looked up at a stranger with large glasses holding a tiny flashlight. I recognized her as a woman, but that was all I knew. I closed my eyes and fell back into the void of sleep.

I heard a voice. It was a woman again, but younger. She was calling out, "I think he's awake!" and a voice answered back about a count being off and how the rate was wrong and how my blood temperature was too high. I couldn't even open my eyes; instead I listened to their voices drawing further and further away.

"Wake up, Dad." A hand gently shook me. "Wake up. Your body is back-synced finally. You're in real time."

I opened my eyes to a dimly lit room with a redheaded Bella standing over me in a white dress that accentuated her dark complexion. There was a sweetness in her eyes that reminded me of my mom when I was younger, a nurturing tilt that made others feel safe. Behind her was Amara, looking like a younger version of Miranda but with a sharpness to her eyes, wearing a dull gray top and black suspenders. The two had grown so much. It was clear they were beyond their teens.

The table I lay upon moved upward silently and brought me to a sitting position, giving me a better look at where I was. I had been moved to the laboratory in the back of our Pennsylvania home, but it looked faded and older. Little to no upkeep had been done on the place, and three cracked windows were boarded from the outside. One of the monitors had a cracked display, although it was still operating. A graying black man in a crisp suit who smelled of lawyer was standing in the background talking to his earpiece while occasionally glancing my way. A woman with wrinkled hands and dyed jet-black hair faced away from me, manipulating something that looked like a pane of glass. Whoever she might be, she was talking to a very young-looking white

Syncing Forward

man with a piercing through his cheek and a concert T-shirt under his lab coat. Tattoos ran from the back of his ears underneath the fabric of his shirt. His hair was shaved high over his ears, stubble descending down along his sideburns to a pointy beard, and his eyes stayed on me the whole time he spoke with the older woman.

"Can we get him out of these monitors, Mike?" Bella asked the younger man.

"I wouldn't recommend it. His syncing was up and down for the last two weeks. We may want to try the nanotreatment we discussed if he starts to dip again." The younger man looked briefly at me and then went back to discussing my condition with his senior colleague.

"Hey, Baby Bella," I croaked. My throat was dry, and I couldn't even clear my voice. She handed me a plastic water bottle with an odd-looking straw poking from the top. The material felt strange in my hand, tissue-thin and more like cloth than plastic.

I washed the water down and tried again. "Hey, Bella. Don't you look so pretty! And is that my big kid back there?"

Amara's eyes were sullen and her arms crossed, but she put on a kinder face when I spoke to her. She took a few steps forward and squeezed my calf as she stood at the foot of the bed. "Hi, Daddy," she said softly. "Welcome back."

I took another sip and replied, "So, where's your mom?"

My daughters looked at each other uncomfortably, and the conversation across the room stopped. Bella patted my chest. "She couldn't make it, Dad."

"But where is she?"

"Can we talk about Mom later? We're on a tight schedule."

"Okay..." My voice trailed off. If she was dead, the girls would have said something, but their evasiveness meant uncomfortable news was still waiting for me. "Can you at least tell me what year it is? How long did I sleep for?"

Amara came up to the top of the bed and held my hand. "You've been asleep for almost nine years since the last time we back-synced you. You're just past the thirteenth anniversary of the Innovo bombing. It's November 8, 2035."

Nine years. "Are you sure?" I asked. It was a stupid question and everyone knew it, but I couldn't keep my head from shaking, from denying the reality. How could they have taken so long? It was 2035! There should have been flying cars and robot waiters and shit that would speed me up without losing a decade in the process!

"Dad, it's okay, just—"

"Nine years?" I shouldn't have been surprised. Amara's college graduation picture was dated 2033, and there had to be time after that for the doctors to work on me. Still, I loved being a dad, and my girls had been at the best age when I was attacked. That age when they didn't need you so much, but they wanted you more than ever. Seven and nine meant roller coasters and games that didn't suck the life out of you, and breaking away from movies that weren't inundated with princesses and magical ponies. I so desperately wanted to be there to warn them about boys, to teach them to drive, to help them find their first jobs. But it seems they had gotten along fine without me. *Unneeded* described pretty much how I felt.

Bella knew I was tumbling from the shock, and she put her hand on my face. "Dad, you're back with us, but we don't have a lot of time. You remember the Dambra 44 treatment Innovo gave you? Well, that isn't what brought you back. This team is from Walter Reed, and they have a plan for fixing you permanently."

"Hi, I'm Dr. Nikonov." A white man in a suit stepped forward from the back of the room, thrusting out his hand toward mine. Despite his Russian name, his King's English placed his education and homeland squarely in the heart of London. His cropped hair was so light I found it difficult to distinguish between the blond and the gray. "I'm working with the Department of Homeland Defense on this initiative, and we're all quite excited to be able to put an end to this nonsense."

Syncing Forward

I nodded and shook his hand. "Sounds good to me, Doc. So what's the deal? I'm guessing by the look in your eye that y'all don't have a fix for me just yet."

Dr. Nikonov hesitated slightly before continuing. "True enough. We used a derivative of the Dambra treatment to sync you back. That's short for 'in synchronization,' if you haven't guessed it. It just means you've been brought up to speed, no pun intended. Anyway, the new treatment is 100 percent chemical. We call it Diox 9. It means no more radiation treatments to work in concert with your syncing."

"Hell, I didn't even know there was radiation involved in the first place!" I rubbed my head roughly, scratching at my scalp, half-expecting to pull out a handful of hair; thankfully, I did not. "So Diox 9, huh? What happened to Diox 1 through 8?"

"Diox 2, 4, and 6 were all failures," Amara said aggressively, causing Nikonov's visage to turn sour. My daughter rattled off the remaining tests. "Diox 5 and Diox 7 almost killed you. Diox 8 they never even administered, since the tests showed it would cause instantaneous death. Oh, I forgot, Diox 1 actually turned the cell sample they tested it on into plastic."

"Holy crap." I looked at Dr. Nikonov. "Are you trying to kill me?"

"If we wanted to kill you, we would have subjected you to thirteen years of romance novels." It was a female voice. The woman with the jet-black hair spun around in her seat, her smile lifting her wrinkles off her aged cheeks. She had been in her late forties when I saw her last, and now she had to be in her midsixties. The black dye job was an awkward look for her, especially when combined with glittery eye shadow. Dr. Gonzales looked like she was ready for Broadway, not for lab work, but who knew what fashion trends women had come up with in the last decade?

"Hey, Doc." I grinned. "Long time no see."

"I wish I could say the same thing," she replied. "I've been staring at your mug for all this time. Will you just synchronize already and get this over with?"

I shrugged. "Well, ma'am, I would, but where else am I going to find a job that pays me to sit on my ass for a decade?"

There were a couple of chuckles around the room, and for a brief moment life felt almost normal. Dr. Gonzales leaned over and gave me a hug. "You sound like your daughter." The doctor gestured to Amara. "I don't know if you know this, but Amara has been helping us find a cure for you ever since we first met."

"Miranda told me last time I was, I was . . . you know . . ."

"Back-synced?"

"Yeah. Why is it back-synced, anyway?"

"Because we synchronize you back to normal time. It isn't a riddle, Martin." She winked.

"Okay, back-synced. Anyway, Miranda mentioned that Amara was quite involved." I looked at Amara, who blushed a bit.

"Hey, I tried to help too," Bella said.

Amara rolled her eyes. "Oh please. Your big idea was giving Dad lots and lots of coffee to speed him up."

The conversation degenerated quickly into a sisterly squabble that remained playful. A serious pause followed as Gonzales settled next to me to give me whatever bad news was lingering unsaid in the room.

"Martin, let's talk about your condition on a very basic level. Whatever material you were injected with reprogrammed your DNA and fooled your cells into operating at a fraction of the speed they would normally work at. Ever since, we've been trying a couple of ways to make your body work the way it's supposed to. Your company has been trying to create an antidote that does the exact opposite of what you were injected with. As you've noticed, the longest they've been able to keep you back-synced is less than a day.

Syncing Forward

"Our team originally tried synthetic catecholamine to jumpstart you—something akin to Bella's idea of pumping you full of coffee, but on a chromosomal level. As you know, that almost killed you and only worked for less than two hours. Diox 9 is a derivative of the Dambra 44 treatment that Innovo developed, but we fully recognize that it's a temporary solution at best. We back-synced you this time so you could give us permission to try step two of the treatment we've developed."

I looked at my daughters, who were doing their best to remain quiet. I could tell they both had something to say. "Go on," I told Dr. Gonzales.

"We have a way of tricking your body into producing fully synced cells that will function normally, but it means there will be some complications for you. We'd like to implant your body with nanorobots that will penetrate your forward-syncing cells and make them operate faster."

"Why does that sound terrifying?"

"It shouldn't. Nanorobots have been around for a decade. They're only robots, but super, super small, and they can be directed with a high degree of precision. This new series of nanos is still experimental, but they show a lot of promise in treating cancer and other genetic disorders. The process could take many years as some cells reproduce slowly, while others don't reproduce at all. The good news is that if it works, you could live a reasonably comfortable life—"

"Tell him about the bad news, Maggie," Amara interjected.

"Damn, you're impatient, Amara. I'm getting to it." Doctor Gonzales shifted in her seat. "Martin, you would be held in sync with this nanotreatment, and we feel comfortable that it will work. The bad news is that the nanorobots will require their own special field that they absolutely must remain inside. Since your brain and nerve cells won't replicate on the scale we need, they need to be regularly adjusted by the nanos. Without that field, part of your body will age normally while the rest of you will sync forward. It could mean paralysis for you . . . or worse."

My brain worked overtime as I tried to process the implications. "Couldn't you just shut the whole thing down? I mean, I don't know anything about these nanos, but if they aren't working properly and it becomes a worst-case scenario, can't you just turn them off?"

Maggie glanced at one of the men in the room and then looked back at me. "Maybe. I can't guarantee that, though. Your cells may slip back out of sync asymmetrically—that's a fancy way of saying that bad things could happen."

"It doesn't sound good. So how would this field work?" I asked.

"You would have to remain in a tightly controlled environment. That means very little moving around, since the field needs to adjust to your movements accurately."

"It means you'll be bedridden, Dad. You'll be stuck in a bed for as long as you live." Amara shook her head slightly, mouthing the words "Don't do it."

I looked at Bella, who got more flustered with each word from her sister. When my eyes fell on her, she jumped up and went face-to-face with Amara. "Shut up! He doesn't know what his choices are! How do you expect him to make a decision if you don't tell him everything? Or were you planning on just keeping it a secret because you don't agree?"

I put up my hands and yelled at them to stop. It was thirteen years ago all over again, and I was scolding my seven- and nine-year-old for fighting over the game console. "Hey! Hey! Hey! Stop it!"

"Martin, nobody is hiding anything," Dr. Gonzales reassured me. "We might be able to get the field to grow in time, but for now, we're dealing with technology that is untested. What Bella is talking about is how your body reacts to the syncing we put it through. You see, since you were first injected, your body has been struggling to slow down as much as it can. Every time we put you through a procedure to speed you back up, your cells stubbornly move back to that slow

Syncing Forward

speed. But somehow we meddle with the rate at which your body decelerates. That means that each time we fail to cure you, it takes longer for you to bottom out. And since we don't want to kill you, we have to wait longer each time we try a new cure. If we don't do this nano treatment now, it could be another ten, maybe twenty, years before your cell speed bottoms out."

I stared at her. She was dead serious. Maggie Gonzales was the epitome of sincerity and wasn't bothering to sugarcoat any of the information. And yet—something in her eyes caught my attention. There was no way to put my finger on it without asking her for a follow-up question, and frankly, I didn't know what to ask if I did.

The man in the suit walked over and introduced himself with an open right hand and data pad that was as clear as a pane of glass in the left. "Martin James," he said, "my name is Randy Lindale, and I represent Innovo in these dealings. This letter declares that Innovo Industries has not signed off on the nanotreatment designed by the US government. Our original agreement with the federal government of the United States regarding your treatment stipulates that Innovo can neither block treatment nor advise you not to take treatment offered by any federal institution. We can only tell you that research conducted by Innovo has not been able to vouch for any claims of viability for this procedure."

Mr. Lindale droned on and on about how my company couldn't tell me not to take the nanotreatment, but that they pretty much figured I wouldn't survive very long if I did. That wasn't what I wanted to hear at all, but I signed the tablet's e-form anyway, confirming that I had been briefed. Lindale transmitted the document immediately and then stood back from the rest of the crowd, relieved that his mission was completed. Innovo was off the hook in the event that my family tried suing them for damages, but my options had certainly not improved.

The room cleared of all personnel, including my aging doctor friend Maggie Gonzales, leaving Amara, Bella, and me together to discuss my fate. The way forward was muddied, to say the least. Did I want to spend the remainder of my life caged in a bed, or did I want to watch fifteen years vanish in thirty-two hours? Would the compound Bruchmuller had injected me with wear off, or were my cells genetically modified forever? The technology might one day come about to make the nanotreatment more flexible and my life more typical.

Then again, the nanotreatment might kill me, failing in one part of my body and ultimately condemning me to a painful death. Without the nanos, a new discovery could cure me entirely or at least wake me sooner than expected. Or, of course, my cure might never come. A budget cut at Innovo would be the end of hope; a simple calculation that their research costs had exceeded any potential payout could spell disaster. Would they continue to treat me? Wake me up as often as they could out of curiosity or compassion? Or might they let me zip through the decades unimpeded? Would I overtake the world in a blur until all manner of care passed from me, leaving me blind and exposed, on display like some statue to be gawked at?

"You should know there is no consensus on how your condition should be handled, not even within the Walter Reed group," Amara started. "That alone is worrying me."

I shrugged. "Well, it doesn't mean it's a bad idea either though, right?"

"Daddy," she started slowly, "you can't do this treatment. They aren't ready. I know it sounds like they are ready, but the Walter Reed doctors aren't considering a lot of variables. It's not worth the risk."

Bella was the more vocal, passionately pleading with me to listen to the advice of Dr. Gonzales. "Dad, do you really want to stay like this? How many times can you do this? What do you think you're going to do when Innovo loses interest in you completely? The money will stop, and so will your care. We don't even know when or if this drug will wear off. At least Dr. Gonzales is offering you a chance to live with us. Please, Dad, just do it—"

"No!" Amara interjected. "Don't just do it—Bella is wrong! They're all wrong!"

Syncing Forward

"Screw you, Amara!" Bella screeched, her face flushed. "What makes you so flipping smart?"

Amara disregarded her sister's protest and looked me dead in the eyes, "Daddy, you have to trust me. I just know this isn't going to work. It isn't hard to read between the lines. Innovo doesn't even believe it will work."

"How can you tell him that? What makes you the expert?"

Amara finally caved to Bella's antagonizing. "Because I don't trust Maggie. She's lying."

"She's your friend! How can you say that about her? She's been taking care of Dad for—"

"She's lying, Bella! Sorry if I don't trust every living soul I meet like *you* do, but she's lying to us. God, I don't know how you can be so gullible all the time."

"Oh, Ms. Secret Agent gets a badge and then she has all the answers!" Bella picked up an empty plastic vial and chucked it at her sister's head. Amara ducked and covered the distance between the edge of the room and her sister in a hot second. They were standing nose to nose when I shut the row down.

"Stop this argument *right now!*" I bellowed.

The girls jerked their heads around to look at me and instantly stopped their commotion. Two pairs of dark-brown eyes stared at me wide-eyed. I must have triggered some parental memory from years back when yelling at them for fighting over the television, a toy, a sofa cushion. In one respect it was flattering that they both cared enough to defend their positions about my health, but it would do no good if my girls let the matter devolve into a feud. And hidden beneath it all, I was angry with them both for bickering like children while my precious moments of synchronized time trickled away. I wanted every normal moment to be perfect—a quality that was sorely lacking from the last time I saw them . . . and Miranda.

I held up my index finger as if to conduct the conversation. "Please, let me ask some questions. Bella, I listened to what you had to say, but let me talk to Amara alone for five minutes."

"But Dad—" my younger daughter started, clearly hurt.

"Please, Bella. Just five minutes. I'll hear you out too—I promise. This will go quicker if I talk to each of you one-on-one. As it is, you two are giving me a headache."

"But you're taking her side—"

"I'm not taking any side. I'm trying to hear both sides."

"Fine," she snapped. "I hope you're still synced after five minutes." Grabbing her glittery purse from atop a table, Bella walked out the door with a slam.

Chapter 16

It was just Amara and me and a room full of soft chimes from the medical instrumentation surrounding me. My older child sat sideways, and it dawned on me she had been concealing something on her hip this entire time.

"Is there something you want to show me?" I asked Amara quietly.

She gave me an embarrassed approval-seeking smile and rotated her body to reveal a shiny gold badge and some unrecognizable model of sidearm. She picked at her cuticles nervously. "There was no time to tell you before."

"Who are you working for now?"

"Homeland Defense. It used to be called the Department of Homeland Security, but things got reorg'd with the uptick in IEDs being set off in shopping malls. It's a national police force dealing with terrorism, interstate gangs, and whatnot." She tried to suppress her smile; Amara was clearly pleased with herself.

I looked at her curiously. "But you were majoring in bioengineering and computer forensics last time we spoke. And a full scholarship to boot! What happened to your education?"

"I finished it, Daddy. You saw my graduation pictures; I know you did."

"I did see them, but I didn't think you were going to just end your education. You've got a tremendous mind, Amara. Why wouldn't you push into what you're good at?"

"What makes you think I'm not good at investigations? You're a great investigator, and I am way smarter than you." She was joshing me, but when she looked at the displeasure on my face she must have mistaken it for a lack of humor, "Seriously, Dad, you taught me all sorts of things when I was a kid about reading people. I'm a natural."

"Sweetie, I do investigations—or at least did them—for a living because it's the only thing I've ever been good at; it doesn't mean you have to. You could be doing so much more. Certainly making a hell of a lot more money than I did. It seems like you're selling yourself short."

She gave me a wounded look, "You know, most people just told me 'congratulations,' Daddy."

I sighed. "Amara, I'm proud of how well you've done for yourself, but frankly I don't understand your career choice. You are a genius by anyone's standards. You have been since you were little. And you choose a career that has you dealing with terrorists? In the field, no less?"

"How did you know I was a field agent?"

"I know the look. Jesus, Amara, I wanted to become a field agent before you were born. But I got lucky, and budget sequesters ended up with me getting canned. It was the best thing that happened to me. Do you know how dangerous a job you've signed up for?"

Amara picked away at her fingertips now, ripping off little bits of skin. A quick glance at her hands told me the habit was well established. Her sad eyes shone with every word of my disapproval. "I know how to handle myself, Daddy. I'm not a little girl anymore."

She would always be a little girl to me, a mind-set she wouldn't understand until faced with her own son or daughter at this age. The whole idea of her working law enforcement scared the crap out of me. "I can see that. But tell me—have things gotten better in the country over the last thirteen years? From the news articles you pumped across the screen to me, I'd say they look a heck of a lot worse. That fancy pistol you're packing isn't going to do you a bit of good when your car gets T-boned by a truck, or a bomb goes off in your building, or they set your sister on fire because you were poking around too much."

Her jaw jutted out. "It's not like Innovo did anything to protect you from being attacked. Somebody's got to stand up to these people!"

Syncing Forward

I shook my head and gave her a dissatisfied stare. "Somebody, yes. But not you."

"Why can't it be me?"

"Because you're my child."

"Why are you being like this?" she whined. A single tear escaped Amara's right eye and landed on her leg, soaking into the material and disappearing from view. She avoided eye contact with me now. "I thought you would be proud of me," she whispered.

I shrank to about one-inch tall at that moment. "Sweetheart, I am proud of you. I am, honestly. I'm just worried about you in this line of work. You understand my reservations, right?"

Amara said nothing. I continued, "Please, you may not be a little girl, but for me it wasn't more than a few days ago that you were nine years old and incapable of eating your cereal without spilling it everywhere." I made it worse. Dang it, I was such an ass.

A second tear joined the first. "Can we drop it, Daddy? Just . . . drop it. Let's talk about your treatment, okay?"

I was a terrible father. Amara had graduated from college with honors, obviously applied for the academy, and passed with flying colors by the age of twenty-two. In less than two minutes my flapping gums had reduced her achievements to a bad career choice and terrible judgment. A long silence took up the space between us before I agreed to change the subject and find out what troubled Amara about the nanotreatment.

"So, you obviously have your old man's eye for spotting deception. What makes you think Dr. Gonzales is hiding something?"

Amara composed herself with a sniffle and wiped her cheek. "Her facial cues are all wrong when I ask her about your safety. Clearly she either doesn't believe it is a good choice or she feels at least it could be safer. But there is more to it than just her face. I've spent years corresponding with her and talking with Innovo researchers. One thing I can tell you is that the government doctors have something else they are working on."

"That should be obvious, Amara. They want the drug Millennial developed. And any antidote they might have as well."

Amara got close to me and lowered her voice. "No, Dad. There's something else. I don't know how it is possible, but there is somebody else out there, just like you, who they are taking blood from. Blood that is out of sync, like yours, but not from you. Human blood. Dad, somebody else has been injected with the Millennial drug, and the Walter Reed doctors have that person in their care."

Amara's reasoning was circumstantial, but when she gave me the details I understood why she believed it. Certain phrases, glimpses of e-mails, the sequence of testing, requests sent to Innovo for large quantities of the Dambra 44 antidote—the list went on. I would have come to the same conclusion myself. What I didn't understand was how that could be, or why it would impact me.

"Wait a sec." I stopped her. "Let's just accept that you're right for now and that there is somebody else out there who is affected by this Millennial drug. Wouldn't that be a good thing? They'd have *two* people to draw information from, *two* sets of data, *two* ways to test if a treatment works. Maybe they figured out the nanotreatment because of the other victim? Assuming he or she is a victim, that is."

"Dad, you don't understand. Every set of data was yours, followed at a later date by this other patient. Every time." There was the sound of somebody coming —doctors most likely—and Amara leaned over to whisper in my ear. "The Walter Reed scientists—Maggie included—have been testing everything on you. Whoever they have, the government believes you are less valuable."

Tell me about the rat . . .

I remembered uttering those words to the late Dr. Bruchmuller. Thirteen years later, nobody had uncovered an antidote or found a soul alive who had originally designed it. The Walter Reed scientists were bound and determined to crack open the secrets buried in my cells, and if Amara was correct, it was without concern for my wellbeing. I was an animal, trapped in a fancy cage, and reasonably expendable. I was still the rat.

Syncing Forward

Bella didn't know—Amara had hidden her suspicions from her sister and everyone around her. The doctors and Bella returned to the room as my elder daughter went to get some fresh air. My younger daughter began picking my brain, wondering what decision I was going to make. I admitted to her that the legal document I had signed letting Innovo off the hook wasn't endearing me to the treatment. Bella countered that Innovo would benefit from keeping me untreated since the reverse engineering of the Millennial drug would be a breakthrough worth billions.

Bella, true to the compassionate child she had always been, steered the conversation back to what mattered most to her: the people she loved. "Dad, think about it. You can talk to your friends. You can talk with us. With Uncle Jacob. God, he misses you so much! We've been lying to him for so many years because we can't talk about you. Think about that! Your own brother thinks you are in a coma. You could talk with him, and have him visit, and have normal conversations that don't last nine months. You can read books. Read news articles—whole news articles—not just headlines. We can play games. Watch movies."

"It would be good to know what your mom thinks I should do . . ." I let the statement linger, watching Bella for her reaction.

She looked at me for about five solid seconds before answering. "Dad, I don't know how to tell you this, but Mom isn't coming back. She was barely here after the last time you went out of sync, and when I turned eighteen, she moved out."

"Did she say why?" I asked, shifting uncomfortably.

"No, but she didn't have to. It just got to be too much for her. She's living in Ohio now, close to Grandma and Grandpa."

"Maybe I could call her? Ask her what she thinks? Maybe it will make a difference."

Bella frowned. "Dad, she isn't living alone." I felt her eyes upon me as well as those of the doctors who had been eavesdropping on our conversation.

My stomach tightened, and I felt clammy all over. The pulse meter on the machine nearby recorded every racing heartbeat. The feeling of betrayal was like a flame in my chest, and my anger—sudden and violent—felt as if it would rip off my skin and storm out of the lab on its own. So that was it then. Miranda had walked out on me. After twenty-four years, Miranda had elected to walk away from our marriage and shack up with another man.

I should have been understanding of my wife's feelings. I should have acknowledged that the strain on the marriage would be too much for even the toughest woman. That waiting around for your husband to awake from the ice of time after thirteen years was unreasonable. I should have felt that way, but I didn't.

"Get out," I told them all. Nobody responded, and I found myself flinging a data pad across the room, watching it shatter into plastic shards and scatter across the floor. The lab coats slowly filed through the door, but not fast enough for me. I screamed at the top of my lungs, "Get out! All of you! Out! Out! *Out!*"

Inside, I cursed God for putting me through this nightmare, for subjecting me to the cruel fate of separation from the world. I don't know how long I sat there, but it felt longer than all the years I had sped through put together.

Syncing Forward

Chapter 17

Bella returned by herself, timidly approaching the shattered father she had left in the lab. I could tell she hadn't wanted to tell me the news about Miranda, but—like many things these days—the news had to be told. She placed her soft little hand in mine and put her face against my chest. She was seven all over again, snuggling into her dad.

"I'm sorry, Dad." Bella's voice was muffled, with her left cheek stuffed into the hospital garment these people insisted on dressing me in. "We didn't want to tell you."

"It's okay," I reassured her, knowing full well it wasn't as I ran my fingers through her hair. I felt hairspray in my daughter's locks, another stony detail to tell me my condition was not a dream. "It needed to be told. I guess I should have figured she might leave, but I didn't expect your mom to move on so quickly."

Bella sat up, looking sullen as she maneuvered to avoid sitting on my urine bladder tube. "It hasn't been quick, though. That's what you keep missing. Thirteen years is a long time. Mom waited for them to come up with an antidote for more than ten years before she finally . . . left. She and Amara haven't spoken since—no vidcalls, no texts, no visits. Amara wiped her completely."

"Wiped her?" I asked.

"Sorry, that's a new expression, I guess. Wiping means that Amara is ignoring Mom, acting like she's dead. Anyway, it's been tough on Mom. She feels like she lost her husband and a daughter at the same time." Bella patted my arm gently, jiggling the IV line gently against my skin.

"Can we talk about something else?" I asked.

"*Can we talk about something else?* You sound like Amara," Bella pointed out, not realizing her sister had uttered those same words minutes ago.

I ignored the observation. "So tell me what's going on with you."

"Please, Dad. You can't put this off. I don't know how much time you have to make a decision, but it wasn't much when we woke you. It's even less now."

It felt as if I was missing something, that no matter what I chose it was going to be the wrong decision. I put my face in my palms and rubbed my cheeks vigorously, popping off several sensors they had stuck to my temples. Unlike the ones I'd worn years ago, these were wireless and no larger than a dime. How could Miranda walk out on me?

"Listen, I need to talk to your mom. Can you call her please? I reckon she doesn't want to talk to me, but I really need to talk to her."

The technician Mike Gandry came in for about one minute to check my vitals and then was scooted out of the room by my daughters. Amara stood off-camera with her arms tightly crossed and an incensed expression as Bella dialed up Miranda's number on the vidcall. My younger daughter stood next to me at my bedside, holding my hand supportively as we waited for the video connection to go through. It rang several times before Miranda's face showed across the screen.

"Hi, Bella . . . hello, Martin." Miranda looked about as awkward as could be. Trying to appear both friendly and distant, caring and disconnected, she ended up looking like a woman who wanted to flee a party when confronted by her ex-husband in front of her friends. There was no graceful way out of the mess. I was positive I looked the exact same way.

"Hi, Mom," Bella responded.

"Hi, Miranda," I said, controlling myself as best I could. "You look good." She actually looked fantastic: she had aged well and didn't look like a woman in her midforties. The weight Miranda had gained from nine years ago was gone, and the bags around her eyes had vanished. It was burning me up inside. Some cruel part of me wished she had gained a hundred pounds and broken out in hives for betraying me and walking out on our family.

"Thanks. You look the same. Identical, really. The bruise on your eye still looks fresh."

"Yeah, I guess it would."

"So, Bella messaged me that they were waking you up, that you had some decision to make on the treatment?" Miranda kept looking back and forth between Bella and me, her eye movements exaggerated on the screen because of the close-up shot of her upper torso. Had she zoomed the camera's capture back a ways, it wouldn't have been so strange-looking. But people frequently did that even fifteen years ago in order to hide what was behind them. It might have been a mess in the house, or maybe another person just off-camera. The other man.

"Uh, yeah. I didn't know you were in the loop on all that, but yeah, they've got a way to treat me, to sync me permanently. Maybe. It's got some risks involved. I figured maybe you would have some opinion on which way to go. I don't have much more time before I've got to tell them what I want to do. If I slow down again, I'll lose my window. What do you think we should do?" Every word seemed to make a terrible thud, like one brick upon another.

"I don't know, Martin," my estranged wife said unhappily, looking away from the screen for a moment. "You can't ask me . . . I shouldn't be involved in these decisions anymore. I had Innovo transfer over power-of-attorney privileges to Amara and Bella. The house isn't even in my name."

"Miranda, I'm not looking for your permission—I'm looking for your advice. Jesus! I need your help. This is my life here!"

"Martin, don't put this all on me. Please, it's not fair."

"Why? Because of your new boyfriend?"

She stopped and looked at Bella regretfully. "You told him?"

183

Bella shrugged her shoulders. "What was I supposed to tell him, Mom? He kept asking. You want me to lie and tell him you are out shopping at the mall? He deserves to know."

Miranda looked back at me full of shame. "Martin, I wanted to explain personally. I really did. Things just got complicated."

The words I had for my wife were downright vile, and I was on the cusp of spouting them all, but the look of shame on her face told me there was little I could call her that she hadn't already called herself. This was my wife, the love of my life, the mother of my children. The only thing I was left with was a pitiful question: Why hadn't she come visit me at least?

Miranda replied irritably. "You can thank your older daughter for not letting me come down. She refused to let me on the property. I believe her exact words were 'Whores are not allowed in my house.'"

I turned and looked at Amara, who was glaring at the vidscreen with as much hatred as I had ever witnessed. "Amara?"

Amara's arms were still pressed against her chest as she strummed her fingers on her forearm. "That's not exactly right. I told her *sluts* are not allowed in my house."

I didn't know how to react. Amara seemed to be defending me, but I felt a strong paternal instinct to admonish her for acting so disrespectfully to her mother. Miranda and I had made a point of not arguing in front of the kids; we called it "the united front." We had tried to support each other on everything so the kids couldn't play us against each other. My support stopped shy of escaping my lips at that moment, and instead I simply sat there gaping at the vidscreen.

"Martin, it's okay. I'm used to it. If *slut* was the worst thing she called me over the last few years, I might actually have had my feelings hurt." I didn't buy it. She acted aloof, but Miranda was clearly wounded by the comment, not to mention Amara's unrepentant repeat of the insult.

"What's his name? Actually, on second thought, I don't want to know. Just tell me one thing: Does he treat you right?"

Syncing Forward

She nodded uncomfortably. Miranda and I spoke in a jagged conversation in which I didn't ask too many questions and she did not provide too many answers. She couldn't counsel me on my decision, and the real reason I had called—to figure out if there was any chance of reconciliation—had been answered. Three minutes into the call we had barely exchanged any words, but—as heartbreaking as it was—I knew my marriage was over. I also knew what choice I had to make. My home lost. My wife had walked out. My job as a parent stolen from me. I couldn't risk losing any more. "I'm sorry I wasted your time, Miranda."

"You didn't waste my time, Martin. I'm . . . I'm glad you're okay. If you need me, just let me know, okay?" We were both crying, and Miranda could barely look at the screen anymore.

"Same here. I don't know what I can do for you, but—"

"Martin, there is one thing I need from you. I feel terrible asking this because . . . Because . . ." She broke into sobs, her words barely comprehensible through her weeping. "Because you were always so good to me and the kids, and you didn't deserve to have this happen . . ."

I knew what she wanted, and it didn't matter how much I hated it. "Just let me know what I need to sign, and I will."

She nodded and mumbled her gratitude. "So, what are you going to do?"

"I'm going to take the nanotreatment."

Amara muttered something unpleasant under her breath and left the lab exasperated. Bella exhaled in relief. She whispered thanks in my ear and ran out of the room to tell the doctors to start the procedure. Miranda and I were speaking privately now.

"If you want to come and visit, you can. I'll talk to Amara and make sure she doesn't give you a hard time."

She evaded my invitation. "You're a good man, Martin. Tell Amara I miss her so much. Tell her I'm sorry."

"I will. *Te amo.*" The phrase was ingrained in me.

"Good-bye" was all I got back, and she disconnected. I wiped my tears and snot on my sleeve, not caring what anyone thought of me. Bella gave me a weepy stare and leaned in to hug me. I leaned over the bed railing and grabbed her around the waist, dropping my face against her shoulder and letting out a stifled cry. My wife. Gone.

I wasn't going to lose anyone else. I couldn't.

Chapter 18

Bella called the Innovo crew and all of the Walter Reed doctors back into the room. The laboratory was abuzz with activity as they prepped me for a spinal tap and other highly invasive methods for getting the nanos into my body. I had questions, lots of questions. Dr. Nikonov explained that, once inside, billions of these creepy little robots would invade my system and implant themselves into key cells. Their positions would be tracked by the reader above me, and then, depending on how effective they were, ten times the amount would be sent in to join the first wave, and then ten times that amount would follow. Even after hundreds of billions of little robots were swimming around inside me, they would still affect less than 1 percent of the cells in my body. The goal was to have the nanos invade the most important systems in my body and reprogram my cells to return to normal.

Dr. Nikonov was pitching the procedure to me, explaining how lab testing on my blood had shown promise of certain cells reprogramming, including epithelial or hormone-secreting cells. Other cells, governing my nervous system, muscles, and brain, would be supported permanently by the nanos. Without them, my mind would slow and my body would age normally. I could conceivably wake up with the brain of a thirty-eight-year-old and the body of a ninety-year-old, riddled with age and falling apart.

The back of my hair was buzzed in preparation of having an injection placed in the back of my skull. I caught my reflection in one of the monitors. I looked awful. My face was still bruised, and tufts of shaved hair were clinging to the side of my head. The black-and-blue marks around my eye gave me flashbacks to Bruchmuller injecting me, my body struggling against the straps of the gurney as I screamed into the washcloth gag. Strangely, this process seemed scarier.

"You need to calm down, Martin," Dr. Gonzales warned me. "Your pulse is way too high, and we need you calm."

"Sorry, but this is freaking me out."

"Bella"—she turned to my daughter—"talk to your dad. I'm sure he wants to be caught up on world events, especially recent ones."

My Baby Bella looked nervous too, but she put on her game face and came to my rescue. You would think that I wanted to be distracted by stories about fluffy puppies, see pictures of rainbow afternoons, to hear inappropriate jokes. But Dr. Gonzales had skillfully dangled the world news topic for me to nibble on, and I bit. What I got was more information than I bargained for on all fronts, from personal to international.

She picked up a new tablet and showed me firsthand the new technology of glass computers. The tablet was flexible and as clear as water and looked more like a rectangular plastic lid than a computer. Bella assured me it was glass and swiped her finger across the surface, which brought to life a display of unfamiliar icons. This device was the first of many advances I found baffling. Improved data lines, skyscraper farms, genetic samples for voter identification, and budding colonies on the moon and Mars. The moon colony was funded by the Russians, while the Mars-One colony was privately funded. I asked what the United States was doing, and I got my answer, unfortunately.

The country was collapsing fiscally and socially. Gangs ran rampant in most cities. Churches were razed, food was scarce, and gas sold for more than fifteen dollars per gallon. Both Bella and Amara had tried to move me several times out of the country town we lived in, but Innovo would not have me anywhere close to a major city with the fires and riots that regularly plagued major population centers. I asked why I wasn't holed up at one of the other Innovo facilities if I was that important. Bella explained that David Tsai had tried to get me moved to San Francisco, but Innovo attorneys put a kibosh on the deal, stating that my presence would represent an "undesired variable to the safety of our property and employees." Beacon, Pennsylvania, was where we were to remain.

Natural disasters hit the US, causing floods in the East and turning the Midwest into a dust bowl. Politics had not changed except that the fringe groups had become worse than ever. And then, in the

Syncing Forward

midst of an ever-growing stack of tribulations, the perfect storm struck America.

The most recent election had been called into question by competing fringe groups, and the current president suspended the election indefinitely. This split the country, and now Texas and North Dakota were leading the movement for secession. Arizona, Wyoming, and Oklahoma were following. It was a standoff the likes of which had not been seen since the Civil War. The whole matter was chilling, yet somehow I pictured my brother Jacob reveling as the Southwest prepared their National Guardsmen to defend their borders. The insanity of it all was surreal . . . but America wasn't alone.

Europe had fallen apart completely. France had split in half, with the southern regions joining the Islamic Crescent that now spanned all of Northern Africa and part of the Middle East. The UK's government was in turmoil as Sharia law was infused into their existing legal system. The result was a tangled legal knot that nobody could undo. The Nazi party now controlled the Greco-Italian Coalition, which had declared war against Southern France.

Germany had built an electronic fence along the French border, and over the last ten years had stopped immigration completely. Displaced residents eventually took up refuge in the mountains near the border. The Vogesen became a breeding ground for a whole new generation of terrorists. With its southern region in turmoil, Germany signed economic treaties with the new Coalition of Russian States—a benign new name for something that looked an awful lot like the old expansive Soviet Russia. The whole world had turned on its head.

"I wish I had some better news for you, Dad." Bella closed my world education with a swipe of her finger on the glass display and rolled it up, then slid it into a gaudy purple carrying bag and stowed it in her purse.

I shook my head slowly. "You're not kidding. Listen, are you okay here? It's just you and your sister, and I don't like the idea of you not having family you can count on close by."

"What are you saying?"

"I think maybe you should move. I'm sure that we could convince Innovo there are other places just as safe. Closer to Jacob maybe? Or your cousins in Ohio?"

"Mom's in Ohio too. You want us to move closer to Mom?" She huffed. "Amara would rather douse herself in gasoline and burn herself alive. I guess maybe we could move to Arizona, but things are really bad down there with the gangs. I know you're worried, but honestly, I feel much safer having us here in Beacon. Besides, Uncle Jacob said that small towns are safer when society collapses."

I rolled my eyes. "You realize your uncle is insane and in serious need of medication, right? He's been talking about the end of the world since I was your age." Jacob was a classic right-wing survivalist nut job. He had a gun collection that was illegal in thirty states and freeze-dried food that had to be pushing three decades old now. He thought that the government and megacorporations were conspiring to turn us all into drones to serve the collective. Or that society would break down into roaming gangs and crazed maniacs. Or we would all be implanted with microchips to track our every move. Or a zombie apocalypse would devour the population. Of course, now the world really *was* falling apart, and the only thing missing were the microchips. And the zombies. As I said, he must have been reveling in the chaos with chants of "I told you sos."

I sighed again. "Well, I hate saying it, but in this particular case I'd say, listen to Jacob. You've got money in the bank, right?"

"Plenty. I'm just not sure what to do first."

"Your mother should be taking care of this—"

"I have good friends here now. They don't know you, but they know me and Amara. We'll be fine here." Something in her tone made me look at her more closely—there was a gleam in her eye and a secret just waiting to burst forth from underneath.

"Okay, let it out. Who is it?"

Syncing Forward

She drew a deep breath, "His name is Keith. He works on one of the smaller properties as a farmhand for now, but he is looking to go into machining."

She poked the tablet and brought up several pics, mostly of them together. He looked like a typical country boy, broad shouldered with light-brown hair and a confident grin. He dwarfed Bella in sheer size; her petite frame must have been half the width of her new beau.

"The two of you look very . . . close," I told her. "What does your ma think of him?"

"Mom says he's a nice boy but that I could do better." She rolled her eyes. "She and Amara are more alike than they want to admit. Anyway, Keith lives with his mom and dad and two brothers. But it's not like he's a slacker or anything. His dad lost his mechanic shop and went bankrupt. So now the whole family is pitching in to buy their home back from the Division of Secured Housing, which is not easy."

That government program wasn't familiar to me, but that was to be expected after so long. "Does this Keith of yours know about my true condition?"

"No," she answered, "Nothing at all."

Bella was a terrible liar. I was pretty sure Keith knew something, if not everything, but it was a dumb question for me to ask given that she could be sued or fined for breaking confidentiality, and we were surrounded by folk from the government.

It dawned on me that the laboratory prepping was done. Dr. Maggie Gonzales was filling a giant syringe with a serum the color of gun-bolt metal.

"You're not going to stick that in my legs are you?" I joked.

"No, of course not," the doctor said with a smile. "We're injecting it into your brain."

What? I looked from her to Dr. Nikonov, and both of them were doing their best to appear friendly. Instead they both looked deranged.

"Dr. Gonzales," I said, "not that I'm not appreciative of this cure, but why is it that Dr. Bruchmuller only injected me in my arms and legs, and now you are going to shove a four-inch needle into my brain?"

"We don't know," Maggie responded. "Nobody does. I can't be sure if I told you before, but your condition should be medically impossible. Of course, almost everything in this lab was impossible thirty years ago. It's only a matter of time before we figure out what you were injected with. Until then, we inject your brain."

Dr. Nikonov gave her a sideways glance. Not that the look I was giving her was any better. I didn't want a needle in my brain.

"Are you doing okay, Daddy?" Amara asked protectively from across the room. Sometime during my history lesson from Bella, my older daughter had returned. She looked as sour as a Granny Smith apple and was hawking the government doctors and technicians.

"Yeah, I guess so." My hands were clammy, and I wiped them on the sheet before I directed my attention back to Dr. Gonzales. "So, what if this doesn't work? What happens to the nanos? Could they damage me?"

"No. These are very small. If we wanted to, we could direct them to move out of your body, turn off, or even break apart on command. Until we start the treatment of reprogramming your cells, you'll be very much yourself. However, once your cells start replicating in sync, there is going to come a point when we won't be able to shut off the nanos. Powering down at that point could be bad." Maggie wasn't looking at me; instead, she was busy prepping the first dose of nanos for delivery.

The details weren't improving my confidence. "Bad? What exactly do you mean by 'bad'? How long before we reach this 'bad' point?"

"We don't know. Computer models say we can nanosaturate your nervous system in about three days. Your body may sync forward by then, so we're prepared to monitor your cell generation rate across

Syncing Forward

your body. We'll do our best to target any failing organs with massive nano injections." Maggie still wasn't looking me. Was she avoiding eye contact, or was I becoming mistrustful? Were Amara's concerns valid?

Now that my head was shaved, I turned to Maggie and probed a little. "So if I might sync forward anyway, why the big rush to inject me? Can't you just treat me when I'm all slowed down? Wouldn't that make more sense?"

She stole a glimpse of Dr. Nikonov before she met my gaze. "I suppose we could, but it would be better to know how your back-synced body reacts to the nanos to make sure they can maintain you." Her words were slow and calculated. Or maybe she was simply concentrating on prepping the army of robotic rescuers that would soon be in my head. Or maybe she was trying to scare the crap out of me on purpose—to send me a message, maybe. A message that this was a bad idea.

Amara's hand was already resting on her hips like a rookie police officer's, thumbs slipping around her pistol holster and the edge of her badge. Her cautious stride took her about the lab, lingering at one instrument or another, clearly disinterested in any goings-on but the doctors' efforts. Bella appeared anxious too, but for completely inverted reasons.

Dr. Gonzales and the others gathered near me, and the medical dance began. Dr. Nikonov was holding a needle poised to slide into my intravenous line when I finally spoke up. "Maybe this isn't such a good idea," I croaked.

"You'll be fine, Mr. James," Dr. Nikonov soothed.

My heart was pounding in my ears rapidly. This seemed wrong—all of it. Were Amara's suspicions of another victim of Millennial's drug valid, or had my daughter become paranoid? What did it mean if she was right? What if this whole exercise was simply for data collection? I put up my hand. "Hold up a sec. I'm changing my mind."

Nikonov looked down at me. "Martin, relax. You're in good hands. We'll take care of you." He reached up and positioned the plastic line that fed down into my arm. Who knew what was in that syringe, but I didn't want it in me. I didn't want any of it in me.

"My father said stop!" Amara appeared, grabbing the man's hand and bending it forward so forcefully that the syringe dropped from his grip and into my daughter's fingers. She brandished it menacingly as he bent over his hand, eyes flaring. I knew Amara was capable of taking care of herself, but never seen her so downright aggressive. Given she was coming to my aid, however, I wasn't about to criticize.

"What the hell is wrong with you? This is just a sedative, you crazy bitch!"

She didn't move. "Be careful. Maybe this bitch is crazy enough to bury this needle into your throat. My father said he doesn't want the treatment." Amara grunted, still bending Dr. Nikonov's wrist in some type of aikido submission hold that had him immobilized from the waist up. The man had no choice but to shuffle along uncomfortably. "Now, come over here and let's talk about how no means no."

Bella stood up. "Amara, let him go! He's just trying to help."

Amara released the wrist lock she had on Nikonov, who backed away from her. The room erupted into arguments that went well beyond the sisterly bickering earlier. Little Maggie Gonzales picked up a plastic tray and whacked it on the metal bed rail repeatedly like a gavel until everyone was stunned into silenced.

"Amara, what has gotten into you?" Maggie shouted. "Have you lost your mind?"

I answered for her. "No, she hasn't. She's just trying to take care of me, that's all. I . . . I changed my mind. I don't want to go through with the injections."

"Dad, why are you doing this?" Bella threw her head and arms back in exasperation, storming past her sister as she did. She screamed into Amara's ear, "This is all your fault!"

Syncing Forward

Dr. Gonzales set the tray down and gently put her hand on me. "Martin, are you okay? What's wrong? Tell me why you don't want to go through with the treatment."

Did I dare tell Dr. Gonzales what Amara suspected? Or share my concerns about how everyone was conducting themselves? Amara still held the sedative away from the technician, and she was eyeballing him like a tiger ready to pounce. At five foot six inches and a buck thirty, I wouldn't think my elder daughter a terribly imposing person, but there was a swiftness to her movements that revealed she was not to be underestimated. The other government technicians were frozen, clearly caught off guard by the pseudo fight that had broken out, unwilling to draw any closer to Amara than absolutely necessary. Mike from Innovo shifted his gaze from Amara to Maggie, unwilling to say a single word. The attorney Randy Lindale poked his head in the lab to check on the commotion, only to disappear once more; he was probably consulting with the office on how they could proceed within the boundaries of their agreement with the feds. Typical lawyer.

The room was locked in a stalemate, and it was clear nobody but me could break the tension. Turning to Maggie, I forced a smile. "Hey, Doc, don't take it personally. I want to be sure about this procedure, and I'm not. That's all. I just think that between you and the other doctors at Innovo, you'll have this figured out in no time."

Maggie's features relaxed, and I thought I recognized relief on her face. Was she being forced into this? Was she being monitored? Perhaps she had never wanted the nanotreatment for me at all—or it could just be that she was happy the anxiety level in the lab was abating. "Martin, it's your decision, and I respect it. We'll do the best we can for you, okay?"

"Thanks, Doc."

Dr. Nikonov walked over cautiously and patted me on the leg. "Sorry I didn't listen to you, Martin. No hard feelings I hope?" The friendly demeanor was a façade—anyone could see that.

"No hard feelings," I replied. "Although if you call my daughter a bitch ever again, I'm going to give her permission to shoot you."

He chuckled nervously, and the insincere smile vanished when he passed Amara with her hand resting on her hip. She tossed him the open syringe. It bounced from one hand to the other before he pricked himself and dropped the needle on a nearby counter. Rather than picking it up, he left it there and snapped at Dr. Gonzales, "Maggie, we need to have a meeting off-site. All of us. Now."

She started to protest, "Somebody should stay back to—"

"Now!" he glared at her.

Maggie looked back at me and waved. "Good-bye, Martin. I hope you'll see me soon."

The wording struck me as odd, but I understood the meaning. "Me too, Doc. Watch over the girls for me, will you?"

Maggie looked at Amara. "I'm not sure they need watching over anymore." With that, she stepped out of the room.

Chapter 19

I didn't know how long the Diox 9 was going to last, but I planned on making the best of it. I needed to follow up with Agent Franciscus to see if there had been any headway in finding the Millennial terrorists. He and I also needed to follow up with Innovo to see what they were planning, if anything—with me turning my back on the US government's help, I was limiting my options. And in between all this I desperately wanted to catch up with my daughters. I was so fortunate that they had remained loyal to me when they could easily have turned their backs. Like Miranda. The thought stole its way into my brain—fresh and jagged.

The lab was cleared of everyone except Bella, who was holding two clear plastic bags in her arms for me to take. The monitoring bracelet dug into my wrist, but I left it there, figuring it wouldn't be long before somebody removed it. Besides, the pain was strangely enjoyable. After sitting for so long with hardly any physical sensation, even the poorly engineered bracelet pinching my skin was most welcome. The bags were vacuum sealed with a pair of shoes in one and blue jeans and a gray crewneck long-sleeved shirt in the other. Breaking the seal, I found a pair of socks and underwear too. Turning around to give me some privacy, Bella told me how she had sealed all my clothes years ago in anticipation of me being cured. She had only brought them out of storage when her enthusiasm over the nanotreatment grew.

"Don't blame your sister, Bella," I consoled her. "It was my choice to back out."

"But why, Dad?"

"The idea of all those nano-bits floating around in me gave me the willies."

"You know, you sound like Amara. Now I know where she gets her evasiveness."

"I'm not being evasive, just a smart-ass." I stretched high to the ceiling of the lab and yawned. "Speaking of your sister, I might have upset her. Okay, I know I upset her. I got overly critical about her career choice, and—well, we left it dangling." I mentioned that I didn't understand Amara's career choices and that she was setting the bar low working for Homeland Security.

Bella corrected me by calling it Homeland Defense and went on, her soft hand reaching out to mine. "You know she did it to save you."

I asked in confusion, "You mean Amara joined this Homeland Defense for me? Why? To prove something?"

"You haven't figured it out, Dad? My sister is only two years older than me and holds a dual degree in bioengineering and computer forensics. I'm a mental retard compared to her. She is the smartest person I know and could have gone to graduate school anywhere on a dozen scholarships. She had universities beating down her door. Instead she joined Homeland Defense because she thinks she can find the people who did this to you faster than a cure can be discovered. She's never been able to accept what happened."

This information was a gut punch. Amara was sacrificing a lifetime of opportunities because she felt she could somehow figure out how to crack Millennial open and discover its secrets. *To save her father.*

"She hates it there, but don't try to talk her out of it, Dad," Bella warned. "I've tried, and she only gets more distant."

Bella looked after me with concern, and I realized how terrible everything must be for her. Amara was leaving, her mother was estranged, and now her father was disappearing again for who knew how many years. "I'm so sorry, Bella. I'm sorry that I haven't been there for you all these years."

My daughter frowned. "It's not your fault, Dad."

It certainly felt like my fault. I supposed I could have justified thinking that I was only partly to blame, but how do you tell your loved ones that you're only 50 percent to blame for ruining their lives? And when I'd had a chance to get a sliver of my life back, I had turned it down.

I asked softly, "Bella, are you mad at me for not taking your advice? About the nanotreatment, that is."

Her expression of sadness told me yes, but she shook her head. "No, I'm not mad at you. I know it was really scary, and it's hard to be sure about anything. I just wish things were different. I miss you a lot, Dad. You're in the house but not really. It's like—never mind. I'm not explaining myself very well."

"No, I get what you're saying," I said, hoping I really did. "But I don't want you thinking that I love you any less because I agreed with your sister. And I hope you know by now that there's nothing I want more than to be there for you. You're still my Baby Bella."

I reached out and touched her sweet face, and she held my palm to her cheek like a warm blanket. "But you need to promise me you won't fight with your sister anymore," I scolded her gently. "You two are going to need each other as you get older. Probably more than ever. Family is where we start and end."

"Fine," she said. She smiled. "I promise I will be on my best behavior with Amara, and I'll do what I can to get Innovo to move us someplace else. Maybe get Uncle Jacob in the loop. Now you need to promise to try to be more optimistic."

I stretched my legs and stepped outside. The denim fabric felt rough against my skin even though I had worn these jeans soft two decades ago. A chill touched the air as the sun dipped toward the cleared cornfields below us. Night was coming to our tiny town in Pennsylvania, and smoke spiraled up from one of the closer properties. A fireplace stoked with wood from a walnut tree as some unfamiliar family no doubt struggled to keep warm. Under different circumstances, I would have known my neighbors, but I didn't exist to these people. I hoped that Bella knew them, that they were good people she could count on, but I didn't dare pretend to understand what was truly happening around us.

Instead, I took some time to speak with the girls about their lives. Amara was moving away for work and leaving Bella alone, a fact I was keenly unhappy about. She reassured me that she would be coming up to check on Bella and me regularly. The house already had a generator for the laboratory, installed in anticipation of a power outage interrupting the nanofield emitters. That was a relief. When I was growing up in the South, my mother and father had always kept a generator on hand. I remember us having one of the only houses on the block with lights when the storms would come. That was until the hurricane took our home and generator with it. I always wondered where that thing ended up.

I thought about Bella at twenty years old, living basically alone in a house twice as big as the one she grew up in with a large bank account at her disposal. She hadn't balanced the checking account ever—it was a task Amara and Miranda had done for her. I was worried. If Bella couldn't take care of me and the house, she could easily lose both. That scenario couldn't happen no matter what.

The three of us walked over to the garage where Amara was parked. She wanted to show me her new compressed natural-gas car (or CNG, as she called it), when her phone began chiming. "Sorry, it's my field supervisor calling. I'll be off the call quick." She touched the thin plastic loop that wrapped around the top of her ear and began speaking. Unlike the open wireless technology I'd grown up with that connected to a cell phone, the "Bridge," as they called it, sat on top of the ear and was the entire phone. Somehow, without inserting a bud into the ear canal, the voice transmitted directly to the eardrum while simultaneously reducing outside noise.

"Dad, do you want to go back inside? You look cold." Bella put her arm around my waist and gave me a sideways hug.

"Nah," I answered her. "I like the cold. It reminds me that I'm alive. Let's go for a walk."

"Can we do that?" she asked, surprised.

Syncing Forward

"The doctors left. That Mike guy and the attorney are the only ones left here. Why not?"

"Okay, where do you want to go?"

"Not far. I just want to walk. To smell. To feel."

Bella smiled and took me by the hand as we walked down the stone driveway littered with broken twigs and leaves from a recent storm. I drew a deep breath, and the smell of autumn triggered a flood of memories.

I remembered three-year-old Bella grasping my hand and pressing it against her little cheek as she dozed off at the family picnic. Her first day of kindergarten, beaming as the faded yellow bus rounded the corner. Bella's fifth Christmas Eve, lying in bed, worrying that Santa Claus wasn't going to show up the next morning because she had been misbehaving. My Baby Bella dancing with me in the living room sweetly asking me, "Daddy, will you marry me?" There were nothing but snippets to fill the gaps between then and now, but I wasn't about to squander the moment.

"Bella, what are you doing?" Amara called out incredulously, trotting up from behind us. "He can't go this far from the house!"

I told her I was going to be fine, even though I had no idea how long I had before the Diox 9 treatment wore off. It might be minutes or hours or days. I didn't dare hope for weeks.

"Daddy, we have to keep you safe," Amara pressed. "Please, let's walk back to the house."

"Amara, I love you, big kid. But I need to spend time away from a hospital bed or I might as well give up. I need a slice of normal right now. Just walk with us. Me and my girls taking a stroll, like we're a regular family. Tell me about the new job. You got a career plan yet, or are you still getting your feet wet?"

My older daughter sighed, resigning to the fact that we were strolling down the hillside whether she liked it or not. She told me how Millennial attacks were her area of preference, and the team she was assigned to worked within the scientific community to find out who these people were. It turned out Millennial had conducted sixteen acts of terrorism, but only four had resulted in anyone's death. University labs destroyed, databases wiped out, companies hacked. Their public statements after one particular attack expressed concern that the genetic research being done would result in the end of humanity. I asked her if there was any relation between the targets, and Amara said only that they were all technology based.

We bent around a corner, and the sunset previously hidden by the tree line lit up the horizon gloriously. Amara tried to steer us back to the house, but we could have keep walking toward the sun forever for all I cared. The temperature outside wasn't as bad as the girls yammered about; I took it as downright pleasant.

I listened to Amara talk about her supervisor and how dedicated he was to capturing a Millennial terrorist. "He says these crypts they use are their hideouts. Instead of holing up someplace, they slip in, pop the drug, and doze until they are ready to come out. Six months later or six years later."

I interrupted. "That's bizarre. I figured they were using them to help sick family members. Not as safe houses. Are you sure about this?"

"It could easily be both. These people use the drug they injected you with to skip forward, hoping we'll give up on finding them. We won't, though. We're going to find them. We're going to crack open one of those crypts, and . . ."

Amara was dreaming, rambling, letting go as she all but spelled out how she was going to fix me. She stopped short of finishing her sentence and chuckled apprehensively. "Don't worry, Dad. We're going to get these guys who did this to you."

"I hope you're right, kiddo. I would be a liar if I told you living like this has been pleasant." I was still reeling from the developments on Millennial. Maybe it was good that Amara was doing investigations after all. "It sounds like your supervisor is just as motivated as you are."

She looked at me as if to say "nobody is as motivated as I am."

Syncing Forward

"Just about. In fact, he asked me to give you something."

Amara reached into her jacket pocket and pulled out a small folded white card. I took it from her, stopping on the road to read it in the failing light. The sharp angles of the words gave it away as script from a man's hand.

13 people at Innovo lost their lives on my watch. I don't intend to lose a 14th. Stay strong, Mr. James. I promise I'll keep her safe.

~Darren Franciscus

PS: You were right about the illnesses.

I looked up at Amara, not knowing what to say. It wasn't that long ago I'd thought Agent Franciscus hated me. He certainly didn't trust me. But I was so caught up in my own problems I never recognized how he must have felt after the Innovo bombing, how everyone must have Monday-morning-quarterbacked his decisions that day, how he felt just as much to blame as I did for the choices he'd made. My decision to push Dr. Bruchmuller in the interview had always felt like the straw that broke the camel's back to me—making the events feel like they were my fault. Franciscus had to be ruminating about that day too, about rushing in, about how he might have done things differently. The events had been preying on my conscience for days. He had been carrying that weight for thirteen years.

But now Franciscus was in charge of placing my daughter in life-and-death situations. It slipped out again how uncomfortable I was with Amara's job. I was her dad, what else could I say? But the more we spoke, the more hopeful I grew that maybe—just maybe—they could find one of the members of Millennial. If they found Millennial, they could find the drug, and that could mean an antidote for my condition.

I waved the card in in the air, the dots connecting in my mind as I spoke. "These people are real clever, Amara. Real clever. This drug of theirs isn't just for them to sleep their way to their next terrorist attack. And it isn't just about helping their family members either."

Bella chirped in, not to be left out of the conversation, "What do you mean, Dad?"

I continued. "Think about it. It certainly is an intriguing way to coax somebody into helping you—'We'll save your kid from leukemia if you help us blow up a laboratory.' Plenty of people would take that offer."

Amara squinted, as if it didn't quite make sense. I had a similar feeling—that something about my theory didn't quite add up, that there was some missing piece of the puzzle that didn't allow the existing pieces to fit together. But I was close; I was sure of it.

We were a good half-mile from the house by now, and the moon was closing in on the hillside. The twilight was fading, and the moonlight wasn't going to last long. I didn't want to, but was time to turn around, signaling a change in conversation. Besides, I could see my Bella had gotten her tail feathers ruffled with all the talk revolving around Amara. So we spoke about her new beau, Keith Heffley.

"He's a real gentleman, Dad. You would like him! He's handsome, and funny—"

Amara interrupted with a drone. "A redneck, barely employed, lives with his parents—"

"—and is really good at fixing things. Oh, and you should see him with his dog. You can just tell he's going to be a good dad . . ."

There was no wrong Keith could do, according to twenty-year-old Bella, who had been growing up in a town with a population of fifteen thousand. Of course I should have admonished Amara for making fun of Keith. I was a displaced redneck myself. But it was fun listening to them go back and forth, so I chuckled my way through their argument.

Syncing Forward

"You know he's dumber than a stump, right?" Amara chided. This drew Bella's ire, and she berated Amara for her lack of a love life, and the two ribbed each other till we could see the house lit up on the top of the hill come into view.

"So sorry that Keith doesn't have an education. Some peoplecan'taffordtogooffto-schoolyouknow . . ."

They were walking ahead of me now, their bodies jerking unnaturally, their silhouettes blurring in the darkness. The fear returned once more. Maybe I should have been resigned to the fact that this moment was coming, but my body felt decidedly different. My left eye went blurry as it slowed independently of the rest of my body, throwing off my equilibrium and racking my head with such pain that it made a migraine feel like a massage.

"DaddydaddyBellagrabhisarmliftimupgottagetimbacktothelab fohelp." My daughters caught me just as I was toppling over. I felt my feet dragging along the gravel but soon found myself able to prop myself up. Bella's voice was synchronizing up quickly: "He'stooheavyIcan'tkeep holding him up like this. Wait, his feet are back on the ground. Dad, are okay? Can you understand me? Dad?"

"Yeah, I'm fine. I'm just . . . starting to slow down." I wasn't fine at all. My whole body felt shaky, as if it were coming apart at the seams. Amara was already on the phone calling up to the lab, yelling at somebody to get the laboratory prepped and for Randy Lindale to bring the car down the road.

"I don't give a crap who he's talking to . . . tell him to be useful for once . . . It's a driveway . . . I think he can handle it." She turned to Bella with accusing eyes. "I told you it was a bad idea to bring him down here."

Bella threw an angry "sorry" back at her sister and reached out to help me just in the nick of time. My knees buckled, and I collapsed on the gravel. "Crap, I can't feel my feet!" I squeezed my legs several times and found the sensation was missing from my thighs on down.

205

Amara came rushing over to grab my other arm. "Dad, it's the Diox 9. Something about it is causing your body to synchronize asymmetrically. You aren't slipping forward the way you originally did. Damn it, I told them this could happen!"

"What do we do? What do we do? Oh my God." Bella was panicking, grasping my arm, trying to lay me down.

"No!" Amara chastised her. "We need to keep him moving! To the labwe'regoingtohavetoliftimcrcmgstikinsd . . ."

I grayed out, vaguely feeling my body dragged up the driveway; noticed the swirl of a car, a series of lights.

Syncing Forward

Chapter 20

I was back in the lab in the back of our property. Amara and Bella were helping Mike hook up the wireless electrodes to my head and chest and back and arms and legs. Dang it, the things were everywhere. Gonzales and Nikonov and the others were supposedly on their way back, but they were a half-hour away. I couldn't exactly be taken to any old hospital, and Beacon, Pennsylvania, didn't have one anyway.

Amara was pacing the floor, pointing her finger at thin air as if the person on the other end of the phone could see her. "Screw you and your excuses, Ping! You knew he was going through the Diox 9 procedure months ago. Somebody should have stayed here to help Mike out in case things went to hell, *which they have!*" Amara began a long string of what could only be curses in Chinese as she pushed the lab door open and slammed it shut. We could still hear her yelling outside when Mike finished testing my vitals and confirmed I was fully monitored.

I was worried. For those couple hours in Beacon the world had seemed almost normal, and I regretted not taking the nanotreatment. Maybe it would have worked? Maybe I might have been able to scrape together a life worth living? Doubt plagued me as I stared at the door through which Amara had exited.

Bella and I were quiet for a moment, unsure how to fill the silence. I didn't want to depress her, but I didn't want to act too aloof either. These were precious minutes that we were never going to get back. I was sincerely frightened by how much time might pass before I was able to synchronize once again. I tried to speak to her, to kill the quiet, when suddenly I couldn't breathe. The room felt as if it had been purged of all oxygen. My chest wouldn't expand to take in air, and panic set in quickly. Alarms across the instruments sounded, and Amara and Randy Lindale came running into the lab.

"His diaphragm and chest muscles are syncing forward!" Mike announced, answering their question before either could ask it. "Help me get the oxygen on him now!"

I flailed my arms as terror set in. I was going to suffocate. The exact thing Amara had warned me would take place with the nanos was happening with the Diox 9. No prayer came to mind. No final words for my children escaped my lips. *Damned if you do, damned if you don't* was all that passed through my consciousness as I grabbed at the bedrails and fought helplessly to breathe. I could feel a tiny bit of air passing through my mouth and nose, but not nearly enough. It was the end of the line for me.

Before they could even set up the oxygen mask, I gasped, my lungs filled with air, and I was breathing normally again. My muscles had synced back and the panic was over, leaving behind only my shaking body and a very nervous group of people. The alarms turned off, and the blips and beeps of the instrumentation returned to their quiet chiming song.

"Mike, we can't let this happen again," Amara told the technician.

Mike was poring over a map of my body, barely listening to her. "I know."

"It could be his heart next time."

"I know."

"What are you going to do then?"

"We, uh, we . . . I don't know. Gimme a minute to think!"

"We don't have a minute, Mike!"

The young tech video-conferenced Lenny Chari, who was ten minutes out. He mentioned a flat tire kept him from being there at the procedure, but Mike spoke over him, trying to get the others on the conference. The gaggle from Walter Reed joined the call as they drove quickly back from wherever they had slinked off to. All their images were transferred to the monitor overhead, and the talking doctor head chatter went into full stereo. Mike didn't bother to look at their faces

Syncing Forward

as he and Amara pored over the readings coming from my body. Bella sat by me, squeezing my hand.

"Administer a second dose of the Diox 9," Dr. Nikonov suggested. "It will stabilize his system."

"It would work," Dr. Gonzales confirmed.

A stranger, another man who was with Lenny Chari, put his face up close to the camera, "You're putting off the inevitable, Dr. Nikonov. He's going to sync forward at some point, and we can't dose him over and over. You could kill him after the second dose, definitely after the third."

Painful death now or painful death in a few hours. Not quite the ideal options.

"It would give us time to administer the nanos. Those would stabilize Martin's nervous system, which is what I suspect has gone asymmetrical."

Amara yelled up at the screens, "No, even if you had time to administer your brainchild, the Diox 9 will wear off too fast. The drug is not fading uniformly. Any solution that involves the Diox 9 is going to kill him. We're going to have to use the Dambra 44."

The doctors from Innovo concurred. After a hurried discussion, the three finally agreed that the only way to keep me from dying was to administer the Dambra 44 antidote that had back-synced me ten years prior. I closed my eyes, letting that sink in. Dambra 44 had also caused me to lose that decade as my body couldn't handle another treatment until my vitals bottomed out.

"Amara, it is entirely possible that the Diox 9 and Dambra 44 antidotes would combine to cause an adverse reaction," Dr. Gonzales warned. "Nobody bothered to test for any harmful drug interaction, at least on our end."

The truth was out. Dr. Nikonov and the other Walter Reed scientists never counted on me turning down any treatment. They never could have predicted my daughter would rush to my defense if I did refuse. I was the lab rat, after all.

209

W Lawrence

Mike tested a sample of my blood with a combination of the two antidotes. The wireless microscope transmitted the readouts to the doctors, who had turned off their video cameras and dug into the data to figure out if they were about to save me or kill me. During the wait, various parts of my body synced forward, but nothing as critical as my diaphragm. No interaction showed up in my blood sample, but that didn't mean I was out of the woods. The minutes ticked by as, one by one, the professionals gave their opinion. I couldn't even vocalize how I felt. The terror of suffocating to death was still fresh on my mind as I looked to Bella, who was as helpless as I was.

That's when my breathing grew shallow again. The room grew dark, and I was suffocating in a room full of air. I tried to calm myself, to tell myself it was going to pass like last time. No relief came. I pushed Bella's hand away, flailing about as my daughters tried to steady me. The ceiling floated away as I watched from a sinking tunnel, their voices echoing from far away.

Amara shouted. "Inject him now, Mike! He can't breathe!"

"They're saying we shouldn't!" He pulled at his hair.

"I don't give a shit what the others are saying! Inject him or I'll beat you to death and do it myself!"

My eyes closed, and the voices abated further from my consciousness. A warm rush washed over me that made the room peaceful and light. It had to be the Dambra 44 working my body back into synchronization. As the drug worked its way into my system, I took in a large breath and exhaled in tranquil relief . . . and then seized in pain. My chest felt as if it would split open, and my head throbbed with such intensity that I could think of nothing else. And then there was a still black.

Chapter 21

"Daddy? Can you hear me?"

My left eyelid unsealed just enough to see Amara's face hovering over mine. Her hand was on my chest, shaking me awake gently. The totality of my being was sore. Not the sharp pain of before, but a colicky throbbing, a residue of trauma that my body could not shake off. I nodded and opened both eyes.

The lab was dimly lit by a single table lamp on the desk in the corner and the faint glow from the instruments. I sat up with some difficulty and noticed the crash cart next to my bed with the paddles dangling from the side. Bella was sleeping in a chair on the other side of my bed, while Mike had fallen asleep on the counter.

"What happened?" I whispered.

"Your body went into shock. It's fighting to go back into chemopreservation. The antidotes are like poison to your cells—too much and they'll kill you. We managed to bring you back, but it was close."

"Thanks for saving my life. Again."

Amara smiled, and I took a moment to look out the windows. Nothing but darkness. The dim outline of an SUV parked by the lab told me somebody had made it back, but whether it was Innovo's people or the government's, I didn't know. Or care.

"What time is it?" I asked her.

She pointed at the digital clock readout on the wall. It read 4:13.

"Four? Why aren't you sleeping, sweetie? You've got to be exhausted."

She held up an Rx tablet, "I'm working on some numbers, trying to figure something out."

"Can't it wait?"

Amara shook her head with a frown. "Not really. I'm calculating how much time you have before you sync forward."

"Oh," I said. "So, how much time?"

"It won't be long, Daddy. Even if I am off on my numbers, you won't make it to sunrise. I'm sorry."

After the asphyxiating terror from before, the prospect of quietly syncing forward again should have been a relief. There are plenty of ways to die, but I now knew suffocation had to be one of the worst. When I'd turned down the nano treatment, I knew that this chemopreservative state was unavoidable, but it didn't make it any easier a pill to swallow. It meant that years would pass by without being able to have a normal conversation, without eating, without the simple pleasures of music or the sensation of a hug.

"Those numbers tell you how long before you're able to get me back to normal?" I asked.

"No, but I've got a theory that your body is building an immunity to the antidotes. It isn't just the Diox 9 we can't use. The Dambra 44 won't work for more than an hour next time we sync you back. It means we have to come up with something new, or there is no point in bringing you back at all. I wish I had better news . . ."

She held up some sort of spandex underwear and asked with an embarrassed grin if I needed help putting them on. I probably could have used a hand, but I wasn't about to have my daughter see me without my skivvies; she looked relieved when I declined and turned around. They were waste collection shorts. Thank God somebody had invented these things that I could slip into instead of being catheterized. The latex-like diaper somehow collected urine, broke down fecal matter, and ejected it all out a tube on the side. At least some of my pride would be maintained this go-around.

Lying back in the bed, I patted her shoulder and tried to appear stronger than I was feeling. "Amara, this isn't your fault—you know that, right? I am so grateful to have you as my daughter. So grateful for both you and your sister. But you can't let it eat you up like this. It's not healthy. It's going to ruin your life."

"I'm fine, Daddy, honestly."

"Are you?" I questioned her. "Are you really happy with your choices? I mean, if I had never gotten myself into this mess, do you think you would have ever chosen this career path?"

"I don't know. Maybe? Probably not."

"What would you have chosen then?"

She bent her head far away, not wanting to answer. "Does it matter? I mean, this is reality, and I can't change it. I've got a job to do now and a house, a sister, and a dad who are counting on me. I can't afford to screw around finding myself."

"I'm afraid to ask if you have any friends."

"I do," my elder daughter protested softly. "I have a few close friends. I'm not a social butterfly like some women. So what?"

"Amara, I want you to be happy. And if you're happy, then you won't get any complaints from me. I just want to be sure that *you're* sure. You're my big kid, and I worry."

"There's nothing to worry about. Trust me, okay?"

"I'll trust you on this." There was a pause in the conversation that I filled with words that needed to be said. "Amara, I'm very proud of the woman you've become. It was wrong for me to demean your choices."

"It's okay, Daddy. I understand why you said what you said."

"So are we okay?"

"Yeah." She looked over at her sister. "Should I wake up Bella?"

I looked over at my baby girl, snoring away in the chair next to me. "Not yet. I need to talk to you about something important."

Amara adjusted herself in her seat, pulling herself closer. Reaching out, I pushed her bangs out of her eyes and back behind her ear like I used to do when she was younger. Gazing into her face, I could still see my nine-year-old looking back at me.

"Amara, this isn't the easiest topic to bring up," I began with heavy hesitation, "but I want to talk to you about your mother."

Amara shrank back into her chair and looked away. God, I didn't want to bring Miranda up any more than Amara wanted to. My wife leaving me was a pain far worse than the physical trauma I had endured. Still, I couldn't avoid this.

I leaned over the rail and tried to get her attention. "Please, just listen to me. I miss your ma a lot. I miss her more than you know. From my viewpoint, she walked out in the middle of our marriage. But as much as it hurts me to say it, your mother has every right to a happy life. She isn't perfect, and she isn't as strong as I would have hoped, but I think your sister is right: she hung in there as long as she could. Regardless of what happened between your ma and me, you shouldn't alienate her like you have, or call her names, or kick her out of this house."

Amara stood up, her face reddening, still careful not to wake her sister. "She walked out on you, Daddy! She left us here so she could 'have a life'! Why would I want somebody so selfish anywhere near me after she turned her back on her own family? Left us here to take care of you? So her wedding vows mean nothing to her? You didn't see Bella and me run away from our responsibilities! She disgusts me!"

"Amara, that's not fair. Nobody should have to go through what your mom and you kids have had to go through. You've been so strong when it comes to dealing with my condition. Don't you think you can be strong enough to find some forgiveness in your heart for your mother? This is the woman who carried you, birthed you, who stood watch over you when you were sick in the hospital, who helped you with your homework and fed you and loved you—*loves* you—with her whole heart."

"Where's all that forgiveness for your own mother?" she cut at me.

Syncing Forward

My daughter had to feel pretty cornered to pull that card. Dang it if she wasn't right, though. The apple hadn't fallen very far from the tree. Rather than dig in my heels, I relented. "You know, you're probably right. And this whole situation has given me a new perspective on how I've handled problems with my own ma. So how about this, Amara. Let's both make some changes. Can you let go of all this resentment and call your mom? Just one call? Maybe it will be the first step for you two to begin reconciling—"

Bella groaned, waking up to the sounds of our hushed dispute, her eyes still heavy from exhaustion. I turned briefly to see if she was fully aware. She was not. When I turned back, I watched Amara walk to the laboratory door. "Where are you going?" I asked. She simply stopped in her tracks and looked down for a moment before turning her head my way.

"I love you, Daddy. But Mom . . . leaving us . . . I just can't let it go." Her apologetic tone only underscored her lack of forgiveness. Amara slipped out the door and shut it quietly behind her. A cold puff of air invaded the room before it vanished in the heated laboratory.

Bella rubbed her eyes, and unaware of the time or the topic of our conversation, asked where Amara went. I swallowed hard. "Out for some fresh air," I said. Bella put the rail down on the bed and rested her face against my right side. She couldn't have been very comfortable, but regardless, she grabbed my hand and put it on her cheek. I stroked her soft skin with my thumb and felt my daughter smile before she dozed off again, completely unaware of the tears that crept down my cheek.

I felt a familiar dizziness while the sounds around me became increasingly muffled. I looked up at the digital readout on the clock. It read 4:20, and then quickly flipped to 4:21. Then 4:22. Then 4:23, 4:24, 4:25, 4:26, 4:28, 4:31, 4:36, 4:41 . . .

Chapter 22

The evening came, and the view outside my sitting room was veiled once more. Watching the sun rise and set in a matter of seconds was a peculiar sensation, one both of loss and wonder. Each time the sun came up, another day ticked off on the electronic counter at the base of the screen. And then another. And another. One look at my heartbeat ratio showed it at 1:1,950. My body was almost at the halfway mark for bottoming out, and twenty-six more months had flown by in a matter of hours. The best guesstimate was that from the time I was injected to this moment, my perceived journey had lasted under seventy hours. Three days to move forward fifteen years.

For the first time, I was no longer wearing goggles while in chemopreservation. A new headband gingerly sat above my ears like a pair of glasses and shot microbursts of saline at my eyes. Rather than a blanket spray, the saline was directed by tiny sensors that moistened my eyeballs with perfect precision. A needle-sized projector complemented the saline component, shooting tiny blasts of air at any pooling of my tears. I didn't know who had designed the device, but it provided me with clear vision, for which I was thankful. Reading was much easier now, and I no longer had to struggle to see through the goggles to get my correspondence.

"'Stand Your Ground!'—Governor Hollister Calls for Louisiana to join Separation"

"CDP Confirms Hantavirus T Strain Infects Human-to-Human"

"Four Hundred Killed in Northern France Bombing"

"Orion Rising Probe Launches—Expected to Arrive at Neighbor Star in 2072"

"US Civil Unrest Carries to Quebec Riots"

Syncing Forward

"Australia Turns Away Second Refugee Freighter, Claims Non-Isolation"

"Dollar Disappearing? Customers Use SDRs in 30% of New York Purchases"

"Millennial Terrorists Destroy Moscow Lab—Issue Warning to Scientists"
—A—*Daddy, read this!*

It was this last headline that caught my attention the most, and not because of Amara's electronic scribble to the side. The topic of Millennial had dual meaning in my life now. The capture of anyone from their elusive group meant the potential of recovering an antidote for me. But it also meant that my daughter was placed in harm's way.

I pressed the link and brought up the article on my news display and began reading.

&&&& Translated by OwtFoxxed &&&&

Millennial Terrorists Destroy Moscow Lab—Issue Warning to Scientists

By Ivan Stemka

The Biosynthesis Lab at Sechenov First Moscow State Educational Facility was destroyed by a large explosion killing 37 students and teachers and wounding at least 700. The terrorist group identifying themselves as "Millennial" took credit for the attack that took place on January 18, 2037 at 0815 hours just as students were beginning their classes.

W Lawrence

> *Millennial issued a public warning on an anonymous webby broadcast that Sechenov research violated "the purity of human DNA to such a degree that it warrants a death sentence" for the researchers as well as the research. See the entire message here.*

> *A university staff member reported anonymously to our agency that the databases for over one hundred research teams in and around Moscow were purged or infected with neoviruses and that cloud backups were breached as well. Sechenov spokesperson Oleg Dimatrov would not comment on the type of research being conducted but stated that the cost to the university would be well over [19 million SDRs] to repair the lab.*

I clicked on the link, and it immediately played a news clip in an unfamiliar language—Ukrainian maybe?—but the video player automatically lowered the volume of the clip and dubbed over it in a broken artificial Spanish. Bella's searches on the system had been recently done in Spanish, so I figured maybe the house computer just assumed that was the correct translation. I muddled through for a few seconds before giving up. Not because I couldn't understand—my Spanish was decent enough—but because the audio interface still wasn't perfect for my chemopreserved condition. My body was always slower than normal, but not always at the same rate. Sometimes one second to me would be fifty-six minutes. Other times the ratio was one second to sixty-five minutes. The biochronometer Innovo had installed was connected to an electronic glass display, but rare was the day that it was able to keep up with my body's changes. The result was half-coherent audio warbling through the wireless audio transmitters resting above my ears. Warbling Spanish translated by computer from Ukranian. Forget it.

Syncing Forward

I suppose I could have asked the girls for another copy, but after scanning the screen I found another link that brought up a transcript of Millennial's public statement.

> *We are Millennial. We are responsible for the recent bombing of the Sechenov Laboratory in Moscow. While we cherish every human life, there are sacrifices in every war. Mothers, fathers: your children are soldiers in a conflict against humanity. The universities, government facilities, megacorporate laboratories, and public research institutions are indoctrination centers where your innocents are transformed into weapons that will destroy our world, and yet you stand idly by and allow our species to perish. This we cannot allow.*

> *Scientific progress has been a staple of civilizations for hundreds of years, but there are a growing number of people who wish to reengineer the world in their own image, to play God with the earth and everyone living on it. Progress is made for the sake of progress itself. Advancement made without ever asking why it is needed. Genetic engineering of children, bio-implants to feed a decadent lifestyle, cloning of human beings to harvest their organs—these are but a handful of activities that have been perpetrated against the human race for forty years. These are movements toward the Singularity, an event sure to create a slave society in which your existence will no longer matter. The end of individuality and the human experience is at hand unless it is stopped.*

W Lawrence

> *Your governments are pushing for Singularity. Your corporations are moving toward Singularity. The so-called enlightened scientific community has been coopted by those insistent upon reaching Singularity. And make no mistake—we will not allow Singularity to be reached. For the good of humanity, we declare war on everyone and everything associated with these goals. To those ignorant to these facts, it is time to rise up and demand answers from those who would steal your humanity. To those who are complicit in these attempts, this is your final warning.*
>
> *We are vigilant. We are eternal. We are coming for you. We are Millennial.*

I closed the article out, and the main screen filled with dozens of news links that Amara had downloaded to my viewer. Each one a bombing, a hacking, an assassination—with Millennial taking credit. I scrolled through the headlines and managed to read a few paragraphs here and there. The terrorist attacks were global and carried out against scientists, engineers, and developers. The entire family of a Sydney software developer was burned to death in their home. Datashove, an information mining company, had their offshore facility blown up by a hijacked yacht packed with explosives. A US Army building was the target of a corrupted drone stolen from the Department of Agriculture and armed with an EMP weapon. A symposium in Geneva was butchered as four gunmen used machine guns and grenades to kill more than a hundred professors who were discussing the benefits of nanotechnology on curing leukemia.

This whole time I had thought Millennial was unique to the US. What was it I had stumbled inadvertently into? They were everywhere. Attacking everywhere. Then my mind dipped back to the investigation I had been running a few days—*years*—ago, and how

Syncing Forward

deeply ingrained Millennial had been in our company's shipping as well as our lab work. What if the drug had been dispatched right under our noses? Sent globally to equip the crypts of Millennial before they began their exercise of terror on the world? It dawned on me that my investigation back at Innovo might have exposed them if only I had moved faster. Or called the authorities.

I typed out a quick message to Amara.

**CHECK 2021 INNOVO SHIPPING RECORDS
COMPARE HOT SPOTS FOR MILLEN—**

Amara sent me a voice message back immediately, anticipating the rest of my message. "It's a match. They used Innovo as a network to get the drugs out to their cells. Now it's everywhere, but you nailed it. Wish we knew they were global when the Innovo attack happened, but . . . Good job anyway, Daddy."

It was a maddening situation to be in. Too slow to react to a world that already moved too fast for regular folk to keep up with it. I looked down at the dual time display below the electric glass. The left number showed the passing minutes and seconds as I perceived them, estimated by the computer from data on my heart rate, response time, pupil dilation, you name it. The number on the right showed the actual date, hour, and minutes that the rest of the world recognized as real time. I don't know why they bothered to add minutes to the display—the hours ticked away faster than a second. It reminded me of the hundredth-place decimals at gas station pumps that would blur to become a flashing number 8 on the readout until they finally stopped. I mused that my flight to the future was progressing so quickly that there might not even be gas stations anymore.

Amara bombarded me with news on Millennial. It took me eight days just to read the first article and three weeks to skim the rest. Sometimes she would overwrite what I was reading before I was done and put a new article or picture up for me to see.

What was Singularity, though? What was so threatening about it that Millennial would slaughter innocent people to stop it? I clicked on a hotlink and was met with a wiki answer: a hypothetical moment in time when artificial intelligence surpassed human intelligence. Sounded like a dozen movies I'd seen. Robots take over the earth. Computers come to life and withhold free apps from humanity. It was the type of plot I'd shrug my shoulders at and wait for explosions to start lighting up the big screen.

As glibly as I took the matter, however, the topic had gone beyond Hollywood scripts and marijuana-laced intellectual discussion. There had to be hundreds, if not thousands, of Millennial terrorists who were willing to kill to stop a theoretical moment in history that would probably never occur. The madness that would drive someone to conduct these atrocities only made me question my judgment again. How had I not seen the crazy in the late Dr. Bruchmuller, let alone my friend Rajesh?

I took a moment to actuate the photovoltaic glass in my sitting room and gaze at the farmland on the outskirts of Beacon. My eyes needed a rest, and focusing out at the distant points was restful and worry free. With a touch of my right hand, I brought up a telescopic app that I could point and zoom in with. On this particular occasion, I chose an orchard of apples that went into bloom before my very eyes. With some effort I could see some of the golden delicious apples growing on the branches when the wind wasn't bad. Otherwise the trees simply blurred with their gentle swaying, looking more like an oil painting than reality.

The display shut down, and upon it appeared a handwritten note from Bella.

Dad, I know I shouldn't have, but I told Keith about your condition. I can't send you a message or the DHD will know I broke confidence. He's been to the house, and he promises not to tell. You've seen the pictures of us together, and I hope you can tell that we are in love. He is such a good man, and I want him to be part of our family. Keith

Syncing Forward

told me that he would never ask me to marry him if you didn't approve. I know this must be hard, but please trust me. I know he is the one. I love you, Dad, and I will take care of you as long as I have to, but I love Keith too. Please let me know if you approve. It is important to me too.

Yours always, Bella

This was a young man with barely a pot to piss in asking for my seven-year-old daughter's hand in marriage. Of course she wasn't seven; Bella was in her twenties and a young adult who had taken care of herself and me for years. With Miranda living in Ohio and Amara jumping all over the Eastern Seaboard from assignment to assignment, I counted on Bella to handle my care.

The thought occurred to me: Would she still want to take care of me if she got married? Would I still have those Sundays when she would religiously sit with me for hours just so I could feel her holding my hand for a few forward-syncing seconds? And that bison of a man would be having sex with Bella. Sex with my daughter. In my house. Dear God, they were probably already having sex here! How could I be so foolish as to think they would be doing anything otherwise? I lifted my hand and rubbed hard between my eyebrows, the weight of my arm magnified by the fact that I had lifted it for fifteen hours.

I didn't know how to respond. Life wasn't waiting for me to catch up. All I wanted to do was sync back into my normal life, to get off the ride. The days pensively ticked by, and Bella came and sat with me for a Sunday—virtually the entire day. She left an "I love you, Daddy" note taped to the screen. I was able to hold her hand for a good fifteen seconds before she vanished in a flash of movement. I blinked and the note was gone, replaced with a new message.

DADDY WHAT DO YOU THINK? I WANT YOU TO BE HAPPY FOR ME AND GIVE ME AWAY.

Give her away? I'd had her for seven years. It was too early to give her away. But what was I going to do? Stop time for everybody? Forbid the marriage? What power did I have? Not like I would have any control if I was synced back permanently. Whether I acknowledged the fact or not, Bella was her own person making her own choices.

Bringing up the virtual keyboard, I clicked, "Okay." Followed by "How?" I hoped she would figure out that we needed to back-sync my body for me to be at the wedding. A response didn't come for several of my minutes, which gave me a chance to look through some pictures, articles, and other items sent by Amara.

A news article entitled "Singularity—Our Destruction or Our Hope?"

A picture of the American flag with only forty-one stars, captioned "The New America . . . for Now."

A document resolving my divorce from Miranda. That one stung worse than Bella wanting Keith to marry her. I drew a deep breath and gave it an electronic signature. When I clicked Send, I felt flushed and queasy. My marriage officially over. I closed my eyes for a few days and let the finality set in. When I opened my eyes, the season had changed again.

I needed a distraction, and thankfully my daughters had plenty to show me. A clip of text from the news, presumably about Amara's accomplishments. I clicked on the link and read "Homeland Defense Agents Thwart the California Drug Cartel's Assassination Attempt on US Congressman Hong. Four DHD agents captured fifteen members of the . . ."

A picture of Amara and three other agents all smiling and dressed in fitted black uniforms, their hands on a large pistol marksman trophy.

A picture of Bella and Keith holding hands at a lake.

A news video with the Internet address w2.//New-York-bankrupt-5th-state-bailed-out-full-story.m6t.

Syncing Forward

I was ready to try watching the video, when the screen was hijacked again and I found myself being bathed by an unknown person. The alcohol bath was a blip of my time, but it disoriented me; my inner ear took a few seconds to catch up to being laid down, spun about, and then set back in my chair. When I got my bearings back, my eyes trained to the EGD and a message from Bella. Hope returned.

Chapter 23

DAD, WE HAVE A POSSIBLE SOLUTION FOR THE WEDDING. HERE IS THE MESSAGE FROM DR. KIAKOWSKI.

2043 DECEMBER 22

*****CONFIDENTIAL CORRESPONDENCE*****

Bella,

Thank you for contacting us. We were going to vidcon you and your sister after the first of the year but I thought you could use a Christmas present. Please read on with the understanding that we are still in our final testing phase and we won't be able to commit to the application until after May.

We have developed a hyperelectrostimulator that should bring your father in-sync for one to three hours. This may not seem like a long time, but the good news is we can administer it every eight to fourteen months. A secondary drug would be injected shortly after syncing forward that would enhance his deceleration and eradicate the original compound.

We concur with Amara's findings that the previous antidotes will not have the desired effect. Martin's DNA has developed a resistance to the drugs that make them less effective.

Syncing Forward

This is not a long-term fix, but it does mean that you will have a chance to spend time with your father more frequently. Once we field test it this upcoming summer, we should be able to create a self-administering system that you, Amara, or any other caregiver can employ.

I will be on vacation starting tomorrow and will not return until January 10. I will call you then to start making arrangements.

Merry Christmas,

Dr. Jerry Kiakowski

Vice President, Advanced Medical Solutions Division

Innovo Industries LPC

    Call me suspicious, but I couldn't stop thinking of the words *field test*. Amara thought the Walter Reed facility had somebody else in my same condition. Was it possible that Innovo knew about this other patient and was in cahoots with the feds? Paranoia, paranoia . . . My contact with Jerry Kiakowski had been brief, but I'd gotten good vibes from the man. The rest of his correspondence seemed straightforward, and I grinned when noting he had been promoted to vice president. Was it his research on my condition that had propelled his career? Maybe I would have the chance to ask.

    Typing was always a risk of time for me since every second that passed was a premium. Quickly I banged out, WUT AMARA THI—

    Amara's video image popped up before I could finish typing. Her dark hair was down, and she had a big smile on her face as her voice sloshed through the audio transmitters. "Daddy, I think it looks great. Lenny sent me their data, and I think it looks good. Looks like

W Lawrence

Innovo co-opted some military tech they are using to enhance battle speed. See you in a few minutes! Love you!"

"In a few minutes" . . . I would pass through several major holidays to be thrust into a wedding for a daughter I only knew as a child. The instruments recorded my blood pressure and pulse going up, which made my synchronization ratio screwy. Movement in the corner of my eye caught my attention, and I turned to see Amara, Bella, Keith, and somebody I did not recognize decorating the room. It might have been Mike from the lab, but with the blurring motions, it was all just guesswork really. The trio hustled through my sitting room, draping festoons and hanging stockings. The Christmas tree went up in a heartbeat and was decorated in one long breath. Somebody spun me around as night came and decided that turning out the lights was a good idea. Facing the photovoltaic glass, I could see it had been programmed to flash the words "Feliz Navidad" and "Merry Christmas" in a luminescent display of colors. It might have taken the kids hours to program this or merely a matter of seconds.

It was October 2038, and I had been syncing forward for nearly seventeen years. At this point I had no real connection to current technological advancements. Sure, there were things that I was aware of from my contact with the gismos around my room, such as the audio transmitters or flattening car seats. Other things I had read about or seen pictures of—like exoskeleton-powered soldiers and sonic crowd control devices. For the most part I was a simpleton when it came to the daily advances that touched the normal person's life in the 2030s. I had grown up with advances like Bluetooth and eleven different generations of Smartphones, ultrathin televisions, and ever more complex multimedia game consoles. The briefest glimpse of what lay out there in the world told me I was a man displaced from history.

As the holiday swept past at breakneck pace, I watched the girls pillage a few presents at my feet. Christmas morning lasted less than two seconds. I think one of them gave me a kiss on the cheek, but there was no way to be sure. They brought over two chairs and sat with me for a bit. Amara couldn't sit still for long and left for her own bed.

Syncing Forward

Bella stayed for a while, her hand on my arm. She must have gotten sore and left, but not before typing a note on my display.

DAD YOU ARE THE ONLY CHRISTMAS PRESENT I WANT. I LOVE YOU.

Did she know she had written those same words to me when she was a kid? Her whole life she'd been wanting one thing, and it was the one thing I was powerless to give her.

Bella placed a present on my lap wrapped in simple gold cardboard and tied closed with a red ribbon. The note said "To Dad from Amara and Bella." It was December 27 before I could finish opening the ribbon and December 28 before I could lift the box lid off. It was December 29 when I reached inside to find a beautiful picture of the three of us smiling side by side, printed on some plastic material that I did not recognize. The girls' images were from when they were five and three. It was not a picture I remembered taking, and I didn't take long to figure it was a Photoshopped picture—and well done at that.

But the image wasn't just a static photo. As I looked, I saw the girls growing right there in front of me. Each second that ticked by for me showed them getting taller, their hair changing length and color, their faces maturing. Somehow the summer dresses they were wearing never changed—only they did. Embedded within this marvelous material was a program that rapid-aged my children's faces so I could see them at any point in their life. The programming no doubt had to be customized to meet my out-sync perception, which meant Amara had tinkered with it.

In the bottom right of the picture was a slide bar that allowed me to flick my thumb and put them back to any age I wished. I tried pegging it at ages nine and seven, but the program slowly pushed the girls forward, growing up, growing older. I couldn't even get the picture to stop moving forward in time. Below the image was an engraving that read "Daddy's girls at any age!" It was a cute gift that I pushed myself to smile at. Out of habit I flipped the thing upside down and noticed two clear plastic sleeves attached to the reverse side, one labeled A and one labeled B. Within them were two lockets of hair from my beautiful girls.

My heart ached knowing they were growing up so fast. I had to get out of this chair, and I was ready to do just about anything to do it.

Months flew by, and even though the passage of time meant very little to me, I remained anxious about the new treatment they were developing. Amara told me she was still pressing them for more research on a permanent solution, but Innovo had insisted on trying out the Pause antidote, as she named it. Pause. That's all it was, really: a pause in my journey forward in time, a pause from the company's research, a pause in the financial aspects of the research so that funds could be diverted to other programs at Innovo.

My tension level only increased as the terrorist attacks claimed by Millennial increased in intensity and frequency. Tokyo, Seattle, Luxemburg, Toronto. Corporations put out legitimized bounties, international intelligence communities stepped up investigations, and our own government continued to deny the ever-increasing outcry that the intelligence community was failing to protect them from Millennial's deadly efforts.

Pulling the keyboard closer, I typed out a message to Amara: HOW GOES THE INVESTIG—

Her face popped up on a video feed that looked sharper than before. The media player had been upgraded somewhere between my blinks, and while the warble was still there, it was decent enough to watch and listen. "Hey, Daddy, doing okay. I sent you a few messages about what's been going on, but you haven't seen them yet. We interviewed a man from Singapore visiting Maryland. We don't know if he's Millennial, but I think he is. Check these facial cues out."

Several still images of an Asian man popped up: in his thirties, shiny oval cheeks, thinning hair in the front. The first was labeled,

Syncing Forward

"When asked if he knew anybody who was part of Millennial." I clicked on the image, and the man answered that he knew of nobody—but his lips pursed tightly right after answering. Subjects often did this when they had more information; it was a subconscious way of buttoning your lips so that you didn't ramble.

I went through the four videos Amara had sent me as quickly as I could. I spent maybe four minutes checking them out, but realized a week and a half had flown by. This miserable condition kept me from devoting time to any real analysis, but I had to trust Amara knew what she was doing. I rattled off a quick message that she was spot-on with her analysis.

I added, TAKE HIM DOWN, KIDDO. After hammering Amara for her career choice last time, I was trying hard to be encouraging. The truth was I hoped she would take this suspect down. Still, my parental instincts were screaming at me, telling me I was a horrible father for encouraging my own kid to be in such a risky job. What kind of man was I that I would put my own child in harm's way for my benefit? But could I stop her if I wanted to? It was a damned conflicting position to be in.

Those fleeting strips of angst were not the sole result of Millennial but of Bella's wedding as well. My career was indefinitely suspended, my marriage was over, and after all these losses, I lamented the loss of Bella's childhood the most. Amara had always felt like she was born a grown-up, despite her obsessive compulsions. Bella, on the other hand, was a funny little girl who did kid things. Spinning around in circles until she got dizzy. Telling her mom that she was just joking when she got caught hiding her vegetables in her glass of milk. Naming all her stuffed animals and then renaming them the very next day. Taking fifty-eight giggling pictures of her butt with the tablet. Wanting to snuggle on the sofa on a Saturday morning because she had missed me all week.

It pained me to think of all the mornings I'd been cheated out of, all the experiences stolen from us, all the moments that defined me as a parent that I would never have. I hated Bruchmuller more than ever, and there was nothing I could do. No act of vengeance or justice could be perpetrated upon a man who was long buried except to destroy his work. The fact that my cure was tied to discovering anybody who was involved in Millennial played into my desire for revenge in equal measure. It was strange how Rajesh's blame in all this seemed to have all but vanished from my mind—I had my villain.

These simple broodings brought my calendar forward another three days. It was April now, and if Innovo stayed on schedule, I was one step closer to syncing and spending time with the kids. It felt strange to be waiting for something to happen, since my new life was almost entirely about free-falling through the weeks and grasping at anything I could manage to comprehend. While my body felt lazy, my brain felt mentally exhausted, as if I had driven four hours in a dangerous rainstorm on a dark Mississippi highway and had to concentrate just to stay on the road.

A creased sticky note appeared in front. This note was stuck to the screen instead of being typed into the display—not meant for prying eyes. Pulling it off, I recognized Bella's handwriting and unfolded it. Inside it had small neat print that my younger daughter had perfected over the years.

Dad—

Amara was hurt on the job but is fine. She asked me not to worry you but i wanted you to know. She may be sore on her right side so just don't hug her there. Don't say I told you anything. The wedding is going to be small. We have a suit waiting for you. Thank you for being so supportive. Can't wait to talk to you like normal.

Love you,

Bella

Syncing Forward

The prying eyes were Amara's; otherwise her sister wouldn't have bothered with the paper correspondence. I folded the note closed, and Bella swiped it out of my hand before I could even perceive her presence in the sitting room. The evidence was gone. Amara must have injured herself something fierce for her to hide it from me. There was no way to know if she had been attacked or shot up or if she had merely tripped and taken an embarrassing fall while in the office, but given her profession I could only guess that Amara was into something that would give sleepless nights to any parent.

— **Part 4** —

Remedium

Chapter 24

I was groomed a good three weeks before the wedding. Mike and another man—presumably from Innovo as well—carted me to my bedroom, scrubbed me down, shaved me, cut my hair, and arranged my clothing on a hanger. The outfit remained undisturbed, waiting for me to occupy it. I closed my eyes because the tossing about they put me through made me nearly vomit.

While they got me dressed, the audio transmitter had stopped working in my left ear. Thankfully the right one was working, and I waited for them to set me upright. Once in my chair, I got several short messages while I banged out a message to fix the earpiece. As was the case before, there were dozens of messages from both my children, from Agent Franciscus, from Innovo's legal department, from Walter Reed. There wasn't enough time to keep up with them all. While I typed, the computer just pumped the audio by me one voice message after the other, a constant stream of information that made my head spin.

Amara: "Hey, Daddy, I can't wait to see you at the wedding. Love you."

Amara again, sounding out of sorts: "Hi, Daddy, I just wanted to tell you how much I miss you and how important you are to me."

My designated attorney: "Mr. James, this is Randy Lindale. Your brother Jacob and his family will be communicating with you at the wedding, as well as members of your wife's family. They have been made aware of your condition and have signed nondisclosure agreements with DHDF and Innovo. It is important that they say nothing specific as part of the agreement. We must also remind you that you cannot speak of your condition to any other party save for your daughters, your brother, and his immediate family."

Jacob: "Hey, Marty. I'm glad I am finally able to talk to you. The kids have done their best to catch me up to speed, and I'm glad you are okay. I wish I could have been there for you in person, but I didn't know. Miss you, little bro. So glad you are not lost to us."

Amara: "Don't forget to tell Bella that she looks thin. She has been starving herself all month, and I can't get her to eat. She's afraid she won't fit in her dress. Oh, and sorry Uncle Jacob and the rest of the family won't be able to make it. I know they really tried, but there was no way to swing it with his job and the border problems. See you soon. Love you!"

Two messages waiting for me in the queue went by un-intelligibly due to the warble from the sensors unsuccessfully trying to match my body's speed. The sensation of movement finally stopped, and I opened my eyes to the fluorescent lighting attached to the laboratory ceiling. Something about my recumbent position had the tear jets malfunctioning and the room was hazier than it should have been, although it wasn't as bad as it could have been, I suppose. I could have been blind like I was when first injected. I shut my eyes anyway.

The technician, Mike, was speaking to me through the system and into my earpiece. "Martin, we're going to administer the treatment as soon as this transmission ends. You may feel some discomfort, but it won't last long."

Every muscle in my body seemed to tense simultaneously, as if I had gotten a head-to-toe Charlie horse. My eyes were shut, and I couldn't open them to save my life. Roughness ground my wrists, and I thought maybe they had strapped me down with canvas straps. But the more I concentrated on the feeling, the more I knew it was something softer, like supple leather. When I managed to pry open my eyes, I saw that it wasn't a strap rubbing against me but skin. Hands were holding me in place as I shook about, my arms banging against the bed railing.

I was hearing actual noise. Banging. Banging and grunts and heavy breathing as Mike and an unfamiliar black man hindered my movements. They stood over me. My movements were fluid and quick and abreast with the men who pinned my arms down. The unknown man was speaking in a deep voice that was coming in clearer:

Syncing Forward

"ComeonMartinyou'realmostthereyacandoitcomeoncomeon. You can doithere you gothataboy. Mike, look at his ocular muscles. He's synced. That was damn quick. Faster than projected."

The stabbing pain vanished, leaving my body mildly sore and sensitive. The men let go, and I realized I had been synchronized back with the rest of the world once more. They helped me sit up, and it was then I noticed we three were not the only ones in the laboratory. Amara was chewing the nails on her right hand with her left hand tucked into her armpit. She wore a simple light-blue dress that went conservatively below her knees. Her shoulders were exposed, but her dark, curly hair concealed much of her light-brown skin. Her makeup covered an anxious expression, penciled on with an accuracy that screamed of a formal event, and it dawned on me that the wedding was literally being planned around my synchronizing.

"Daddy, are you okay? Can you hear me?" Amara asked, stepping forward hesitantly as she did.

I took the earpieces and the tear jets off, feeling like my old self again. I tried to speak, but my words were reduced to a crackle. Mike was ready with a thin bottle equipped with a long nozzle that he popped into my mouth and squeezed. A fine, lightly flavored watery mist coated my mouth and throat, but not enough to choke on. I didn't know what was in that bottle, but my vocal cords moistened up quickly, and I spoke with ease after a couple of sprays.

"Hey, big kid! Yeah, I can hear you just fine. You look so beautiful!" My sweet daughter gave me a wide smile and clopped awkwardly across the room in her too-high heels to give me a hug. The embrace was brief, and it was obvious she was in a rush.

"Daddy, it looked painful when you synced forward."

"It was worth it." I grinned while trying to look tougher than I was. "It was a bit rough, but the syncing didn't last long."

I touched my face, and my fingers came back with makeup on the tips. Before I could ask, Amara explained, "We've got some concealer on your face to cover that bruise you've been sporting for two decades. We also added a little gray to your hair. It's not the best disguise, but who's going to suspect you've found the fountain of youth, right?"

I looked into the compact mirror she held up, checking out my face and hair. It would have to do.

"How do you feel? Do you think you can stand?" Amara inquired hurriedly. "Let's try to get you to stand, okay?"

Mike tried to tell her to take it easy, but there was no dissuading Amara. She informed the men in her company that the bride was patiently waiting for her father to walk her down the aisle and had been for more than an hour. My caretakers weren't convinced that I needed to hurry, but I took my daughter's outreached arm anyway and brought myself to an upright position. The transition was surprisingly easy, as if I had simply been sitting around on the sofa for too long. I stretched my arms as much as the stiff suit would allow and took a deep breath to take in the smells denied me for my out-sync time: flowery perfume from Amara, bubblegum that smelled like mangos in Mike's mouth, a sterile plastic scent that came from almost everything in the lab.

All three pulled and poked at me, removing the sensors that had been buried under my suit, pressed into urgency by Amara, who reminded them it wasn't just my tardiness for the wedding that she was concerned about. Dr. Kiakowski had written that I would have between one and three hours before I synced forward again. The countdown began.

It was noon, May 8, 2039, and a flowery aroma hung in the air. Amara was driving me down the country road in a new sedan I didn't recognize. Sporty but dinged up, it had a full backseat into which I glanced to find a steel pole mounted in the center with handcuffs and ankle cuffs, presumably a restraining device for arrests. The cornfields were plowed and bare save for a few fields covered in white crystalline foam. The rows whizzed by the window, gleaming in the sunlight and looking like acres of diamonds. Last year I had watched from the sitting room as one of the neighboring fields was sprayed with foam

Syncing Forward

from the back of a large green tractor, and I wondered what the substance was made from. Presumably it protected the seedlings and was nontoxic in nature, but for the life of me I couldn't figure out if they had disposed of it or it eroded away. My unique perspective made it impossible to tell. One minute it was there and the next it was gone.

While I stared mesmerized out at the crystal fields, Amara spoke on the phone to Bella in Spanglish. I listened to half the conversation and chuckled; their banter had much the same tempo as it had when they were younger.

"*Que va a ser un desastre* . . . There is no way they are going to be able to sit together," Amara snapped. "It's not fair to Dad to make him sit with your mother and her new husband after everything she's done . . . I'm not stressing you out. I'm saying it isn't right, and you are going to have to tell the caterer to move around the seating assignments. You want me to call him? Fine, I'll call him . . . I said I'd call him . . . You are so cranky. I'm not instigating . . . Okay, okay. Do you want to talk to Dad or not? Okay, here he is."

Amara reached up and pointed to her ear, then made a motion like she was flicking something off her index finger and onto the windshield in front of me. A video display shone magically from nowhere, and a close-up image of Bella looking both unhappy and utterly stunning met my eyes. It didn't seem to extend to the driver's side of the windshield, and Amara mentioned for me not to worry.

Bella's hair was straightened and tied back in a French braid that looped forward and over her shoulder. Her makeup was painstakingly applied, making her face look so grown-up. Despite all these preparations for her big day, Bella looked aggravated and stressed. Some of that tension eased when she saw me. One less thing to go wrong.

"Hey, Dad. How do you feel?"

Upbeat, stay upbeat, I kept telling myself. "Great. Better than you, which should not be the case on your wedding day. What's wrong, baby?"

"Nothing." She paused. "Well, Amara and I were just talking, and . . . it's not important. Don't worry about it."

"Baby Bella, I was listening to the conversation. What can I do to make you happy?"

Bella wanted a normal wedding with Keith's parents sitting with her own parents at the table next to hers. This problem wasn't a result of my chemopreserved condition—not directly, anyway. Plenty of families had to navigate the uncomfortable waters of divorced parents brought together in awkward moments. It had never come up for me, as my father was dead before my marriage to Miranda and my mother had walked out on us long before that, but it wasn't difficult to sympathize with her feelings. "Ordinary" was a premium quality when it came to my children; the less they had of it, the more they craved it. In a single decision, I could make Bella's stress disappear. That meant, of course, that I would need to sit with my wife, who had left me for another man seven hours ago.

Amara was on another call, presumably with the caterer. Our conversations overlapped, so concentrating on Bella became difficult, let alone making out what Amara was saying to the caterer. I thought I heard something about cutting the table in half, but I couldn't be sure. Everyone's conversation ground to a halt when our car banked a turn and we almost slammed into a wide-load tractor carrying a tarp-covered load that extended into our lane. Amara swung the car to the right and to the edge of a rut that I figured would snap the axle for sure. At the last moment, she yanked the car back to the left and onto the road.

"Sorry, Daddy, I didn't see him coming around the corner," Amara confessed, then returned her attention to the caterer.

The near miss had my heart pumping, and I shouted out several involuntary expletives before my younger daughter was able to regain my attention. "Bella, if you want me to, I'll sit at the table with your mom." It was going to be painful, but I girded myself and added, "It's not like I am going to have to spend the whole day with her."

Syncing Forward

The disappointment shifted to Amara in an instant. My baby girl lit up and blew me a kiss before hanging up. Amara's dour appearance went hand in hand with a simple "Never mind" that she whined into the phone before hanging up. About three minutes passed before either of us spoke.

"I can't believe you are going to sit with *her*," Amara groused.

"Are you saying you haven't talked to your mother since the year 2033?" I looked at her, exasperated. "Do I have that right, Amara? Really?"

"I've been busy," she answered flatly, her hands gripping the steering wheel at nine and three o'clock.

"For six years?"

"Sorry, Daddy. Sorry that I've been simultaneously trying to take care of my father, who spends his days living like a statue, while fighting organized crime and hunting down a terrorist group that has eluded capture for almost two decades while planning a wedding for my sister. I think I can safely say I've been busy."

"You and I can be as angry as we want, but it won't change the fact that your mother is going to be there. And it's your sister's wedding, so both of us need to suck it up."

"Yeah, and you did such a great job forgiving your mother for walking out on you." Amara's talent for gut-punching somebody with a single comment had not been lost, and the brutal truth panged away at me. But it wasn't as if I had been dragging my heels. When exactly was I going to do this? The nondisclosure agreement alone prevented me from reaching out to my mom. I selfishly took some relief in this fact, as there were years of bitter silence between us that I couldn't deal with on top of everything else.

When we lost our emergency housing in Texas after the hurricane, my father refused to move in with my grandparents. He was a stubborn man to the core, and no amount of pleading by my mother could convince him to do otherwise. They fought for weeks while we moved from hotel to hotel, our money disappearing, the jobs never coming. My mother threatened to take us to our grandfather's house and leave my dad, but my father wouldn't have any of it. Then one morning she was gone. No note. No good-bye. Years later she tried to reconcile with me and Jacob, but I wouldn't budge. Jacob supposedly kept in touch with her, although he rarely brought it up. He knew how I felt.

So here I was lecturing my daughter to forgive Miranda for the same crimes against family—my hypocritical words were like water against a rock. I decided to change the topic quickly to keep her from brooding on Miranda's presence at the wedding.

"You seem to be favoring one arm over the other. Are you hurt?" I asked.

Amara gave me a sideways look. "Bella told you, huh?"

Dang it, the woman was quick. "Wow, you couldn't even let me pretend that I was observant enough to notice your injury?"

"I told her not to say anything. You know, if it wasn't her wedding day I'd smack her." Amara shook her head and took her left hand off the wheel to bite at her cuticles. "Well, whatever she told you, it isn't as bad as it sounds. My right eardrum has been completely repaired, and I can't even feel where they repaired my ribs anymore. It's the burn that's still tender; that and where the orthotic robot was inserted. Ivan—my partner—was burned on a much bigger section of his chest, and he's doing much better. It's because I'm allergic to the new burn treatment, that's all, so I'm stuck with technology from the twenties."

Burns? Broken ribs? Popped eardrum? I'd suspected it was bad, but her injuries were much worse than I had anticipated. I didn't want to sound shocked, though, since Amara assumed I knew more than I did. Instead, I backpedaled purposefully to keep her talking. "You don't have to talk about it if you don't want to," I told her. It worked.

"I do want to tell you, though. Bella always makes things worse than they really are. Okay, well, it's pretty bad taking a slab of concrete

Syncing Forward

to your chest, but we got really lucky considering the size of the explosion. And what Bella doesn't know is how close we got, Daddy. I mean, if I had just shot the son of a bitch, we might have a cure for you right now."

"What are you talking about?" My inquiry was sincere now.

"It was Millennial, Daddy. I found one of their crypts. They sleep in them like freaking vampires, drugged up in a state of chemopreservation, but they don't wake up like you do. I found that out. The fifth vial Dr. Bruchmuller was going to inject you with? It's some type of drug that accelerates the forward syncing process and knocks you out. You fall asleep in one decade, wake up in another."

"So they aren't sitting around in the crypts playing poker?" I joked.

Amara grinned. "It's unlikely. Anyway, we had our suspect cornered in his crypt. They built it into the foundation of an office building in Washington. Daddy, they camouflaged it to make it look like a wall with pipes. It was locked up as tight as a drum, so we called for backup. We were playing it safe, following procedure. That's when he blew the whole damned thing up. If it wasn't for a steel pillar that was in the way, the blast would have killed us for sure. Ivan was banged up real bad, but we pulled each other out of there before the whole building came down . . ."

She was talking but I was getting tunnel vision, and it wasn't from the drugs or the driving. Amara was telling her tale like she had spent the day window shopping at the mall. Every step my daughter described felt as if I had shoved her into the inferno of the explosion myself. Her story of her escape brought me minor relief, leaving a sickly residue of tension in the pit of my stomach.

" . . . as it was, the evidence got destroyed. Nothing left. Not even a molecule." She looked over at my pale expression, and suddenly concern shone on her face. "Daddy, are you okay? Are you slowing?"

I waved my hand. "No, no, I'm fine. Dandy really. No syncing forward or backward or sideways. Just—" I composed myself. "Just trying to get used to the fact that you've got a job that puts you in harm's way."

"You're not going to start in on me, are you?"

"No. It's your life, and I support you. And I hate to say this, but I need you to catch these people. I can't keep moving forward like this."

I meant it. Sort of. I kept telling myself to be encouraging, that if anyone could capture one of these terrorists, it would be my daughter. That maybe she was exaggerating about how bad it really was. I nodded with as much enthusiasm as I could muster while Amara confided in me details kept from the general public. Homeland Defense was working with MI5 from the United Kingdom on what they believed to be the hottest target in the world: the Visser brothers.

I remembered the article Amara had sent me years ago when two scientists —twin brothers, no less— decided to network themselves to each other. If that event garnered the attention of Millennial, they never made it known, but later the brothers combined the genetic material of their children with the networking technology and were able to make remarkable achievements in communicating with their newborns. The collective intelligence of the networked family had reportedly hit an IQ over 200. While I didn't know a darn thing about what made a cell phone work, it sounded like an achievement that could change the world. British Intelligence felt the same way, and they were sure that the Visser brothers were a prime target for the neo-Luddite inclinations of Millennial. Homeland Defense was sending Amara to the UK after the wedding.

I needed that antidote, and there were hundreds of samples of it hidden around the world. It was there for the taking if only somebody could find one of these booby-trapped crypts and somehow disarm it. One dosage of whatever drug they used to bring themselves out of chemopreservation, and my life could be my own again. But how? And at what cost? Unlike my own bad luck at stumbling upon Bruchmuller's unauthorized research, Amara thrust herself into the thick of finding Millennial and discerning their secrets.

Syncing Forward

My own poor judgment had gotten me into this mess, but perhaps Amara's obsession would result in my salvation.

"Any word on the other person at Walter Reed? Were you able to confirm there was another person who had been injected with the Millennial drug?" I inquired.

"All my friendly contacts at Walter Reed were wiped after that debacle with the nanotreatment. I've got nothing from them yet . . ." Amara stopped short of saying the word *but,* as if there was some other tidbit of information she wasn't ready to share. Normally I would have pressed her, but we happened to pull into the parking lot of a church with a weathered steeple and peeling paint. It was time.

My elder daughter rubbed my arm sorrowfully and asked if I was okay. I nodded and took a deep breath. A stranger with a tan suit and a graying mustache opened the back door and hurriedly waved us into the church. I was going from one drama to the next. One child couldn't let go, while the other child I was giving away. Every father feels apprehension on his daughter's wedding day, but from where I was sitting, it had only been about three days ago when Bella was my seven-year-old baby girl. Three days to flush my marriage, lose my home, and watch my sweet daughter marry a man I didn't know. I stepped over the door's raised threshold.

Chapter 25

It was May 15, 2039. The last seventeen years had zipped by as if I'd been encapsulated in some torturous time machine. Now that I was synced back into normal time, I was still being hurried about. The heavyset man who met us at the side door of the church was Robert Heffley, the groom's father. A handshake, an inquisitive look, a hurried pace through the narrow hallway to the rhythm of Robert's labored breathing and I entered the church.

Murmuring sounds grew louder as we made our way to the back of the church, which was filled with strangers on one half and several mildly familiar faces on the other. A sea of Hispanic hair in one section indicated my wife's family, and one of the men looked like Miranda's little nephew Ignacio. Hell, standing there was like being confronted with a vivid dream from my childhood.

Robert whispered it was nice to meet me and went to sit up in the front pew. As he shuffled to the front of the church, I caught a glimpse of Miranda between the bobbing heads in the crowd of a hundred or so. Feet were tapping in impatient anticipation, as the wedding had been delayed by over an hour. Nobody knew the true nature of the delay except, presumably, for our immediate families. I was looking at the back of a blue-haired woman with a tacky orange dress, when she whispered that she'd heard the father of the bride was an alcoholic and the cause of the wait. The middle-aged woman next to the elderly lady tapped her on her wrinkly arm waddle and thumbed in my direction. Several pairs of eyes swiveled my way, and then the hushes spread quickly.

Amara arm-hooked me and pulled me further into the back into the church, where I melted at the sight of Bella. Twenty-three years old and a picture of beauty from a bridal website, it was hard to believe that this was my Baby Bella. I drove my fingernails into my palms, hoping the dream would end, hoping the hallucination would reveal my madness. Neither happened, and instead I was lightly kissing her on her cheek, whispering how radiant she looked and how proud I was of her. Word was spreading like wildfire that the wedding was finally on, and I barely had a chance to say anything else to Bella before the music started playing.

My younger daughter took a deep breath and smiled nervously. "I'm a little scared, Dad."

I smiled, "You said the same thing when you were six. You thought Santa Claus wasn't coming because you hit your sister."

Bella smiled. "I don't remember that."

I chuckled nervously, "Good, I thought it scarred you for life." Bella reciprocated with a tiny laugh and we both stood there nervously, waiting for the musical cue. Clearing my throat, I put on my best parental hat. "Are you happy with your decision?"

"I think so. Yeah, I'm happy. It's just a big decision, and I want to do this right."

"I think you'll be fine," I said, "as long as you are sure in your heart."

She took my right hand in her left and turned to face the doors. "I'm ready."

"I'm not," I half-joked. It brought a smile back to her face, and I didn't have the heart to tell her I wasn't ready at all. But then we were walking down the aisle, listening to the gasps and ooohs and sniffles from the guests as Bella lit up the church with her loveliness. Keith Heffley stood there waiting near the altar steps. Lifting her arm to give her away was a heavy chore, but I strained through it and found my empty seat on the front pew. Amara looked at me from her maid-of-honor position, and I could see that she was doing her best to hold back the tears.

I stole a quick glance at Miranda, who was dabbing her eyes with a tissue while a white man in his fifties with a shiny bald spot squeezed her hand sympathetically. It was impossible to look away from my wife—my ex-wife—as our gazes met for the briefest of moments. We both knew how difficult the day was for me, but there was nothing we could do to prevent it. That shared moment disappeared as all thoughts and eyes went to the bride and groom. Their magical moment was underway.

It was sixty minutes on the nose from the time I was synced back to when the vows were completed. Mrs. Bella James-Heffley stepped past us, broadly showing off her gleaming white smile as she was carried away through the crowd's elation. Amara approached me quickly and whispered in my ear to make sure I was feeling well. I told her I was fine, and she gave me a quick peck on the cheek and told me to stay with Robert before she vanished into the crowd.

The aging Anholt Hotel sat on the edge of the town of Beacon, one of the few reception halls left in the area. Friends and family had brought multiple platters of homemade food, supplying the dinner. The delicious food was almost enough to mask the musty smell of the hall. To be honest, I was pleasantly shocked that Bella had gone with such a modest arrangement for her wedding, and I told my new in-laws as much. Leann Heffley, Keith's mother, filled in the blanks for me, enlightening me about how Bella didn't want to be seen as the rich girl from the top of the hill. With so many people struggling to get by with paying their bills, Bella felt the right thing to do was to have a wedding that was on par with other weddings from the area. The one thing she didn't penny-pinch was an open bar for everybody, and it took a short minute for the line to stretch across the room as men and women waited for their liquid encouragement. Amara held two degrees, but Bella was clever enough to know you keep your guests happy with free booze.

My own seat was clear on the far side of the table, with my in-laws keeping me a good distance from my ex-wife—most certainly the work of Amara. Guests were filing into the room still, and I supposed I should have been on the lookout for family members whom I hadn't seen for many years, but I was distracted by more carnal options. Steaming bratwursts and pepperoni-laced macaroni taunted me mercilessly, food that Amara forbade me from even considering as their intoxicating aromas floated through the room. I asked why, knowing full well the answer would be the same as always: the food would decay within me long before it was digested.

"Beer?" a voice offered from behind me. I turned to see Miranda standing over me in a green dress. She had two long-necked bottles of a brand I didn't recognize. Both were open and frosty and provided too much of a temptation to say no. I stood up and took a long look at my former wife. Miranda had kept herself well maintained—she certainly didn't look like she was fifty years old, even though she was. Her hair had been dyed for sure, and she wore her foundation noticeably thicker, perhaps to cover up wrinkles that were starting to appear around eyes and in her cheeks. My wife's expression must have looked a lot like mine: the poignant moment in our lives had finally come when our baby girl became a married woman. This milestone we could both still share, despite our separate lives.

"Thanks." I took the bottle and dared a sip. It was probably pretty average, but at that moment in time, it was the best beer I had ever tasted.

After enjoying a swig of the carbonated beverage, I opened my eyes to see Miranda staring at me. "How are you doing with all this?"

"Worse than you," I responded honestly.

"I can imagine." She flashed me the saddest smile I'd ever seen. "Martin, I know I'm not your favorite person right now, but I did want to say hello, and thanks for convincing Amara to let me come."

I didn't dare tell Miranda what our daughter said in the car. "Did Amara talk to you yet?"

"No. And I don't think she will. But I miss my daughter, so I'll take what I can get." She nodded as if she had to convince herself that Amara's lack of communication was a good thing. Maybe it was—some form of begrudging forgiveness hidden underneath all that anger. It was awful not having the time to work this through with either of them, watching the fleeting years go by with no resolution. Miranda's heart was as broken as Amara's was hardened.

Miranda pointed to some of her family, catching me up on which kids had grown into which adults. A lovely grin appeared on her face as she spoke of her nephews and their children, and each sentence from my former wife's mouth was a blade that cut deeply into me—making me wish we could reconcile, but knowing she was never going to be my wife again.

"Any word from the doctors on a more-permanent cure?" A glimmer of hope sparkled in her eyes.

"Nope. This is about as good as it gets for now. I've got an hour left, at best."

The glimmer went out as fast as it appeared. She knew how I felt, her dark penetrating eyes looking into me, reading me intimately, not the cold way I would interview a stranger but from years of closeness. "Martin, I'm so sorry that you're still . . . like this."

I choked up a little but managed a "me too."

Miranda looked over my shoulder, and when I turned, I could see Amara glowering back at her with her arms folded. She refused to come any closer—Miranda was a pariah. It was enough to break the moment between us—not that it was anything more than a whisper of hope anyway.

"Es el mismo perro con distinto collar," she moaned. "It appears your bodyguard doesn't want me near you."

I shook my head. "I really wish the two of you would patch things up. This is insanity that she's let this fester. How long has it been since you two actually spoke? Six years?"

Miranda took a big swig of her bottle and looked down remorsefully. "I know I'm not a perfect person, but I've tried to make amends. Every year I send her a birthday card and a Christmas card, and not just an e-card—a real card. I invite her over for Thanksgiving to my mami and papi's. She turns me down every time. She visits her nana and papa when I'm not there, lies to them and tells them that she's working on the holidays. My mother is in early-stage dementia, so

Syncing Forward

she believes everything Amara tells her, but my father isn't stupid. He knows we're fighting. The whole thing is a mess."

"Sorry about that. And sorry to hear about your mom. Please tell them I said hello." The words came automatically, but I had no idea what they knew about me or what they could know about me. I put my hand on Miranda's shoulder to console her and felt a surge of loss. My wife's skin against my fingertips was a cruel reminder of my life as it could have been.

Bella swooped in, gave her mom a peck on the cheek, then took me by the arm to steal me away. I gave a little wave to Miranda as I walked away. She waved her fingers in return as her new husband came back, wrapping his arm low around her waist. He might as well have pissed on her leg to mark his territory. Who knew what he knew about what was going on, but he certainly didn't seem sympathetic at all. The glare of his eyes, his shoulders squared off in my direction: this was a man unafraid of a conflict, but I wasn't about to give him one. I reminded myself that Miranda didn't leave me for him—she simply left.

"Dad, you look really good," Bella beamed. "How are you feeling? Any problems?"

"No, I feel swell," I assured her.

"You look sad. Is it Mom?" She studied me thoughtfully and continued as if I had answered her. "You made me really proud today, Dad. This hasn't been easy for you. I love you so much. You know that, right?"

I hugged her and nodded, afraid that my voice would crack if I spoke.

We walked across the banquet hall, and the back of my knuckles occasionally brushed against the frilly fabric of her wedding dress. "Would you like a big surprise? A really big surprise?" she asked.

"Sure."

"Turn around."

It was Jacob. My brother.

"Hey, little bro."

"Holy crap!" I shouted. "Jacob, how the heck are you?"

His face was wrinkling and his hair was graying, but it was my brother just the same. The last time I'd seen him was at his fortieth birthday party. Now he was in his late fifties, pudgy around the center, with a weathered tanned face. My brother's hands and arms were dotted sparsely with age spots. He still had a full set of hair, combed neatly back so the comb marks could still be seen in his silver top. Dang if he didn't look like our dad when we were growing up.

I reached out and wrapped my arms around him as he did the same to me. We embraced in a bear hug that went on so long, it drew more than a few awkward stares from the wedding reception. I didn't care. This was my older brother. My best friend. We'd had our share of ups and downs, but we always bounced back. Jacob was the one person I counted on after our mother walked out and our dad went off the deep end. Homeless nights living in an old beat-up Dodge. Helping me pay for community college classes. Sneaking my first beer at Charlie's Bar & Grill when I was only seventeen. Gut-punching me when I tried to start a fight with a man twice my size. Dragging my adolescent butt to church and praising God when I thought we didn't have a dang thing to be thankful for. If there was anything positive about my hellish condition, it had to be a fresh appreciation for my older brother.

"You look . . ." Jacob gasped, firmly holding my shoulders. "So young! Is that makeup you're wearing?"

"Yeah," I admitted, suddenly self-conscious. "It's a long story that the girls can fill you in on."

"Look at you!" he kept repeating. "Bella and Amara brought me up to speed on your condition, but I have to admit I had a hard time believing it, even after I signed the nondisclosure agreements your company eemed me."

"Eemed?"

Syncing Forward

"E-mailed, but nobody calls it that anymore. They just call it eeming."

"Ahh. So how are the kids? How is Lily?"

"How do you know about Lily?" Jacob looked confused. "I'm not sure what you know and don't know."

"Hey, Bro, I know you didn't get to find out much about me, but the girls kept me well informed about you. Remarried a pretty blonde. Crystal and Darren seem to like her. Darren is an electrician, last I heard, and Crystal was doing something in clothing sales, I think?"

Jacob chuckled. "Well, your nephew Darren is still working as an electrician, but now he's on the Texas Army base near the eastern border. He'd be here except for work obligations. Crystal lost her job and came back to live with us in Dallas. But overall things are as good as can be expected. They're both right over there talking to Amara."

I looked at my older daughter, who was chatting it up with Crystal and Lily. On more than one occasion, she peered over and checked on Jacob and me. Turning my attention back to my brother, I dug into the details. "The girls told me you were in Tucson. When did you move?"

Jacob threw out his hands in exasperation. "Ahh! You don't know! Tucson doesn't exist anymore. The city, the whole damned city, was invaded six months ago, half of it practically burned to the ground."

I cocked my head and threw him an incredulous look. "Invaded? You're pulling my leg."

"I wish I was. The Cartel Alliance came across the border and took everything from Yuma to Tucson. The Governance Army tried to beat them back, but they were armed to the teeth."

I didn't understand any of what he was telling me. Jacob had to explain that after Texas and other states seceded, the US government engaged them in a standoff in New Orleans that almost led to a second civil war. The president backed off at the last moment, but sealed the borders and imposed an embargo on the new American Governance that cut a swath right up the middle of the United States. While civil war was an unpopular option for the people on both sides, it didn't keep the government from cooperating with more nefarious forces.

Cartel Alianzia, or Cartel Alliance, had started off as a rogue state within Mexican borders, funded almost exclusively by drug money. Legalization of drugs within the US turned the Alianzia into an economic power with unmatched ruthlessness. After years of deadly attacks, the Mexican government acquiesced and gave up on the land near the border. Unhampered in the south, the drug nation took their business full force to the north.

The Cartel Alliance moved in from Tijuana and took the border crossings in California by force, stopping just shy of San Diego. Tucson and Yuma followed shortly thereafter. Jacob, Lily, and the twins got out, but they lost their house and most of their belongings. The Alliance tried to take El Paso but was carpet-bombed by the Texas Air Wing. They tried again until Governor Hollister threatened to nuke every city under the drug lords' control. The violence along the American Governance border finally ceased.

"Turns out the US was funneling arms to the Cartel to break Texas, cut the head off that old rattler. It's a political nightmare for them now. Bastards can't stand the fact that we don't need them anymore," my brother said proudly.

I wouldn't have believed the tale Jacob told me were it not for both his sincerity and the grim faces around us listening on. Of course, had a man from 1929 gone forward seventeen years, he would have been met with news of the Great Depression, World War II, the invention of jet power, and bombs that could destroy entire cities. My situation wasn't so different, even with the girls feeding me information. There was so much to read and so little time. From where I sat, it was only two hours ago that Tucson was still part of the Governance, and seven hours ago that the Governance didn't even exist. I couldn't spend every precious moment I had scouring articles and watching newscasts—and even if I could, I think I would lose my mind doing it.

Jacob and I meandered over to the ladies, and I got a chance to speak to them face-to-face. My niece Crystal had turned into a stunning young lady who looked to be the spitting image of her deceased mother. She had adopted Jacob's Southern drawl and looked every part the cowgirl, and I found my own drawl creeping back in as well. After she lost her job, Jacob had Crystal taking care of the house chores—much to her chagrin. I spoke with my sister-in-law, Lily, who didn't strike me as terribly conversational. Maybe she was uncomfortable in large settings, I reasoned. Then again, I was a virtual stranger to her, and it might have been her way to be standoffish at first meeting. Amara and Bella later swore to me that she was a very nice woman, so I took their word for it.

Amara remained at my side the whole time we spoke, not saying much, probably not wanting to take me away from Jacob. I found her looking at her watch frequently, and I looked at mine in reactionary fashion to see it had been more than two hours since I had been injected. Any minute, I would sync forward again. Jacob, sensing that I wouldn't be able to talk for much longer, got quiet.

Pulling me to the side, he spoke closely in my ear. "Hey, Marty, I need to apologize about something."

"What?" I looked at him curiously.

"You know I don't rightly understand what your condition is, but many years back Miranda told me you were in a coma, and I had no reason to doubt her word. At the time I told her that she should unplug you, let you die, let you have some peace. I have to admit I'm a bit embarrassed about myself now."

"Jacob, you couldn't have known. You weren't supposed to know. This whole thing is complicated, more than I care to say. But there is no way you should feel bad for looking out for me. After Mom left and Dad died, you did nothing but take care of me, and you did a damn good job too. You've been a good brother, even when you didn't know I was looking. Don't you ever apologize for that again. You got that?"

He embraced me again, nodding in agreement and clearing the lump in his throat. "You know, when this whole border thing gets settled, I'd like you to come and visit us in Texas. In fact, you are welcome to immigrate down there if you'd like."

"Heh, and move in with the rebel traitors?" I quipped.

"Yeah, I suppose you could call us that. Just watch yourself up here. Your liberties don't mean much, even in the so-called Constitution State. Don't trust these government sons of bitches."

"Oh geez, Jacob. The years have passed, but you still sound exactly the same. *Paranoia, paranoia, everybody's coming to get me . . .*" I sang an old song we'd grown up to. It was an amazing experience to be reunited with my brother after so long. I daresay it made me near-on hopeful.

"Seriously, though, I'd love to see you down in the Lone Star Nation," he said. "Unless your new son-in-law has anything big brewing here, I bet he'd pick up a job right quick."

Turning to Bella, I asked, "So how would Keith feel about moving to Texas?"

"Dad, can we have our honeymoon before you start moving us to a different country?" She giggled. Texas a different country—that was going to take some getting used to.

"Love ya, little bro. Even if you are a drone."

"Freak." I stuck it back to him with a backhanded jab to the gut. Eye rolls came from the women, reminding us to stop acting like children.

Amara glanced at a minitablet and gave me a look. Actually, it was *the* look. Whatever sensors were still hooked up to me were sending her signals that this pause in time was coming to an end. The disappointment made my shoulders slump and my head bow. It just wasn't enough time.

Syncing Forward

Just then, the DJ made the announcement that we would begin the dancing soon and called for the father of the bride and the bride herself to come up to the front. Bella was laughing and hooting with some friends, her face bright and happy, her cheeks rosy. Two of her girlfriends followed, equally chipper. "Dad! You ready to dance with me?"

Amara shook her head and answered for me, "Sis, Daddy is going to be sitting this one out."

The girls behind her were calling out, "Nooooo, you gotta dance with Bella on her wedding day!" but Bella's smile faded as she looked back and forth from me to her sister. The silent communication between us was enough to tell her my visit was ending. The excitement and joy Bella must have been feeling was stolen from her and replaced with the terrible feeling of falling short. I felt it too. We were so close to making it the perfect day for her.

She gave me a hug around my neck and squeezed me tightly. Her face was wet with tears, and I could see she was on the verge of a breakdown. "Please, Dad," she whispered. "It's my wedding, we can doaquickdanceokay? Justtwominutes."

The jubilant moment of the wedding was crushed by the stark reality of my chemopreservative condition. *I can get through one dance,* I thought to myself. But my equilibrium started to go, and the noise of the reception hall was getting muffled. I was slowing, and there was no stopping it. "I better go, Baby," I told her, the nausea bubbling in my stomach. "God knows I would stay if I could, but I'm . . ."

She hesitated and put her hand up to her cheek to stifle the sadness. "Ilove youDad. Thankyou forbeinghere for myspecial day." Then she slowly pulled her arms off me and stepped back, composing herself so her friends would not be suspicious. She wiped the tears from her face and took a deep breath to steady herself. Her girlfriends were chanting "Dance! Dance!" behind her, ignorant of the drama that was unfolding ten feet from them.

"Amara, is my makeup okay?" she asked her sister quietly.

Amara nodded slightly, giving her the go-ahead to turn around without any embarrassment.

Bella faked an exaggerated a look of disapproval as she turned to face the women. "Nah, I don't need to dance with him. He's a terrible dancer anyway! My mom always complained about him stepping on her feet."

One girl giggled while the other two made sympathy sounds that you might hear when somebody sees a baby crying or a puppy falling. Bella covered the moment perfectly, and Amara guided me to the door. I was stumbling and felt as if I was about to fall, when Keith Heffley came up from behind and grabbed my other arm. My son-in-law said something about not to worry as we moved through the crowd. We passed the older woman from the church, and I heard her say, "SeeItoldyouhe'sadrunk."

I caught a glimpse of Miranda staring, her hand over her mouth. Jacob put his hand up to wave and said something, but I had no idea what. And then I was out to the parking lot. Keith ran up from behind and grabbed the car door for me. It was a good thing he was spry for his size, as I threw up right at his feet. He jumped back, deftly avoiding my projectile vomit by inches. The new groom reached into his tuxedo pocket and pulled out a decorative handkerchief. He took me by the arm and wiped my face as I stumbled against the adjacent car.

"Mr.Jamesyouokay tostandup ordoyou wanttosit inthecar?"

I couldn't talk, but I pointed to the seat. Keith eased me into the seat and put the cloth in my hand. "Heretake thisjustincase." My son-in-law looked up at Amara. "Whatdowedonow?"

Amara was already prepping a hypospray injector with the second drug designed by Innovo—the one designed to help me sync forward faster so I wouldn't have to wait to be brought back. It meant visiting again in ten months instead of nine years. Not ideal by a long shot, but beggars can't be choosers. "Weinjecthimtwice nowandthen twicemorewhen Igethimup tothelab."

Syncing Forward

A blurry figure came out the side door of the reception hall and asked if everything was okay, but Keith waved him off.

"GobacktothepartyKeith," Amara shooed him away.

"Heyhesmyfamilynowtoo I'llhelp."

Amara took a forceful tone. "GoBella'sgoingtoneedyourightnow."

Keith unwillingly stepped back and waved to me. "MrJamesfeelbetterI'lltalktoyousoon."

Amara circled the car, almost slipping on the asphalt in what was left of the beer I'd downed earlier. She was moving at what looked like double speed. My daughter pulled my suit jacket off my shoulder and administered the hypospray right through my shirt. It stung mildly, but at least the pain kept my mind off the desire to heave. Amara zipped into the driver's side of her car and shot me in the left arm too. I watched her take off her shoes, note the smell of vomit on them, and discard them outside the car.

"Ineverlikedthoseheelsanyway," I heard her grumble.

Reaching into the back of the car, she pulled out a plastic bag with hair accessories and hair spray cans. She emptied it in a hurry and put the bag in my hands. I pulled it close to my chest in anticipation of losing more of my dinner on the drive home.

It wasn't possible for me to tell if Amara was speeding or not. She might have been going fifteen miles an hour for all I knew. To me, that car was a fighter jet screaming along the country road. I stuffed my face in the bag and purged my stomach of every ounce of bile.

It wasn't long before I was back in the sitting room. The Innovo techs brushed my teeth and rinsed my mouth out with something minty. The instrumentation was hooked back up, and my tear-jet set was hooked back up to my eyes so I could see normally. The wedding was still fresh in my mind. Bella prancing about with her friends. My new son-in-law looking smitten over his bride. Jacob and my niece. Miranda and me chatting, trying to bridge the passage of time. It was an emotional roller coaster, and I didn't have the strength to do anything but ride out the dips and turns.

Amara looked at me apologetically, her tears flowing, her blurry movements halted as she drew close to my face and spoke slowly, but I was already syncing forward at full speed, and I couldn't make out what she said. She must have realized her words were falling on deaf ears, because she typed a message on the screen.

DADDY I'M GOING TO FIX THIS. I SWEAR I'M GOING TO.

Syncing Forward

Chapter 26

Back in the sitting room, I felt my body cramping from exhaustion. Fatigue set in. By my best guess, I had been awake for a perceived twenty-one hours in a row and managed to fly through eighteen years in three and a half days. I feared closing my eyes, knowing that even barely decent rest could find me two and a half years into the future. I couldn't fall asleep. Not again. What would I miss? Would I wake up at all? I felt painfully aware of how few years there were in a person's life, my mind dwelling on the wrinkles in my brother's face. It was to those thoughts that I succumbed to sleep.

Innovo called it V-5322. Amara called it the Pause. I called it pain.

The second time the drug was administered, I woke to the fiery pain of the V-5322 coursing through my limbs. It was a Charlie horse in every muscle in my body. It was a burn on every square inch of my skin. That's what the Pause felt like.

Make it stop! Make it stop! That was the only thought going through my brainpan while I thrashed about and opened my eyes to a sunlit day that blinded me to anything else. Then the agony was gone, as if somebody had turned off a spigot. But even though the torment vanished, my nerves were as frazzled as a cat playing with a hair dryer cord, and my body shuddered involuntarily.

"WakeupDaddy," I heard Amara's voice. "Comeon comeon you cando it, there you go. That's it. Can you hear me?"

I nodded. She dabbed my lips with a wet cloth, and then used a squeeze bottle to wet my mouth with something that tasted like watered-down lemonade. I grabbed it clumsily and drank as quickly as I dared while I felt her vigorously massaging my calves and then my arms and then my neck.

W Lawrence

I tried focusing my eyes, but the light was very bright. All I knew was that I was in the back of a large vehicle out on the roadside. No, a roundabout street. There were people walking everywhere and more than a few curious heads looking in our direction. Old shops, abandoned grocery carts, large tricycles with two seats and baskets in the back rolling alongside the cars, scooters with diminutive sidecars zipping like daredevils in between them all.

"Where are we?" I managed to squeeze out while sitting up.

Amara was all business as she pulled her long black hair into a ponytail, checked the clip in her pistol, then holstered her firearm. Most of the people who were staring walked quickly away. She said, "Easton, Pennsylvania. Daddy, you need to listen to me, because we don't have much time. I'm here with my partners, Ivan and Everett. Everett is up on the rooftop of the diner across the street. Ivan is out in the crowd. We found Bernard Rendell. Do you remember him?"

"Bernard Rendell?" I repeated. "Bald, tall as a flagpole. Yeah. He's the only one left from the group that kidnapped me."

"I was able to make contact with him. My supervisor doesn't know. Nobody knows except the three of us. We're making a deal."

"Wait. What kind of deal?"

"For the cure. They call it Remedium. Rendell is willing to give it up, but only by injecting you with it. He won't give it to us otherwise."

"Why?" My blood was pumping, and it felt like a migraine was coming on strong. Rubbing my temples, I closed my eyes and tried to digest what was going on, but the hope building in me was tangible.

"They don't want us replicating their drug. My guess is they feel confident that by administering it directly, the Remedium will be absorbed before anyone can draw it back out of your system. Makes sense. It's been their secret for twenty-four years, and we don't exactly have much to bargain with."

"What do they want in return?"

She ignored my question, helped me to my feet, and put a tiny piece of plastic behind my ear. "This is your walk-n-talk. You'll be on our channel. Even a whisper and we'll hear you. I don't plan on leaving your side, but if things go sideways, we need to be able to talk."

I was wearing ripped pants and a dirty sweatshirt with "University of Iowa" in big letters across the front. Amara didn't look any better, with dusty black jeans and a worn flannel shirt that covered her pistol. I gestured for her to stop so I could get caught up on what was happening, but she grabbed a red cooler, locked the SUV, and pulled me along, telling me we needed to get moving.

Amara had managed to make a deal. Even with the unknown looming ahead of us, I felt a pep in my step that hadn't been there for Bella's wedding. This meeting was dangerous and questionable, and to continue forward was risking everything. I kept telling myself that I had to trust Amara's judgment, that she wanted me cured as much as I did. However, this was my daughter—my once nine-year-old daughter—who was leading me into a situation that was almost as uncertain to her as it was to me.

"When are we? How long this time?" It was a question I dreaded asking, but I needed an answer regardless.

"June 5, 2040. Bella and Keith had their one-year anniversary a few weeks ago. We could have woken you, but you were exhausted, so we dosed you with low levels of the Pause drug. It managed to speed up your cellular activity enough for you to get some rest."

She could see the confusion on my face and explained as we walked. "Your body is operating at a ratio of one day to about our 163 days. You still need sleep, Daddy, but if we waited for you to have good night's rest, it would be three and a half years, and we couldn't afford to miss this chance today. So we sped up your cells with small doses of the Pause in order to get you to rest faster."

"That's dang confusing," I responded.

"Please don't make me explain it again." She flashed a wry grin that disappeared quickly.

Easton's Main Street must have been quite upscale at one point. Walking the circle was like looking at a beautiful woman through a filthy window. Façades were crumbling. Paint peeling. Glass boarded up. As we moved through the masses of people, hands went up from the sidewalk looking for handouts. Graffiti covered many of the walls and windows, although it looked more like stenciling than spray paint in some cases. A group of teenagers all wearing blue stood on a corner openly peddling bags of what could only be drugs.

"Are we safe here?" I asked.

"Not really."

"Does your sister know what we're doing?"

"No."

"Franciscus doesn't know what we're doing either?"

"No."

"Jesus, Amara, what have you gotten us into?"

"I'm trying to save you. Now, Daddy, can you please move your ass a little faster? We have a small window to work inside."

"Where are we going?"

"There." She pointed to a broken white monolith poking out of a fountain that sat atop the center of a roundabout. Half the surrounding trees were dead, and the ones that were in blossom looked rather sickly. Weeds popped out of the sidewalk, and people bathed in the fountain's waters at the base of the monolith.

Amara started trotting, and I stepped up my pace to keep up as we ran the gauntlet of tricycles and compact cars. On more than one occasion I found myself cussing, as the drivers seemed bent on running us over. Amara had told me this was Pennsylvania, but had she not, I would have likened it to a Third-World country. While I had never been to Easton before, I was sure that it had never looked so run-down. If this was what other major cities were like, it made perfect sense that Innovo wanted me in the country. By the time we reached the pedestrians, I let out a sigh of relief and sent a quick prayer of thanks to Saint Christopher for not letting me get squashed like a bug.

Syncing Forward

"Now we wait," Amara told me, answering my question before I could ask it. She spoke calmly to the air. "Everett, you have eyes on our target?"

I heard a man's voice in my left ear. "Eyes on South Third and both sides of Northampton Street. No target in sight. You can bet they have peeps on you two already, though."

"Verdad."

Another man spoke right after. "North Third's got nada. Amara, how's your papa over there?"

Amara smiled cautiously at me. "He's on the comm right now, Ivan. Say hi."

"Gentlemen, I have no idea where you are or what you are doing, but I trust you have my daughter's best interests in mind." What else was I going to say? I knew their names from pics Amara sent me, but beyond that I was a man out of place and time and surrounded by strangers.

"Don't you worry, Mr. James." Everett spoke in a thick New York accent. "*Eso está al otro lado.* From where I'm watchin', I'll ventilate anybody who messes with your little girl."

Amara cut in. "Hey, Everett. This little girl is going to shove a boot up your ass if you don't cut the chatter. Eyes open, mouths closed."

He chuckled. "We're off the clock, A. You can't order me around."

Ivan chimed in as well. "A, you gotta be nice to the volunteers."

Amara rolled her eyes. "Come on, guys, I need you two sharp on this. This is my family on the line."

The idle banter died away, and we were left with the sounds of kids laughing and bums fighting and cars honking at scooters and tricycles. We stood there in silence, watching the folk around us conduct their business, waiting for all six-and-a-half feet of Bernard Rendell to show up. I was anxious about him potentially sneaking up on us, although how he could do that when he stood a head above everyone else, I couldn't imagine.

After a few minutes I spoke up. "Amara, can I ask a question without you putting a boot up *my* ass?"

She rolled her eyes. "I knew you were going to make a comment about that."

"Sorry, but I'm not used to you talking like a truck driver."

"Occupational hazard."

"Fair enough." I kept my eyes scanning the horizon. "Are you going to get in trouble for this? I don't want to get cured just so I can visit you in a jail cell."

"Give me some credit, Daddy. None of us would be here if we thought it wouldn't work. My friends trust me, and so should you—"

Everett cut in. "We got Bernard inbound on foot, moving eastbound on Northampton. Scanner shows he's armed with a pistol, and there's a 70 percent chance he's carrying an IED. Stay frosty, Amara. Looks like there's at least one more with him. Male, brown skin, average height, blue jeans, white shirt, Mets baseball cap, nothing on the scanner."

Ivan answered. "I spotted 'em both too. What the hell is it with terrorists and the Mets?"

"Beats the hell out of me," Amara remarked. "I've got them crossing the roundabout. Dear God! Bernard almost got hit by a scooter. If he dies before he gets here, I'm going to be pissed."

I looked across the street, and sure enough it was Bernard, his gait marred by a noticeable limp as he dodged a tricycle carrying bird-filled baskets, then sprinted onto the sidewalk before an old Honda Civic could run him down. He looked at my sweatshirt from about twenty feet away, called to the man in the Mets cap, and walked cautiously in our direction. We walked toward them as well until there were only ten feet separating us. The men were separated by about fifteen feet, but they squared off against us. We stood shoulder to shoulder, and Amara whispered for me to be quiet and let her do the talking.

"That's close enough," Bernard wheezed.

Amara put up her hands. "Fine with me. I don't want you setting off that device you're carrying."

He kept his gaze on Amara. "If you are thinking about trying to disable it with an EM disrupter, think again. It's a hardened switch, and I'll turn you, your father, and everybody within fifty meters into a greasy stain without thinking twice."

"I don't have an EM disrupter, Bernard. Just take it easy, okay?"

"But you're armed." He pointed at her side.

"Yes. I'm armed," she said deliberately. "I've got a pistol on my right hip, but that's where it stays because we are here to make a deal, right? My father doesn't have any weapons. We're cool."

Bernard stole a glance at me and nodded. "Mr. James, good to see you. You haven't aged a day." His chuckle indicated he was pleased with his own humor.

"I wish the feeling was mutual, Hoss. Last time we met, you were voting to leave me under the ruins of Innovo," I said, careful not to move my hands. "I didn't take too kindly to that, Bernard."

He sneered, "Just business. Rajesh and Dieterich tried to save you, and look where it got them."

Amara broke in. "So are we making a deal, Bernard?"

I glanced at a woman with sunglasses who was sitting on the fountain's low wall, sunbathing in the late-spring light, drinking from a bottle of water, handing a piece of candy to a little boy who could have been her son or nephew. My gaze shifted to all the kids playing in the fountain. There had to be thirty of them, innocently enjoying the day, ignorant of the monster who had arrived in their midst. Bernard was definitely telling the truth: the idea that he'd kill every one of those children with the bomb he was carrying was mortifying. It was hard to believe this psychopath had once worked at Innovo under my nose, slapping labels on packages and handing out company mail.

The man in the Mets cap pointed at me and chimed in, "Why is he moving around? Why did you administer the Innovo drug?"

Amara put her hands on her hips. "You didn't give me much choice with your meeting place. How else was I going to get him to this fountain?"

Mets Man spoke over her. "The Remedium might combine with their drug adversely. It might kill him."

"I have the A-542 antidote Innovo designed. It's in this container right here." Amara held up the red cooler she had been toting in her left hand. "There's enough to dose him three times over. We can do it right here. It works quickly. Once he's slowed down again, you can administer the Remedium and keep the rest of the Innovo drugs." She put the cooler on the ground, opened it for them to see inside, then flipped the lid closed again. With her boot she gave it a careful kick, sliding it five yards to Bernard's feet.

Bernard stomped down on the cooler's handle, killing its momentum. He snapped at Amara, "We don't need your attempt at an antidote." He looked about nervously, his hand clasped around something oval-shaped with a wire running up his sleeve. "Who else is here?"

"Just us, Bernard. We came alone."

"Bull crap. You're never alone."

"Bernard, I just want my father back, that's all. He was never supposed to be a target for Millennial. He's a victim here, and he's the only reason I'm on the job. Once he is cured, I'm out of DHD. My resignation will be effective immediately. You'll never have to worry about me looking for you or your people again."

I found myself holding my breath, afraid to move, displaying my hands as wide-open fingers that had nothing to hold. Despite Bernard Rendell's towering stature, his gaunt stare and sunken cheeks made him look more like a skeleton than a giant. He was a man in poor

Syncing Forward

health, maybe knocking on death's door, and that's what made him so terrifying. This man was on the way out, and he didn't have a problem taking out untold numbers of men, women, and children indiscriminately.

"He's going to need to come with us." Bernard instructed Amara as if I wasn't even standing there.

Ivan whispered through the walk-n-talk, "This isn't going so good, Amara. Watch yourself."

Amara took a small step backward and reached carefully for my fingertips. "That wasn't part of the deal. You said you were going to take care of him if I dropped my investigation."

"But the investigation doesn't die with you quitting, now does it?" he retorted. "You've got partners, records, files, pictures, phone records. That's what you told me last time we spoke."

"I exaggerated what we have on Millennial to get you here, Bernard," Amara responded. I wasn't looking at her face, and I couldn't tell if she was lying or not. "We're desperate. Innovo is nowhere close to a cure."

I looked over my shoulder at the woman who had handed the kid candy. She was still sitting up on the wall, drinking from her water bottle, her head pointed in our direction, sunglasses on. The bottle of water had the cap on it, but she kept putting it to her mouth as if she was drinking from it anyway. Nobody forgets to pull the cap off a water bottle unless they are highly distracted.

"If that's the case, you better do what we ask," Bernard threatened. "If you don't, we'll let your father keep going till the world ends. Who knows, maybe he'll outlast us."

I turned my head in the other direction, away from Bernard and Mets Man, and whispered, "There's somebody else here watching us. Female, white, twenties, on the fountain wall, wearing sunglasses and a paisley skirt. Water bottle in her ha—"

"Got her," Ivan answered back.

269

"Send Martin James over to us, and we'll cure him when we feel comfortable that you haven't pulled a fast one." Mets Man had his hand behind his back, maybe sliding it into his back pocket, or maybe grabbing for a weapon. Everett said his scanner was only picking up the one bomb on Bernard, nothing metal on Mets Man.

Amara pushed my hand behind hers while still squarely facing Bernard. "I wish I could trust you to do that, Bernard. How about this: I'll give you passwords to our system. You can wipe out anything you want from our case files."

"Whoa, Amara, you can't do that," Ivan dissented over the walk-n-talk. Everett right afterward.

Bernard and his friend began walking forward. "That might be acceptable, but in that case, we're going to need both of you to come with us to make sure you live up to your end of the bargain."

"Do you have the Remedium with you?" she asked.

"It's close by."

I looked at Bernard, and whether because of my own fear or discernment of his facial queues, I didn't believe him. Mets Man looked too damn eager, and the request for us to go with them was rehearsed. I mumbled to Amara that they were lying while trying not to move my lips. She answered back that she knew, and we both stepped backward.

Amara raised her shaking right hand ever so slightly, sliding her thumb up under the fabric of her untucked flannel shirt. "Bernard, it isn't nice to switch things up at the last minute." Her voice grew more desperate. "How about you cure my father here and now? We leave him here, and I come with you on my own. Is that a good compromise?"

"No," I said out loud, more to my daughter than Bernard. "You can't go with them."

"Daddy, please," she hushed me.

"Got movement behind you," Everett chopped in, "utility van just parked twenty feet on your six and stopping traffic. At least one

Syncing Forward

black male inside eyeballing you from the driver's side. Get out of there."

Bernard grinned. "'Daddy'? How sweet, Amara. Come on, let's get this over with. You can help your *daddy* get better if you both come with us." He stepped forward again, his tone taunting.

Everything happened so fast that I thought I was syncing forward again. Amara said the word *cojelo*, which meant *take it*. A split second later Bernard's hand, which had been gripping the explosive trigger, vanished in a blood-washed stump, pink spray flying up from his wrist.

The muffled sound of rifle shot transmitted through the walk-n-talk, but I couldn't hear a dang thing where I was standing except for the splash of gore striking the pavement. Mets Man looked down in surprise as Amara quick-drew her pistol and fired three shots into him. By the time my eye went from Amara's movements to the Mets cap, he was already dropping to his knees with a red stain through the M in his baseball cap and two more through his chest.

Screams erupted from everywhere, and Amara shouted at me to run for the SUV. Children were being scooped up by mothers and fathers. One woman jumped out into the street and was struck by a motorized tricycle, sending both the rider and the pedestrian sprawling. I heard a horn blaring and screeching tires but didn't look back to witness her fate.

Out of the corner of my eye, I watched the woman with the water bottle sprinting toward the utility van. Amara was in fast pursuit of Bernard's bloody trail. He had lumbered backward into the roundabout, reaching across his body with his opposite arm to grasp the dangling switch.

There were two more popping sounds in my earpiece. Everett must have taken two shots at somebody or something from the roof, but I was moving toward the dead Mets fan. I'd seen plenty of dead bodies in movies and television shows, but this was different. I'd seen bodies at funerals, and when I was a teenager there was an old man who died in a cot next to me at the homeless shelter. I had been unable to sleep, and when I opened my eyes he stared back at me. He took his last breath, and his unblinking stare in the dimly lit room was enough to give me nightmares for years. Now I had seen this Met fan's last breath, but dead at the hands of my daughter and right in front of me. Amara had killed him in cold blood.

My body quivering, I reached out and flipped the bloody body onto its side. A red puddle was forming underneath him, but I forced myself to continue forward, rolling him onto his stomach and checking his back pockets. Half of me wanted to find the Remedium; the other half wanted to find a weapon, something to justify Amara's gunning him down. I found neither. Shoving my fingers into his back pocket and coming up empty-handed, I felt along his belt line, hoping to find anything.

There was a lump, a small egg-shaped plastic ball tucked between his belt and his pants. It could have been just about anything, and perhaps it was a key to where they were storing the Remedium, or a sample, or a clue. But before there was time to inspect it, I heard cars crashing into scooters crashing into cars crashing into tricycles. I palmed the oval and looked up in time to see Amara rolling on top of the hood of a car, then falling to the ground.

"No!" I screamed, sprinting into the roundabout and leaping over a plastic crate filled with broken glass and around a pile of scooters mixed with their riders. I was there at her side as she looked up at me with a road-rash cheek and a black-greased nose. "Amara, are you okay?"

"I'm fine. Help me up." She winced as she grabbed my left hand with both of hers and pulled. "Everett, what's our status?"

"Ivan is on foot chasing after the utility van moving northbound. I took out both tires, but they're riding the rims out of here. Police dispatched an ob-drone, but I took it down. I say we have two minutes before PD puts boots on the ground. We need to bolt, babe."

"Give me thirty secs," she huffed, heading back into the wreckage in the roundabout and moving with purpose to an overturned van. I repeated Everett's concerns, but Amara told me to get to

Syncing Forward

the SUV. Of course I ignored her, trotting on her heels till we came around to a body trapped underneath the vehicle's weight. It was Bernard. His stump of an arm was flailing, crimson trickling from his mouth, his skin even whiter than it had been before.

"Where's the Remedium?" Amara growled as she ground her heel into his chest. "Give it up and I swear on my father's life I will leave your people alone."

Bernard glared hatefully back. "Stuu . . . pid biiitch. You're hunn . . . hunnnting the wronng peop—" He spat up blood. "Ki . . .ll . . . you all."

Amara drove her heel into him harder and snarled at the dying man through her clenched jaw. "Listen, you son of a bitch! You made me. You hear me, Bernard? *You made me* who I am, and I will destroy every last one of you psychotic bastards unless you give me what I want. I will kill all of you!"

I put my hand up and gently slid Amara out of the way. She looked at me incredulously, but with nothing to lose, I bent down close to Bernard's face. "Please, give me my life back. I'm begging you. I swear I will never share the antidote with anyone, just—"

I heard a high-pitched hum and several flickering clicks, almost like the sound of a gas station pump ticking away the gallons on a meter. Bernard heard it too and smiled, mouthing "You're dead" while the blood bubbled up from his mouth. I asked Amara what the sound was coming from, and—as she helped me back up to my feet—she felt the plastic egg in my hand.

"Jesus, Daddy. It's a remote trigger . . . run! *Run!*"

I chucked it as far as I could, but she was yanking me by the hand, screaming it was too late. We sprinted between the cars and tricycles in the pileup, shoving bystanders out of the way as she barked orders over the walk-n-talk. "Everett, clear the roundabout! The bomb is going to go off. Clear it!"

"Crap," Everett squawked back. "Silencer's coming off; keep your heads low. Meet you at Juliet twelve."

W Lawrence

I heard the rifle this time from the rooftop in front of us and to the right. Everyone heard it. The screams resumed as Everett unloaded round after round into anything he could find that wasn't human. Windows, metal sheets, walls. The crowd scattered in every direction at the sound of sniper shots, and Amara and I were almost trampled before we reached the SUV.

The door opened automatically, and I jumped into the back as Amara slid into the driver's seat. Amara was calling out to Ivan on the walk-n-talk, but he wasn't responding. There wasn't any time to strap in, and Amara slammed the vehicle into Reverse, hurling me practically into the front seat as she ran the high-profile vehicle back along the street and wheeled us into an alleyway.

For the second time in four days—or twenty years—I witnessed the scientific prowess of Millennial in the form of an apocalyptic explosion. The flash of white was trailed shortly by a wave of dust and smoke from the direction of the roundabout. The alleyway Amara steered us into protected our SUV from the shock wave, but still we witnessed bricks as they blew from the walls of the building. More people went stumbling and crawling and sprinting away from the hell of Millennial's handiwork.

"Ivan! Damnit, Ivan, answer me!" No answer. "Everett, are you off the roof?"

"Yeah, I'm okay. Juliet eleven heading on foot to Juliet twelve. No sign of Ivan."

Halfway there already, I climbed into the front seat and strapped in as Amara lay on the horn and pulled the SUV out into the crowd. My daughter drove up on the sidewalk and into an alleyway, careened around a turn, and almost ran over a boy in a wheelchair. Our horn blared, and a friend or relative or stranger yanked the boy out of the way. Three more turns and Amara slammed down on the brake.

She climbed out, and I was too stunned to stop her. My ears were ringing from the gunshots and the explosion. My eyes fixed open in shock, I watched Amara run around to the front of the vehicle and hug two men who were dressed like homeless people in the doorway of a closed shop, one carrying a long narrow cardboard box wrapped in "fragile" tape. I barely recognized her teammates from the photos she'd shown me. The reunion didn't last more than a couple seconds before all three climbed into the SUV. Amara was still driving, the men now behind me. The box tipped over on its side, and I could see the barrel of a rifle poking out. Ivan and Everett quickly introduced themselves while we fled the carnage.

"Sorry about that," the large Hispanic man huffed. "I lost my walk-n-talk chasing after the van."

"You're here. We're good," the Caucasian man replied before turning his attention to Amara. "What the hell happened, A?"

Amara stared straight ahead.

"You offered him access to our files?"

Amara said nothing, focused on the road, her knuckles white on the steering wheel.

"We'll talk about it later, E." Ivan slapped his hand on Everett's back.

"Jesus, all those people," Everett mumbled.

The stillness within the SUV was a sharp distinction from the city engulfed in the fire and smoke we were leaving behind. Feelings of relief fought with the tremendous disappointment over failing to find my cure and the terror of Millennial's commitment to protect themselves. And Amara . . .

The only thing worse than knowing my daughter barely lived through Bernard's final moments was the growing recognition she was never, ever, going to stop.

W Lawrence

— Part 5 —

Pause

Syncing Forward

Chapter 27

The third time I experienced the Pause was worse than the second; hopes that my body would grow accustomed to the drug's side effects were long gone. Every nerve in my body fired off sensations of burning, and I wailed myself into a normal speed. Was an animal gnawing its way through my chest? The pain wasn't like the heart attack I had experienced at Walter Reed, but it certainly wasn't any better. All over my body, nerve endings fired off like I was being stabbed with ten thousand pins. I jerked my arms forward only to feel them restrained by burning steel clamps that made my tortured skin scream even more. Coming into clarity, I could see they weren't clamps at all. Instead, Keith and Amara and Bella and the technician Mike Gandry were holding my limbs, grimacing as they watched my misery melt into mere cold chills and shivering.

My eyes swam in their sockets, and every sound clattered against my eardrums. God, I wanted this journey forward to end, to let me spend time with my family, but I didn't know if I could take the pain of the Pause again. The only thing keeping me going was seeing the faces of my kids on the other end of this hell. Two hours syncing back, two hours syncing forward, then enduring another round of anguish . . . Each time I was sure that my body was going to rip open and gush my insides out.

Then, the pain was gone. I could see. Move. Hear. I got gentle kisses from my girls that still felt like scorpion stings to my sensitive skin. I bent my fingers and toes and sat up to a newly painted taupe-colored room. It was Bella's old bedroom, which meant the master bedroom was now occupied by her and Keith. I suppose I might have felt slighted, but I didn't. What use did I have for any room? Maybe the girls felt better knowing I had someplace to call my own. There were pictures of us on the walls and doodads from my past that the kids must have been holding in storage. An old globe still featuring the United States as one nation. A bone-handled knife my father gave me when I was seven. A pewter figurine of the Eiffel Tower from when Innovo flew me out to Paris.

Bella was crying, and Amara didn't look any better. I reached to my baby girl and croaked, "What's wrong, sweetheart? Why are you so upset?"

"Dad, are you okay? We didn't think you were going to make it."

"He's stabilizing," Mike assured everyone while poking at a glass slate. "The V-5322 is fully absorbed. He's good for a couple hours."

Amara wet my throat with the squeeze bottle again, helping me speak. Bella grabbed my hand and looked at me sorrowfully while still speaking with Mike. "Innovo has to come up with something better. This is just torture."

I cupped her hand between both of mine. "I'm fine. This is my third sync. I'm sure it will get better."

Oh crap. I had screwed up. Amara's eyes got as big as saucers for a split second, and she realized my mistake too. "No, Daddy, this is the second time you've used the Pause drug. Not the third. You're confusing this treatment with one of the others."

I nodded and agreed with her, and nobody in the room seemed the wiser. No one knew Amara had used the Pause to sync me out in Easton. Mike Gandry made a comment about how the V-5322 shouldn't have had such an adverse reaction after waiting twenty months, making notes on his pad while walking off. Amara and I shared a look.

It was December 27, 2041, and the family was chomping at the bit to celebrate. After making sure I was synced back, Amara and Bella told me to hurry up and get ready. A comfortable pair of jeans, a sweatshirt, some underwear, and a warm pair of socks were laid out for me to get dressed in. Mike suggested taking a quick shower to rid

Syncing Forward

myself of the chills. I agreed with enthusiasm. Rubbing alcohol may clean you, but a hot shower makes you feel more human.

It was less than two hours ago for me that I was sitting in an SUV, listening to a scanner as police responded to the explosion in Easton. At least five were dead at that point, and who knew how many more after I synced forward. The whole time Amara was cleaning me up so I could return home, I had knots in my stomach. More innocent deaths, more destruction, and I couldn't help but feel their blood was on my hands. On the hands of my daughter. I was going to ask Amara about what had happened, but she held her stare on me and shook her head very slightly. Questions would have to wait.

"Hurry up, Dad! You're missing Christmas!" Bella pounded on the door, yelling for me to step things up. Five minutes and the water was off. I slid into my clothes and felt the water on my back absorb into the T-shirt. Then I was ushered to the sitting room, where I looked upon my chair with dread. I'd have a couple hours, and then I'd be sitting in it once more. The family had decorated the room with holly and tinsel to brighten it up, and I forced myself to tell them how great it all looked. Four days into this ordeal and I didn't know how much more I could take. It hurt to stand. It hurt to sit.

Everyone had been holding off on Christmas celebrations for two days as they waited for the Pause drug to take effect. Now that I was synced back to normalcy, they decided gifts should definitely come first. My presents were small and for the most part useless. Some technological wizardry that would take me more time to learn than was mine to spend, clothes I would most likely not be wearing. These were presents designed to make me feel normal, to make the family feel normal. I took them with gratitude.

Bella was staring at me with her mouth scrunched up and a conflicted gleam in her eyes. "Dad, I have good news and bad news, and I don't know what I should tell you first, with it being Christmas and all."

I was worried at the prospect of more bad news, so I deferred to the good, and good news it was.

"*Estoy embarazada!*" she blurted out in Spanish.

I stopped and looked from Bella to Keith and back to Bella, "That's . . . holy crap! I didn't expect that news. Congratulations! Bella, how do you feel?"

"I'm a little scared, Dad."

"You're always a little scared. And yet you manage to get through everything beautifully. So do you have any morning sickness? How far along are you? Did you find out the sex of the child yet?"

"About three months. I was going to tell you earlier, but I wanted to save the news for when I got to see you. And no morning sickness."

"You know your mom was sick every day she was pregnant with both you girls. You're lucky."

"Yeah, Mom told me already. She says hello, by the way."

The same sinking feeling from the wedding came back again. "Tell her I said hello back."

"You know Mom still loves you—"

"Don't," I cut Bella off. "Please . . . just don't." God only knew what had made Bella say something like that, but I didn't want to hear it. I couldn't hear it. But bringing up Miranda was a lapse on my part, not my daughter's. It made me feel self-conscious and brought the death stare down from Amara onto her sister.

Bella healed the discomfited silence with one phrase: "And it's a boy."

"A boy?" I looked at Keith, who smiled broadly and pointed a thumb at himself. "Nice job, Keith." I gave him a firm handshake and looked back at my Bella. There was no baby bump on her that I could see, but it would be poking out soon. The next time I synced back, there would be an infant in her arms. The word *Remedium* came immediately to mind, and it tore me up inside that a whole new set of moments were coming that I would miss out on unless I got a hold of that elusive antidote. Damn, it was so close, and then the whole deal fell apart.

Bella and Keith already had 3D images of the baby boy, which they brought up on a projector in the center of the room. I could see him moving and breathing, his heart beating swiftly. My stomach knotted up knowing I wasn't going to be there for the birth, knowing that I was one injection away from a cure.

Mike Gandry brought me a small pastry that contained a condensed protein delivery that would digest within twenty minutes. While we had all been celebrating, the man was still working, testing my blood, and verifying I wasn't going to die or go into convulsions or explode. The girls had gotten our live-in tech a present, and we were going to watch him open it, when Amara pulled me aside into the hallway.

She whispered, "Obviously Bella doesn't know where I took you, or it would be me who would be banished from this house."

I whispered back, "What did you tell her? That I was going on vacation?"

"I told her I had a colleague doing independent research on your condition, but that the government and Innovo couldn't know. I told her he had confidence he could cure you, but we had to keep it secret. Bella and Keith bought it, of course."

"And when I showed up not cured?"

"Easy. It didn't work. But I asked them to keep it a secret from you so as to not get your hopes up. They'll never bring it up just as long as you don't."

I looked at my older daughter, who was nervously biting her cuticles as we huddled in secrecy together in the hallway. We talked about her teammates, her friends, who had tried to help us. Nobody had ever figured out it was them, thankfully, but now they were forced to conduct an investigation into the Easton target when they knew perfectly well what happened. Everett had transferred to a different division under the stress, but Ivan was sticking around.

"Amara, what the heck happened back there? I thought you had a deal with Millennial."

She glanced away in disappointment. "So did I. I'm sorry, Daddy."

I wanted to ask her if she'd thought the Mets-cap-wearing man was armed, if she'd thought he was reaching for a weapon, if she'd somehow known he had that remote trigger. I wanted to ask her how many people had died in the explosion. The questions stuck in my throat for fear of the answers.

"What?" she asked, studying my face the way I would an interviewee's.

"Amara? Why . . . ?" I couldn't ask her. Instead, I threw out something that had been bugging me since my daughter joined Homeland Defense. "Why did you go into law enforcement? I know you have been trying to find a cure for me, and God knows I appreciate your loyalty. But why not try to come up with the cure? You're smart enough to figure out anything. Why didn't you set your sights on working for Innovo, or even Walter Reed?"

She looked down thoughtfully for a moment, listening to the laughter and chatter from the sitting room, then raised her head again. "I guess I didn't expect it to take so long to find the Millennial network. Or for it to be so hard. Medical school was another four years minimum before anyone would hire me, and even then there was no guarantee. You know, I've thought about quitting and going into research. But now that has its own problems."

"What?"

"Money. Nobody at Innovo wants to spend the necessary research money on curing one man, especially after so many failures. Until the economy bounces back, this Pause drug you have is all you're going to get. Two hours every ten months, and you and I both know your body can't take too much of this. You see, Daddy, we're stuck. Making a deal with Millennial had to work, and now . . ."

Syncing Forward

She stuck out her lip like a pouting child. I reached out and drew Amara into a hug. My poor girl was taking on the weight of the world, and I didn't know what else to do other than console her. At the sounds of footfalls along the wooden floor we separated, and we each drew a deep breath. It was Mike Gandry coming around the corner with a large box containing what appeared to be a small kitchen appliance, but heaven only knew what the contraption actually did.

"This is perfect, Amara. Thanks!" He gave her a one-armed hug as he tucked the box into his armpit. "I'm going to set it up in the lab. Not that I don't appreciate using your kitchen, but it's nice having my own stuff."

"I'm glad you like it, Mike." She nodded with a smile.

Bella found the three of us congregating in the hallway and yanked us back into the sitting room, where they caught me up on the last eighteen months. It was a joy to be around Bella's smiling face, which glowed with happiness. In some ways I felt guilty about talking with her more than Amara, but with the baby on the way, the conversation fell that way naturally. We shared stories of childhood, and Keith was belly-laughing at one of my old anecdotes, when curiosity got the best of me.

"What names have you picked out for the baby?"

Bella looked to Amara uneasily, then back at me. Keith stopped laughing unexpectedly, and the Christmas spirit that had previously hung in the air seemed to vaporize. "We, uhh . . . We're naming him Jacob, Dad."

I chuckled anxiously. "What's wrong with that? My brother must be loving it."

The room got quieter still. Bella avoided looking at me entirely and instead exchanged eye movements with her sister. It should have been obvious to me, but perhaps I was in denial. I didn't want to think that so much could happen in so little time. That maybe God might throw me a few softballs before gearing up for that fast pitch.

"No." It came out of my mouth against my will. "No, Jacob was just here. Are you sure?"

"I'm sorry, Mr. James." Keith approached me nervously, putting his thick hand on my shoulder to console me, but instead I stood up on wobbly legs and walked to the kitchen.

"Dad?" Bella called after me. "Dad? Are you okay?"

Standing by the sink, I looked out the window at the snow-covered valley. Rolling hills of dusty white covered the outskirts of Beacon and blotted out the windy road that led to our house. Even the trees looked cold. Jacob was gone, and I'd barely had a moment with him. My chest tightened at the thought of his passing, my mind reeling as I couldn't do the simple math to figure out how old he was. All I knew was that he was too damned young to go.

"Bro, you are higher than a Georgia pine!" The memory of us drinking, downing a twelve-pack of beer on the front porch of our house in New Jersey, wormed its way up from some deep recess in my memory. The neighbors staring at us, wondering what manner of redneck had just moved in next door. It was such a crappy house, but Jacob had helped me put up new drywall and redo the wiring and replace a rotted stud. He had burned through a week of vacation just so my wife and I could have a decent place to live. And when the chips were down and Jacob needed help, I'd let his kids go into foster care.

"Dad, I'm so sorry." Bella came up from behind. "We didn't want to tell you yet."

She told me Jacob had died on July 3, 2041, of a massive stroke while painting the kitchen. It was enough to kill Jacob on the spot at fifty-nine years of age. Friends gone. Career over. Wife left. Now my brother. One problem was demanding enough, but having them one after the other in a matter of perceived days was insufferable.

I bent over the sink, taking deep breaths to keep from falling into a panic attack. I stared at the water spiraling counterclockwise down the drain. An egg noodle stuck on the rubber stopper flapped about in the stream. I flicked it and watched it disappear. Another

Syncing Forward

memory of Jacob and me trading shoulder punches in our front yard in Louisiana popped into my head, but I shook it loose and let it join the egg noodle.

It was a terrible sinking feeling, my life flowing forward so quickly. *Sinking forward. Syncing forward.* The double meaning of that phrase had probably never dawned on anybody, but it was sickeningly appropriate.

After splashing cold water on my face, I composed myself and asked that we call Lily, Crystal, and Darren. It turned out that Amara and Bella had planned to call the twins and my sister-in-law all along. Amara set up a holo-emitter in the sitting room, and I enjoyed my first virtual visit with Jacob's family via holograms. Their images were strangely crisp, and half the time it looked and sounded as if they were right there in the room with us. My niece and nephew were as wrecked as I was; this was their first of many Christmases without their father. Lily was quiet and sat uneasily through the virtual gathering, her face paralyzed with sorrow.

Then the drug began to wear off. I quickly glanced at the clock and realized the Pause had lasted 150 minutes this time around. Soon I was back in my chair, watching the weeks tick by, staring out at the melting snow, the frozen land transforming into fertile acreage.

Jacob. I missed him. I wanted him back so badly. I kept dwelling on the arguments we'd had and the times I'd blown him off and the time we lost after I was injected by Bruchmuller. Another two hours from now I would get injected again with the agonizing Pause, but what I dreaded the most was the unknown—the bombshell the girls would drop on me next. While I could have spent those two hours—ten months—shuffling through news headlines and listening to warbled messages, instead I pulled up an archive of my brother and his family. Pictures from the wedding, of me and Jacob with our arms around each other's shoulders, of my big bro stuffing his face with cake—I closed the picture file along with my eyes.

When I opened them, I learned that Jacob Martin Heffley had been born. Eight pounds even, with a tuft of red hair growing out of the front of his head, my first grandson's pictures started popping up to interrupt my brooding. The baby's wide eyes filled the screen, and there was no stopping a smile from growing across my lips. I couldn't help but ruminate at how life had been taken and given so quickly. Was this how it would be for the rest of my life? Losing one person only to have him or her replaced with another?

There was one matter that Jacob had always been on me about, and that was reconciling with my mother. I knew I had to do it to honor his memory. I had to do it to be a good example for Amara. I had to do it for myself, or it would eat at me forever. I typed a note to the girls that I was ready to speak to my ma. I wasn't going to be the man who let his heart be so hardened by past mistakes that he made a whole slew of new ones.

Had I learned my lesson earlier, I might have done right by everyone, but as it turned out I was too late. By the time I was ready to forgive my mother, she had been long, long dead.

Syncing Forward

Chapter 28

Market bombings and terrorist killings were as commonplace in this new decade as they had been back in the 20s. An anniversary of one of these days of remembrance would not carry much public interest beyond the local victims. Memories of November 1 of 2021 would have been unremarkable, hardly worth dredging up, save for the fact that my existence had finally been brought to the world in 2042. Just prior to my syncing, Amara hijacked my computer interface and put up a screen filled with the newest articles.

"World's First Time Traveler Is Revealed!"

"Martin James—Millennial's First Victim?"

"Innovo's Secret Agenda—Capitalizing on Millennial Technology"

"US Government Denies Involvement in the Innovo-Millennial Project"

"Innovo Stockholders Flee as Company Scurries to Make Full Disclosure"

"Time Traveler—Sentinel over Sleepy Town of Beacon, PA"

I pressed the link to the last article, and there was a picture of our house. A second picture was a blowup of the window to the sitting room, and the shadow of a man sitting in the window was enhanced with some sort of optical imagery that was neither infrared nor thermal. Staring at the image was unsettling as the potential ramifications to my future sank in. This could mean no more research into curing me or even a stop to manufacturing the Pause antidote.

W Lawrence

My heart fluttered in panic as I mentally ran through a list of all the people who could possibly have broken confidentiality. Amara? Never. Bella? She would never intentionally say something, but I knew she had told Keith about me long before they were married, long before he'd made the disclosure list from the federal government. She'd probably even brought him into the sitting room to prove it. That brought me to Keith, whom I did not know well at all. He easily could have told his parents. Robert and Leann Heffley might have said something along the way, inadvertently of course. My niece and nephew? My sister-in-law? Who else knew? Everybody has a person they feel comfortable telling their secrets to, and that person had somebody else, and so on. It reminded me of something Jacob had told me about Benjamin Franklin, who wrote, "The only way to keep a secret between three people is if two of them are dead."

The article stated:

This reporter has confirmed that a time traveler does exist, and he is currently residing in the quaint farming town of Beacon, PA. This extraordinary man zips through time, jumping through the years and . . . does nothing?

As reported by the State-Approved Media Department of the Harrisburg Examiner, the designation of "time traveler" is not quite accurate. No bending of the laws of physics or outrageous machines allows this man to navigate history. However, his existence may be even more bizarre than one dreamt up by H.G. Wells. Mr. Martin James, originally of Louisiana, is under the influence of a medication that literally slows his body to near death. A minute passing for Martin James is perceived as several hours for the rest of the world. Currently under the care of Innovo Industries, James is reported to receive treatment

Syncing Forward

that brings his body concurrent with a normal speed so he can "visit" certain years. From the viewpoint of James, he is most definitely a time traveler.

Jackal hackers—anonymous individuals or organizations that illegally access computer systems when they are most vulnerable—first published the information on this popular website three weeks ago, after Innovo fell victim to its second major terrorist attack. The databases were scoured by jackal hackers after their main storage facility was destroyed by high-density explosives. As the information was quickly backed up from a secondary to a tertiary site, the hackers scored tens of thousands of files from the lowered security protocols.

Innovo officials have yet to comment on what information was lost in the data transfer and what was stolen, but stockholders began dumping—

The article was torn from my screen as Amara sent me an audio transmission and a text message; both indicated that they would be reviving me soon. Even through the distortion, I could hear deep concern in Amara's voice. Something bad had happened—something that made her hide the facts from me till she could talk to me face-to-face. So I waited for the piercing sting that would begin my synchronization. I wouldn't wait for long.

Chapter 29

Fourth Pause began. Shooting pain raced along the backs of my legs. My eardrums seemed like they might give way to the pressure and burst painfully inward. I bit down hard and was surprised to find my teeth embedding themselves into a soft rubber guard. If I didn't know better, I could have sworn a machete was being dragged across my rib cage and jabbed into my armpits. My skin felt like it was being flayed off in strips. My mind grasped desperately to focus on the least painful sensation, unable to find solace in any part of my body. And like a switch, the pain all vanished.

My grip relaxed as my senses caught up with my environment. I was in the sitting room; only, this time my chair had been moved from its normal position to a spot closer to the bookshelf. It took several minutes to focus—the Pause had me so frazzled that my eyes wouldn't stop moving no matter how hard I concentrated. When I managed to regain some semblance of control, I found myself staring at Keith's five o'clock shadow as he released his hold on me and gave me a pat on the leg.

"There you go, tough guy," he told me encouragingly, but it was obvious watching me thrash about was not easy on the stomach. I would have felt bad for him, but I was busy nursing my own wounds, and besides that, Keith had hit one of my pet peeves.

I wagged my finger at him, but the words didn't come. He handed me a familiar bottle and sprayed it in my mouth. I tested some grunts and confirmed that my voice had returned.

"Keith," I sputtered, "you can call me 'Martin.' You can call me 'Mr. James.' You can even call me 'Dad.' But don't call me 'tough guy.'"

His jaw dropped a little. "I, uh, sorry . . . Mr. Martin—I mean Mr. James. I mean . . ."

Amara saved my son-in-law from his embarrassment and cut him off. "Don't let him push you around, Keith. He's just in a bad mood because he knows something is wrong but can't figure out what it is."

I looked up at her. "And what makes you so sure that's how I feel?"

"Because I can interpret faces too, Dad. Only, your microexpressions last hours instead of a fraction of a second. You aren't exactly difficult to read."

"Did the thought cross your mind that I might be irritated because taking that Pause medication is like a living hell?"

"Well, there's that too."

"Where's Bella?"

Amara frowned. "She couldn't watch you sync back. I can barely stomach it, and I've seen some pretty horrific crap."

She gave me a hug and a kiss on the head and helped me up to my feet. The pads of my feet felt like pins and needles, and I sprang about the room until the sensation wore off. Amara and Keith guided me and made sure I had my balance before letting go. Amara clearly wanted to talk, but she insisted I get some clothes on and freshen up. A new set of clothes were on the sink counter, and toothbrush, toothpaste, washcloth, and hairbrush were all laid out for me. Keith was talking to me through the door about his new job down at a farm collective, but there was one thought on my mind at that moment that eclipsed all the others.

"There's my grandson!" I called out, holding out my arms as I walked into the kitchen. Bella smiled with the tired brow of a new mother and held up my brother's namesake for me. He was a chubby little monkey with big eyes and a little mouth that kept opening and shutting as if he was suckling the air itself.

"He looks hungry."

"He's five months old, Dad, and he's always hungry," Bella droned. "I love him to death, but I have no idea what compelled you and Mom to have me after having Amara. I'm just exhausted."

"Trust me, you will miss this when it's over. The smell of his little head, his jerky little kicks, his grabbing at your fingers . . ." Little Jacob pulled on my thumb and refused to let go. "You'll miss every sleepless night."

Being a father might have taken some getting used to, but being a grandparent came instinctively. Even when my stomach growls were so loud that the girls heard them, I refused to relinquish little Jacob, instead propping him up on my leg and downing the rapid-digestive tart they served me. Bella apologized for the meager portion, but even with food that absorbed into my system quickly, a larger quantity might survive in my stomach long enough to get vomited up in two hours or go septic in my intestines.

With a lull in the conversation, I took the opportunity to bring up the inevitable discussion. "So, what happened?"

Amara took a breath and dove in. "Dave Tsai called us confidentially. He's Innovo's vice president of global security now. Normally he doesn't reach out, but every once in a while he lets me know important decisions coming from the board. Since your condition went public, Innovo has been experiencing severe financial problems. The board of directors is tossing around the idea that you are the reason Millennial attacked Innovo this second time."

It was the damn deal with Bernard that had set them off. It had to be. Amara's face told me she felt the same way, and the two of us struggled to act normal for fear that Bella would start to wonder. Amara continued. "They think the research Innovo is doing to cure you is what spurred the attacks, and there is talk about dumping all research relating to you in order to make stockholders feel safer. They might decide to sell you."

"Sell me? Can they do that?" I wondered incredulously. "I'm assuming slavery is still illegal."

Bella interrupted. "They wouldn't be selling you to anyone in particular, just cutting you loose as an asset. You are a ward of the corporation, and they can move to have a judge release you from their care. I know it sounds odd, but you might be better off staying in their custody. Even without the research, they still provide the V-5322 drug . . . and a salary. The government could make an argument that they would be the only ones capable of taking care of you and take possession of you."

After everything we'd gone though, this couldn't end with me stuck in the basement of Walter Reed again. I couldn't trust them anymore.

My younger daughter continued. "Dad, we could probably keep up with the bills, but we could never pay for the Pause drug. We would lose these hours we have. You would never be able to sync back again." Bella might sound overly dramatic, but the idea of coasting forward in time with no hope of a cure was terrifying.

I shrugged. "What can we do?"

Bella gritted her teeth as if she didn't want the words to escape her mouth. "Well, we invited somebody to speak with you. She's here now."

Chapter 30

If there was a camera lens on the device between me and the woman, it was either concealed or so small that I couldn't see it. Four inches across and looking more like a black plastic can, the holo-recorder had no cables or cords or projections of any type. The reporter who sat across the table was a white woman in her thirties, blonde, slender, attractive save for the black eyeshadow and whitish makeup that made her look like a raccoon. The dress she wore hugged her features—more of an evening gown than something a reporter would wear. Then again, women's fashion of the future was as disconnected from me as the people who lived in it.

Her name was Margo Sanguine, and she worked for Transworld News Agency. Her name was as fake as her demeanor, but I went forward with the interview regardless of how much she repulsed me. Bella and Amara wanted to reduce speculation about what Innovo was working on, but more importantly, they wanted to let the world know their father was a human being worth saving.

Being interviewed on international television by some plastic female was unappealing to me regardless of how attractive she appeared or how nicely the girls dressed me up. However, with the confidentiality agreements already effectively blown, my ten minutes of fame might be enough to sway public sentiment and convince Innovo's stockholders to keep pumping money into my treatment. Besides, Amara and Bella would beat me senseless if I backed out.

"Welcome to the worlds from Beacon, Pennsylvania. This is Margo Sanguine with Transworld News, and I am here with Mr. Martin James, who has been called the world's first time traveler. Hello, Martin, thank you for inviting me into your home." Margo folded her hands and stared directly at me.

"You're welcome. I appreciate you coming out to visit," I responded with as much pleasantry as I could muster.

Syncing Forward

"Your family has requested that we keep this interview to less than ten minutes, so if you don't mind, I'm going to skip many of the background questions and get straight to business."

"That's fine."

"How do you feel?"

"Nervous, I suppose. I used to do interviews, but I was always in the interviewer's seat."

"I suppose it doesn't help knowing that billions of people around the world will probably watch this, not to mention the Luna and Mars colonists."

I snickered nervously. "Thanks for the added pressure, Margo. I appreciate that. Seriously, I feel great. Innovo designed a remarkable drug that allows me to interact normally for two or three hours. The transition in and out is always rocky, but once I'm past the pain it feels like I'm back to normal." *Rocky* didn't adequately describe it—more like being dropped from a cliff onto rocks. But I had to remind myself not to bite the hand that was feeding me.

"When the news first broke on your story, we discovered that years fly by like days to you. Now, when you are out of 'synchronization' as they call it, you are awake and aware of everything around you, is that so?"

"Yup. Unless I'm sleeping, of course. I actually do need to sleep, which is strange because I could wake up in a different decade."

"What do you experience when you are awake?"

"Well, when I first was injected with the Millennial drug, I couldn't experience anything. Sound is muffled so I can't hear. I can't feel anything unless somebody or something touches me for a long time. My one daughter, Bella, sits with me every Sunday so I can hold her hand for a few seconds. A few seconds to me, anyway. She's recently married, so I was worried about her not having enough time to spend with me, but she's been a great kid and still spends Sundays in this room. My older child takes good care of me too, just in her own way. Both of my daughters are quite devoted."

"Walk the worlds through a typical day from your perspective."

Sanguine had managed to work that phrase "the worlds" in again. I supposed it was their catch phrase for their network, and since people were living on Mars and the moon, I reckoned it made some sense. I cocked my head slightly. "Which kind of day, Margo? I mean to say, my day without the drugs Innovo supplies lasts ten years. One of *your* days to me is perceived as just over twenty seconds."

"Let's do the last day for you, roughly speaking."

I took a deep breath and exhaled slowly. God only knew what Innovo had figured out about Amara taking me to Easton. Somebody had to wonder why Bella had never synced me back when she could. Mike Gandry had to be asking questions. All those concerns and memories crisscrossed my mind in a split second.

Margo Sanguine was staring at me, and I realized I had to say something. "Let's see, my daughter Bella got married to a nice young man, and she had a baby boy she named Jacob, after my brother who just passed away. I found out that my existence has gone public—that was a big surprise. Because of my condition I can't walk around, so I spend most of my day reading the news, corresponding through letters and voice mail. It's like I'm on a desert island and can only send a message every once in awhile because things move so slow-like. Typing is the fastest. I can't speak because my vocal cords won't vibrate strongly enough to make sound. My ears don't work because all the sound waves buffet my ears all at once—"

"Is it loud?" Margo asked.

I shook my head. "Fortunately, it all sounds muted instead of like a cacophony. It's like being underwater in a public pool, but quieter."

The interview went on, with Margo asking the questions I figured she would ask. Showing the world—the worlds—how I could see with the tear jets and hear with the earbuds, how technology developed by Innovo was specifically directed at me with no real function for the rest of the world.

Syncing Forward

"Best estimates indicate over one hundred million SDRs spent on you and your family over the last twenty years." Margo leaned toward me with a hard focus, getting in my personal space. *Yeah, I know that trick, Margo.* "How do you justify such resources being expended to save one person?"

Just because I knew the interview trick she was pulling didn't mean I knew what to say. I didn't even have an equivalent to understand what a hundred million SDRs translated to. Then I thought about what the girls had told me—that I needed to give people a reason to like me, to want me to live. What was I to do? Give them a sob story? With the world so twisted up, sympathy for me didn't seem like it would get much traction.

I took a stab at toeing the company line. "Innovo has been very good to my family, and I think of them as not just trying to save me personally, but my family as a whole. And there is no doubt in my mind that if they figured out how to fix me, the medical breakthroughs could help a lot of people. I'm not a genius by any stretch, but it doesn't take brilliance to realize how slowing somebody down might be helpful for surgeries or other medical procedures."

"Quite true. How do you feel about the Russian Coalition bidding to purchase you for space travel research?"

"I . . . I didn't know about that."

"You didn't know?"

"No."

Margo held up the bendable computer display and flapped it in front of her. She read through a short list of businesses, state-run facilities, and quasi-government agencies that had all made public statements about wanting to "acquire" me. "Do you find that disturbing?"

I frowned. "Not nearly as disturbing as if Innovo sold me."

"Many people are criticizing your company as engaging in twenty-first-century slavery. Do you think it is right for a business to be able to own a person?"

That question was loaded, and the reporter knew it. I had no idea who Margo Sanguine was, but she was certainly shrewd in her attempts to stir up controversy. "It's hard for me to judge the ethics of owning a person," I began, "when I'm the person benefiting from the help of my company. I suppose I don't like the concept, but I try to think of Innovo owning the information *inside* me, not necessarily me as an individual. If I was a slave, I don't think I would be benefiting nearly as much as I have. Innovo has been good to us."

"Do you miss your wife, Miranda?"

I stopped breathing. My eyes locked with Ms. Margo Sanguine, and as much as I'd disliked her before, I outright despised her after that question. "I think you'd have to be stupid to think otherwise."

My sharp retort barely made Margo flinch, but I noticed it just the same. She must have been used to people throwing nasty comments back at her because she composed herself like a true professional. "If you could talk to her now, would you want her to come back? To be a part of your life?"

"Maybe we should talk about something else, Margo."

"Sorry," she said with barely enough feeling to make it sound like a real apology. "I know this must be tough for you. Family is very important to you; that much is evident. You're a new grandfather. What's that like?"

I rolled with the question and grinned. "I'll tell you when we're done with this interview. I've had very little time with the newest addition to our family."

"How do you feel being in a split household?"

"Split? How so?" I tried not to show how out of touch with the rest of the world the question made me feel—it was clear she wasn't talking about my divorce anymore.

"Our records show that your brother Jacob James and his family have been huge supporters of the Texan-led separation. Prior to that, he was part of the Tea Party, which engaged in terrorism against the government. Your nephew Darren works on one of the paramilitary bases that have made attacks into the United States."

I hoped to God that holo-recorder wouldn't show the worlds how badly I wanted to slap this woman. I had never supported my brother and his political agenda, but I would be damned if I let her disparage Jacob's memory. "My brother is dead, Ms. Sanguine. My nephew is an electrician."

"And I'm sorry for your loss, Martin. But your nephew and niece and sister-in-law are still Separatist supporters. Contrast that with your daughter, who works for the Homeland Defense Force. Like many American families, you must have a difficult time resolving those political rifts within your own family, correct?"

"No, not correct," I expressed irritably. "We don't talk politics. We don't have time to talk politics. What little time I have is spent catching up on my condition and any possible cures and staying up to date with my daughters."

"Do you think the self-declared American Governance should acquiesce and rejoin the USA?"

I bobbled my head. "I have to tell you that of all the news I've read, this has got to be the most insane. I don't know who is right and who is wrong. I was never political like my brother or even a very patriotic person, to be honest. I've barely had a chance to read into the matter. But I just can't figure out why a bunch of grown-ups could let things get to the point where we would be ready to kill one another."

Margo nodded her head slightly. "Americans on both sides of the borders would agree with you, at least in part." I must have said something that agreed with her agenda because her tone became more pleasant after my comments. I only hoped I hadn't ticked off too many folks with my politicking response.

"Let's move on to the big topic." The reporter swiped her finger slightly over the display in her hand, and a new set of notes appeared. Reading them was near impossible since I was looking at them upside down and backward through the transparent sheet. "The nondisclosure agreement you have with Innovo. Yours is a mystery you've known about for a lot longer than the rest of the world. You are aware of the media attention you've received recently?"

"Yes. I get news that I can skim through while I am syncing forward. Just the highlights of the highlights, if you follow. But for the record, it was Homeland Security that insisted on the nondisclosure agreement—not Innovo."

"Did the Homeland Defense—Homeland Security at the time," Margo corrected, "Did they give you any reason?"

"They only told me it was a confidential matter, and we couldn't speak about it."

"Why is it they didn't want you talking about Millennial, do you think?"

I pondered that question. "I really don't know. It seemed rather odd. The agents didn't have a lot of information, so maybe Homeland Security was more in the dark than I thought at the time. Or maybe they were afraid I might compromise an existing investigation."

"People are calling you the worlds' first time traveler, but clearly that isn't true. Millennial terrorists were presumably injecting themselves before you were attacked. How long do you think they were operating before you discovered them?"

"I don't have the faintest clue." I made no mention of my investigation, not wanting to cast Innovo in a bad light.

"This mystery drug they use—what do you think they use it for?"

"I'm guessing just like the rest of you. Obviously it means a great deal to them to keep it a secret."

"Any idea why they would use something so valued by their ranks on a civilian target?"

There didn't seem to be a good reason to play ignorant on that question. "One of the members took pity on me. Rajesh Jotwani. After I was attacked, it was Rajesh who refused to kill me when the others wanted to. So they injected me with their drug to slow me down, hopefully to release me later. Maybe they were going to ransom me—I don't know."

"What do you think about Millennial? About their agenda?" Margo inquired.

I knew what they were capable of, but I found myself unable to make the step to denounce them publicly. They certainly deserved every disparaging remark I could make, but I still needed that cure, and they still had it secreted away somewhere. Call me a coward, but some tiny seed inside me hoped against hope that somebody from Millennial's organization would take pity on me.

"I really don't know," was all I committed to. "I'm still shocked by what they've done. I'm still angry about what they've done to me. But if one of them gave me the cure to get me to sync back permanently, I wouldn't turn it down."

Ms. Sanguine swiped across the clear display on her lap and read the last of her notes. A little yellow symbol flashed in the corner, presumably to tell her that ten minutes were almost up. "The files that were jackal-hacked from Innovo indicate it was a man named Dieterich Bruchmuller who injected you with this mysterious drug against your will. Is that correct?"

So Margo had more information than I originally thought. I went forward cautiously. "Yeah, that was him. Him and a few others were involved, but yes, mostly Bruchmuller."

"You sound so angry at the mention of his name."

I adjusted in my chair. "Wouldn't you be? He stole twenty years from me, ruined my marriage, destroyed my career . . ."

"How did you feel when you found out he was dead?"

"Part of me wished I was the one who pulled the trigger. Not that it would have done me any good, I suppose. Part of me—the reasonable part—wishes he hadn't died. If they'd captured him, maybe I'd be cured by now."

The yellow symbol on her display transformed to red, and the ten minutes were up. Margo refreshed her plastic smile and closed the interview. "Martin, I know we're out of time. Just three closing questions if you don't mind."

"Sure."

"What do you say to the people out there who are accusing you of working with Millennial?"

"I didn't know there were people saying that. I . . . I'm at a loss. All I can say is that I'm not. I'm a victim just like the poor people who have been murdered and injured by these terrorists. I certainly would have never volunteered to be injected with this drug. It's a living hell."

"What do you want people to know about you?"

I scratched my head and looked off to the side to ruminate. Slowly I answered, "I would like them to know I am not here by choice. That the help I get from Innovo, as generous as it may be, barely makes my life tolerable. If it wasn't for my kids, I think I would have lost my mind. I just want a chance to be a normal dad again with a normal job."

"How much time have you been in this condition, from your perspective?"

"I don't quite know. Four days? Five days? It is hard to say."

Margo Sanguine shut off her display and straightened up in her chair. Her final question of the interview came to me. "You are as close to a time traveler as there ever was. What do you think about the world two decades later?"

"Wow, uh . . ." I rubbed my jaw, running my hand along my freshly shaven skin. "Cloning, a moon colony, a Mars colony, Europe ripping itself apart, America broken in pieces . . . I'm sure today feels like just another day for you, but I feel disconnected. It's strange, because I remember as a kid wishing I could see what was going to happen in the future. Now all I want to do is go back to the past."

"Thank you, Martin. It was a pleasure to finally meet you."

"Thank you for the opportunity, Margo."

Chapter 31

Syncing Forward

As I said good-bye to Margo Sanguine, Keith thanked her and her assistant for coming while escorting them out of the house. The two of them disappeared as Keith's broad frame obscured them from view, and eventually their voices trailed off with the closing of the front door.

Bella gave me a one-armed squeeze while tucking baby Jacob under her other arm like a football. "You did great, Dad," she said. I was thinking the same thing. Not that I was the type to fish for praise, but I certainly needed a big helping of positive attitude now. The one thing I didn't want was backlash from Innovo or the public.

The chime of the house phone rang in stereo from the sitting room to the living room to the kitchen. A look at the smartglass interface showed Innovo as the caller. Then another ID showed underneath that—Unknown. Then another. Then State Affiliated Media Ctr. Then another Unknown. The pleasant chimes were beginning to grate, so Bella touched the glass and pressed a few commands, and the sound went away. With the house quiet, we could hear Amara on her cell phone in the kitchen talking in Spanish, probably to her supervisor.

Mike Gandry came quickstepping down the hall from the back of the house, probably from the lab. His face was flushed, and I'd be lying if I said he didn't look ready for a fight—an argument at the very least.

"What the hell did you do?" he yelled at Bella. "You put Martin on the news?!"

"We did what we had to, Mike," Bella said in defense. "People need to know what my father has been through. Innovo isn't doing anything, and the government would take him back to Washington DC if given half a chance."

"Well, you could give me a warning instead of blindsiding me like that. You'd think after all the years I've taken care of this family you owed me that! Do you have any idea how stupid I look to my boss and his boss? That I had no idea you were planning this stunt?"

"Mike," I said, trying to break in, "don't get angry at them. This was my fault."

He looked at me, and his tone changed. "Martin, I know this wasn't your idea. I'm not stupid. I wouldn't even have reported it to Innovo if you guys had told me, but if you don't trust me enough to at least tell me *Margo Sanguine* is in the house so I don't look like a complete ass, then maybe I need to transfer."

We both called after him, but it was no use. He stormed out the back door and slammed the laboratory's door so hard we could hear it in the house. After a bit, Bella, Amara, Keith, and I congregated in the living room and discussed what to do once Innovo and the government gave us our lashings. My younger daughter and her new husband felt the only thing we could do was wait to see how things went. My older daughter hesitated voicing any optimism. Not that Amara was ever a beacon of positive thinking. With the phone messages stacking up and the clock ticking down, everyone wanted to know what I wanted to do.

I pointed to the pink bundle in Bella's arms. "Can I take the next hour and enjoy my family? We're not going to get an answer from anybody on anything today. And maybe I'm being selfish, but the next time I want to hold that little baby, he'll be walking and may not want to be held. This is my last chance to hold my first grandson."

The simplicity of being a granddad. It meant juggling my attention between my grown children and an infant. It meant I could put on my "daddy" persona once more. It meant diapers all over again, of course. As a father of two girls, the one thing I wasn't expecting was getting a face full of urine when I changed Jacob with his feet pointed toward me. Girls don't have aim like that. That brought a big laugh from Keith and my daughters, not to mention a toothless smile from Jacob, who seemed outrageously amused at christening his grandpa with pee. I washed off and quickly changed shirts before returning to the living room. I hadn't laughed like that in twenty years.

An uncertain future, crazed terrorists, a life in shambles, but none of it mattered with a baby in the room.

The interview caused a buzz immediately. Legal briefs were issued. Attorneys went into overdrive. The Justice Department threatened to press charges against me. Congress wanted to subpoena me. Innovo went into damage-control mode, weighing their options of dumping me and facing the public backlash that could come with that, or retaining me and weathering the stockholder concerns over safety and financial commitments. Beacon, Pennsylvania, was overrun with visitors for months, people who came to see the famous time traveler, Martin James. Those visitors were met with the same cold greeting of a new security detail that the unwanted reporters were already well acquainted with. I watched vehicles parked at the bottom of our property line sit for days before moving on.

Transworld News paid handsomely for my interview—money that Bella was able to pump into improving the alarm system on the house as well as money for attorney fees. Innovo paid for the added security details—an additional cost that didn't make keeping me in their good graces any easier for them. The company had plenty of other problems to muddle through, and they were just hoping to get out of the spotlight before rendering a judgment on me. David Tsai managed to keep us clandestinely informed on the decisions made by the board of directors—most of which amounted to putting off any resolution until public interest faded. I managed to record a quick message for Dave before syncing forward again, and once back in my chair I got some mail from him as well.

Friends I hadn't seen in years wrote to me after seeing my interview. My uncle Joe from my mom's side got in touch after returning from a fishing trip and seeing my interview. He was 104 years old and pretty fit for a centenarian. I don't know why, but his correspondence gave me some hope that, despite my rush through time, I might still be reunited with the people I cared about.

I was back in my typical place by the window; only, this time small devices were set up in the corners of the window to prevented sensor cameras from penetrating the reflective glass and invading our privacy. Amara wrote me more often, but even through the brief messages we sent each other, I knew something was amiss. There was rapidity to her verbs that made even her typed communications seem exhausted. I asked if she was okay and was answered with her typical dismissive response. Her voice mails were off too—sketchy, as if her attention was being drawn in a dozen directions.

Bella left me a note one day confirming that Amara was off her medication. Heck, I had forgotten Miranda mentioned that our daughter was taking meds in the first place. Another note from Bella showed up shortly thereafter, saying that Amara was having problems at work. A third note was swiped before I could read it.

Syncing Forward

Chapter 32

Fifth Pause began on August 22 of 2043. It was eleven o'clock in the morning, a blistering summer day that made the cornstalks stretch and the air conditioners strain. Despite the repeated messages from Bella and Amara to hold off, I would not let the pain dissuade me from getting back to them. Innovo kept saying that the V-5322 should work, but apparently Mike Gandry had left a final message for the girls in which he discouraged us from using it anymore and promised the data was forthcoming. An unread message from Mike sent to me personally before he left still awaited my reading it. His going seemed inevitable after what happened with the interview, and I didn't blame him.

Keith and a replacement technician by the name of Felipe Aguarro were there to guide me out of the next particularly painful transition. I thought I could handle it. Once it began, I regretted making the decision to start. Pause was a bone snapping and snapping again. Pause was a demon scratching at my spine, trying to dig out each vertebra. Pause meds fried my nerve endings like a burn upon a burn, and this newest synchronization had me panting like a dog.

Keith and Felipe tended to my skin with cool washcloths, but the instant relief I'd felt after syncing the last few times was absent. Instead, my body throbbed in pain that subsided only after ten minutes or so. Felipe left after I was able to calm down and told us he would return after analyzing my data.

Keith grimaced, talking to me only after he knew I was calming down. "You okay, Mr. James?"

I felt tears on my cheeks and realized the synchronization had really screwed me up this time. My hands shook as I wiped them away, and I simply shook my head. "That wasn't a bee sting."

Bella and Keith took me outside and let me stretch as they gave me their most recent news.

"Dad, we're pregnant again," she told me timidly.

"That's wonderful news!" My arms wrapped around my Bella, and we spoke about baby Jacob, who was now fourteen months old. He toddled and tipped his way about, scurrying around like a roach and making his parents barrel after him. He was calling me "Pop-pop." It must have been strange for him to see me actually moving and hear me speaking. To a child's eyes, my frozen self must have been an awkward sight indeed.

The stroll took us down the hill to a view of a glorious Pennsylvania horizon. I stretched my stride slightly as my equilibrium fully returned, feeling less like a cripple and more like a functioning man. We discussed how Innovo was still deciding what to do with the research into the Millennial drug, and as such was effectively deciding my fate. Supposedly Dave Tsai would give us a preview of whatever was coming down the pipeline, but for now we waited. That wasn't easy for me, even when I was syncing forward at one-four-thousandth the rate everyone else was. Conversely, Bella seemed optimistic that things would bend our way soon.

As we enjoyed the sunlight, the happiness from my younger daughter peeled away and revealed her deep concern over Amara. Amara had told her sister that she'd applied for another division within Homeland Defense, but the field investigations into Millennial seemed to continue. Amara had come home for the Easter holiday with her partner Ivan Fagundes but spent her days off on the phone, secreting herself away from everyone, including Ivan. Bella threw around words like *disturbed* and *twitchy*. Even Ivan mentioned to her that Amara was acting strange and wanted Bella to talk to her. There were disciplinary issues at the department—nothing career-ending, but they were frequent and foolish. A sharp tongue, a bad attitude, OCD had kicked in big-time, and to top it off, Amara was irritating the wrong people. But there was more.

Syncing Forward

Amara and Ivan had tracked down another Millennial member, and once again they'd almost lost their lives. The explosion leveled an abandoned warehouse and set four hundred acres of Georgia woodlands aflame as the cornered terrorist killed himself to avoid capture. That was eight months ago, and since then Amara had been skittish and short on conversation. Both girls had failed to say a word about the incident when it happened.

"What do you want me to do?" I looked to Bella, who clearly wanted to ask the same question of me. "I could barely get your sis to listen to me when she was nine years old."

"Dad, just talk to her, please. She hasn't been home in two months, and it took everything I had to get her to come up here. You know I didn't want to sync you back, but I also know you wanted to see Jacob, how important that is for you. Well, she begged me to not sync you back and got angrier than I've ever seen her when I did. She's so mad at me she won't even come into the house." Bella held a wiggly Jacob in her arms as Keith opened the back door for her.

"Where's she at?" I relented.

"The lab."

What I really wanted was for my daughters to figure out a way to work through all these problems and not leave them to me to fix in the two-hour window I had with them. I turned and headed to the laboratory alone. Running into Felipe Aguarro outside, he wanted to talk about the test results. I brushed him aside, telling him to discuss the numbers with Bella. The new technician tried to engage me but gave up as his words only got my back end's attention. I don't know if he appreciated how important my minutes were, but there wasn't even time to explain my rudeness as I opened the door to the lab. White plastic sheets covered all equipment save for a few computers that were exposed and running. Amara stood near the wall, talking to a man on the video screen when I entered.

"Yes, I told you I would be there by tonight. Yes, alone! Just relax. Listen, I need to go. Okay, bye." Amara slid her finger across the screen, and it went gray with inactivity. I saw her palm a small rectangular shape from the counter nearby and surreptitiously pocket it. When she turned my way, her face was tense. My daughter's hair was much shorter, and I wondered if that was a style change or a result of the firestorm she had barely escaped.

"Do you have time to hug your dad?"

Amara closed the distance and gave me a largish hug. "Hi, Daddy. I'm glad you're awake. Sorry about the call, but I tried to tell Bella not to sync you back. Work is really busy."

"What's the little doodad in your pocket for?"

She grew an embarrassed expression. "It's a scrambler. We use it for cases we don't want monitored. Everyone is under the microscope."

"Even law enforcement?"

"Especially law enforcement."

"Oh." There was a knot in my stomach, a familiar tension that reminded me of the meeting with Bernard. The bomb. The missed chance to get the Remedium. "Still working on the Millennial case, huh?"

"Among other things," she answered uncomfortably. There were words hanging off my daughter's lips that would fall off. A matter that was devouring her from the inside.

"Working *alone* on something? That sounded ominous."

"I'll be fine, Daddy. Some cases are like this."

"Aren't you worried? About getting hurt, I mean?"

"Trust me, Daddy. I'm learning there are far worse things than Millennial out there."

That observation sent a shiver down my spine. "You know you aren't making me feel any better. Is it anything you can talk about?"

"Some things I've seen are . . . awful. We lost some people to the new mods."

"Mods?"

Syncing Forward

"That's short for modifications—changes that people get. Artificial implants, genetic enhancements, limb replacements, engineered babies. Most times they're a good thing—my ear and left shoulder and arm are mods—but it didn't take long for black-market mods to start popping up. The sad fact is we've always been outgunned, but now criminals are faster and stronger, to boot."

My attention was split between what Amara told me and a visual inspection of Amara's ear and arm. They looked totally normal—no scars or flashing lights or mechanical sounds emanating from them. "Your . . . parts . . . don't look artificial at all."

"What were you expecting, Daddy? A metal claw?" she scoffed.

"I don't know. Just something different, I guess." I paused and asked, "So, who did you lose from your team?"

She told me that Franciscus and two other agents were killed while raiding an illegal modification lab in Staten Island. Several of the suspects had been surgically modified with the ability to spit cobra poison from their mouths. One agent was blinded. Two more were killed from bites. Franciscus was struck in the eyes with the venom, but some of the poison also worked its way into his blood through an open wound. He died two days later.

Franciscus definitely wasn't my friend, yet I felt the odd connection between us cut by the news of his death. I told Amara how sorry I was for her loss but couldn't help but ask questions about how a human being could manage to be modified to such an extent. That technology seemed impossible, but Amara assured me that it had been around for ten years. The genie was out of the bottle now for anyone to use.

Her left arm looked just like her right arm. If scientists could grow an arm or build an ear, it seemed pretty logical that maybe technology was catching up with my condition. I asked her if any of the tech could be applied to fix me.

Amara's expression turned suddenly remorseful as she stroked her left arm. "No. I've checked already, extensively. But even if it could, I wouldn't want you getting mods. Sometimes they just don't feel right."

"Those mods you took for your shoulder and ear—are those enhancements? Or are they repairs from getting injured on the job?"

Amara glanced at me, then turned away. "Why are you always asking me questions when you know you won't like the answer? You know why I got them."

My older daughter looked so miserable—not a one-off bad-mood demeanor but a lingering sullenness that hung off her like a weighty pack. "Amara, I want you to resign. This job of yours—"

"Daddy, don't start in on me. Now is not a good time. I'll transfer soon, okay?"

"You know, when you were little, you did this. You'd be working on a picture or a book or a game, and your answer was always 'now isn't a good time.' Which, translated from Amara-code, meant 'I'm never going to stop.'" I paused for comedic effect and tagged on "I remember it like it was yesterday."

I was waiting for a smile, or an "I'm not a little girl anymore," or anything. She wasn't paying attention. Either that or she had something on her mind that was pushing out all other thoughts. We walked outside and down the driveway. I took some enjoyment in the sunlight beating down on me despite the rough conversation. Amara looked uncomfortable in her long dark pants and dark shirt, so I steered us toward a shade tree on the edge of the property. Once we crossed under the large birch, we stopped and spoke more.

"Your sister is worried about you," I said. "She tells me your most recent boyfriend left you. That your job is keeping you from having a family. Don't you want children? You didn't even tell me you had a new boyfriend, by the way. It's something you don't really like to talk about, is it?"

Syncing Forward

Amara rolled her eyes. "Bella is a busybody. You know that, right?"

"Was he one of the agents lost in that raid?"

Amara said nothing.

"Bella says you aren't taking your medication."

Amara shot me a cockeyed look. "I never take my meds. I haven't taken them since I was eleven. They make my thinking fuzzy."

I shook my head, not knowing if any medication would be able to slow Amara down. I pushed her on what Bella had told me. "She said you got blown up again. That's why you got the mods, isn't it? Amara, how badly hurt were you to need entire parts of your body replaced?"

Amara looked away, her right hand rubbing her left shoulder instinctively. I repeated the question, which caused my daughter to whip around and snap at me, "So what? It's what I do, Daddy. It's my job."

"It doesn't have to be your job. You can transfer or quit or—"

"But it does! Don't you get it? I was *this* close to finding another crypt. *This* close!" Amara was shouting, holding her index finger and thumb a centimeter apart. "I don't know how they knew we were there, but they detonated the freaking crypt remotely. We lost the suspect in the smoke and fire. But he's out there."

"Bella told me the Millennial terrorist killed himself."

Amara circled the tree, barking at me. "That's why I don't tell Bella everything. She can't keep a secret to save her life. I told her what they reported in the news. No, he didn't die. He got away, but I've got something big I'm working on. I can get the cure this time, I know it—"

"Stop!" I bellowed. The excuses, the procrastination, the justifications caused me to boil over. "God, Amara, just stop! Please! A piece of me dies every time I hear about you out there, don't you understand? I know you're trying to save me, but don't you see that

313

you're killing me? I want to be cured, but it doesn't do me any good if there is nobody to come back to. Damn it, listen to me!"

Amara was walking away, but I grabbed her and spun her around. My daughter swatted my hand away instinctively, grabbing my wrist and prying my grip from her arm with the ease of peeling a banana. Her other hand cocked back slightly. It was unexpected, partly because I wasn't seeking a confrontation, but this was also my child, and perhaps my mind still locked her permanently at nine years old.

"What? You want to take a swipe at your old man?"

"No!" she said, letting go and shaking her hands as if she had touched something vile, disgusted with her reaction. She stuttered through her pleading. "I just want you to-to-to-let me do this! I'm so close to getting the Remedium. The cure for you!"

"Please, Amara, please! I'm begging you. Please, listen to me . . . let it go. Just let it go. I've lost Jacob, I've lost your mom. I don't want to lose you."

"But you won't lose me, Daddy. I promise!"

"You can't promise me that. Don't you see? These people . . . these Millennial terrorists. They are fundamentalists. They are organized. They believe in what they are doing. Their very survival is based on keeping those crypts hidden, and twice I've seen up close what they are capable of. If they are willing to kill themselves to keep their secrets, they won't hesitate to kill you."

Amara rolled her tear-filled eyes, wiping her nose with her twitching fingers. "You don't think I know that? I am out there every day . . . *every day* dealing with people who are *barely* human. People who are *more* than human. I've killed eighteen worthless pieces of crap, degenerates who have punched me, knifed me, shot at me. I have spent years studying these bastards. I am the number-one expert on Millennial in the United States. I've turned down three promotions to keep my field investigation going. I'm the only person *in the fucking world* to track a Millennial crypt down, *and I've done it twice!* So *don't you dare* tell me what I can and can't do!"

Syncing Forward

She stormed away from the tree and into the brightness of the noonday sun, arguing with herself as she went. Halfway to the house she drew her firearm and aimed it at a wooden stump near the garage. Amara barely took aim before emptying twelve rounds from her pistol into the dead wood. The register on the gun remained open, and she stood there with her chest heaving. Turning around, she looked at me and went to say something, when she stopped, holstered her sidearm, and trotted to the car.

Keith and Bella came sprinting out of the house with Felipe close behind. "What the hell are you doing, Amara?" Bella screamed at her sister.

"Target practice!" Amara yelled sarcastically without turning around. She climbed into the car and screeched out of the driveway.

Little Jacob cried from the noise. Bella ran to me and made sure I was okay. I told her that I was, although that reassurance only applied to my physical well-being. Inside, my stomach churned and my heart thumped. We walked past the stump and looked at the grouping of bullet holes no bigger than the palm of my hand, a grouping she'd shot from forty feet away. I supposed I should have been impressed, but all I could think was that my child had become an obsessed, vengeful, and lethal woman whose life was spinning out of control. Amara was coming apart at the seams and dangerously so.

I watched her car kick up a snake of dust as it barreled down the road. Bella tugged on my arm and encouraged me to go inside, but instead I stood there, fixated, as my elder child disappeared from view.

"Come on, Dad, let's go in," Bella said softly.

We went back inside and tried to make the best of the time we had left. Bella suggested that we plan a trip for the next time I synced back. "That way your whole life won't be spent indoors." I agreed it would be nice to do as a one-off, but it was difficult to pick an activity with so much on my mind—not to mention the terrible pain I would endure when taking the Pause. Would I even recover enough to stand next time? Still, we fantasized about what we would do as a family.

In the end, we decided that the newest baby boy who graced our lives would be enough entertainment for everyone. We played some games, watched a video on the Mars-One colony expansion, and talked about the next baby. Bella explained that many of the newest generation of babies were being genetically modified, enhanced with select DNA. India and China led the way in the largest population of "enhanced" humans, but communities were springing up everywhere. These weren't superbabies; they were merely screened for genetic diseases and other less-desirable traits; but I couldn't help but wonder if my old friend Rajesh Jotwani had been right all along. Were we going too far? Genetic manipulations of children, humans equipped with poisonous venom—were these the concerns that had driven Rajesh to join Millennial so long ago? Was he madder than a hatter, or did he have foresight the rest of us didn't?

"Did you do the screening for the new baby?" I asked.

"No," Bella answered strongly. "The church spoke out strongly against it. And Mom would kill me if we did. Besides, it just feels wrong to me."

Keith mentioned cost was too much of a factor in the US anyway, with the economy still reeling. Looking into his eyes, I was certain that cost was one of the only things keeping him from considering a DNA modification to my newest grandson—that, and Bella's opposition to the procedure. Certainly, he didn't seem to share her convictions.

The dizziness started to kick in, and it was time to head back to the sitting room. Bella gave me a big kiss on the cheek and told me in a weepy voice that she loved me. I told her not to upset herself as it would make the baby she carried fidgety. We were pulling up some display options for my computer that would make communicating back and forth faster, when Amara walked in.

"Daddy?" my dark-haired daughter called from the doorway. Amara ran across the room and embraced me, crying uncontrollably like a child, gasping in sobs. "I'm sorry, Daddy! I'm so sorry!"

Syncing Forward

"It's okay! Shhhh! It's okay . . ." I stroked Amara's hair as Bella came close and turned it into a group hug. Bella finally let go and whispered that she would go get some tissues. Keith stood there awkwardly until I silently waved him out of the room.

"I'll quit, Daddy. I promise, I'll quit. Just don't be mad at me." Damn, she sounded like a little girl all over again. Had she ever grown up? Was Amara trapped in the past as much as I was? I reminded myself that she had always been like this, unable to let things go until they were fixed. Presumably that made her an excellent investigator, but it meant she couldn't grasp the idea that her life could move forward without resolving every problem that got in her way.

"I'm not mad at you, Amara. You're my firstborn, my big girl, the smartest *woman* I know. It's not that I don't believe in you; I just don't want to lose you."

My daughter finally calmed down, but I felt myself syncing forward slowly. My head was spinning, the world accelerating.

"IknowDaddyIjustgetstucksometimesDaddyIthinkyouareslipping . . ."

"I love you, Amara," I managed to get out in cracking syllables.

"IloveyoutooDaddy."

Fifth Pause ended, and I once again sped toward a new future. I checked the clock-calendar on the computer display. Half an hour had gone by, and it was just after Thanksgiving of 2043. Bella had sent me a silly cartoon of a turkey wearing running shoes as it fled a meat cleaver wielded by an elderly woman. Correspondence from the family was good, and my attention was torn between my worries about Bella's pregnancy, my concern for Amara's stability, and my secret questioning whether I'd survive another syncing back. While Bella appeared to be progressing normally, Amara dipped once again into strange voice mails and cryptic messages.

AMARA, YOU OKAY? NEW T-R-A-N-S-F-E-R YET?

Certain words and phrases were preprogrammed for ease of transmission, but occasionally I was forced to type words that didn't show up on the list. I risked taking the time to send a message.

The response I got back filled me with dread.

I'M SORRY, DADDY. I CAN'T LET IT GO.

I clicked out a new message, begging her to come home for a visit. Responses were relatively instantaneous for me since the girls moved so fast compared to me. So when the seconds ticked by, I grew more concerned. I sent off a quick message to Bella to check on her sister, but by then it was too late.

It was the last message I ever got from Amara.

Syncing Forward

— **Part 6** —

Rajani

Chapter 33

My sadness carried on in silence, my throat unable to make a sound, my ears unable to hear my own breathing. All that reached me was the white noise hum they transmitted to keep me from going insane. Even the tears I shed for Amara evaporated long before they could reach my cheeks, whisked away by the rush of time. There were messages, dozens of them. Voice mails too, stacking up, but I couldn't get past the first one from Bella.

> DAD I DON'T KNOW HOW TO TELL YOU THIS BUT AMARA WAS KILLED.

Lifting my heavy arms, I pulled at my hair and fruitlessly tried to scream. I clawed at the wireless sensors affixed to my temples, only to have someone stick them back on a split second later. Trapped in a temporal cage, I wasn't even afforded an opportunity to grieve. Instead I settled for the pathetic existence that I dared call my life.

Once I calmed myself enough to read my messages, I found that Innovo was suggesting this might be the last time my body could sync back. Bella didn't want me to sync at all. I told them I needed to come back, if for no other reason than to see Amara's grave, to say good-bye.

The weeks ticked along three minutes at a time, and I sat numbly in my chair, scanning the information fed to me from the outside world, praying that it had all been a mistake, a sick joke, anything.

A click of my finger brought a news reporter's grisly description of how my child met her death.

> *Special Agent Amara James was killed in the line of duty while attempting to apprehend an escaped terrorist in West Virginia. Amara James was the older daughter of the so-*

Syncing Forward

called time traveler Martin James but was single and had no children of her own. According to inside sources, the explosion was so massive that it leveled trees and set cars from a nearby road on fire. A ceremony was performed in Washington, DC, and a more intimate service was conducted in James's hometown in Pennsylvania. Agent James was part of the Homeland Defense Force's Antiterrorism Division and an eight-time decorated officer. Three civilians were also killed, including . . .

I shut off the video and clenched the arms of the chairs, trying to rip them off, my muscles fatiguing long before I could do any damage to the furniture. Bella sat with me for a full Sunday, something she hadn't done in a long while. I looked down at her motionless body and her round pregnant belly, and for a split second I could have sworn I saw her belly extend and grow. Probably not, I told myself. She was there for a few hours, and that was all. When she vanished, I felt the loneliness creep in once again.

A few minutes more passed when I closed my eyes to rest, but I opened them to a message from Bella.

DAD, ARE YOU SURE YOU WANT TO SYNC BACK? INNOVO IS SAYING IT COULD DO PERMANENT DAMAGE. I LOVE YOU AND CAN'T STAND TO WATCH YOU SUFFER AGAIN.

I wrote back, IF I DON'T SYNC BACK THIS LAST TIME I'LL GO INSANE. PLEASE, BELLA.

She relented and told me to prepare. That was the worst part—just waiting for the onslaught of anguish to overpower me. Knowing it was going to beat me down hard, but not knowing how long it would take.

The sixth Pause was the most physically painful syncing I had experienced yet. The convulsions came on top of the burning and freezing and aching and stabbing. At one point I passed out, only to wake up to a slightly lesser version of hell. I had to stay focused on the end. Ending. It was ending. Was that moment less painful than the last? Maybe? God help me. Yes, the pain was less. Still more than I could stand, but that's what I said a day or a second ago. I caught a glimpse out of one eye and saw I was in a hospital bed. It looked like it could be our laboratory, but the sting of sensation forced my lid shut.

There were voices. Keith's voice. A woman I didn't recognize.

"Doctor, he's practically a vegetable," Keith complained. "Can't you do something to wake him up? This is all the time he's got."

The woman took a reproving tone. "Do you realize our treatment is the only thing that kept him from going through excruciating pain?"

"Can you do anything or not?" he pushed.

The woman explained that the injection she was preparing would clear my head enough to keep me awake for the next hour, and Keith thanked her. I put up my hand to let them know I was awake. At least, I thought I put up my hand. There was something burning touching my fingers, and I flinched, only to realize it was Bella's soft hand holding mine. With my eyes prying themselves open, I saw my child, my only remaining child, waiting patiently by my side.

"Hello, Dad." It was all she could manage before putting my palm against her cheek and tucking her chin down into the covers of my bed.

The woman whose voice I'd heard earlier was talking with Felipe, and she approached me quickly once I made a motion to my throat. They wet my whistle as before and managed to prop me up, the pain still prominent in my limbs.

Syncing Forward

"Hello, Martin. I'm Dr. Khatwani. We're managing your pain the best we can, but we're already struggling to cope with syncing you back. Any more pain meds and you won't be able to stay awake. Any less and I can't guarantee the level of comfort you're experiencing, as limited as that may be. Do you understand?"

I nodded and answered in my fatigue, "Yeah, I got it. Not your fault, Doc. How much time do I have?"

"You have an hour left. Maybe a little more, but not much." I remembered complaining about doctors trying to soften bad news by delivering it with innuendo. This doctor went right to the cold, hard truth, and I found myself hankering for more palliative words.

With Keith and Bella standing by, Dr. Khatwani continued. "The V-5322 is overloading your nervous system, and it is doubtful you will survive another injection. It could still be used in an emergency, but your body will require at least a week before we administer it again safely."

That was a week in "Martin time," meaning more than seventy years before they could use the Pause without risking my life. *What life*, I wondered? Did I have a life without the people I cared about in it? The blows kept landing, taking me down to the mat. One precious hour left. Amara murdered. I would have endured the pain of the Pause for the rest of my life if it meant I could bring Amara back.

Keith pushed a wheelchair with me in it out the door, down a newly installed ramp, and out to a veranda that still smelled of fresh-cut wood. Jacob toddled about as he barely managed to avoid being run over by the rubber wheels. My eyes trained in on his little shoes, his feet scampering around. I wondered if he truly understood at his age what a grandpa was.

"Dad, I want you to meet your newest grandson," Bella tried cheerfully. She brought over the sleeping child wrapped in a light cloth and a thick diaper. "This is Riley Martin Heffley, born at three o'clock in the morning on May 16. Tomorrow will be his two-month birthday. Say hello."

Two-year-old Jacob bounced about, chased by Keith. "Daddy get!" he kept repeating as he toddled about outside. Bella watched her husband and older son make laps around us and then down into the yard. She strained to make a smile appear—a desperate effort to improve the mood.

My poor petite daughter had given birth to Riley, this nine-pound behemoth of an infant whose chubby cheeks were flushed from the heat. The baby woke and began swatting at the air. She held him out for me to see, but I couldn't make a connection. My soul had shut down. And to think I actually told myself nothing would hurt worse than Miranda walking out.

"Dad, do you want to hold Riley?" Bella offered.

I gazed vacuously at my child and grandchild going through a ritual that should have been quaint and familial. Instead, my innards were twisted, wounded, and numbed by Amara's death.

"Dad, come on; hold him. He's such a good boy," she said, smiling.

I snarled. "I don't know how you can sit there grinning like a fool knowing your sister's been murdered."

Bella stopped bouncing baby Riley and set him down in his seat. She strapped him in, then approached me and grabbed my tear-soaked face. "Listen, Dad. I don't know how to make this better for you, but don't you dare suggest I haven't cried myself to sleep every night after losing Amara. If I look even remotely sane, it's because I've had seven months to learn how to cope. I miss her too. I sit in Amara's room so I can feel close to her again. But I've got a family of my own now. I don't have the luxury of sitting around and weeping."

Those words might as well have been a slap to the face. And from Bella, no less. Was I going to tell her she was wrong? Was I going to just give up and die? My daughter drew the line: grieve, yes; surrender, no. She retreated back to the baby and took a slow, deep breath to calm herself.

Syncing Forward

She unstrapped Riley, then raised him to her face and dressed up in an exaggerated smile, a singsong tone to her words. "Somebody I love once told me babies know when their mommies are upset, and they pick up on it, don't they? We don't want a sad baby, now do we?"

His little legs kicked as he listened to his mother's voice, but as soon as Riley looked away, Bella's saddened eyes returned. She stood and brought the child to me, kneeling by my side. "Dad, you know how you told me I'd always be your baby? Well, this is *my* baby, and I want you to be a part of his life. Now hold him. Hold your new grandson."

She held Riley up and let his arms and legs whirl in the air as he grasped for anything or anyone to cling to. Hesitantly I reached out and settled Riley into my arms. My little grandson was a plump one, with big folds in his legs and thick fingers that pulled at the hair on my arms with a tight grip. He stared at me with full brown eyes and opened his mouth wide.

"Hey, Riley," I said, letting out my best baby voice. His legs kicked in excitement at my voice and then stopped as he watched me intently. "Hey, big boy." My words once more animated my grandson with jerks and wiggles.

It brought a smile to my face—a smile that seemed impossible just moments ago. Bella watched us giggling as I took delight in this new member of the family, but my laughs quickly turned to sobs as I held my grandson for consolation. Bella reached out to take Riley away, but let me hold him anyway, let me grieve for Amara as I held this innocent boy.

There should have been joy in the house. There should have been laughter. But Amara's death was a deep wound that I couldn't ignore. She had been thirty-one years old. I realized there would be no legacy of family from her, no child to call out to her. She would never be a mommy who would get cockeyed looks from her disbelieving kids when she talked about the old days of chasing down bad guys and analyzing bioengineering data to help save their grandfather. No reconciling differences between Amara and her mother.

God, up until now I hadn't even considered how awful Miranda must feel.

"Miranda?" was all I could ask my daughter.

"Mom came to the funeral," Bella answered with teary eyes. "It was two weeks before Christmas, and we had to go through Amara's clothes to find, well, an outfit for her to rest in."

"Do you know if she and Amara . . . you know . . . spoke?"

Bella shook her head with the strength of a soft breeze. All of those moments of what-could-have-been were finished, replaced by the cold reality of consequence. Miranda must have been out of her mind with grief. If I didn't think it would make matters worse, I would have called her then and there.

I once read that the death of a child is like a period placed before the end of a sentence. The insight had never truly found its mark within my heart until this moment.

From Bella's wedding to this moment, five years had whizzed by, and yet it felt like less than twenty-four hours. In a single day my younger daughter had gotten married and had two children; my brother had died from a stroke way too young; and my older daughter had been murdered. The Pause was wearing off—the last of the V-5322 I could take for many, many years. The technician was setting up my chair, and fear grew within me as I pondered that I might never sync back again. Innovo still hadn't made any decisions on whether research into Millennial's chemopreservative drugs would continue. The Pause would kill me if I used it again. My body would reject the other treatments. I settled into the chair, unsure of my fate, reticent in the face of doom.

The moment was interrupted by Keith, who cleared his throat to catch my attention.

"Martin?"

"Yes, Keith?" I whispered.

Syncing Forward

"Uh, I know the timing is bad, but there's somebody here to see you."

"Is it family?"

"No."

"Then I don't want to talk to whoever it is. Tell them to come back in a decade or two." My sarcastic comment didn't amuse him, and he stood there motionless. "Who is it, Keith? A reporter?"

"It's Ivan, Amara's partner from the DHD. He says it's important."

Ivan Fagundes hadn't been with her when she was killed. I hadn't seen or spoken to him since the bombing in Easton, Pennsylvania. Bella had mentioned that he was there at the funeral and was the last person to leave Amara's gravesite. Now he was at our front door uninvited, but something about the impromptu visit inclined me to give the man a minute. Maybe two.

At my approval, Keith let him in, and we cleared the sitting room at his insistence. Ivan had trimmed down since our last meeting, but he was a big man who looked like he could still do some damage if anybody was unlucky enough to get within his grasp. His goatee was missing, replaced with a clean-shaven square jaw.

"Mr. James, I was hoping to extend my condolences before you—" His tone was hurried and quiet.

I interrupted. "Ivan, I know you were friends with Amara, and I appreciate you stopping by, but I literally could start slowing any minute now. I hoped to spend this time with my family—no offense."

"No prob. I wouldn't be bugging you except Amara gave me instructions to get ahold of you if . . . well, if, you know, anything happened." Ivan looked down regretfully.

Anger I didn't know I felt welled up at him. "Why weren't you with her, Ivan? I know I'm twenty years out of sync, but I figured partners still stuck together on dangerous assignments. That's why they *assign partners*, you know." My accusatory tone caught me off guard. It

327

wasn't my aim to make the man feel more terrible than he obviously did.

"Mr. James, trust me when I tell you I would have been there if she had let me. But your daughter was pretty stubborn. She didthingsthatsheshouldn'thvdnbut Amara went rogue . . ." Ivan's voice sped up for a good portion of his explanation and then slowed once more—my body was in its last synced moments. "Everything you might have read about her last assignment, the subject she was pursuing . . . it's all a fabrication."

I found myself holding my breath. "What are you talking about?"

"I could be arrested for coming here . . . or worse." Ivan Fagundes rubbed his head nervously. "There's a facility near Washington, DC, that is completely underground. It's under Walter Reed. They've been holding another man who's got your same condition. Amara said to tell you never to trust them—the researchers at Walter Reed. She said the man was sleeping as he synced forward until just over a year ago when he woke up. He was under the influence of another drug, one that let him sleep when he was slowed down."

I was growing impatient. Something was on his mind, and he was dancing around the important details. "Jesus, Ivan, I'm starting to slow down. Just tell me what you're supposed to tell me!"

Ivan was talking with his hands, desperately trying to get the words out. "Everything the feds tried in order to wake him up failed. They figured out they just needed to wait him out, let the drug run its course, but they couldn't do that unless he was synced up like you. So they kept testing all their drugs on you first, but it wasn't for you, get it? Everything that didn't work on you they passed on. Everything that did work, they stuck him with. So then one day he woke up, and that's when the interrogation started. They wanted what he knew. But their chance only lasted a couple of hours because the Pause didn't go long-term.

"Amara found out about him. She found out and did everything she could to get at him. After things went south with our

Syncing Forward

meeting with Bernard, she met another member of the Millennial terrorists. That's when she started working with them, hoping they'd help her, you see? Amara went rogue. She corrupted our files at DHD. She destroyed evidence."

"No, Amara would never do that. She hated them as much as I do." I shook my head in disbelief while knowing Amara was fully capable of all of it all.

"No, no, Mr. James! I loved Amara, but you know as well as I do that she was willing to do anything to save you. I swear on my life I had no idea she was working with Millennial, or I would have stopped her. You gotta believe me."

I couldn't. "You told me Amara gave you instructions to talk to me in case she died?"

"A month ago I found a note she hid for me. I didn't show it to anybody because I knew I'd be finished if I did. In it, Amara wrote about the Millennial terrorist at Walter Reed. The other man, the prisoner there? It's Bruchmuller. Dieterich Bruchmuller is alive. They've got him . . ."

Chapter 34

The chimes from the monitor rang their alarm. Bella, Keith, and the doctor rushed in past Ivan Fagundes to my side. They were asking me questions, but I was already syncing forward, and their faces were blurred by both motion and fatigue. They placed my eye gear on and set up the monitoring pads and poked at me in all the usual places. Bella typed a quick message telling me she loved me and not to give up hope.

Hope. I had it again. Hope and anger. Amara was dead, but somehow that son of a bitch Bruchmuller was alive. All those years Walter Reed had him in their care, testing their treatments on me so they could bleed him for Millennial's secrets. Amara had figured it out, maybe even years ago, but never could capitalize on the information. Maybe I wouldn't either, but I would try.

I was fighting fatigue and sedatives, my nervous system was racked from a half-dozen medications and treatments, and my soul was tormented by loss, but I still reached for the keyboard to try to send a message to Bella. She had to know, and I couldn't be certain that Ivan would share the information with her. If Bruchmuller was syncing forward just like me, that meant Walter Reed didn't have a cure yet, but that could mean the government was still doing research.

I closed my eyes and suddenly didn't feel like opening them again. I was floating on water, or maybe it was the laboratory bed. The room was warm and inviting and dark and I couldn't wait to sleep away all the problems, all the worries. Maybe I'd wake up and this would be a dream? Yes, this was all a dream, and I was waking up in my old bed in my old house. Miranda's arm wrapped around me from behind. Having breakfast. Sitting in traffic on the way to my old office at Innovo. Parking in front of the A Building and watching it gleam in the sunlight until it exploded like a grand crystal vase packed with dynamite.

Syncing Forward

"It's your move."

"I can't move. If I move my king, I'm going to lose."

"You still have to move him."

"You won. I'll be checkmated in three moves. I give up."

"Why do you look so sad, Amara? It's just a game."

"I'm not sad about the game."

"Well, what is it, kiddo?"

"I don't want to say . . ."

"Come on, big kid. You can tell me anything; you know that."

"Daddy, it's time to wake up."

"Wake up? Wake up from what?"

"From this. It's not real. I'm not real."

"What are you talking about?"

"This is a dream, Daddy. And it's time for it to end."

"Will you be there when I wake?"

"I'm gone now."

"I'm sorry those people killed you."

"They didn't kill me, Daddy. You did."

"Amara, I'm sorry! Please don't go . . ."

Chapter 35

As I came to, I slowly realized I wasn't in my bed or my house or even in a room. Amara's painful words faded away like a storm passing over the mountains, but their impact lingered. She had died because of me.

At first I had the strange sensation that I'd wet myself and the warm urine was running all over my body, some strange flashback to my childhood combining with the unusual sensory input I was experiencing. Floating, swishing, weightlessness. Was I dreaming? Where was I? And a sound came from all around me, an echo of bubbles like a fish tank or a hot tub.

My eyes opened to an alien sight: I was suspended nude in a liquid that felt vaguely different from water. Strapped around my head was a piece of gear that covered my eyes, mouth, and nose. Air came through that smelled antiseptic. I became increasingly aware of a soreness around the straps that held me loosely in place and figured that I'd been attached to this thing for a long time. There were tubes feeding out of my arms, legs, and abdomen. Even though my vision was fogged, I could still see my arm hair swaying in the amber-tinted liquid, alternating between standing straight up and falling flat against my skin. A small but defined pulse to the fluid in which I was suspended kept me centered in the tank.

The tank . . . It was cylindrical, maybe ten feet tall and four feet across. I tried to see outside of it, but my vision was impeded by the fog in the goggles, the distortion of the liquid, the curve of the container walls, the lack of illumination from beyond. Was I syncing forward or synced back? In Beacon, Pennsylvania? A medical facility? How long had I been sleeping? Hours? Years?

I looked up to see if there might be some sort of door through which I could climb out, but I saw only a plastic grate with no handles or latches. I felt around anyway, hoping my fingers would find a control or handle, but found nothing except smooth surfaces. I was trapped.

Syncing Forward

My concern growing, I knocked on the tank walls and heard the banging echo back to my ears. At least I could tell that I was synced back; being submerged gave sounds the same muffled quality as being out of sync, but the amplified gong of my hand against the wall made a sound I definitely could not hear when slowed down. But where was everyone? Where were Bella and Keith? Where were the Innovo doctors?

I knocked on the tank. Everything on the other side was still. Had the medication Millennial injected me with run its course? Maybe. Nobody had a solitary clue about how the drug had been manufactured or what timeline it would operate on. Perhaps it only lasted twenty years. Perhaps it lasted forever.

I banged on the side of the tank again. Something was definitely wrong. If whoever had me here really had my best intentions in mind, surely they would have put a call button within reach, or a way to signal somebody—anything! I banged on the glass with my open palms, beating at the glass like a madman. My breathing grew rapid and erratic. The oxygen wasn't coming in any faster, and I grew lightheaded. Dear God! Would I suffocate in this watery prison?

Then, to my relief, lights went on in the room, and I could see a figure moving quickly about. A second joined him, and then a third. There was a sound coming all around me, low and powerful. My feet descended to the bottom of the tank, and I could feel the suspension I was in rushing between my toes and into the drains below. I looked up and noticed the fluid level dropping steadily. A face pressed up against the glass—distorted like a fun-house mirror. Still, I could tell it was Bella.

She was yelling something, but there was no making it out. Two words, one syllable each. Her hand made a motion like she was pushing down on something. Down . . . down . . . did she want me to crouch down? Sit down? Look down? She was definitely saying "down," but I didn't understand the first word. I looked frantically at the floor of the tank and didn't see anything but a set of small drains spaced evenly about a plastic grating.

333

W Lawrence

I looked up at her and shrugged my shoulders. I had no idea what she wanted me to do! The fluid level finally passed my ears on its way out of the tank, and I could see Bella better—but more importantly, I could hear her better.

"Calm down! Calm down! You're okay . . . just relax, Dad."

I put my hands on the sides of the tank and tried to slow my breathing. *Calm down.* I must have panicked and set off every damn alarm they had. It dawned on me that the only thing causing the lack oxygen was probably me freaking out unnecessarily. Disoriented, frightened, I waited for the details to come.

I was also embarrassingly aware that I was bare-ass naked in front of my daughter. As the suspension liquid swirled down the drain, I knelt at the bottom of the tank, covering my groin as best I could. I didn't have long to wait, as the top unsealed and the entire tank slowly rotated sideways. I inched forward on my knees, sliding forward carefully so as not to let my nude figure fly awkwardly out of the slippery tube and onto the floor in front of everyone. A man was reaching into the tube, and I grabbed for his hand. He slid me gracelessly along on my knees, past the top, and into a waiting oversized towel. There were hands all about me, pulling at tubes and lifting me up into a concave padded bed. There was no keeping my pride after all that handling.

A woman in zebra-patterned scrubs got very close to my ear and announced loudly, "Martin, we're going to be removing the breather. When we pull it off, I want you to exhale as hard as you can. Can you do that?"

I nodded and gave a thumbs-up.

As the apparatus was pulled from my face, a seal broke, and something moist came out of my chest. It felt like vomiting out of my lungs. Lying on my side, I watched the discolored water spew out of my mouth and into a clear basin. I continued to squeeze my diaphragm tightly, chin down, until the last remnants of the oxygenated fluid dribbled from my body.

Syncing Forward

I took a deep, painful breath as the icy air chopped at my lungs. I could not avoid the sting except to deny myself oxygen. I blew out and drew in again, this time with far less discomfort. Within a half-dozen breaths I was breathing normally and on my back. My eyes were having a difficult time focusing, but I managed to make out Bella in the background, peeking over the shoulders of the people working on me. A man with a surgical mask spoke with my daughter and then disappeared from view.

Bella managed to creep to my side in all the ruckus and put her hand on my face. "It's okay, Dad. They're going to put you under again for one last treatment. I'll see you next year."

How many treatments had I gone through? Were they purging my system of the Millennial drug? Why did I have to wait a year? I tried to ask her what was going on, but the injection was already flowing through my body, and I was lost to darkness once again.

Chapter 36

"Welcome back, Dad," Bella's voice startled me awake. I drew the air in quickly, holding it in my lungs till I could feel each muscle in my chest stretch. She wore a plastic cover over a blue dress as she stood among a dozen men and women in white lab coats. Where? How? When? The questions beat their way out of me, and behind them all was an almost malevolent desire to find Bruchmuller.

Doctors controlled the room, unfortunately, pushing my daughter back to the wall, ignoring my questions while I endured hours of prodding. They explained how my nervous system had been fried by the V-5322 and—while many repairs had been done in the recovery tank—some procedures had to be done while I was synced back.

Lights, machines, strangers, all working underneath the familiar Innovo logo on the wall. Distracting me from all of it hung two thoughts: I wanted the Remedium; I wanted Bruchmuller to suffer. And I didn't care which order those came in.

As I bounced from one set of hands to the next, I gleaned the staples of information I needed. Nine years had come and gone. It was 2053, and we were in an Innovo facility in Fort Worth, Texas. Techs and docs confirmed with enthusiasm that their new *Accelerate* treatment was stable. Accelerate. Funny how the name of the treatment was flashier now that the public knew about my existence. And it wasn't just an improvement on the name V-5322. No painful transition, no dizziness, no terrible aftereffects. It had taken some time, but Innovo had finally put more resources into helping me.

Innovo intended for Accelerate to permanently counteract the effects of the original injection I'd received at the hands of Millennial. Unfortunately, it failed. It did, however, allow me to sync back for nearly a full day before I would sync forward. The mechanics of the treatment were beyond me, but one of the technicians explained that my cells were dosed with a targeted radiation within a specially designed chamber, and the end result was my syncing back. After

Syncing Forward

twenty-two hours, I had to return to the chamber where the computer would monitor my return to chemo-preservation, dosing me as needed to make sure everything remained uniform. Whether I was syncing forward or back, I learned back in Beacon that "uniform" equaled "good."

It sounded like a crap-load of radiation—and it was. The cumulative effects would certainly have killed me if it hadn't been for an available medication that purged my system of radiation. The only drawback they mentioned was the anti-radiation treatment was somewhat toxic to the human body—it was designed for battlefields and terrorist attacks, not for regular use. Because of that, I had to wait six months before I could do it all over again.

Two days per year. No torturous transition. It was a far cry from normal, but given what I had lived through, I'd take it. Another nine damn years I had lost on top of everything else. Nine years floating naked in amber liquid, waiting for my nervous system to recover from the last treatment. Who knew what the true effects of Innovo's new treatment were? Not me, but solutions weren't exactly beating down my door either.

After leaving the hospital, a limousine drove us westward out of the DFW Metro. and I finally had a chance to catch up with Bella on my missing decade. My daughter sat by my side, handed me a clear electronic reader as thin as paper, and pulled up a copy of a court order. It read:

> *Innovo Industries International, doing business as Innovo Industries Incorporated within the boundaries of the State of Pennsylvania, United States Proper, has neglected its custodial requirements relating to Mr. Martin H. James (National ID A6-NBC-77439-333044H2) under agreements with the United States Department of Homeland Defense. Pursuant to National Defense Act ND-*

W Lawrence

> *65993 (Section T2, Para. 12) Martin H. James will be remitted into the custody of...*

"What the heck is this?" I asked her.

"The government came for us, Dad," she said calmly. "They were ready to take you back into custody, and our guess was you were never coming back. And it wasn't just you. The house, the lab, and everyone associated with it. Our whole family."

I scanned through the legalese before handing her back the reading device. "How did you get out of this?"

"We didn't." Bella shrugged. "We were done for. Dave Tsai has a friend in the Justice Department who tipped him off before Homeland Defense raided Innovo and our house. Dave called me in the middle of the night telling us you were being shipped to their Dallas facility on a cargo plane. We caught a private jet out of Harrisburg and fled the country. Innovo sent moving vans to get what they could from the house, but it was too late. We lost everything."

"I'm so sorry, Bella."

"It's fine, Dad. It's just stuff, right?" She gave me a sideways hug and a kiss on the cheek. "We saved you, and that's the important part."

"And I appreciate that." I nodded slowly. "So, give me the lowdown. We're in a limousine going where?"

"We're going home. Jacksboro, Texas. We'll be there in an hour and change."

"Why Jacksboro?"

"Keith found work on the railroad, and it's a good city. You'll like it."

As the limo carried us along, I buried my daughter in question after question. What happened with Ivan Fagundes and his claim that Bruchmuller was alive? Bella found nothing but dead ends. Ivan's

Syncing Forward

phone had been disconnected, there were no public records, no mention of his life or his death. It seemed implausible that a Homeland Defense agent—a public employee—could disappear so completely, but life in the United States had become increasingly dangerous. A few months after Ivan disappeared, the government came for us as well.

After the move to Texas, Bella's optimism diminished with each failed attempt to glean more information about Dieterich Bruchmuller or Ivan Fagundes. E-mails, notes, videos—Bella had scoured them all, only to find nothing. Years sped by, and my surviving child sadly concluded that whatever secrets Amara had uncovered she'd taken with her to the grave.

Swallowing that pill proved hard indeed: that all Amara's efforts had amounted to nothing when it came to curing me. My daughter—my firstborn child—had left an empty legacy that fell short of everything she'd wanted to accomplish. It tore at me knowing Amara's life was a mere collection of regret and tears and hopelessness and questions that would never be answered.

I clasped my hands together and bent over to stare through the floor of the limo. It was over for me.

"Don't, Dad."

"Don't what?" I asked her.

"Don't shut down on me. Aren't you the one who told me to live my life?" She held my hand comfortingly. "You need to do the same. We have a new home in a new country, and the Accelerate treatment could easily lead to your cure. We're not giving up on you, so don't you dare give up on us."

Bella always seemed like the weaker of the two kids, but when I looked into my daughter's eyes that day, I knew I had been wrong. She was the one that kept trucking no matter what.

"I wish I could take credit for you being such a strong woman," I admitted, "but truth be told, you earned that description all on your own." I told her I would break out of my funk, shake off the blows, and keep fighting. God knew I didn't want to, but I would do it for my daughter.

Through the window I saw how Jacksboro sprawled across the open Texas land, a growing center of industry and commerce that crept steadily in every direction. The city was bright and clean and fresh with construction. Factories dotted the landscape—at least what I assumed were factories. The architecture of some of the buildings included deep angular cuts and pyramidal windows that seemed anything but practical. Others were shimmering rectangular boxes coated in solar panels.

We finally passed through a gate and turned onto the driveway of a walled property. That's when I caught my first glimpse of "the dome." Our new house shaped the property, a single-story ranch frame with a steeple rising an additional fifteen feet above the roof. Atop this steeple was a reflective top shaped like an egg. The sunlight shone through it just enough to reveal a chair within. My chair. This was to be my new perch from which I could watch the world.

"What's up with the tower?" I asked Bella as I stepped out of the limo.

She took my hand, "It's an observation chair. It's also where the Accelerate treatment will be administered. It's a hundred-percent automated, and the radiation won't harm us in the house with you so far up in the air. You'll like it! It's perfectly safe when not in use, but I told the kids they would get radiation poisoning if they went inside, just to keep them out."

I chuckled. "You're a mean mama. I like it. The secret is safe with me."

The front door to the house opened, and I was treated to a larger family than I had left in Pennsylvania. Victoria Heffley was my newest grandchild, seven years old with a face that looked nothing like Bella's or Keith's or anyone's in the family. She gave me a small handshake and ducked behind Keith's imposing frame. Riley, now ten years old, circled me like a mad thing, saying all his friends wanted to time travel like me. Jacob was a different story, however. He was twelve

Syncing Forward

years old and struggling with walking with some thin assistive device on his left arm and leg. I waited to speak with Keith and Bella alone to find out what happened.

That night, my daughter explained that when he reached four years old, Jacob had been diagnosed with sinistropolio—a new and crippling twist on polio that affected only the left side of the body. Since the epidemic had started in Arizona and spread across the American Governance, rumors flew that the disease had been engineered by the United States military. It wouldn't be the first time a new—or old—disease had been cooked up. Keith told me that National Socialist scientists in Greece had tainted the water supply in France with a genetically modified version of the flu that targeted only Muslims. Two hundred and thirty thousand people, mostly children, died as the flu ravaged Europe's Muslim communities. I shook my head in defeat as she told me the news—life had become incredibly cheap in forty years. I feared what terrors my grandchildren would find all too common when they reached adulthood.

The rest of the evening was spent with the children buzzing about, while I tried to catch up on the world and get a grip on lost history. Most of all I delved into the correspondence between Bella and Innovo regarding a cure. I promised Bella I would be optimistic and thankful, but my heart sank every time something reminded me of my brother, my mom, my wife, my daughter.

Keith spent some time showing me the observation dome controls with Victoria peeking at us the entire time. The egg-shaped capsule was downright space-aged, but I took to the controls intuitively. The folks at Innovo did a bang-up job and must have spent a pretty penny on it. I guessed the secrets inside my body were still worth something to them.

The most unusual part of this new arrangement was sleeping in a bed while still synced back. I had twenty-two hours, and the doctors insisted I get my rest. The next morning I would climb into the capsule and spend six months detoxing, waiting for the anti-radiation drugs to filter out of my system. Six months to me was easy——from my perception it was just over an hour to burn. The hard part was sleeping. I got my good night kisses and was given a dark, quiet room with a comfy bed.

I kept thinking about Bruchmuller underneath Walter Reed, how the US government would have probably pulled me apart to cure him. The betrayal stung me, made me feel worthless.

I kept thinking of Amara. My child was dead.

I turned the light on and stared at the wall restlessly. Framed in wood was a letter addressed to me.

2049 September 19

Office of the Governor
J. Pelletier
Xavier Dorn Building
1100 San Jacinto Blvd.
Austin, Texas

Mr. Martin James,

On behalf of the sovereign nation of Texas, I am delighted to offer you asylum and residential status effective as of the date of this letter. You have been sponsored by Lily Oland-James in accordance with the American Governance Refugee Act of 2039 and as such have declared yourself an able-bodied civilian or as having the means with which to support yourself...

Syncing Forward

Chapter 37

"Dirty Bomb Kills Tens of Thousands, Clears London—Millennial Credited"

"China Liberates South Korea, Delivers Message of Unity"

"Washington State in Meltdown—Riots Draw Unenforceable Curfew for Seattle"

"Mars Celebrates 200th Resident"

" 'We Are People Too!'—Clones and Civil Liberties"

"Islamic Crescent Envelops Italy—Refugees Reportedly Slaughtered"

    I sat in the dome. The Harrison Tower was twenty-nine stories high and counting, and I watched with a sense of wonder as the last half of it was built in half an hour. The shiny glass office building was definitely the tallest structure on the horizon, looming over the station where magnetic rails brought in cargo on trains that looked more like streak-of-lightning freight cars. Watching the city grow industriously was a pleasant break from the headlines, which only showed the world ripping itself apart.

    The unknown material composing my observation chair felt more like a sponge than a fabric-covered cushion, and it adjusted to my movements easily. The egg-shaped dome I sat under shed away rain and dirt and gave me an unobstructed view of the urban skyline. With a turn of my head, my chair smoothly rotated so that I could look down at the small, distinctive homes that stretched to the north and east.

A computer monitored what I looked at and made incredibly accurate determinations as to how to enhance my vision. As the sun dropped below the horizon, the smartglass in the dome enhanced the view of the skyline wherever I fixed my gaze. The clear view made everything crisper, more discernible, but whatever algorithm allowed it to function was beyond me. When I looked up at the stars, the computer illuminated a projected azimuth for the moon's pathway as the stars spun on their axis. Anything I wanted to view in the heavens was mine to explore, but before I could survey the night sky further, the sun crept back into the world and the photonics within the glass shaded my eyes from the bold sunlight that beat its way into my shell.

"Dad, we'll be bringing you down shortly. I've set your clock to read the new countdown. Remember to compliment Riley on his new big-boy teeth." Text complemented Bella's warbled voice, appearing to hover before my face in 3D imagery. I couldn't be sure how the words were projected; I didn't know how most of the technology around me worked.

"Thanks, sweetheart," I mouthed. "I love you."

THANKS, SWEETHEART. I LOVE JUICE.

The same computer that monitored my eyes could read my lips, interpreting my mouth's movements and converting it to speech for the family to hear or read. It was . . . not as accurate at figuring my speech. While my vocal cords couldn't make sounds when I was syncing forward, my lips and jaws didn't move like a normal person's either. My muscles fatigued and my lips dried out, but I silently mouthed my way through conversation anyway. I repeated myself slowly. "Not juice. I meant I love yooou."

NOT JUICE. I MEANT I LOVE JEWS.

There was a recorded response with the whole family laughing hysterically in the background. Bella responded brightly, "Thanks, Dad. We love the Jews too."

Syncing Forward

I smiled thinly, not quite able to bring myself to the laughter that was captured on the recording. While I still dwelt on Amara's passing, I had to acknowledge that many years had passed for everybody else. My fresh wounds were well-worn scars for Bella and the others. The calendar showed May 2054 and ticking. An artificial voice informed me that my second Accelerate treatment was complete. I was going home to visit again.

The autumn sky was slowing down, and my chair descended from its perch atop the house and into Keith and Bella's home. The observation bubble descended smoothly and spun to face the living room of our new house. A seam appeared in the glass that cut its way in the shape of an ellipse, ultimately slipping to the side and melting back into the clear material behind me. A glance at the rate meter next to my chair read 0.55 and rising—I was moving about half the speed of everybody. I watched the numbers change: 0.78. 0.89. 0.94.

Victoria was the first to greet me, surprisingly. Over those six months she had corresponded minimally, but now she wrapped her arms around my neck and kissed me on the cheek before I could get out of my chair.

"So, Grandpa," Victoria told me with heaps of precociousness, "I suppose I am going to have to show you how to use our new computer since you don't know anything about it. Don't worry—the interface is extremely easy for old people to use." She was a brown-haired beauty with blue eyes that hid a dozen thoughts behind them. She smiled and handed me a tablet with a gorgeous moving picture of a cityscape displayed across it. Cars zipped along wild lit roadways under impossibly arching buildings. "By the way, I made this for you. I hope you like it."

Bella peeked around the corner, waiting for her daughter to clear out of the room before she came over and helped me out of the chair. "Welcome back, Dad."

"Same to you. Victoria warmed up this time. She gave me a hug *and* a picture, although I don't recognize the city."

345

"Actually, Dad, it's a freehand sketch of Ibadan." Bella pinched the bottom corner, and the whole sheet went blank, followed by a time lapse of how Victoria had gone about drawing it on the computer.

"Where the heck is Ibadan?"

"Come on, Dad, you don't know? It's the second largest city in Nigeria."

I looked at her and raised an eyebrow.

"Okay, fine," Bella said. "I had to look it up. But it's incredible, right?"

"Wow, I'm impressed," I said, this time sincerely. "She did this all herself?"

"The drawing and the movements, yeah," my daughter answered nervously. "It's gonna take some time to get used to her being like this."

My newest grandchild was another education in how there was no stopping progress. Just after moving to Texas, doctors diagnosed Jacob with his new disease, and Bella miscarried for the second time. The doctors presented Keith and Bella with the option for genetically selecting their next child, and given the circumstances and the means to do so, they took the option.

Using Keith and Bella's DNA, engineers pieced together the highest quality genetic bits of my daughter and her husband and bound them together with nanorobots and designer retroviruses. Victoria was guaranteed to never contract a disease or even a cold for thirty years. Her bones knit twelve times faster than a normal human's, and she learned six times faster than her peers. In addition, her nervous system came standard with implantable upgrades so that she could accept further mods with little chance of rejection. My grand-daughter sounded superhuman to me; in reality, she was one of millions of mods whose population was growing and changing the face of humanity.

At our first meeting, before I knew anything about the modifications, I found Victoria mature in ways that surpassed Amara

Syncing Forward

at seven years old: a large vocabulary, clear communication, a clever demeanor. However, Victoria had an eerie stability to her. She wasn't emotionally distant like Amara was—she was more aloof than anything else. When I asked Bella why she'd had a change of heart about having a genetically enhanced child, she answered only by looking sympathetically on her polio-afflicted son limping about the house.

Syncing back for a full day not only meant sleeping but showering and going to the bathroom like a normal human being. And dinner was certainly a more enjoyable experience now that I could eat some real foods. With newly improved rapid digestive enzymes, I could eat some proteins and fats. Turkey burgers were in—steak was still out. Cheese and butter were back on the menu, which I had a bad hankering for. Alcohol was still a no-no, and the Lord only knew how badly I needed a drink. It was still important to moderate my food intake as I couldn't take the chance of having food left in my system while syncing forward, but I didn't mind. The Accelerate treatment allowed me to have the closest thing to a normal life that I could have.

"So, Dad," Bella began, "Keith and I have some good news for you."

"Pregnant again?" I asked, perhaps more enthusiastically than I should have.

"No," she enunciated, "that ship has *sailed*. No, this is a different bit of good news. Come with me."

We walked into the wide-open living room that was sunbathed with a large bay window. The sofas were arranged in an L shape with a square coffee table between them. When we stepped in, Ivan Fagundes stood up from the sofa and worked his way to me with an outstretched hand.

347

Chapter 38

"Mr. James, welcome back."

Ivan looked pretty good, although the gray hair in his beard and on his head was a stark reminder of the passage of time. His reaction complemented my own. "Man, it is twisted how you don't age. You look exactly the same. Even your eye is still a little banged up."

I touched it reflexively. "I reckon it is, but Bella says it's getting better."

"Oh yeah, it looks a little better, I guess." He nodded. "It's been a while, though."

We sat down catty-corner from each other, my lap quickly occupied by Victoria, who jumped up on me and snuggled against my neck. It reminded me of Bella, who had done the same thing a week ago, from my perspective. The first question on my mind was where Ivan had been, and his answer was as much of a surprise as I might have expected.

"Prison."

"You're kidding."

"Don't I wish. DHD brought me before a tribunal and found me guilty of obstruction of justice, perjury, and a few other various and sundry items."

My stomach churned. "Is this because you came to me and told me about Amara?"

"No. Maybe a little. I dunno. They had charges trumped up when they flipped my apartment and came up empty-handed. They knew I had something, though. Eight years after they arrested me, they put me in a work detail near the West Virginia border. I was able to bolt, cut into the Governance and down to Oklahoma, where I've been laying low, seeing how far DHD can reach, trying to avoid being picked up by Governance deporters. I finally was able to make contact with Bella and Keith a few months ago."

"Hey, I'm sorry, Ivan. I really—"

He waved his hand dismissively. "This is not your fault, Mr. James. I had info, and I refused to share it with my superiors. That was my choice, my way of respecting Amara's memory."

"So what did you find?" I asked him. "I mean, was she close to finding one of Millennial's crypts? Or a sympathetic member? Did Bruchmuller give up information on the Remedium?"

With an uneasy reach, Ivan handed me a handkerchief from his pocket. A piece of paper was wrapped within, sealed in a plastic bag with a faded *2/I F/A* written in marking pen. To Ivan from Amara.

"Our team always called each other by our first initials. A, E, I, and O. We were always joking around that we were looking for U." It was a long-distant memory for him, the kind forged in misery. A look of embarrassment marked his face as he handed over the precious note.

Kissing Victoria, I handed my seven-year-old granddaughter off to her mom and asked for a moment alone. The two scurried away, Bella discouraging the boys from interrupting as she went. I undid the bag and unfolded the words, wrinkled and ironed flat again by time and pressure.

I,

There is a lot I can say to you, but first I want to say I'm sorry that I hurt you. You were the best friend I could have, and I couldn't give you back what you were looking for. In the beginning it was bad timing, then later it just didn't work out, and after O was gone it was just too soon for me. Now I'm going to have to say good-bye. I made a deal with the Devil to save my father, and it's time for him to collect. I

W Lawrence

know you would try to stop me, which is why I didn't tell you.

Millennial is fracturing. There are those that are resigned to the fact that we are going to destroy the world, and they want to be there to inherit it when everyone is gone. Then there are the ones we've been hunting: those who want to stop certain types of technology from being developed and produced. The people I'm meeting, I don't know where their intentions lie. To be honest I don't know where mine lie either. I don't know who I am anymore.

There aren't any good choices left, I. If things go bad . . . If that happens, I need you to get to my father. You'll know by the time you read this which way things went.

If my dad is still syncing forward, tell him to never trust Walter Reed. The man they've been holding there is Dr. Dieterich Bruchmuller. He's in chemopreservation, and every suspicion I had about using my father as a test subject has been confirmed by Maggie Gonzales before she passed. They have lied to us from the beginning. They found DB dead after the 2021 Innovo bombing but he must have injected himself, assuming that he'd appear dead, be buried, and recover. But they figured out he was alive, and now he's a prisoner.

If things go right for me for once, we'll be on opposite sides, and none of this will even matter.

The V-5322 antidote was shared with WR and they've managed to wake up DB, but it's killing him just like it's

Syncing Forward

killing my father. They won't risk losing DB, and so you know who they will experiment on to crack him open. I can't let that happen.

I made sure you had an alibi, but if you're smart, you'll burn this letter and never mention it just in case.

You may not believe it, but I'll say it anyway.

With love,

A

PS: tardus, somnus, remedium

It might have been written after the brief message Amara sent me, perhaps before. There was no date. Ivan must have treasured those parting words, an eleven-year-old memorial to his friend, his partner, and whatever else Amara was to him. For me, the note sliced over the fresh wound of my daughter's death. A death that had occurred a mere two days ago.

Drawing a deep breath, I let it out and held the note out to Ivan. "Thank you for sharing this with me."

"Hey, Mr. James, it wasn't my intention to upset you . . ."

I patted him on the shoulder and explained that he shouldn't apologize, that not knowing was worse than knowing. It turned out that whatever plan Amara had, she'd timed it with Ivan's vacation so he wouldn't be suspected of aiding her. Her plans hadn't protected him, though, nor had they succeeded in getting the Remedium. I thought of my poor daughter in the end, wondering what she felt in her last moments.

I sat still for a long time before I spoke.

W Lawrence

My finger ran over the postscript at the end of the letter. "I recognize the word *remedium* at the bottom, but what are the other two words?"

The largish man leaned in and pointed his finger at the note. "Well, she never said, but it didn't take much to figure it out. They're all Latin. *Tardus* means slow. *Somnus* means sleep. *Remedium* is a remedy or a fix. Those are loose translations, but I'm positive they are the names of the Millennial drugs. One makes you slow, one makes you sleep, one makes you wake up. Makes sense, right? When you were held hostage at Innovo, they were going to inject you with a fifth vial. That had to be the Somnus. They were planning on taking you with them to the crypts, and I doubt they wanted you waking up in transit."

Ivan and Amara only knew the word *remedium* because Bernard had called the drug that, and Ivan was sure Amara would have told him the names of the other drugs when we met in Easton if she'd known them then. They were only words, after all. However, it stood to reason that my daughter learned the names *Somnus* and *Tardus* after the meeting with Bernard. I didn't want to believe Ivan about Amara conspiring with Millennial in the end. There had to be more to the story. It had to be some elaborate ruse my daughter concocted to get in with these people.

It was as plain as day that Ivan was holding something back. It took some needling and convincing him that he couldn't hurt me more than I already was hurt, but I still had to drag it out of the man.

"I could be totally wrong, Mr. James. But after I got out of prison, I did my own snooping, looking into this. One of my old buddies in the analytics department told me he'd heard about a rogue agent who had been killed, and that the files had been ordered purged afterward. I mean, anyone assigned to that event was wiped from the records, along with dates, places, you name it." He cleared his throat. "I'm not convinced it was Millennial that killed Amara. This is just me theory-hammering, and it hurts me, knowing the people who work there, but I think agents from Homeland Defense killed Amara."

Syncing Forward

"Why, though?" I asked, wishing I hadn't pushed him on the subject. "Why wouldn't they just capture her?"

I regretted the question the moment Ivan started answering it. "The only reason I can think of is if they thought she was a terrorist. If they thought she was working for Millennial. If they thought she was going to kill them first."

Chapter 39

The information Ivan provided me I hid from Bella and the rest of the family. I spent the remainder of May 20, 2054, doing what I could to stay hopeful. Ivan Fagundes stayed for lunch at Bella's insistence, but in many ways I was relieved when he left. His suspicions about Amara seemed to add up regardless of how badly I wanted them to be untrue. Those thoughts were the last thing on my mind when I went to bed and the first thing on my mind when I woke. I spent my early morning prepping to slip back into chemo-preservation and receiving radiation poisoning treatments to clear my system out, just so they could dose me all over again six months later. The dome was my second room.

While I synced forward, Bella messaged me about a woman who had reached out to her, offering to help me. Ivan's message was right behind Bella's that he was running background checks to find out if she was Millennial, ex-government, or just three pills short on her prescription. The woman kept reaching out for Bella, wanting to speak to me directly. Ivan discouraged Bella from responding or giving any information on where we lived, let alone arranging a meeting. We knew to heed his warnings. If this woman was indeed Millennial, she would be capable of anything. When Ivan sent me a biography on this mystery woman, I found there was more public info than I could read in an hour.

Her name was Rajani Tjhia, born shortly after the Pakistan-India ceasefire in 2024. Her father was a Hani from Hunnan, China, and her mother a Pakistani refugee who'd fled to the east to avoid the nuclear fallout that spread across the northeastern corner of the country. Rajani's teenage years were spent as a captive; she had been imprisoned by a Swedish billionaire who specialized in human trafficking. She moved from one compound to another, strung out on drugs and suffering one violation after another at the hands of her captors. The young girl's misery was numbed by constant drugging and mitigated by the fact that the billionaire had several other concubines who spread his attentions thin.

Occupiers in Seattle caught up with Rajani's oppressor in 2041, and during a volatile protest on his front lawn, they stormed one of his mansions and beat him to death with bricks from his own wall. Rajani's black hair was clean and her body shaved, her lips plump and luscious from forced Botox injections, but the teenager was a far cry from a supermodel. When they found the seventeen-year-old girl, her arms and back were pocked with hypospray scars from injecting Twist, a drug three times more potent than heroin.

Saved by the Occupier movement in Washington, she was cleaned up, dried out, well fed, and given an education. She was a media star in the 2040s and the poster child for anyone speaking out against the corruption of the rich. Ivan Fagundes had found articles and interviews spanning several years, but most were told in the context of a history with which I had little familiarity.

With a swipe of my finger in the air, I hyperlinked out of Rajani's bio and found that back in the 40s, the West Coast of the US had suffered far worse from the US splitting up than the East. The United States had already lost over half its square miles when the American Governance took everything from Texas to Louisiana and on up to Montana. The Cartel Alliance carved out southern portions of California and Arizona. The isolated remnants on the West Coast could not stand on their own, unable to pay for their own infrastructure, let alone the growing debts in the East, and as a result the governments in East Washington, Northern California, and Oregon collapsed like dominoes in 2047. Occupiers swept through the state capitals, dragging politicians from their abodes. Police made only nominal attempts to stop the toppling of the government, given that most couldn't be paid. From Washington on down to Santa Cruz experienced the unthinkable: abandonment. The US federal government disengaged from their West Coast holds.

W Lawrence

Left without any legal support, big businesses scrambled to withdraw from a population bent on seizing every bit of property they could get their collective hands on. Companies loaded cargo ships with whatever assets weren't nailed down, leaving hollowed-out factories and empty stores for revolutionaries to discover. What was supposed to be a monumental achievement for Occupiers became a hollow victory at best.

Learning those facts helped the video from Ivan make much more sense. I watched the recorded footage from Transworld News of the Seattle Innovo manufacturing plant. As my company tried to clear out its assets from the facility, protesters blocked the gate with the full intent of confiscating whatever lay within. Men and women donned typical Guy Fawkes masks and black capes that had been worn for fifty years. Some carried signs; others carried Molotov cocktails. A few carried makeshift cattle prods.

The live footage had been safely captured by drones that buzzed over the unruly crowd, interviewing people remotely. The news bar flashed on the bottom of the screen that the "shackle corps" had blockaded the gate, while the drone filmed hundreds of protestors handcuffed both to the chain-link fence and to each other.

A remote interview between a middle-aged reporter and a young mixed-race woman followed, the information bar identifying her as Rajani Tjhia. Her face was glowing, and the man beside her was jubilant in both his protest screams and his attempts to kiss Rajani while she spoke. The interview cut off as the drone spun around to capture a more aggressive group of protestors hurling Molotov cocktails at a truck within the facility's fence line.

The drone moved up and back to capture the scene. The video showed a larger picture of the protest, the throngs of angry people, the truck's windshield on fire. Even while syncing forward, the warble in the recording could not hide the reporter's apprehension. In those few seconds he narrated the scene as the truck accelerated, the driver blind from flames, then slammed into the shackle corps that had secured themselves to the gate.

Syncing Forward

The drone footage drew closer to the carnage, but I turned off the video. I had seen enough. Rajani Tjhia survived the nightmare, but Ivan's bio made it clear that her boyfriend did not. It was after this incident that the woman vanished from the public eye, and she hadn't made any statements or done any interviews since.

I mouthed a message to Ivan, asking if he thought she might have gotten involved with Millennial. His response said that anything was possible. But what was her motivation for reaching out to me? Ivan tried to convince her to meet with him, but she insisted on meeting me in person. I wanted to risk it, but he warned me that patience was best exercised in this case. You would think that waiting would have been easy, but I was keenly aware that every second I spent under the influence of Millennial's Tardus drug meant my family grew an hour older.

Chapter 40

Thanksgiving of 2054 I synced back, feeling both frustrated about Rajani and guilty that I had spent nearly all of my syncing forward time on articles instead of keeping up with the family. It was important for me to trust the people around me to get things done, and for now, Ivan became my new eyes and ears. It wasn't that he was discounting the option of meeting Rajani, only being cautious. This November day had to be family focused, although one whiff of the enchanting scents told me my attention would be split regardless. The glass pod descended into our house, where the air was drenched in the smell of spices and sizzling turkey fat.

Riley and Victoria guided me to the kitchen with Keith standing behind us, making sure I wasn't too wobbly on my legs. Hugs and kisses and a bombardment of personal updates greeted me. But after living in a bubble devoid of smells, my attention was drawn to the kitchen like a moth to a campfire. My daughter was basting the turkey and grumbling about it cooking too fast.

"Can we get to the dinner part of this visit?"

This got me a full eye roll from Bella. "Dad! Six months of ignoring all of your correspondence, and food is all you care about? Go play with your grandkids. I'll be in to visit with you in five minutes."

As I anxiously walked through the dining room, it dawned on me that there were too many place settings. I made a mental count: three grandchildren, son-in-law, Bella, me, niece, nephew, and sister-in-law, which left two chairs remaining empty. I grabbed Riley from behind, threw him up the air, and roughhoused with him while seeking out Bella in the kitchen. I found her still fiddling with the turkey while Keith popped a bottle of wine.

"Hey, Baby Bella, what's up with all the chairs? Are you expecting somebody else? Is Ivan coming?"

Syncing Forward

Bella and Keith exchanged quick glances, and then Keith mumbled something about how he knew I would notice. My daughter turned and handed me some string beans in a serving dish. "No, just some friends of ours. I hope you don't mind."

"Oh, okay." I shrugged. "No big deal to me." I walked out of the kitchen and to the dining room to unload the vegetables, knowing full well she lied, dreading it would be Miranda and her new husband. The wounds were still very fresh from that betrayal, and I couldn't see myself getting through Thanksgiving with them.

I didn't have to wait long for the mystery guests to arrive, and I took to shoving my face against the window like a dog waiting for its owner, curious to see who was climbing out of the car. Definitely not Miranda. An elderly man with white hair and tan skin, wearing a light-tan sweater, stepped toward the house smoothly. His body was propped up with some thin plastic-looking support on his legs and back. Young Jacob had to wear a similar device on his legs and arm to cope with his disease, and had it not been for my opportunity to see the support in action six months ago, I would have been perplexed by what I saw.

A younger man stepped from the driver's side, and I was smacked with a blast from the past. The straight black hair, the narrow smile—all characteristics of my good friend that were still fresh in my mind from decades ago. The two men were at the doorstep when the house computer announced their arrival over the intercom.

"Mr. David Tsai and Mr. Li Tsai are at the front entrance. Would you like me to open the door?" The voice—unlike the synthesized voices of my childhood—was seamlessly human. Only the precise enunciation gave it away as artificial. There was no form to attach to the voice, however. It was merely software, albeit sophisticated.

"No, Alfred, Keith will get it!" Bella called out to the computer.

Keith couldn't have beaten me to the door if he tried. I strode out of the living room, passing and almost knocking over poor Jacob in the process. I shot a quick apology to my grandson as I reached for the door and swung it open.

As I looked at Dave, my mind had a difficult time connecting the man I knew from a week ago to the man standing at the front door. Even with the peculiar exoskeleton, I could see him leaning forward and barely able to maintain his own balance. His face was drawn and withered, and the spark in his eyes had vanished. I struggled to reconcile how much Dave's son, Li, looked like his father from so many years ago. In his late twenties, trim and affable, Li carried himself as confidently as his old man had when we first met.

"Hello, old friend," Dave said with a grin.

I gave him a wry smile in return. "Who are you calling old?"

That early afternoon, I really made an effort to give thanks. I was thankful for my Baby Bella and her husband, my three grandchildren, my old friend from Innovo, for Ivan Fagundes, for the company providing for us, for the roof over our head, for Lily being loyal enough to the memory of my brother to stay close to Darren and Crystal, as well as sponsoring us so that we could take refuge in Texas. That one act changed everything for us. A flash of Miranda's face came to memory, and the pangs of loss throbbed heavily—I missed my wife.

While the turkey itself was off my menu, Bella had made ground turkey meatballs. The digestive enzyme I had to drink with the food was bitter and warm, but I muscled it down since it meant gravy and mashed potatoes in my belly. I spent a great deal of time speaking with Dave's son, fascinated by the work he did. Li worked at the Wéibō Yànshōu station, which collected microwave power beamed down from the Lunar Colony solarplants. Huge fields of solar panels on the moon collected vast amounts of energy, which engineers had figured out how to transmit back to earth. They were so prevalent that I could see them on the moon's surface when I was in my dome. It was a fantastic invention that brought cheap energy to all of Southeast Asia. That afternoon I came to respect this young man, who grew into very much a youthful version of his father.

Syncing Forward

After our feast, the kids scrambled about and showed me the virtual classroom where they received their education. The nook in the corner of the living room projected a classroom setting where other students met and interacted with their teachers in a holographic environment. The school was a private cooperative of parents, some of whom volunteered to teach, while the other parents provided administrative and financial support. Bella and Keith "didn't do teaching" and were happy to work behind the scenes. It seemed so alien to me, and I reprimanded Bella quietly, telling her that it would be better to put the kids in public school, only to find out public schools didn't exist in Texas anymore.

While the immediate family scrambled to clean up the dishes and leftovers, Li insisted on volunteering to clean up with them. Dave Tsai and I sat together and chatted on the sofa as a soccer game played out on the holoprojector in front of us. Occasionally the three-dimensional image would launch a soccer ball right at us, and I instinctively ducked; this wasn't my father's 3D. The sound was muted, but the computer butler, Alfred, would call out when either team managed to score a goal. I could hear Bella and Riley in the kitchen yelling out hoots and howls at each announcement.

Dave brought me up to speed on his wife and her business, on his retirement from Innovo, on his condition and how it had affected his decision to leave. My friend was dying of cancer. Despite the wild leaps forward in medical technology, Dave was decaying away and had been since his fifties.

"It's painful to move." Dave sipped at his coffee and continued. "The doctor installed neuroblockers to help manage the pain, but they don't work as well as advertised."

"Who makes the neuroblocker things?" I asked.

Dave smiled. "Innovo—go figure."

"How long do you have?" The question was direct, but I saw no need for discretion or tact at this point. Those were the social constructs of people who had time on their hands.

"Months. Maybe more. Maybe less. Pretty soon I'll be flying back to China so that I can put myself down legally. It's illegal here in the Governance, so—"

"What?" I interrupted. "What did you just say?"

"I said suicide is illegal in the Governance. In fact, it's one of the only places you can't perform—"

"That's not what I meant. Put yourself down? It makes you sound like an unwanted alley cat. What the hell is wrong with you?"

"Nothing. It's just time."

"Why would you kill yourself?" I became suddenly angry with his coolness. "Are you insane?"

"Not at all. It's the right choice."

He could see the horror in my eyes. Dave looked down, swirling his coffee with his spoon. "Martin, the world you know is gone. I'm lucky to be able to choose the time of my passing. Here it is illegal. But there are some other countries where assisted suicide is not exactly voluntary. At least in China I have rights—"

"China has more rights than here?" I asked, exasperated.

"On some matters, yes. Since the 2041 reforms—" Dave stopped suddenly and put up his hand. From the distressing look upon his brow, I could see he was coping with another spell of agony. When it eased, his wrinkled eyes looked back up at me. "I don't want to do a history lesson for you; it isn't that important. I just want you to understand where I'm coming from. It isn't my mind that is going, Martin—it's the rest of me. I'm so tired of being in pain."

"But what if they come up with something to fix you in two months?"

"And what if I spend the next nine months in misery, or my hip breaks again, or I'm drugged into a stupor so that my wife and son can watch me piss myself uncontrollably? I know how you were brought up and that you believe suicide is a sin, but it's not like I'm making some rash decision in a depressed state. I know who I am, and I'm happy with the life I've lived."

What was there to say? That he was wrong? That the suffering he was going through could be endured? Suicide was an abhorrent option, downright detestable. How conflicted I was, sitting face-to-face with my friend, who had done so much to preserve my life and now was discussing ending his own! Being so close to the problem muddied my uncompromising position on the matter. Not that he needed my permission or even my approval. But I knew that I wasn't just concerned for his immortal soul; I was selfishly worried about living in a world without him.

"You can't . . . do this, Dave. Please. All of my friends are dead." My meek words were matched by my broken posture. Dave put his palm on my head to console me, and I reached up and held his wrinkled hand in place, hoping that if I held onto it long enough he would change his mind. I prayed for God to forgive him, to take Dave home before he could take his own life.

Li came over and sat with us, no doubt sensing his father was upset. "Everything okay, Dad?"

Dave nodded quietly. "We're fine."

"You tell him the bad news about Innovo?" Li asked.

It took a bit for me to realize that there was more bad news—news not tied to my friend killing himself.

My gaze narrowed. "What's going on?"

That's when Dave delivered what he'd come to say. Over the years, multiple members of the board of directors at Innovo had debated the logic of supporting the research into the Millennial drug and continuing my financial support. After thirty years, a growing number of people felt the research was a dead end and a waste of money. In an age of corporations being targeted by political groups based on the "moral" direction of their expenditures, Innovo rubbed people as being rather callous. Public sentiment was a fickle matter. Dave kept close tabs on these discussions and at times intervened to keep me in the company's care. With his departure, however, his involvement ended.

"A decision is coming soon, Martin," Dave warned me. "You won't want to make it, but it will be yours nonetheless. There is a strong possibility the board will vote to sell you off in the next six to twelve months. At that point, you could be left with a decision as to whether you want to be financially supported—or owned, if you will—by another company."

Syncing Forward

Chapter 41

My sprint to the future was reduced to a brisk jog with the Accelerate drug, comparatively speaking, of course. Five synch-ronizations over two and a half years went smoothly with no sign of damage to my nervous system or any part of my body. As paltry as some would feel a single day to be, those were cherished moments in which I would do my darnedest to soak up six months of living. I was able to visit the beaches at Galveston Island and swim in the Gulf of Mexico. I ate my first burger in thirty-three years and downed it with a nonalcoholic beer. I was able to see Riley play soccer and get beaned in the head with the ball. I watched young Jacob persevere through his polio affliction and grow into a handsome young man. I stood amazed as my young granddaughter, Victoria, learned calculus by the age of ten and could recite entire passages of *Moby Dick* from memory. I took Mass at the church in Jacksboro. I snuck a half a piece of bacon and ate it despite it being against the rules.

At night, alone in my room, I let everything out. My father always told me that real men never cried, but I must have spent hours weeping when I should have been sleeping. I mentally chronicled everything and everyone that had vanished from my life. It was during one of those low moments when my grandson—my brother's namesake—told me how lucky I was to be the youngest grandfather in the world. While that might not have been wholly accurate at that moment, it was only a matter of time before I became the oldest man alive.

Ivan found stable work in Dallas with the police but managed to stay in touch. Correspondence from Rajani Tjhia came sporadically, each video a soulful request to meet. Ivan, Bella, Keith—everybody but me—thought granting her request was a bad idea. It seemed folly to dismiss anyone's offer of help, but the jury was in, and the verdict was this woman was a crackpot. Bella surprised me by saying there had been plenty of others promising help, but all were simply looking for a con or a claim to fame.

In March 2056, a vote at Innovo to sell off the chemopreservative drug research division was narrowly defeated. Bella immediately scheduled another interview, an old move from her playbook to keep public opinion sympathetic and stockholders nervous about appearing coldhearted.

Another leap forward six months and twelve days. My sixth day of normalcy came into focus; only, this time we were in a limousine on the move through my home state of Louisiana. New Orleans was a "neutral haven," a border city between the American Governance and the old United States. As part of some agreement, the city was run independently. Keith explained it worked like the District of Columbia would if it sat between two angry gorillas. Bella also thought that a trip to see the rebuilt sections of New Orleans would be a fun activity for us after the interviews. I didn't understand what she meant by "rebuilt" until we drove another ten miles up the highway.

My eyes gazed upon a horizon vaguely familiar to me. Lake Pontchartrain extended up and out to the north, but also deeply eastward. The signs on the road told me we were driving the Louisiana SR10, but the causeway that ran over the water was something quite new to me. I looked down into the water to see the ruins of the old causeway bisecting just underneath us. Pontoons decorated with artwork and flowers told me New Orleans must have taken another bad hit. Katrina had changed my childhood and my life, and one would have thought that seeing this new devastation would bring up old memories. But it dawned on me that I felt no deep connection to this land anymore. Too much time had passed. Too much history had swept underneath me for me to be touched personally.

"It was pretty bad," Keith said softly. "A tsunami struck the city after the Florida earthquake six years ago. It killed over four thousand, most of them drowning in their cars."

Syncing Forward

I shook my head. No hurricane this time. I should have been shocked, but after being bombarded with awful news, I was growing numb to the tragedies that had befallen the world. I had leapt through thirty-three years in ten days, and so I added this knowledge to the general melancholy that came with learning new history.

Bella asked me if I knew what special date was coming up. I knew she meant well by making light of it, but I quietly asked her not to remind me. She looked a little hurt, but I supposed she'd understand eventually why I didn't want to discuss it.

The Transworld News Building cast a shadow on our car. As we reached our destination, a mob of protesters appeared, shouting hatefully at us, pounding on the plastic doors as we pulled past them and into a secured underground. I caught glimpses of their signs: "CURE THIS MAN OR CURE 1 MILLION CHILDREN," "MJ = FAILURE, INC." I didn't know how they knew it was me. Heck, maybe they didn't. They might have accosted every car that drove into the office building in the hopes that they would be right one time. Their screams disappeared as the limo vanished underground.

Margo Sanguine of Transworld News Agency was one of two interviewers scheduled for me as I reluctantly prepared for the sit-down. Bella had promised Transworld half an hour instead of ten minutes. Another thirty minutes was allotted to Tremundo Verdade News. A precious hour of my life would be spent answering questions, but it was an hour that I would have to sacrifice in order to preserve any hope of Innovo continuing their studies. Their extensive research had brought the wrath of social movements, the members of which saw the money spent as squandering resources that would be better off used on the poor and suffering. I didn't fully understand the mentality behind the protest, but the whole spectacle was unsettling.

I sipped on a cool glass of water, peering down at the group of eighty or so college-age adults whose chants were muted by the soundproof building. They didn't look as angry from several stories up. I took a final look down at the mottled crowd below, ran my hand over the sensor next to the window, and watched as the glass gradually tinted back to its standard reflective shade. Smartglass was everywhere—one of the few technologies with which I was both familiar and comfortable.

"You're on the set in two minutes, Mr. James. Please come with me," a young man with a soft voice said as he gestured politely toward a door. One look at him told me he was . . . different. His eyes were large, his cheekbones pronounced, and the manner in which he carried himself was plum different.

We walked into a small but comfortable room with a strange shade of flat blue on the walls that was easy on the eyes and yet robbed the room of its depth. Margo Sanguine met me with a soft handshake and gestured to a place to sit. Before I could manage another polite glance at the stranger who had brought me here, the man exited the room.

"Robert is a mod," Margo explained. "I could tell you were confused when you looked at him. Partially integrated, tremendously educated. I never have to worry about him getting sick."

"What does that mean?" I asked. "Partially integrated?"

"Oh, all the mods are doing it these days. They network to various hubs via implants in their heads. It means he can check his mail while going to the bathroom, or watch his favorite television show while doing his filing while collaborating on our next interview set. It never seems to slow him down, so you won't find me complaining. And to be honest, if we had three more of him I could fire my entire staff." She gave an indifferent laugh as she gestured for me to sit. I wanted to ask what it meant to be fully integrated, but I never got the chance.

Once we were seated, the lights in the corners of the room swiveled to maximize illumination while minimizing glare. My chair seemed to contour and move underneath me, adjusting to my height and weight for maximum comfort. Margo Sanguine sat catty-corner to me in an identical chair as an assistant attended to her. Only a tiny four-inch rod, thinner than a nail, occupied the table that sat between us. The tip of the rod twinkled red, and the interview began.

Her face was as plastic as ever; surgery had only augmented the woman's practiced tone and calm façade. "Welcome to the worlds from New Orleans. My name is Margo Sanguine with Transworld News, and I am here with Mr. Martin James for only his second interview in fourteen years. How are you, Martin?"

"I'm better in some respects, worse in others."

"You look the same."

"So do you."

She smiled. "Yes, but my looks are from a talented enhancement technician. You, on the other hand. . ."

"I figured out it's been only a week since you last interviewed me. I must be pretty important." It was meant as a joke, and Margo rolled with it professionally, giving a little chuckle.

"One week, fourteen years—who's counting?" she joshed. "So, how is life better?"

"Well, the new treatment Innovo developed is stable so far and allows me more synchronized time back than I've ever had. From my perspective anyway. It's only a couple of visits a year, but it's way better and not nearly as painful. The last medication almost killed me."

"What do you do with your extra time?"

"Try to stay up on events, keep informed on my condition, play with my grandkids. The visits go fast though—too fast."

"You saw the crowds outside." My interviewer switched gears quickly.

"Yeah, they didn't look so happy to see me."

Margo's tone was a serious one. "These protesters aren't nearly as bad as some of the others, but they have been here all day. Political activists from at least three different groups who all see you as the face of oppression. Here, let me show some of the holo-highlights we've been taking." Ms. Sanguine summoned up a 3D image on the table that showed a group of protesters—whether they were the same ones outside the studio office, I couldn't tell—holding signs with my face plastered on them. Slogans such as "WASTE NOT WANT NOT" and "CURE THIS MAN OR CURE 1 MILLION CHILDREN" ran across my image.

Margo waved the image away. "How do you feel when you see those signs?"

"I reckon they have a valid point. We could take money from everywhere and use it to feed the poor and take care of the sick. I'm not unsympathetic to the plight of the unfortunate. I was a teenager and living in the back of a car with my dad and my brother after we lost our house and Dad lost his job. I know what it's like to not know where your next meal is coming from.

"But look at the incredible things people have accomplished in the last forty years! There are people living on Mars and the moon. I just found out that they are harvesting solar energy from the moon and beaming it to Earth. That's amazing to me. But if companies and governments had never bothered to put the money into those endeavors, you wouldn't have all that energy."

"You're saying there has to be a balance," Margo tried to fill in.

"Exactly."

"Let's move on to the topic of Millennial. Considered to be the most notorious terrorist group of the twenty-first century, their final act of terrorism was setting off a dirty bomb outside London's parliament. Fifty thousand dead from radioactive exposure, another eight hundred thousand injured or suffering from ailments associated with radiation. Seven years later, nobody has heard a word from them. No attacks, no assassinations, no demands. What do you think happened?"

"Margo, when I heard about the London attack I couldn't believe it. I was under medical care at the time and was unaware, but my first reaction was . . . I was dumbfounded. I know that a dirty bomb was always a fear when I was in the security industry, so to see the effects was awful. But, and I hate saying this, I wasn't surprised. My daughter—"

I began to choke up. I was no longer in the interview room. I was someplace else, some*time* else. Amara was three years old and stacking lettered blocks in alphabetic order. Amara was five years old and telling me I was the best daddy in the world. Amara was six years old and bawling her eyes out because her toy set was ruined, all due to a single piece missing. Amara was ten months old repeating over and over, "Dada. Dadadadadada." Amara was nine years old and hugging me in the hospital, asking me, "Do you think there is something wrong with me?"

"Martin? Are you okay?" Margo Sanguine asked with her best imitation of concern.

"Can we stop the interview for a couple of minutes? I just need some air."

"We can talk about something else if you want."

"No, I need a break. I promise you'll get all the time you were allotted." I put up my hand and breathed slowly to calm my nerves.

The mistress of media gave a frustrated eye roll as the rod in front of us changed from red to light blue. "Ten-minute break, Helena!" she barked over her shoulder.

"Sorry, I'll be right back." I walked out of the room and passed Bella in the lobby. She asked me if I wanted some company, but I simply shook my head and climbed into the elevator.

"Dad, I don't think you should go off by yourself."

"I put on my big-boy pants today, Bella," I snapped. "I just want a few minutes to myself."

"What floor, sir?" the elevator's computer asked.

"Lobby, please," I responded. The doors shut in Bella's confused face, and the floor dropped gradually. It wasn't just Amara's memory that disturbed me, but Margo's utterly uncaring attitude as well. I knew why Bella had scheduled an interview with her: money.

W Lawrence

My daughter wasn't being greedy, just smart. Even if the bigger plan—pressuring Innovo to keep me on—didn't work, we would need every penny we could get. As the years turned into decades, there had to be money. Transworld was willing to pay big bucks for my back-to-back interviews. At that moment, though, I didn't give a lick.

Chapter 42

The lift zipped smoothly down nine flights and opened up to a glass-door lobby that emptied out to the protester crowd. They had no idea what I had gone through. What I was going through. Somehow they equated me with Innovo. Who knew—maybe they had some sort of legitimate gripe with the corporation. But how was that my fault? My melancholy had transformed to frustration as I pushed the doors open and stepped out in front of the mostly young crowd. Two armed security officers turned toward me, surprised to see anyone stepping through the doors.

"Sir, please step back inside the building," one commanded, putting his hand on my chest to guide me back into the edifice.

The crowd took only moments to realize it was truly me before they burst into chanting, *"In-no-vo must go! In-no-vo must go! In-no-vo must go!"* I was guilty in their eyes for receiving help from Innovo. I was a resource sponge, and they detested me. To these people, my life had been utterly conflated with the perceived wrongdoings of every corporation in the world, and I'd had it up to my eyeballs.

"Screw you! You people are idiots!" I yelled. "Do you have any idea what you are even talking about?" My words were drowned out by the crowd as they lurched forward and up the steps toward me. I didn't know if they wanted to yell at me or kill me or simply get close enough to take some video shots, but the guards didn't afford me the chance to find out. Both men shoved me forcefully back inside and pulled the doors shut, locking them from outside right before the crowd overtook them. The angry young men and women banged on the windows and pushed against the uniformed men, crushing them against the doors. Fortunately both men stood a half a head over the reprobates that were pressing in on them, and they used their muscles to shove the men and women back. A few of the protesters cowered away, unused to the physical conflict. More were revved up at the thought of confrontation, and they had their wish granted by the other end of a baton.

A pair of police trucks pulled up, and more chaos ensued as the frothing crowd began banging on the hoods. Four short-haired dogs that were nearly the size of ponies jumped out of the back of the trucks. Their paws had elongated digits that gripped the edges of the trucks while they howled in some incomprehensible language. They even had actual uniforms on and little helmets. Doggy helmets—how cute. Except there was nothing cute about them; they looked terrifying and unnatural. The crowd shrank backward as a half-dozen police officers in riot gear joined the gigantic dogs.

As for me, I stood on the flip side of the glass entrance and gawked at the rumble outside. Two security officers slowly beat back the rowdy crowd whose attention had been split between the guards and the cops and the dogs from hell. Had they been properly motivated, the mob could easily have overwhelmed the security officers, but instead they felt it better to serve their cause by taking up their chant once again.

"Hello, Martin," a soft voice said from behind, startling me. I turned and saw a mixed-race Eastern woman in a janitor's outfit pulling a wheeled trash can out of the closet. She appeared to be in her twenties, although she might have had one of those youthful faces too. Her skin was smooth and shiny like toffee, and only her eyes reflected a grim adult stare. She wheeled the can in my direction and stared intently out the window.

"Do I know you?" I queried, wondering how she knew my name, aware that I had seen her face before.

"No, but I know you. Practically everyone on the planet knows who you are: Martin James, the time traveler."

I scoffed. "Ha! Time traveler. I don't think anyone would like to travel through time the way I do. It's more like 'time prisoner.'"

"Aren't we all prisoners of time?" she asked. Her words were so smooth, almost prearranged, like the practiced lines of a play.

Syncing Forward

I took the bait. "How so?"

"We all move forward, and we can never go back. There are plenty of things we'd all like to change. I know what I would change." She held out her hand, staring at me in a manner that made me feel terribly awkward. "My name is Rajani."

The eyes hadn't changed, but her face and hair had gone through a major makeover since the time the videos of her had been taken. I shook her hand cautiously. "Nice to finally meet you, Rajani. Although it appears you don't have the right ID card."

I pointed to her uniform identification card, which read "Maria Torres." Rajani cocked her head and grinned thinly. "You know, you're the first person to look at my ID card. I came in through the basement, hoping to meet you on your way out of the studio. Getting in wasn't easy, but like any company, there is always somebody who is willing to break the rules for money. It's fate that we have met in such a way."

A voice chirped in my earbud. "Dad, where are you? Margo is throwing a fit wondering if you are going to finish your interview." It sounded so crisp compared to the cell phones of my day.

"Yeah," I replied. "I'll be up in a couple minutes." The phone made an audible click to indicate the connection had been severed. The people outside renewed one of their earlier chants about profits over compassion.

"They frighten you," the woman observed.

"They're idiotic, acting like I did something wrong," I mumbled.

"Don't hate those people out there, Martin. They don't hate you. They just don't understand you or what you've been through."

"They could ask."

"But that assumes they see you as a person, and they don't. You're a symbol, Martin. People don't hate the symbol but what the symbol stands for." Rajani's voice was steady and kind.

375

I agreed grudgingly. "You seem to have the pulse of what's going on out there."

"I know something about the subject. I spent years with those people. I also know what it's like to be a symbol, to be a victim of expectations." The woman's eyes gazed out in recollection as she continued, "People want to categorize you, explain you, and justify you and your actions. And the whole time you want to scream at them and tell them how you are a human being with dreams and feelings and regrets."

She was staring at me again. I didn't like it, but I pressed her. "Rajani, you've been trying to reach me for years. My friend Ivan said you claimed you could help me, but he was dubious. And I'll be honest—I've had my helping of disappointments. I really hope you're legitimate."

Rajani turned and faced me squarely, her mouth open as if she wanted to say something but was held back by some invisible force.

"Are you with Millennial?" I asked her frankly.

"No." She shook her head. "I'm not with anyone anymore."

"But you used to work for them?"

"No."

The hair on the back of my neck rose, and the awkwardness of the moment ratcheted up. "I don't want to be rude or thankless, but why are you here, Rajani?"

"Because . . . because I love you, Martin."

It was time to leave. Undoubtedly I had made a mistake in talking with this woman, and the I-told-you-sos were already echoing from the future. Her face oozed desperation as I slowly backed up. "I'm sorry to cut this conversation short, but I have my own set of expectations I'm dealing with. It was nice to meet you, Rajani."

I pressed the button for the elevator and waited for its return to the lobby.

Syncing Forward

As she stepped forward, I stepped back once more and felt my heel rub against the wall. She must have noticed a change in my demeanor, because the young woman moved closer yet again and tried to soothe me. "Wait! Don't be upset. I just wanted to meet you, Martin. It may sound crazy, but we're kindred spirits, you and me. I know about your pain, about your wife walking out on you, about your daughter and brother dying—"

"Please don't bring up my family," I warned. "I don't know you." The elevator doors slid open with a *ping*. I walked backward away from Rajani and into the lift. The computer console that ran the elevator verbally prompted me for a destination, so I called out "ninth floor."

Rajani placed her left sneaker against the door so it couldn't close. She continued. "I've had losses too, Martin. My freedom was taken from me at an early age. My one true love was killed by the same people who keep you imprisoned now—"

"Imprisoned?" I scowled at her. "What are you talking about?"

"Innovo, of course! They hold you captive while raping the world, Martin. They abused the people of Seattle and then discarded us like some torn diaphragm. When it came time for them to pay their fair share, they packed up their equipment and ran. That facility was built at the expense of the people, and they just left."

I lied to her. "I don't know anything about that, but—"

She spoke over me. "At the protest in Seattle, we handcuffed ourselves in a long chain in front of the gate to keep them from fleeing in the middle of the night, from stealing what they owed us. Their convoy refused to slow down. They figured we would move, step out of the way before the trucks reached the gate, but we couldn't. We shouted and screamed, but it was too late. My fiancé, my best friend— he was ripped apart, Martin. I was knocked aside with his arm still handcuffed to mine, only it wasn't attached to his body anymore. And Innovo's response? They called it 'a regrettable incident.'"

Angry tears rolled down her cheeks. On the defensive, I said, "You can't possibly think I'm responsible . . ."

The woman's eyes were soaked with sympathy as she took a step closer to me. "No! I don't blame you at all. I blame Innovo. Their greed has left you like this—trapped—just like you said. Keeping you hoping, keeping you waiting, wondering. You're a slave to their agenda, Martin. That's why I'm here. I've come to free you."

She was insane. Her impassioned views only intensified my impulse to flee.

"That's very nice," I said, "but unless you have a cure for my condition, I won't ever be free." I forced my shoe against hers and pushed her foot away, causing the doors to slide slowly closed.

Rajani threw herself into the threshold of the elevator, the doors squeezing her slightly before reopening. The computer responded with a triad of chimes before it announced, "Please step away from the elevator doors."

"I need you to leave me alone now. I've got to go." I pushed her this time. I didn't like the idea of laying hands on a woman, but she was crazier than a dog in a hubcap factory.

"But I *have* the cure!" Rajani cried out.

The sliding doors were just about to shut, when she reinserted her foot once more, causing the doors to freeze and then reopen. The young woman stood there nervously and repeated, "I have the cure, Martin!"

I stared at her in wonder. Could it be Rajani was telling the truth? That she had discovered what scores of researchers had been unable to discover? No, but perhaps she had befriended somebody at Millennial to get an antidote? The elevator called for pedestrians to stand away once more, and I helped her open the door with my hand, leaning forward, shocked that my long journey might finally be coming to a close. I remember thinking that—even with the wrong intentions—this woman might be holding my salvation.

"Do you have the Remedium?"

Syncing Forward

Rajani's brow furrowed, as if she had no idea what I was talking about. "I have the cure," she restated, "for both of us."

What did she mean? If she had obtained the Remedium from Millennial, why didn't she know what it was called? I had so many questions and no time to ask them.

Without warning, Rajani reached into the janitorial apron she wore and pulled out a small pistol. Before I had a chance to show my shock, before my mind could register that I should flee, she aimed it at me and fired two shots at my chest. While reeling in pain, I heard her steady voice say, "You're free now, my love . . . and so am I."

The doors to the elevator shut just as she aimed the pistol under her chin and pulled the trigger. The look on her face was that of a person completing a long journey: weary but satisfied that she had made it to her goal. The sound of the third and final shot was muffled as the lift carried my bleeding body back up toward the ninth floor.

Chapter 43

"Sir, please return to the standing position," the computer directed. I looked down at the crimson stain that spread over my shirt and spilled warmly down my back. There was a throbbing feeling in my chest, and my hands and feet felt numb. The chrome-plated monitor on the wall registered that we had passed the second floor, then the third. I tried calling for help, but the words wouldn't come.

"Sir, do you require assistance?" the synthetic voice asked when it was clear I wasn't moving.

I struggled to breathe as my right lung filled with blood and fragments of bone from my ribs. The world was spinning, and the tearful agony of the gunshots was finally registering. Fourth floor, fifth floor, six floor . . .

A human voice broke over the intercom. "Sir! Remain calm! We are, uh, we're getting you help. Just don't move!" I remember distinctly how ridiculous the notion was of me actually moving. I didn't see a camera, but a type of monitoring system must have kicked in and contacted the security officers monitoring the building when I didn't follow the computer's instructions. No doubt their attention was fixed on the protesters outside until they observed my collapsed body in the elevator.

Seventh floor, eighth floor . . . When I coughed, I felt blood gurgle up in my throat and dribble out the side of my mouth. Did something land on me? I could have sworn an invisible metal plate had dropped from the sky and landed on my chest. My breaths were small and getting shallower by the second. I remember thinking, *Yeah, getting shot? That's nothing compared to the Pause!* In my mind, I was bragging to some imaginary bystander.

The elevator voice announced cheerfully, "Sir, you have arrived at the ninth floor. Have a good day!" The panel on the wall was flashing an alternating red and yellow light, but beyond that the ninth floor was

Syncing Forward

white and unfocused, as if the walls and floor and ceiling were gone and the elevator emptied into the middle of a cloud. Maybe I was speeding up, because everything looked so slow, so very slow. Voices filled the void, separated by indefinable breaks.

"Dad! Oh my God! Help! Somebody help! Help!"

"—bulance three minutes out. They're on their wa—"

"—hear me? Can you hear—"

"—so much blood . . ."

I saw tubes. Tubes everywhere. Some were thick and gray, others clear, one filled with blood. A bundle of fiber-optic cable was connected to a plastic plate on my chest. A hand with eight fingers moved over my face. A beam of light. Reality faded in and out. My view was machines and masked faces and gloved hands. Broken conversations were all I could make heads or tails of.

"—stop the bleeding before he syncs forward— "

"—worst round of golf I ever played—"

"—maneuver the las-stitch over the—"

"—looks much better—"

"—my mother still makes the best chili . . ."

— Part 7 —

The End

Syncing Forward

Chapter 44

The sun jumped off the horizon as it frequently did when I was out of synchronization. Instead of rocketing across the sky, however, it seemed to slow down and stop, almost as if it might plunge back to the east and erase the dawn. The long shadows from a row of yellow oaks shortened and rotated, then halted as the sun sat immobile. The hundred-foot-tall trees dwarfed the small shrubs at their bases and appeared as monuments in the largely empty yard. The grass was short and manicured, albeit patchy and brown in parts. Hot wind blew a lonely cloud across the sky and tickled the hairs on my arms.

The chair I sat in was reclined back, and there were dark sunglasses over my eyes. Somebody must have dressed me, because the shorts and button-down shirt were unfamiliar—not to mention something I would never have picked out for myself. A small glass table was set up to my right with a glass of lemonade sweating and ice cubes melting. An empty outdoor recliner sat opposite the tiny table.

Everything felt real . . . The aroma of flowers and hot earth wafted to my nostrils. I heard shoes swishing across the grass and turned to see a young man with hair parted sharply on the side and slicked down across his head. Were it not for the Bermuda-style shorts and bare feet, he would have looked snipped from *The Great Gatsby*. He wore a largish ring that projected a thin holographic image of a phoenix onto the back of his tanned hand. His face had changed considerably, but I recognized him anyway, chiefly because of the considerable limp he carried on one thin leg.

I tried speaking but found my voice just as dry as ever when I would sync back. With shaky hands I took a sip of the lemonade and tried again. "Jacob?" I called out, uncertainty still a part of my waking state.

"Hey, Martin. Welcome back," he said with a boyish tone still to his voice. "I had to go take care of Molly. Sorry if I left you out here by yourself. How long have you been awake?"

I shook my head. "Uh, maybe a minute or ten? I'm not sure. Where am I? And who is Molly?"

"You're at the Venario Convalescent Facility in Houston. And Molly is—"

I heard scampering and took notice of a two-year-old girl toddling across the grass after Jacob. "Daddy! Daddy! Daddy!"

"Molly is my daughter." Jacob finished his sentence, then swooped the little girl up in his arms and twirled her around the lawn.

"Congratulations," I stammered, "although the good news has me wondering—how long have I been out?"

Jacob sat down on the seat and bounced his daughter on his knees. My great-granddaughter. "It's July 3, 2063. You were messed up pretty bad. Three shattered ribs, shredded lung. It's a miracle those shots didn't take you out. Rajani Tjhia missed your heart, your arteries, your spine. Still, recovery has been a pain in the butt because of the Tardus drug. You've been in a rehab tank for seven years. Off and on."

Another rehab tank. Another seven years. I tried to stand but found the pain noticeable across my chest and abdomen. Jacob warned me to stay put and said he'd get help if I needed to go to the bathroom. I looked down at my chest and noticed square patches of skin, with something rectangular underneath each patch.

"Any word on if the Remedium was found? Or a substitute discovered? Or . . ." I looked at my grandson and stopped. "I can tell from the look on your face that's a big fat no."

"Sorry, Martin."

Jacob continued to explain what had happened to me. "You haven't been fully synced back in a while, but doctors dosed your system with low levels of the Accelerate treatment so that your recovery time wouldn't stretch out so long. If they hadn't, you'd be waking up another five or ten years from now."

Syncing Forward

I shook my head. Apparently having your DNA modified by the Millennial drug and being shot in the chest was a bad combination.

He sat on the edge of the chair, bouncing Molly on his good knee. She looked at me and giggled a few times, but then hid her face in his chest. Jacob took a breath and started. "So here is the worst of it. Research has not been picked up by anybody since Innovo went bankrupt, so you're stuck with the Accelerate treatment."

"Innovo's bankrupt?"

"Yup, last year. They tried to dig out of it but eventually got broken up and bought out. We made some inquiries as to who bought the rights to your research, but so far the details of the sale are sketchy. It sucks, but there's nothing we can do about it."

"Wow. You couldn't break that gently to me, Jacob? Geez." The kid had made no attempt to soften the blows. Maybe he thought that getting all the lousy news out of the way was the better way to go. Maybe he was right. It still stank, though. With Innovo gone, my only hope remained with Millennial giving me the Remedium drug. Or their crypts being discovered.

"You're a free man now. Nobody owns you. How does it feel?"

"Terrifying."

"Well that isn't good. I was hoping you'd say 'liberating' or something to that effect."

"How is Ivan Fagundes?" The question was a matter of desperation, but I tried to pull it off as casually as I could.

"He's okay. Met a nice lady and speaks highly of her. Got hired with the Texas Rangers, and that keeps him busy. He isn't looking into Millennial anymore, if that's what you're getting at."

"Any particular reason?" I asked in disappointment.

"There's nothing to look into. They've disappeared. Nobody knows if they are waiting to strike or giving up or if they just don't exist anymore. Ivan left you a ton of correspondence in the first year after you got shot, but after that . . . well, people need to move on, you know. He needed to find work that agreed with him."

Molly was tugging on Jacob's arm, impatient with the conversation. She was a cutie for sure, with a silly smile and chubby cheeks.

July 2063, I mused. Near on forty-two years I had moved forward. Staring at the toddler, I furrowed my brow. "Wait a second. If it has only been seven years, how do you have a kid already? That would mean you were . . . nineteen when she was born?"

Jacob gave me a sheepish smile that reminded me of his father, Keith. "Eighteen, actually. Me and Renatta were dating when she got pregnant somehow."

"Somehow, huh?"

"Well, you know, some of the anti-F drugs don't work a hundred percent of the time."

"Are the two of you . . . you know . . . married?"

"Yeah." He nodded. "Dad make it abundantly clear what I needed to do. We were talking about it anyway, so we made sure Molly had a good home to be born into."

"Jacob," I said, changing gears, "how did I get out here? Normally I get synced back in the house or in a lab at least."

"Oh, that was my idea. We weren't sure how long it would take for your body to adjust to the Accelerate treatment after recovering from the gunshots, but I got the notion we'd have you wake up someplace nice for once. Mom had to take my sister to an event, and Dad is working."

"Where's Riley?"

"Basic Training. He said to say hello and recorded a bunch of messages for you. We can pull them up from here, no problem."

The heat was getting to me, so I asked Jacob to wheel me into some shade. Jacob showed me how to actuate the controllers, and I soon found my chair was equipped with a dual-track system akin to what you'd find on a tank, although much lighter and fancier-looking. Molly bounced ahead and disappeared into the building from which she originally came. It was a two-story structure built out of high-strength foam and sculpted beautifully. I had seen a few of these structures in videos when we first moved to Texas but never had a chance to visit one. The concept behind the buildings was actually quite old, but the application was much less expensive now, apparently.

A woman's holographic face appeared on the arm of the chair. The automatic doors slid open, and a female voice chimed through the speakers built into the wheelchair arms. "Hello, Mr. James. Will you be needing assistance?"

"Uh, no. No thank you." I looked up at Jacob, who explained that Nurse Nikita was a typical program these days—fully interactive and networked to the nurse's station. Sounded more like a stripper name than a computer interface to me.

"Turn here," Jacob directed as we moved into the building and toward an open glass elevator.

The three of us climbed into the elevator, which lifted us silently to the second floor. Molly scampered about, looking down through the glass in amazement at the people below. It was strange that my synchronizing would be taken so casually. I chocked it up to real-life interference and figured that I couldn't get everyone to drop their whole life just for me. It stung a little all the same.

The world was feeling awfully weighty, so I pressed Jacob. "So, do you have any good news for me?"

The doors slid open, and we exited the elevator and rounded a corner toward a large conference room decorated with streamers and balloons. Jacob smiled. "The good news is I lied about everybody being busy today."

"Surprise!" the group called out. Bella, Keith, Riley, Victoria, Crystal, Darren, Lily, Ivan, and a dozen other people I didn't recognize—mostly convalescent staff, I surmised—sprang out from the corners of the room and from behind the table.

I looked at Jacob in pleased astonishment. "You fooled me! Nobody ever fools me!" It was true—Miranda had tried for years to pull off surprise parties and failed miserably. I'd catch a strange inflection in her voice or an asymmetrical facial expression that allowed me to discern she was up to something. Miranda would tell me to leave the job at the office.

My grandson smiled broadly, feeling cocky that he had pulled off what nobody in the family had ever managed to do. I was fixing to give him a punch in the shoulder but couldn't reach him from where I sat. Besides, lifting my arm felt like I might rip open the holes in my chest. I looked about to see if there were any other familiar faces. Dave's, specifically. I didn't see my old friend. I put my hands to my face and rubbed the stress out of my cheeks. Bella had made me promise her I would live my life, and I couldn't let her down. It was time to enjoy what I had. I would deal with the setbacks later.

"Welcome back, Dad." Bella's heels clicked across the floor as she enveloped me in a loving hug.

It hurt my chest when she squeezed me, but I ignored the pain. She gave me a kiss on my cheek and then wiped off the lipstick marks she'd left on my face. I studied her gleaming face and found the moment bittersweet. Our family was reunited, and everyone looked wonderful. Jacob's sinistropolio had been halted, and I had the privilege to meet my great-granddaughter. However, the realization that I had crossed a threshold did not bode well for the future.

My daughter, my Baby Bella, was now seven years older than I was.

Syncing Forward

Chapter 45

Thirty-eight years old. That's how old I was when I'd been attacked by Bruchmuller. It was the age I was trapped within when Miranda divorced me, when my brother passed, when Amara was killed, when Dave took his own life, when I was shot in the chest, and when my grandchildren and great-grandchildren were born.

In less than two weeks I had rocketed forward through more than forty years of history. I had met two Texas governors and three other governors from other states. I was filled with wonder as Mars filled with hundreds of colonists and mortified as war ravaged Asia and the South Pacific. Central and South America were on the verge of unifying into a single mighty nation while Europe licked its wounds and tried to find peace after years of genocide. I was there when Occupiers, struggling to form a new government on the West Coast, were met with a new type of occupation: that of the People's Republic of China.

In 2063, we tried suing the United States government for information relating to Dr. Dieterich Bruchmuller, but their response was both frustrating and expected. No such research existed. No such person was currently in their care. The November 2021 death certificate of Dieterich Bruchmuller was sent to add insult to injury.

I caught up on some of Ivan's messages, most of them clues as to the whereabouts of a Millennial crypt, all of them a bust. A news report detailed how an older building being torn down led to the discovery of a crypt. The explosives contained within detonated, tragically incinerating the demolition crew. Those poor guys hadn't done anything wrong; they just showed up for work and were burned to death because they took a wrecking ball to the wrong building. But that wasn't the end of the news on Millennial.

A new product called Conference became popular all over the globe—the result of technological advances that were uncontainable by laws or social mores. Modified human beings who were engineered on a genetic level had begun connecting with each other in the ultimate social networking experience. This seemingly benign collaborative service must have been important enough, though, since it drew Millennial from their crypts after decades of silence.

They destroyed networking hubs and ripped apart communication towers in attacks that resulted in relatively few casualties. The victims were all modified humans. Computer viruses were released that were intended to wipe out Conference, but the sophistication of the operating systems turned out to be far more resilient than the terrorists had expected. We hired private security to protect me and the family for months, but Millennial never showed.

After dozens of global attacks fizzled into mere annoyances, the group issued a public statement:

> *We are Millennial. For decades we have guarded against the efforts of those who would re-create the world without any forethought or consideration for their actions. We have attempted to thwart their efforts. We have warned you of the dangers presented by these so-called redeemers of the human race. However, it is clear that neither fear nor death, reasoning nor imploring, have shaken the global community to its senses or brought about a sense of responsibility. We can only warn that the path you are set upon will cause your destruction. We are watching. We are immortal. We are Millennial.*

The phrase "We are coming for you" was noticeably absent from Millennial's statement, and the talking heads and international officials went into a frenzy, breaking down the tone of the speech and their lack of zeal. An alleged member of Millennial came forth anonymously to do an interview with a member of the press. He said that the direction of Millennial was going to be one of detachment. We as a people had gone too far, and they only wanted to be left alone. These rat bastards had killed more than a hundred thousand people, and now they wanted some type of truce with the world.

Even if he spoke for Millennial, I was not convinced. After we canceled our security detail, all I could think about was my granddaughter and how her mods could make her a target, about how I might lose another member of my family to the plotting of Millennial.

Victoria was fifteen years old, a graduate with a master's degree, and considerably more articulate than the seven-year-old I was introduced to before being shot. After being synced back at the hospital, I could see a distance between her and Bella, although at the time I chalked it up to mere adolescence.

Over time, though, I could see the coldness wasn't limited to her mother but to the rest of the family and neighbors. My granddaughter was part of the ultimate clique: one that included only mods. They studied together and hung out together and left everyone their own age in the dust. Bella and Keith did everything they could do stay involved, but Victoria was changing. My granddaughter was what they called partially integrated, but Conference mods meant she would be fully integrated with every other mod on the planet.

Bella refused Victoria's requests for the Conference mods. When she did, Victoria appealed to Keith and even to me. Truth be told, the idea of my granddaughter networking her brain to a million other people gave me the creeps. I explained that it was probably best to heed her mom's advice, and after that, my granddaughter withdrew even further. My meager attempt to dispense wisdom was rejected openly—to teenage Victoria, I was merely a mouthpiece for her parents.

In late 2064, Victoria left home in the middle of the night. Supposedly she left a note for Bella and Keith, but they refused to show me what she wrote. It seemed a bad idea to press the matter;

W Lawrence

Bella was clearly shaken, and Keith warned me that we should just wait for Victoria to come back of her own accord.

In spring of 2065 there was still no word from my granddaughter. The police refused to investigate. According to Governance law, she was now sixteen and considered an adult. On the day I synced back, Bella wept in my arms about how she missed her baby. I tried to console her, to explain that Victoria was just going through a phase, that she could take care of herself. She might have been sixteen, but she held a master's degree and was highly employable. She'd come around in time. My words brought little solace to my daughter.

Syncing Forward

Chapter 46

In the autumn of 2069, I was surprised to receive an offer of the most unusual kind. When Bella sent me a message that I had a job interview scheduled for my next synchronizing, I chalked it up to her pulling my leg. I synced back, played the typical catch-up game, and did my best to be Mr. Positive for my daughter, who was still wounded by Victoria running away from home. An hour into our visit, the house computer, Alfred, announced that a Mr. Taras Negnevitskii had arrived at the door.

Taras was a tall, slim man who appeared to be in his early forties. Jacob invited him in and cleared Molly out of the living room so this visitor and I could speak without interruption. Taras introduced himself as a representative of the Sino-Russian Joint Space Operations, which believed my chemopreservative state was most uniquely suited their recent endeavors. Their agency had resurrected a NASA project from more than a hundred years ago, and using improved technology, they intended to investigate a planet that was more than four light-years away. I had read a brief article about a similar but unmanned mission from about thirty years ago; its expected arrival date was the year 2072—three years from now.

The new plan was to send a person to the star Alpha Centauri to confirm what scientists believed was a pair of habitable planets. The problem was, even with the best technology, the trip there would last more than forty years. It would be impossible for a normal man, but I was no normal man—not any longer. Still, what Negnevitskii was proposing ran along the boundaries between strange and absurd.

"Mr. Negevinksi—" I started.

"It's Neg-ne-vit-skii. But please, call me Taras," he said.

"Sorry. *Taras*, are you asking me to go into outer space? That's crazy!" I laughed.

393

"Not crazy. You are still very popular in the eyes of the public. The mission isn't scheduled to launch for another four years. There is plenty of time to train you for the launch, and we are fully capable of changing the launch specifications to accommodate you. Everything else can be learned along the way."

"Four years for you. That's eight days for me. Are you telling me I am going to be ready in a week?"

"With time to spare." Taras waved his hand dismissively at me as I shook my head in disbelief. "Mr. James, let me cut your chase, as you say. The *mooshkoy*—in English you say robot, I think—will be the pilot, the scientist, the doctor if that becomes necessary—"

"If this mooshkoy can perform all these vital tasks, why send me? Why not send it alone? Or send two or three of them?"

Tara drew closer to me. "Fifty years ago, colonizing Mars became successful because Mars-One was able to show humanity struggling to establish a colony. Joint Space Operations began construction of the Luna colony several years later, and it was not nearly as captivating. Why? Because rovers performed most of the beginning work remotely from earth. *Da*, this was smarter, safer, but to this day the Mars colony remains vastly more popular than its counterpart on the moon despite being smaller and less practical. The world wants to see a man succeed, not a machine. Not to mention that the initial cost of Mars-One was paid for almost entirely by advertising. Our expenses were . . . shall we say, burdensome? Did I say that properly? My English is not so good."

"Taras, your English is better than most Americans." His accent was thick indeed, but I paid my compliments where they were due. The message he was conveying, however, was so ridiculous that I was shocked it was even being proposed. "Getting back to this outer space mission . . . you just want me along for the ride? I'd be gone for decades."

"Do not underestimate your importance. You would still be working, I can promise you. The ability to see things with your own eyes, to experience things the way only a man can. This would bring

Syncing Forward

trust to the entire mission—that is something not even the best machine can achieve. And the trip would last only a few weeks for you," he clarified.

"But my family is still here. I'd be coming back after my daughter and grandkids were long dead. That doesn't seem appealing."

"Perhaps I was not accurate in my description." Tara cleared his throat. "Like the early Mars-One colonists, this mission is *one-way only*. Bringing physical things, like a person or a machine—that takes time. But we have a new technology that allows messages to go across light-years like a phone call. With that, your experiences would be instantly communicated back to Earth and help make the way for the first colonists. They would bring with them materials for the habitats and food and such. Perhaps by that time we will have a new cure for your condition, and you will have a chance for a most exciting life on a new planet. You'd be a hero—"

I had already stopped listening. "No, this is not going to work," I told him.

"How can you be sure? We have excellent scientists—"

I stood up. "No, Taras. It's not a matter of me being afraid of dying or concerned about the quality of the flying saucer or whatever you'd strap me into. I mean, this is not going to work for *me*. I don't want to go on your mission. I don't want to be a hero, I don't want to be your token redneck astronaut—I don't want any of that. I want a normal life. I want to wake up tomorrow and have it actually *be tomorrow*, not six months or six years later."

"We believe we can find a cure for you," Taras said, pulling a single circular chip about the size of an old US quarter out of his pocket. He set it down, and electric current from the smartglass table powered an invisible emitter within the tiny square. A holographic display showed multiple commands in Russian, which he quickly toggled through to get to a document display. The image in front of me was filled with words in Russian, the first page of a lengthy document.

Taras uttered a command in Russian to the computer. The document's words quickly morphed to English. I read about four sentences into the mammoth document and gave up. "It was better when it was in Russian," I quipped. "What does all this say?"

Taras was growing impatient, but he steadied himself, desperate to make me his rocket man. "Martin, this is a guarantee of funds to research your condition, to find a cure for your—the English word is too difficult—your slowness. In any case, this document details our budget and plans for continuing the research done by Innovo. You should note we are prepared to dedicate a tremendous sum to assist you."

I mulled over this new facet of Taras's offer. After Innovo was bought out, I was faced with the ominous prospect that there would be no permanent fix to my condition. Now the Sino-Russian Alliance was willing to dedicate four times the total money Innovo had spent on curing me, all for the low price of climbing into a spaceship and never returning to earth.

"What if you find a cure for me before I leave on the mission? Will you give it to me?" I asked dejectedly.

"You know we could not. Your condition is precisely what makes you perfectly suited for this mission. Curing you means you would never survive the flight to Alpha Centauri, let alone the wait for the colonists."

I turned and looked into the kitchen and saw Bella doing her best to eavesdrop. Even from the living room, I could see her concern and sadness. I had no idea how much she'd heard, but I guessed Bella was as conflicted as I was.

"Did you ask the Millennial group? There has to be some way to find them. I saw a news clip where they interviewed a member."

"No. That interview was done in secret many years ago—the contact has again disappeared. If we could have found the Millennial people, do you honestly think we would need you?"

Syncing Forward

"Then ask publicly! Offer whoever steps forward immunity. Somebody will take the offer. They are scientists, after all."

"So you want us to not only place a terrorist on our flight but advertise for them as well? You clearly have no idea what the public will do to us."

"Taras, you are offering me the possibility of a new life while simultaneously demanding I give up everything I've been fighting to keep. Without my family, the cure means nothing. It may seem pathetic to you, but even when I am synchronized, I am out of sync: out of sync with the world, with the people in it. My daughter is all I have left of my old life."

"And you would be allowed to communicate with her as often as you wished."

"I don't want to do it, Taras."

"Please, Martin." His tone became distressed. "There is no one else who can do this job!"

"I said no!" Gesturing toward the hallway, I stood over our guest. "I don't want to be rude, but I'm thinking you should go."

The thin man stood and straightened his bland tie. He spoke softly, sensitive to Bella's prying ears. "Martin, we are very well informed. We know that nobody is even considering reopening the research into Millennial's drug—nobody except us. Your daughter, your grandchildren and their children—they are all going to pass. This is tragic, but it is also a fact. The only thing you will accomplish by staying here is watching them die. Let them die knowing your life had some purpose and that you are helping humanity reach the stars. They can proudly take that memory to the next life."

I hung my head and said nothing.

"Take some time to reconsider. The offer will be on the table for at least a year. After that, we will need to proceed without you." Taras Negnevitskii stepped quietly out of the living room, thanked Keith and Bella for inviting him into our home, and walked out the door.

Impulsively, I ran after him and caught up as Taras climbed into the back of the limousine waiting outside. The chauffeur pointed to me, and Taras looked in my direction quizzically. "Yes, Martin?"

I was suddenly hesitant to say anything, but now that we were face-to-face, it seemed I should get what I had to say off my chest. "My daughter, Amara—she was a special agent before she was killed. I found out after her death that the man responsible for putting me in this condition was still alive. Dieterich Lenhart Bruchmuller was his name—*is* his name. He is supposedly in a state of chemopre-servation as well. I don't know how he escaped death or why they have been hiding him, but I do know where: Walter Reed Medical Center."

Taras closed the distance between us, his face awash in surprise. "Are you sure?"

"No, but I trusted my daughter. Amara may have had her quirks, but she knew how to conduct an investigation. Ivan Fagundes was her partner, and he knew something as well. He works as a Texas Ranger now. He may know more."

"And this man you speak of—would he possibly know how to re-create the drug that is responsible for your condition?"

"That's the impression I got."

"Why are you telling me this?"

"Because, if there is a chance my daughter was right and somebody can get information out of Bruchmuller, you'll have what you need. Then somebody more qualified than me could take the Alpha Centauri trip."

"And you could have your life back," Taras added.

I nodded.

"You know, you could have traded this information for a guarantee that we would provide you with the antidote." He cocked his head and waited for my response.

"I reckon I could have," I replied, disappointed that I had not considered that option before opening my mouth. "But I hope you'll have some sense of consideration if it turns out my information gets you what you want."

"I will take this to my superiors," he concluded slowly, climbing back into the limo as he did. "Thank you, Martin, for trusting me."

As he closed the door, I muttered, "Don't make me sorry I did."

The subject of my "job offer" was given a wide berth for the remainder of the day while the family fell into what little ritual we had. It was two weeks before Christmas, but we celebrated anyway with a trip to church and a small gift exchange. Catching up with the ever-growing family tree was a fun challenge that I had no issue with reviewing. The evening grew more uncomfortable when the subject of Victoria came up—her vanishing, not knowing if she was alive or dead. We tried to make the best of the evening, but the air was thick with questions and angst. It wasn't till late that night that Bella and I had a moment alone to talk about the day's visitor.

"Are you going to do it, Dad?" she asked out of the blue, sipping on her coffee and snuggling her feet underneath her on the sofa.

I was tempted to be coy on the subject but didn't want to waste any more precious minutes on Taras's proposal. "No, I'm not."

"Why won't you?" Bella asked contritely. "You don't have much of a chance getting cured if you stay here. I hate to be the pessimist, but your prospects aren't looking so great."

"Baby Bella, you are all that's left of my old life. I won't have any chance of seeing you again if I leave, and I'm not ready to give up. I'll take a small chance over no chance."

I was there—four years later—when the Shenzhou 75 launched from orbit and headed for Alpha Centauri, piloted by one of the most advanced computers made by man. I watched with mixed enthusiasm as the craft moved away from Earth, taking with it the aspirations of mankind along with any chance of my cure. The launch of the interstellar craft stirred up childhood dreams of traveling to outer space and seeing alien worlds. I would be lying if I said I wasn't filled with a sense of remorse as video of Saturn flying past was transmitted back on the Shenzhou's superluminal communicator. My imagination had me corresponding with ground control, making some clever statement that would make viewers smile and my family soar with pride, words that would be archived among the great historical phrases.

When years of nothing but endless transmissions from the blackness of space came from the Shenzhou craft, the romance of leaving Earth wore off. The reality of what it meant to cross the great expanse between stars finally set in—even at one-fifth the speed of light, people around the world truly understood what an enormous ocean of nothing our planet drifted upon.

Chapter 47

Taras Negnevitskii never contacted me after his initial visit, nor did anyone from the Sino-Russian Joint Space Operations. I tried a few times to find out if his people had found out anything about Bruchmuller, but my vidcalls were declined: Taras was not in, Taras was busy, Taras was now in a different department. The offer they'd made to have me as part of the mission was never disclosed to the public.

In 2069 my daughter had Miranda moved to Jacksboro, Texas. Bella didn't ask for permission, and I didn't oppose her. I synced back in December of that year, and it was the first reunion in over three decades, since the wedding. I barely recognized this woman I had once called my wife.

More than a month of perceived time had passed for me by then, and the ratio of time I had syncing back had grown considerably. I would have been eighty-six years old if Bruchmuller never injected me. So strange it was that I was still a young man, and yet all my prospects for a normal life had vanished.

Bella prepared me as best she could, detailing how Miranda's husband had passed away a few years back. Not that Miranda knew. When Miranda had a rare moment of lucidity, it usually pertained to our daughters. The dementia was advanced, and virtually everyone who approached her was a stranger. As bad as the condition was, it wasn't the reason Bella had brought her to Texas. Miranda's immune system was failing, and there wasn't a treatment around that could help. Doctors said she had at best a year in her. Out of all the tragedies I had dealt with, this one felt the easiest to avoid. And yet I found myself drawn back one last time to the woman who broke my heart.

We drove thirty minutes to an advanced hospice center in the next town. I stood nervously at the door to Miranda's room while she stared out the window at a barren tree. Bella took my hand in hers, and we walked in together. The only sounds were Miranda's ragged breathing and the holoprojector from two doors down blaring away.

"*Hola*, Mama," Bella spoke quietly, brushing Miranda's gray hair from her face. "How are you feeling today?"

Her eyes were wide against her wrinkled skin, fearful and uncertain of everything. "You were here this morning."

"No, Mama. That was yesterday. I brought you an orange, remember? You love oranges."

"*No me gusta,*" she snapped. "I told that fat man with the mustache to take it away. I hope he threw it in the trash."

Bella tried to get her mother to remember anything: a food, a name, a place. But Miranda's mind was emptied out by the crippling disease that had ravaged her mother. I watched helplessly from behind until Miranda pointed her bony finger at me. "Who's that?"

I inched forward, trying not to frighten her, smiled as best I could, and greeted her. "Hello, Miranda. It's good to see you."

She stared at me for a solid ten seconds before she repeated to Bella. "Who is that?"

I walked closer and crouched at her bedside. "Miranda, it's me. Martin."

"Martin is my husband's name," she spoke shallowly. "Martin, Martin . . ."

I smiled and looked at Bella, relieved that she was recalling anything.

"My husband is out with my daughter, Amara. I don't think he would like it that you are here."

My heart sank. From my point of view it wasn't that long ago that my wife had been a whole woman, dedicated to her family, feisty, unafraid of a hard day's work. To see her here like this, her body dying, her mind lost to the effects of disease . . . I tucked Miranda's blanket in, helpless to do anything else. It took all I had to stay in the room while Bella brushed her mama's hair, the whole time Miranda calling her a stranger, telling me she didn't know me. My daughter finally reached her limit and stood up to leave.

"I love you, Mama," she told her, kissing her on the cheek. "I'll come by tomorrow, okay?"

"My daughter is a police officer," Miranda glowered. "She'll arrest you if you harass me."

Bella and I walked arm in arm out of the room, both of us devastated. I suggested we go to church, because at that point I wasn't sure I was going to be able make it through the rest of the day without divine intervention.

We drove to Iglesia de Santa Teresa and just made the evening service. Father Gutierrez had been a friend of our family's for many years, and he picked us out of the sparse attendance rather quickly. After service we told him about Miranda, and he prayed with us for guidance and solace, promising to visit with her. As Bella went off to use the restroom, I confessed that my faith was anything but solid after what I had been through, and I meant it. It was nearly impossible to see God at work in the world after all I had witnessed, after all I had gone through.

The father put his arm around me and told me to take courage, that divine providence was made evident after our darkest trials. It was small comfort.

Miranda passed away five months later from pneumonia. Some new form of lupus had shut down her body's ability to fight disease, not that she even knew she was dying. I was there to console Bella—my daughter equally comforting me. Inside I never stopped loving my wife, even after she remarried and moved away. I couldn't bring myself to admit to Bella how ashamed I was that I hadn't kept in contact with Miranda when she was still lucid. She was as good a wife as anyone could have expected, and she went to her grave without me acknowledging that.

Bella told me there were dozens of video messages of my former wife as a young woman —the woman I knew—showing her reaching out to Amara with pleadings for them to reconcile. Amara never did, of course, and when our daughter died, Miranda was wounded to her very heart.

I swore that I would make the best of the time I had with those around me. While making friends was nearly impossible, we did our best to keep the family as close as possible, even when fights would break out and differences seemed irreconcilable. Still, time has a way of slipping out of all of our hands, and the family reunions became less frequent and less popular. Each day that passed for me brought me closer and closer to the inevitable, a day that I dreaded more than death itself.

Syncing forward. Syncing back. The pages of history relentlessly flipped by whether I read them or not. At Bella's fiftieth birthday she told me about Riley's recent divorce—six months into their marriage, and they were already splitting up. While my youngest grandson wasn't winning any prizes in my eyes, I was impressed with how well Bella rolled with the changes.

"You know, Bella?" I told her. "I am very proud of you."

She looked at me cockeyed, surprised by my comment. "Why? I haven't done anything."

"You raised three kids, you're still happily married, and you've taken care of me all these years. I'm astonished at how well you've handled everything."

"Let's see . . . my oldest son knocked up a girl at eighteen, my daughter ran away from home, and I wouldn't call Riley being divorced at twenty exactly awesome. Oh, and I might poison Keith if he doesn't get his snoring fixed."

I chuckled but tried to steer the conversation to a more serious tone. "Seriously, Bella. How did you cope so well?"

Syncing Forward

"Honestly? It was you, Dad. I know I never had a flashy job or invented anything or even figured out how to fix our washing machine, but I knew what I wanted to be when I grew up."

"What was that?"

She shrugged matter-of-factly. "I wanted to be as good a mom as you are a dad. I figured if I could do that, then I'd make you proud."

A tear crept out of my eye. "Well, you've certainly done that, and then some."

Bella flexed her hands open and shut while wincing just a smidge. She looked up at me, and we shared for a moment the same look of concern. My daughter brushed her hair back behind her ear. "It's nothing, Dad."

"You better get that checked out," I said, mildly concerned. "It could be arthritis."

Chapter 48

Syncing forward. Syncing back. Bella came home from the hospital and told me that her health problems were degenerating quickly. After accepting the Accelerate treatment, I found my Baby Bella crippled by her new condition. Two years later—a mere four days for me—my grandsons began prepping me for the reality of Bella's shortened future.

It was March of 2073, and Bella had been battling AVIDS—Advanced Immune Deficiency Syndrome—for years. The condition had been misdiagnosed for more than a decade, and shockingly about a quarter of people over forty suffered from the disease. What was worse, Jacob relayed rumors of the condition being more widespread than was publicly discussed. It seemed to be caused by genetically enhanced food being incompatible with the digestive system of some people. Eating naturally simply wasn't affordable anymore; genetically modified foods had become prolific and tainted crops globally. Animals suffered from Krukk's Disease, a livestock version of AVIDS—unless, of course, the animals were gen-enhanced as well. New modified animals only exacerbated the spread of AVIDS as their proteins wormed their way into the people who drank their milk and ate their meat.

Generations of modification upon modification had led to a global food supply that was increasingly foreign to the unmodified people who were consuming it. AVIDS worked like many immune deficiencies, painfully sucking the life from the man or woman who was unfortunate enough to contract it as whatever disease chose to set up shop destroyed the body. Gen-modifications could be done to counteract the effects, but that was only if your body didn't reject them. The older you were, the higher the rejection rate. Scientists called it "a regrettable side effect of necessary technological advances." I called it "my child dying."

Syncing Forward

She was asleep in her favorite chair when I synced, and so I sat there with Keith, waiting for her to wake. For hours I sat, wondering if I was going to be able to speak with her one last time. The doctor holo-messaged in and—after checking her vitals remotely—told us it wouldn't be long. Riley was on leave from his military duty in the Gulf of Mexico and brought his new wife and son. Jacob made a showing along with a few of the great-grandkids. They had spent the last few years watching her degenerate, while each time I saw my daughter it was a snapshot of her decline. I don't know which experience was worse.

Father Gutierrez had shown up earlier to administer last rites and now was mingling quietly with others in the house, being his typical encouraging self. Despite the father coming to our home three days in a row, I found myself unable to speak to him. The way I saw it, his presence in our home was akin to being a harbinger of death.

Jacob unsuccessfully tried to prod me off the chair. Twelve-year-old Molly tried to tell me there was still a chance Bella could pull through. I told her to leave me alone. Keith brought me a small sandwich and digestive enzyme for me to eat. I managed to stuff the food down my throat while still holding Bella's hand, which was kept warm only by our contact. She still breathed raspy, laboring breaths that made it seem as if she might go at any moment.

That's when Bella woke up. Disoriented at first, she stared at Keith and smiled. He reached out and held her other hand, leaned over, and gave Bella a bristly kiss with his overgrown mustache and unkempt beard. "Hello, love," she greeted him. "Where are the kids?"

Jacob and and Riley came in, squeezing into the crowded corner and hugging their mother gently.

She smiled painfully at her husband. "No Victoria?"

Keith shook his head.

Bella frowned, and tears escaped down along her temples, "Where's my baby girl?"

"I don't know, honey." Keith gripped her hand tightly. "I'm sure she would have come home if she could have."

Bella's wounded face was not so optimistic, but she managed to force a smile through the physical and emotional pain. "I love my family so much. Thank you, Keith, for making them with me."

"How do you feel?" Keith asked her, his jaw trembling.

"I think I feel better," she answered with a slow, shaky exhale.

Keith smiled brightly and patted her hand. "That's wonderful, honey. Wonderful! Can I get you anything?"

Bella looked over at me and then back at Keith. "Would you brew me some . . . of that herbal tea?" Her laborious breathing interrupted almost every sentence with a pause.

"Sure, sure," he told her. Keith gave her another kiss and trundled from the greenhouse.

"Kids, go help your father, please. I want to talk"—she took a deep breath—"to talk to your granddad alone."

It was just Bella and me, and I could barely hold it together after knowing she had lied to Keith. "Please, tell me how you really are, Bella."

She looked at Keith's empty chair. "I'm dying, Dad . . . I can't breathe too well. I didn't want him . . . . . . him to hear me say as much, though."

When she looked back at me, I did not see the crippled fifty-five-year-old woman everyone else saw. All I could see was my little angel, seven years old, struggling to breathe and grasping my hand with a pitiful grip. I looked at the father, who was deep in prayer. I tried, but the words wouldn't come together to form a sentence, not even in my head.

She looked up at me, and I could swear it was my Baby Bella's tiny voice that said, "I'm a little . . . scared, Dad."

The words thrust me back to her Christmas experience—of her thinking that Santa might not come—to her first time riding a bicycle, to her wedding just before Keith took her hand in marriage, to when she was giving birth for the first time. It was my job as her dad to tell her she'd be okay, to tell her everything would work out. Instead, the only words I could manage were, "I'm scared too."

"Will you take care of Keith for me, please? After I am gone?"

Why did she have to ask me that? I didn't know what I could do in my condition. I nodded in agreement, mostly because I didn't dare speak a word for fear of losing control. We sat there for another couple of minutes quietly, when she pulled my hand to her face and guided it to press against her cheek. My thumb stroked her wrinkled skin affectionately, the way I used to when she was a child.

"I'm . . . ready," was all she said. Her grip relaxed, and then she was gone.

"Please, no," I sputtered through snotty tears and quivering lips.

The monitor on her wrist gave off a solid audible tone that called the rest of the family to the greenhouse. Keith rushed over and dropped to his knees to hold her. The teacup and saucer fell to the ground, widening out in an uneven earthy stain. What little warmth was left in Bella's face slowly faded. Jacob gripped his kids, telling them that their grandma's suffering was finally over. Riley was calling the hospital to arrange for a coroner. The children looked on with confused and saddened faces—for them this was the first death they had experienced.

Father Gutierrez finished his prayer over Bella's lifeless body. "*. . . sellado con la sangre de Cristo, que puede volver antes de que usted libre de pecado. Amén.*"

The torment of losing Bella gnawed at my soul. What was I, besides a wayward father who dropped by a couple of times a year? I had failed Bella. I had failed everybody. My sweet child had been ripped from me, and all I could do was stare and watch it happen. I wished to go back in time, climb aboard the Shenzhou, and plunge myself into the void of night. I wished that Rajani's two bullets to the chest had

W Lawrence

put me out of my misery so that I would never have lived to see this day. I wished to go to sleep and never awake.

Syncing Forward

Chapter 49

After Bella passed away, I spent a half-dozen of my days with Keith and Jacob and Riley. Great-grandkids came and went, and our visits were simple. They tried to arrange special trips for me, but my ailing son-in-law was not up for heavy traveling, and I refused to leave him alone. I was obliged to make good on my promise to Bella to take care of her widower husband, and that was what I tried to do.

Keith managed to hang on for a few more years before AVIDS took him as well. He passed away while I zoomed through the months, and I selfishly thanked God that I didn't have to see him die. I couldn't sync until three months after Keith died, and when I did my morning was spent at the cemetery. Father Gutierrez drove Jacob and me, and they spoke of newsworthy items that barely made sense to me any longer. Bella's plot was right next to Keith's, and each tombstone showed a recycling video of the two of them holding hands and kissing in their younger years. The quote's origin escaped me, but the meaning was fully understood.

In loving memory of
BELLA JAMES-HEFFLEY
2020–2078
"A happy family is but an earlier heaven."

Family. It was all I ever wanted. From the time I was a teenager, making a home for a family was all I cared about, and it had been ripped from my grasp. Despite all efforts, despite my prayers and the resources at my disposal, I had failed. Once my little girl was gone, the only thing I had left was the word I'd given her to look after her husband, and my promise to Bella was fulfilled with Keith's death. I was utterly spent with living. There was no hope of a cure and no reason to continue as I was.

I recalled sitting with Bella the first time I got synced, and how she said she would kill herself if anything ever happened to me. I remembered admonishing her, telling her "Bella, even in the worst of circumstances, I'd never take my own life out of sadness. If you learn nothing else from me, I want you to do this: live your life right to the end."

Gutierrez approached from behind and put his arm around my shoulder. "Martin, are you going to be okay?"

I nodded, staring down at the pair of graves.

"What's on your mind, Son?"

"Father, is it still a sin to commit suicide? Even assisted suicides? You know, if somebody is suffering a lot."

"It has always been a sin, Martin," he said. "The only difference is whether we choose to recognize it as such. The world may change, but God doesn't, nor do his expectations of us change just because suicide is accepted by the world. I know you are troubled about your friend David, but you can still pray for his soul. And Bella never went in that direction despite her condition—you should be proud of your daughter. Neither did Keith. They fought the good fight to their very last days. Your daughter and her husband are at peace in heaven now."

I said nothing.

"Who are we talking about, Martin?" he probed.

I said nothing.

"Martin"—the father took me by the shoulders firmly—"God has no doubt handed you a challenging life, and I don't propose to truly understand your grief. Of this I have no doubt, however: there is a plan for your life. God doesn't make mistakes. You may not like it, you may actually hate it, but you still need to accept it. Your own death isn't going to bring back Bella, or Amara, or anyone else you love. Suicide will only dishonor their memory and separate you from them in the afterlife."

Jacob watched helplessly as I pulled away from Father Gutierrez and stormed toward the car. I stopped in my tracks when the priest called after me, "Martin! Please! Don't give up now. You still have family left. Jacob, Riley, your great-grandchildren—"

"For how long, Father? How long do I have them for? Hours? Days? Weeks?" I turned and walked off into the cemetery, not really knowing or caring where I would end up.

"Are you sure you want this, Martin?" Jacob asked. He never took too well to calling me Grandpa like Riley or Victoria had. I suppose it made our relationship feel more like a friendship than the one I shared with the rest of the family.

"How many more times are you going to ask me that?" I asked dejectedly. "We've had this argument over and over."

"I just figured you would want to ring in the New Year with us. It's only a single jump for you. One more day. Come on."

"I've said my good-byes, Jacob. Don't make me go through them again."

I knew what he was trying to do: get me in a celebratory mood so that I would reconsider. But there was no fighting me once I made my mind up—not this go-round. Either he would help me or the attorneys would cut him out of the decision-making process completely. Jacob—my grandson—was now almost my age, a widower from a traffic accident and a machinist by trade. Out of the whole family, my brother's namesake had stuck by me the most, almost stubbornly, one could say. We spent hours debating my decision, and sometimes angrily. I supposed his losses of temper were signs of affection.

Jacob sighed as the doctor hooked up the dermal applicators along my abdomen and the neural impeder across my forehead. When he put his hand on my arm, I noticed a few sunspots forming on his skin and imperceptibly shook my head in disgust. It might not be disease or an accident, but age would soon take him too. Even Victoria, wherever she was, would finally die. Three grandchildren and their children and their children—to watch them lost to time like their mother or father or aunt was too much for me to bear.

"I love you; you know that, right? I won't give up on you, Martin. Not ever. We'll continue to push for a cure," Jacob said.

"You do that."

"Are you sure you don't want to see the others?"

I shook my head. I didn't want to see or Riley or the kids. I wouldn't have stopped even if Victoria came back to visit. Hell, I didn't want to see Jacob or even the doctor. I didn't want to see anyone. I just wanted to close my eyes and die, but I couldn't even do that. My life was a living hell, but I didn't want to risk eternal damnation by committing suicide. My only remaining solution was to sleep.

If they found a cure, I would be forced to cope with whatever bad news was brought to me. But I knew that they wouldn't find a cure. I would continue to sleep through the decades till somebody decided the space I occupied wasn't worthy of me holding it. Then they would dispose of me, and I wouldn't be responsible for my own death. I'd finally be dead and reunited with the ones I loved. God forgive me, but I just couldn't go on anymore.

This was why Rajesh Jotwani had apologized to me years ago, standing in the freight elevator as the doors were closing, looking down on my pathetic body strapped to the gurney in the corridors underneath Innovo. He knew the hell my life would become without the Somnus. The fifth vial Bruchmuller was to administer to me would have put me to sleep so that I would never have experienced the passage of time. It had to be the secret to how the Millennial terrorists had survived throughout the years, reappearing decades later from their stealthy crypts. They slept their way through the ages, fully prepared to find a new world each time they emerged. They went voluntarily, either reconciled to losing their families, or having none, or bringing them into the crypts themselves. And for them, the Remedium was available, always within grasp.

Syncing Forward

Had anyone been able to duplicate the antidote for the Millennial drug, I would have simply woken up in a different decade or century and been none the wiser. Sadness most certainly would have overwhelmed me, but it would have been far better than watching my children murdered or decaying from disease before my eyes. I would never have known my grandchildren or great-grandchildren only to lose them. I would never have experienced the destruction of my country or the illness of my friends. I would never have known the detailed horrors that people perpetrated on each other in this sick world.

The doctor cleared his throat. "Okay, Mr. James. We're going to put you under now. It will take only a few seconds for the neural impeder to put you into a coma. This won't be a coma like you might experience if you were injured. It's like a switch, really. We turn it on and you sleep; we turn it off and you wake up. There is no pain involved."

"I don't care about pain."

He looked at me awkwardly. "I see. Well . . . do you have any questions before we proceed?"

"Will I dream?" I asked.

"No. No you won't dream."

I turned away from him and Jacob both. "Good."

— **Part 8** —

Exodus

Syncing Forward

Chapter 50

The doctor lied. There were dreams. Broken, disturbing dreams of faces and places and feelings of loss that came in irregular intervals. Darkness swirled around my fleeting thoughts as flickers of memory and imagination invaded my silent black.

Miranda on the bed. "I can't do this anymore..."

Dave warning me, "I told you they were terrorists..."

My Baby Bella hiding her face from me. "Mommy, he's doing it again! Turn it off! It's scary..."

A doctor from the waiting room in New Jersey notifying a woman about our Innovo employee. "We did everything we could to revive your husband..."

"Mom is seeing somebody else..."

"Amara's dead..."

"Bella won't last long..."

"Uncle Jacob had a stroke..."

Deep in my soul, I screamed for somebody to help me. *Please take me out of here!* Was I in hell? Was I dead and being punished for my sins? That was it—I was dead. It was my greed that had caused all this. My greed and vanity both. I should have listened to Dave, I should have walked away, I should have...

Amara, nine years old and holding my hand. "I love you, Daddy. Don't worry."

Blue water, moving rapidly, waves on fast-forward, night, day, night, day, streaks of light across the sky like shooting stars, clouds screaming by, a dark storm rolling in and dissipating in seconds, palm trees vibrating like tuning forks in the gusts that battered them.

Slowing down, watching the world decelerate. A semicircular room where I reclined in a half-dome of smartglass with flashing displays and luminescent white floors lighting the room. A doorway with no door to my right, and a video screen with images of industrial construction flipping by to my left.

Two chairs appeared in front of me, both clear and thin and looking like they would snap if anyone sat in them. Whoever had carried them blurred by, but I could tell it was a man in white clothing. Where was I? A mental hospital? Perhaps I had been insane this whole time? A psychotic break that detached me from reality? That would have been preferable to the reality I experienced.

I heard two sets of feet clip-clapping their way to the room. A man and a woman, both dressed in body-hugging white outfits, sat down across from me and waited. Neither spoke to me or to each other but instead sat patiently as I fully synchronized. The woman then stood, grabbed a drinking glass with a straw from behind me, and held it to my mouth. I sipped the subtly tart drink, swishing it about my mouth and gargling with it before swallowing.

As the woman sat down, I tried to speak but found myself struggling a bit. I cleared my throat. "Who are you? Where am I?"

"Hello, Martin James," the man greeted me. "My name is Walter Vergas. I am the chief of this facility, and we welcome you to Panama."

"Hello, Martin. My name is Anisa," the woman said. "We transported you here sixteen months ago, and we have been taking care of you during that time."

"What year is it? Where's Jacob?"

They both continued to look at me, but I couldn't help but feel a moment's hesitation in which something transpired between them, something hidden. Anisa spoke up first. "It is 2125, Martin. You have been asleep for forty-three years and three months."

It was worse than hell. I was still alive. Still syncing forward, sinking forward through time, only to be jerked back and have the nightmares of the world thrust upon me. Before it had been my family, but now it was strangers, unfamiliar faces, bringing me back into a

Syncing Forward

world I didn't want to know. "What do you want from me?" was all I could manage.

"I apologize for being the bearer of bad news, but Jacob passed away shortly after we took possession of you," Walter answered. "He could no longer tend to your care and so made ar-rangements with us for your hospice."

Jacob was gone now too. I was shell-shocked with regret, knowing my last act had been to turn my back on my grandson, on his love, on his compassion. Why was this happening to me? Why did they wake me just to shove another death in my face? Why?

Within that minute of conversation I realized how deep into the future I had plunged. But the torment of sleeping all those years was fading away, wisps of regret and horror and loss disappearing into the air. So many thoughts and feelings tumbled around inside me, but all that managed to escape my lips was the question, "You're a mod, aren't you, Walter?"

He smiled. "That's an old-fashioned way of putting it, but yes, you are correct. And my companion?" He gestured to the beautiful woman as if challenging me, testing my observation skills.

Inhaled, exhaled, I needed to calm down, to shake the confusion off me, to focus on something that had nothing to do with me. I looked at her perfect face, her solid expression, her deep-blue eyes. "And you, Anisa—you aren't human at all."

Walter Vergas smiled. Anisa did not. "You are a very clever man, Martin James," Walter said. "Very clever indeed. How did you know?"

Chapter 51

Chief Walter Vergas appeared to be in his late twenties, but his voice carried a maturity that did not match his age. It wasn't just his vocabulary and tone but the quality of his actual voice that seemed like that of a person in his forties or maybe even his fifties. His skin was smooth and youthful, tan and soft, as if he had never worked a day in his life. His posture was excellent, like a military figure, yet relaxed enough to make him approachable. His body was sculpted from exercise, toned from top to bottom. But it was his eyes that gave away the secret.

Yellow, almost golden, the irises were an unnatural color, and they didn't look quite right. The size of his eyes were slightly too big. Not alien-creature big—just big enough to not be any normal man's. He reminded me of the enhanced humans I'd met in Louisiana and Texas.

Anisa was different for a whole set of reasons. Like her counterpart's, her body was a picture of perfection. Flawlessly balanced measurements from her bust to her hips, long blond hair that cascaded off her shoulders and down to her waist, slender yet powerful legs exemplified through the white skin-tight pants she wore. Her skin was flawless, with neither a freckle nor a hair to mar it in any way. Her face appeared completely devoid of makeup, and yet she seemed tattooed with dark eyeliner, and her cheeks achieved the perfect blushing color as if she were ready for a photo shoot.

To find such a beauty anywhere would be rare. However, when Anisa spoke, she was incredibly still—not locked in a position but still moving, almost pattern-like. She blinked in perfect intervals, even when answering questions, and I could see no carotid artery pulse to speak of on her gorgeous neck, something that should have been visible on somebody so slender and sitting in such a position.

The mod, Walter, was still chuckling even though I hadn't answered his question. He was saying something in a low tone to the

Syncing Forward

blonde. I heard the words *remarkable* and *keen*. Somehow these compliments only frustrated me, took me to the reality of my situation, the futility of even being alive.

"Who are you people? Why am I awake?" I asked them again, not really caring who answered.

Walter Vergas responded, "We are your new custodians, Martin. And you are awake because we are close to a cure for your condition. We need your assistance, however, and unfortunately there was no way for us to move forward without rousing you."

"I gave explicit instructions that I was not to be revived." My hands were still shaky from the images that haunted my dreams, my mind slipping back to Bella's death.

"Technically, your request was to be resynchronized once a cure was discovered," Anisa responded evenly.

I pulled my eyebrows together. "Not to be rude, but what the heck are you?"

"I am a synthetic multiform companion." The mere fact that it responded so quickly told me that this question was both processed more quickly than a normal human being would be able to and fully anticipated. Anisa answered smoothly, "You would probably define me as an android. I have been created for the purpose of interacting with you and assisting you with your transition to our facility."

I was put off by that last comment. "Did . . . did you say *created* for me?"

Walter broke in. "Martin, we have a lot to discuss, and our agenda is quite full. However, my guess is you will be far more cooperative if you are able to fill in the gaps between when you fell asleep and when you arrived here. My suggestion is that you spend the next hour with Anisa. I apologize, but we cannot spare more than that. She is at your disposal. She will show you the facility and answer any questions you may ask. I believe working with her alone will be both more comfortable and private for you."

Walter stood up and put out his hand to shake mine. I obliged out of habit more than anything, but was surprised when he turned and walked away. I called out to him, "Wait, what is going on here? You said you have a cure for me? Is it true?"

He paused and looked at the blond woman—the android—then turned back to me. "Anisa will tend to you. We will meet in one hour."

"Wait, how did you sync me back? How much time do I have?"

"We used the Accelerate treatment, so our time together will be similar to what you have experienced before." He started to leave again.

"Hold on one damn minute," I called after him again. "What's going on? You can't just leave me in here with this . . ."

I started to walk after him but heard motion close behind me. I turned and found Anisa standing in my personal space with a subtle smile on its face. "Shall we begin, Martin?"

I gave an up-and-down to this thing called Anisa. Alone with a robot that looked like a supermodel and acted like a person. The sigh I let out expressed the helplessness I felt, not to mention be-wilderment at what these strangers had thrust upon me.

I exhaled slowly and nodded. "Uh, sure. Fine, I'll play nice. So, Anisa, to be sure about all this, you are not alive?"

"No, I am not. I mimic 3,046 aspects of human life, however, including warmth, breathing, blinking, body language, facial expressions, and heartbeat. I can eat, drink, and even blow bubbles in chewing gum."

"May I leave?"

Anisa frowned slightly as if confused. "Leave? Where would you go?"

"I mean, will you try to stop me if I walk out of here? Detain me? Give me a beat-down?" I twanged my speech and tossed in some slang to see if it would keep up with me.

Syncing Forward

"Martin, first, I cannot allow you to come to harm. It is my primary function to protect you, so giving you 'a beat-down' would run contrary to my programming." God, it was so realistic! Anisa even did air quotes around my words. "Second, I would be happy to take you for a walk around the facility and answer your questions."

It gestured to the doorway, and I stepped out into warm salty air and a downright pleasant breeze carrying fresh smells of tropical plants and sounds of unfamiliar birds. The room had been climate-controlled, and this was like walking through a barrier. No door separated the outside environment from the inside. We descended down through a series of steps separated by large observation platforms and eventually met the comfort of the Panamanian beach. Looking down at the water allowed me to see how perfectly clear it was, so much so that I observed a school of fish darting about for a moment till the sunlight blotted them from view.

"So have I been cured? Is there even a cure?" I asked it.

"Those are questions Chief Vergas will answer for you." Anisa cast a curvy shadow on the ground, her near-translucent hair glimmering in the sun.

It wasn't going to give me the answers I wanted, so I did what this Vergas character had asked of me—I tried to catch up. "What happened to Jacob Heffley?" I asked quietly.

"My apologies, Martin. Jacob Heffley died in his sleep, with no adverse cause of death recorded." I looked out at the water, kicking up a scoop of white sand. I felt the granules work their way into the soft-soled shoes these people had dressed me in, with each small irritation combining to form an unbearable sensation. I slumped down in the sand and banged my shoes to shake it all away.

"What about my other grandkids? Riley? Victoria?"

"Riley was killed at the age of fifty during a rescue operation in the Gulf of Mexico while serving his last six months in the Texas Navy. Victoria's whereabouts and status are still unknown. Her last known link was a Conference node in Luxembourg, June 15, 2078."

"Fifty years . . ." I muttered.

"Forty-seven years, six months," Anisa corrected.

I sat on the beach, running my fingers through the hot sand, feeling both relieved at not having seen their deaths and guilty for not being brave enough to spend time with them in their last days.

"If it is any comfort, Jacob, Riley, and several other members of your family recorded messages for you to watch upon your awakening," Anisa informed me. "There are more than twenty-seven hours of holo-records from your grandchildren and another twenty-five hours from their progeny. I can make arrangements for you to watch them at a later time if you wish."

Why on earth would I want to watch anything? I didn't even want to be awake. Anisa simply stood over me, staring down in a way that would make most people feel awkward. "Can you please sit with me, Anisa?"

"Do you require companionship?" it asked.

"I just want you to sit," I answered with a perturbed tone. "You're freaking me out just standing there. Please sit down. Unless, of course, the sand will do something to your circuits."

"I don't have circuits in the traditional sense, and my system is fully enclosed. I can even swim." Anisa sat next to me. "I am curious—how did you determine so quickly that I am not a human female? It is widely circulated information that less than 4 percent of naturally born human men can identify my model type."

It was odd that an android would be curious at all. I went through the list. "First I noticed your carotid artery, or the lack thereof. You may have a faux heartbeat, but they should have put one on your neck as well. That, and your blinking is not human. Plus, your chief, Mr. Vergas, right? He hinted to me there was something different about you. Oh, your speech is impeccable. And then of course you appear way too sculpted for most human females. You look like a Photoshopped model."

Syncing Forward

"If you mean that my form is distracting, am I to assume you would prefer a different one? I am capable of altering my appearance if you would prefer."

The throbbing ache of loss was building in my chest. Perhaps it was my desire to run from that pain, but I decided that the distraction of Anisa was preferable. "You can change how you look? How is that?"

"It is part of my function as a companion. Do you have any preferences?"

"Surprise me."

Anisa's form shrank vertically and slightly narrowed at the hips. Its skin became olive while its eyes widened and took on an almond shape. The black color poured from its scalp and filled its blond hair while it shortened to shoulder length. Its nose and cheekbones moved with smooth precision, telling me this was not a clunky machine underneath. Where before there sat a lithe blond Caucasian, there was a Korean female masterpiece. The transformation was complete.

"That's incredible!" I told it, transfixed by both the speed and complexity of what I had just witnessed. "Are these, uh, presets for you? I don't have a better word to use right now. You've got me stunned."

"Yes, but I can mimic other forms as well. I can scan a picture or see a person on the street and transform to their parameters. Observe." The new Asian grew taller once again as its skin changed in complexion and its hair turned dark brown. Its hips widened a bit and its cheekbones, mouth, and eyes all morphed into the familiar face of my daughter Amara.

I jumped up from the sand and stumbled backward, my hands shaking in enraged sadness. There Amara was, standing before me, wearing Anisa's snug-fitting white outfit, smiling slightly as she held eye contact with me. "I took the liberty of uploading images and video of your family," it said with a voice that was eerily similar to my daughter's. "Perhaps interacting with a more familiar face will help you adjust to your new environment."

I turned and stared off in the opposite direction. My heart was beating quickly, and I felt a panic about to overwhelm me. My voice quivering, I instructed my companion, "Anisa, change back to how you looked before."

"Is there a prob—"

"Change back now!" I screamed.

When Anisa walked around me to face me again, she was in the blond woman's form. "My apologies, Martin. It was my intent to put you at ease, which I have clearly not done."

I put up my shaking hand. "It's okay. Just promise me you will never do that again."

Anisa gave me a curious look. "Would it be safe to assume that taking the form of anyone from your past should be avoided?"

"Yes, please."

"Forgive me. It was not my intention to upset you."

I took a few moments to listen to the sound of calming waves crawling up the beach. "There is no cure for me, is there, Anisa?"

"The chief would prefer to discuss that matter with you directly."

I shook my head and let out an exasperated laugh. Anisa's face gave zero clues as to the actual answer, but I got the distinct impression that if they did have a cure, this Walter Vergas would ask something from me in return.

Anisa reached for my hand and grasped it gently. The android had mentioned that its artificial body had warmth, but I was shocked at how human it really felt.

"Not that I'm ungrateful for the company, but why are you holding hands with me?" I wondered aloud.

"Do you wish for me to let go?" it asked.

"No, I'm just curious if this is part of your program."

"It is. I am a companion. It is part of my base programming to put you at ease. I may not be human, Martin, but I still understand the need for physical contact."

"Interesting," I mused. "Well, thank you. After everything I've been through, it's . . . it's nice."

"Do you wish to have a sexual encounter?" Anisa asked matter-of-factly.

I pushed its hand away and stepped back. "What? Me? No! No, I do not."

"Is my form unpleasing?"

"No, Anisa. That's not it," I answered, flabbergasted by the offer. "Your form is definitely pleasing. It's just that I don't feel like doing anything like that right now. My mind is so far away from *that* subject, I can't even fathom it. Plus, the fact that just a minute ago you made yourself look like my deceased daughter pretty much ruined the idea of sex with you *forever.*"

"Perhaps you wish a different companion then?"

"No! Anisa, you are fine. Just . . ." I took a breath and closed my eyes, "Just, can you not bring this topic up again?"

"Of course. Perhaps we should head to Chief Vergas's office then, Martin."

Was Anisa hurt by my refusal? It seemed like it, but that was probably my mind filling in the blanks, inventing observations I would make from a real person. Regardless, I was on my way to finally finding out why these people had woken me. We walked back across the sandy beach, shoes in hand, toward the building complex. A massive dirigible carrying a translucent cargo container on its underbelly flew silently overhead out to sea, and my sadness was further eclipsed by my astonishment.

We were ascending a long flight of steps that snaked up the cliff-side, when my morphing companion announced, "Chief Vergas will be detained for another hour. He apologizes for the delay but assures you he will meet with you as soon as possible."

I hadn't seen Anisa lift a finger to press a button or glance down at a phone to read a text. The thought crossed my mind that it had been programmed to drag this meeting out—to what end I had no clue—and I confronted Anisa about it.

"So why the long delay?" I began digging. "Why not just wake me up and get down to business if you need me so badly? There's no need for pretending with me. I've got no place to go and nobody left to see."

Anisa looked at me with a puzzled expression. "I don't understand your questions, Martin. They seem to imply a distinct lack of trust."

"Well, that's because I don't trust you. How did you know that this chief of yours was delayed another hour, for instance?"

"I am networked for communication, Martin. I can receive and send messages via text, voice, image, or hologram and process them while performing other complex actions—much more complex than the simple act of guiding you around our facility. For example, in the last thirty seconds, I have already swept the security perimeter, authorized your entrance to the Tres Carga section of our facility, and conveyed your concerns to Chief Vergas. He asked that you relax."

"Oh," was all that came out of my mouth. I felt a bit embarrassed, although why, I didn't know. This was a machine I was talking to, I reminded myself. "So . . . why the delay?"

"The chief is engaged in a project that he wishes to share with you personally. The timing of such has been difficult to manage. The details I cannot share, per his request. Shall we continue into the facility, or do you wish to return to the beach?"

I looked down the seventy feet of cliff we had ascended and out at the fine sand that lay beyond. I realized my heart was beating fast from the physical exertion, and it dawned on me that I didn't want to talk anymore. "Anisa, can I have a moment to myself please?"

"Certainly, Martin. I will come back to check on you in fifteen minutes."

Syncing Forward

I stood there in reflection for some time at the platform's edge. Anisa eyed me from a second platform above while talking with two uniformed men but kept the three flights of steps between us, leaving me alone in my thoughts. Seeing Anisa transform herself into the likeness of my late daughter had shaken me like a struck tuning fork, and I couldn't get Amara's death out of my mind.

Daddy, is there something wrong with me? My daughter's voice echoed from the past.

It was easily fifty feet down before anything—or anyone—falling would make contact with the cliff's edge. I was sure the fall would kill me, and no one would have the time to catch up to me before it was too late. I rested one foot on the bottom rung of the rail fence. My leg shook. I put my second foot on the rail and boosted myself up, when a sharp clap sounded from behind me and Anisa suddenly appeared at my side, a hand firmly resting on my shoulder. I didn't see how it had cleared three flights of steps between us so quickly, but I could only assume it had jumped thirty feet.

"May I ask what you are doing?" Anisa asked in its typical even-toned voice. Two uniformed men trotted down the steps at a brisk pace toward me as well.

I shook my head. "I'm not doing anything, Anisa. Just relaxing."

"Why are your feet on the bottom rail, Martin?"

"I told you, I was just relaxing."

"My apologies, Martin. Chief Vergas warned me that you might need monitoring, and I cannot allow you to come to harm."

"I thought you were my companion. Aren't you supposed to do what I ask?"

"Yes, that is correct in most cases."

"Then why don't you just go inside for a little while, Anisa?"

"Martin, it is my fundamental program to protect human beings and you above all else, even if that means protecting you from yourself. Perhaps we should go inside together?"

I gripped the handrail tightly. "No."

"Martin, you are attempting to commit suicide, and I cannot allow it."

My knees got week, and damned if I wasn't collapsing into a pathetic little ball. "I can't do this anymore." I covered my face in shame and tried to calm myself, but it was no use. Flashes of everybody I ever knew assailed my consciousness, and I started to hyperventilate.

"You're the love of my life, Martin. Of course I'll marry you."

"Funny Daddy! Do it again! Do it again!"

"It's okay, Bro. We're family, and we stick together."

"I'm a little scared, Dad."

I covered my ears desperately, unsuccessfully trying to keep the voices away.

"I just want to die, damn it!" I screamed aloud. Several heads of onlookers swiveled in our direction.

"Martin, please calm down."

"Calm? *Calm?* Everyone is dead! They're all dead, and I don't know what I am anymore! I don't know how to fit in here! I'm trapped, and there's no way out of this-this-this fucking cage! This isn't my world, don't you understand? You live here! I don't! And that guy over there, and him, and her, and Walter Vergas, and everyone I meet will be dead, and it will just be me! Alone! I'm sinking. Dear God, help me, I'm sinking!"

It didn't matter what I did anymore, if I failed or succeeded to do whatever my new custodians wanted me to do. I was a ghost, doomed to walk the earth until the ground underneath me decayed away and vanished from existence.

Anisa knelt and put its arms around me, its warmth like a soft hug from my wife after a rough day. I knew it wasn't real; Anisa was a construct, a thing, but it was all I had. I clutched my companion as if for dear life, unable to still the crying fit I was driven to.

"God help me. Anisa, I see their faces everywhere I go. I close my eyes and they are still there. My Baby Bella . . ." My poor daughter, crippled and suffering as her body consumed itself. All the moments I should have had with her as a father ripped from my grasp, and it was all because of a single moment.

"Tell me about the rat."

From a ring on Anisa's finger, a holographic display of smiling faces beamed from the gem and in front of my face. They shuffled from right to left; some posed for their picture with a thoughtful smile while others were more candid. Anisa spoke softly. "Do you know who these people are?"

I shook my head, my lip quivering as I tried to steady myself.

"Take a close look, Martin. They are your kin—generation after generation of your family who have survived to this day. Your children live on in them, do they not? You have an opportunity to be a part of their lives. You are not alone. You still have family. And you can help them."

I wiped the tears off my face, confused by Anisa's words. "Help them? How?"

"Come, let us speak with Chief Vergas. He is ready to answer your questions."

Chapter 52

A tropical breeze blew across the lush coastline and countered the humidity. I hated it for making an otherwise miserable day feel like an absolute paradise. The multilevel facility was a stunning work of architecture that rose and dipped in impossible arches and spanned farther than the eye could see to the north, but still managed to blend into the green landscape of the Panamanian coastline to the south. Thick leaves and pliable palms filled in the gaps between buildings and concealed large portions of the walkways from view.

Maybe it was the walk, maybe it was the air, maybe the cold water I ran over the back of my neck, but I managed to calm down enough to appear sane. When I stepped out of the restroom I felt all eyes upon me, and the awkwardness grew. I don't know if I would have jumped or not, but I do know I didn't like how the folk here stared at me now.

I felt compelled to act normal again. I walked alongside Anisa and asked, "So why am I here? Why Panama? I mean, how does this place fit into the world?"

"The first two questions Chief Vergas will answer."

"Maybe a wiki page would be easier to read," I groaned.

"You won't find any 'wiki pages' anymore," Anisa answered, "as the Internet you knew is very much gone. It is much more complex now. However, I can summarize a bit for you."

We went up a set of steps and then another and then a ramp to a corridor, passing the observation room where I originally woke up, then walked across a bench-spotted courtyard to a labyrinth of hallways in which I was sure I would be lost if left alone. But I was far more sure that I would never be left alone in this place.

Anisa continued. "Panama is part of El Sur de las Naciones Consolidado. Most people will refer to it as the Esse-Enne-Sey . . . SNC, if you wish to Anglicize the acronym. Eighteen countries and

Syncing Forward

dependencies from Central and South America united under a single flag, currency, and military between the years 2083 and 2088. The Southern Consolidated Nations run from Nicaragua down to the Falkland Islands and enjoy strong economic treaties with the American Governance, Canada, Quebec, and Eastern Mexico. El Día Unificación is celebrated on August eighth, although most citizens call it Ocho-Ocho. Given the intervals between your synchronizations, I'm afraid you will miss the festivities by two weeks. I am told they can be quite exciting."

It sounded unappealing. Festivities meant being festive.

Anisa escorted me to a room with a single sliding door and no windows. The ceiling was dome-shaped, and the blue color of the walls extended up from the floor to overhead, making the room feel like we had stepped into twilight. Walter Vergas sat with his hands folded at a table, waiting uncomplainingly but with a clear sense of purpose in his expression. The three of us sat down, and I found that my new hosts had laid out fare similar to what I ate back in Jacksboro: simple foods with low quantities of proteins, lots of vegetables, and a drink laced with rapid digestive enzymes so that whatever I swallowed would not rot in my small intestines.

It didn't take long for Walter to get down to business. "So, Martin, you've seen our facility. Do you know what it is for?"

"Not a clue," I admitted. "Anisa was not very forthcoming with those details."

"Forgive her; I asked her to let me deal with this particular subject." Walter seemed pleased that his instructions had been followed, which made me wonder if these androids sometimes failed to follow the directions given to them. "This is Ground Control for the Atlantic Cargo Lift Center. We move freight into space as well as returning it Earthside. Our operation is to the twenty-second century what the Panama Canal was to the twentieth century. It is vital to the SNC—that would be the Southern Consolidated Nations—as well as to the Mars and Lunar colonies. However, over the last eight years we've been working with other organizations on a much more important mission. You are familiar with the Shenzhou 75 mission, I am told?"

I ran my fingers through my short hair, realizing it had blown full of sand in the wind from the beach. I wanted to be polite with these folk, but the sight of food—even this food—still managed to trigger my baser instincts. I shoveled a cherry tomato in and spoke with my mouth full, not caring how rude I was being.

"Yes sir. I was invited to fly on the contraption. They had the idea that sending a man on the mission would make it more palatable to the public. Seemed like an insane idea at the time." Had it been a mistake it was to pass it up? Had Taras Negnevitskii been right after all? Maybe it would have been selfish to leave, to spare myself the pain of watching Bella die. Rolling that about in my head made me sick to my stomach.

Walter Vergas dabbed the corner of his mouth with a cloth napkin. "Eight years ago, we signed agreements to work with the Sino-Russian Alliance on a bold initiative called Renascentia. The plan is to send multiple starships to Alpha Centauri, where the Shenzhou mission discovered two habitable planets. The problem we are still having is the time involved in getting there. Simply, we can't go fast enough for anyone to arrive at a meaningful age. It is the reason we contacted your grandson Jacob Heffley in the first place. It was my intention to solicit your help directly, but we discovered you had left specific directions not to wake you unless Millennial's Remedium antidote was found."

I stopped chewing, staring in disbelief. "So you are saying that you have the antidote?"

"We do not."

I was puzzled. "Then why did you wake me?"

"Do you know what Singularity is?"

"Is there a reason you are answering my question with another question?"

Syncing Forward

Walter Vergas didn't react to my nasty tone. Instead he went on. "Martin, I am fully aware of your low-profile meeting with Taras Negnevitskii many years ago. I also know that he never disclosed to you the true reason the mission was being launched in the first place. You see, Singularity was not some campfire ghost story that Millennial terrorists would spout to scare the public. It wasn't a theoretical concept either. It was a true event that resulted in the emergence of what we now call Conference."

"I know about that. It's that social networking thing for mods."

He shook his head. "It is far more than that now, Martin. Conference is very real and widely considered to be dangerous. This may rub you the wrong way, but it appears Millennial may have been doing all the wrong things for all the right reasons. Originally Conference was a product, like a cell phone or holo-emitter. Genetics, robotics, information swaps, nanotech—these technologies were designed to enhance our lives. However, when they converged, people called this event the Singularity. What had been several disciplines of technology soon became one endless sea in which the men and women involved became lost. It wasn't a simple merging of man with machine but of man with man. The individuals became a network of collaborative thought that increased with each new member and each new child."

"So, excuse my ignorance here," I interrupted, "but you keep referring to the mods as 'they.' Aren't you one of them?"

"I am an independent enhanced modified human," Walter elaborated. "Like your granddaughter Victoria was. Genetically superior, engineered to be disease free, nearly injury free. Now somebody like me is typically infused with the Conference technology at birth, which networks us with others. Unlike your granddaughter, Victoria, however, in my adolescent years my body rejected Conference for reasons that are not very interesting. Thus, I am considered an independent. And I cherish that independence, Martin. I know how they think, and I can tell you the rest of humanity has reason to be concerned."

435

He took a sip of ice water, eyeballed me from across the table, and set the glass down. "You used to call them mods; we call them *sheng ji*. Do you speak any Chinese dialects?"

I knew a few phrases and curse words Dave taught me, but not enough to make conversation. I shook my head.

"It means 'upgrade,' but it also implies 'better' or 'superior.' The sheng ji don't just think faster and live longer and fight better and know more. They believe themselves above regular human beings and have good reason to. The group has exceeded the individual with the help of Conference. In all respects they *are* Conference. The result is now a whole new species of mankind: they work together, collaborate together, procreate together, and build together. Anyone outside of that species is . . . unimportant."

My granddaughter. Victoria. I wondered if she ever took the Conference modifications, and if perhaps that was what had drawn her away. "It doesn't sound so terrible," I countered. In truth it sounded appalling, but somehow I felt like I was betraying Victoria by saying as much.

"No, I suppose it doesn't. But those modifications don't just positively affect the people who are born to them. Some children end up rejecting the bio-implants—like me. Others become deformed. While independent sheng ji are simply disposed of, the deformed are experimented on or transformed into biological network hubs. Think of that, Martin . . . children being used as equipment."

Vergas was an imposing man, cut like a superhero out of a comic book with a keen intellect to boot, but I had seen a vulnerability about him that shone in his eyes and in his face. This was personal, maybe even familial. I didn't press.

As disturbing as the topic was, Vergas managed to become even grimmer. "Thirty years ago a South African scientist discovered the gen-engineered foods that fed the bulk of the world had been surreptitiously recoded. This was no oversight, no display of corporate greed in shaving a few pennies off each bushel to boost their stock price. Proteins were purposefully resequenced in basic crops across the

Syncing Forward

globe so that they would slowly poison the people who ate them. These resequences had no effect on anyone within Conference, of course. Their biology was designed to digest the new foods. That's how illnesses such as AVIDS developed. That is how your daughter and son-in-law died, and most likely how your wife died as well."

Suddenly I didn't feel like eating. I put my fork down and pushed my food away.

Walter put his hand on mine. "Please, Martin. Eat. The food you are eating is quite safe. And even if it were not, the single consumption of a meal or even a hundred meals would not kill you. These modifications to the foods are quite subtle and designed to work in the very long term."

"But why?" I asked. "Why poison everyone over a period of decades? That's psychotic!"

"Why not?" he retorted. "Conference is not composed of humans. Not anymore. What started out as a simple networking of twin brothers became a laboratory of scientists working with an efficiency never achieved before. That led to breakthroughs in genetic modifications that used nanotechnology to continue their advancement and robotics to protect it. Over time this experiment became an institution, which became a lifestyle, which became a society, which became a species. Now when the sheng ji look at regular human beings, they do not see their brothers. They see obstacles, inferior resource drains.

"Conference no longer thinks of itself as a group of self-actualized individuals. They don't use networks; they *are* the network. They think long term. And so we continue to find their work in soil bacteria, feeding fish, even pollen. In Europe, the Islamic Crescent is falling after eighty-five years of rule. Nanorobots no bigger than a fleck of paper swarm across the landscape, embedding themselves in the bodies of women and sterilizing them. The birth rate in Southern France has dropped to 0.8 children per family. In thirty years, Europe will have a population smaller than that of Colombia."

437

W Lawrence

"Well, Mr. Vergas, you've managed to scare the crap out of me," I said, "but you still haven't explained why you misled my grandson in order to bring me here."

"Please, Martin, it would be easier to show you." Chief Vergas pressed a button on the table, and a tiny holographic display appeared at eye level: an ocean platform with massive zeppelins taking off and landing. *"Aumenta, máxima,"* the chief commanded the computer to enlarge the image, which filled the room. The table at which we sat seemed to glide about a hundred feet above the ocean, tiny rectangles floating on the water's surface growing larger as we approached them virtually. I wasn't prone to vertigo, but I was surprised by the clarity of the images, the sounds of wind and waves. I found myself gripping the table edge for fear of falling.

At first they loomed as great scorings in the sky that rose from the platforms and reached into the heavens, appearing and disappearing from view. Then, as the image drew nearer, what I thought were cuts looked more like ribbons tying those massive floating platforms to the darkening atmosphere. We quickly reached one of the superstructures where a ribbon was secured. What may have been commonplace for my hosts to me appeared a marvel beyond imagination. It dumbfounded me to the point where it even managed to provide a distraction from my time-traveling nightmare.

"What you are looking at," explained Walter Vergas, "is the newest orbital cargo elevator to Adelante Space Port. It sits four hundred kilometers from the Panamanian coastline and is one of four orbital elevators controlled by the Atlántico Centro de Carga de Elevación. We receive cargo from the Luna and Mars colonies while ferrying out supplies to the colonists, launching satellites, and constructing ships in orbit.

Anisa pointed to a cylindrical shape descending from the sky and down the ribbon. "That is a cargo lift returning from orbit. While this is a simulation, we actually do have a lift returning today. Its manifest indicates it contains sixteen empty containers, four tons of rare metal samples from Luna, and two passengers."

Syncing Forward

I watched the ribbon twist nominally with the wind and grappled with the idea that it reached into space. "What is that thing made out of?" I inquired.

Anisa responded with a textbook answer: "The tether is made of graphene nanotubes—ultra-lightweight material woven together, dropped from orbit, and then secured at these stations."

"But even if they are super light, how does it not fall down from its own weight? They've got to be hundreds of miles long."

Walter elaborated. "Actually they are thousands of miles long, and they don't hold themselves up. The lifts are suspended from the platforms. Were the tether to be severed, it would fall up into outer space."

I cocked my head like a dog hearing a strange sound.

"If you had a rock on a string and you swung it around in a circle, centrifugal force would hold the string taut. Cut the string, and it flies away with the rock. The lift operates under the same principle, Martin. The tether is connected to Adelante Space Port, which acts as a counterweight—the rock, if you will. The elevator is an affordable way for us to move cargo in and out of orbit. But our most important project is still not complete, and that's why we need you."

As the holographic image drew closer to the tether, our table seemed to insert itself into the elevator, then lift itself up at tremendous speed. There was no sense of motion, but the visual was incredibly real as we "climbed" through the atmosphere and out into space.

"In reality this trip would take three days," Walter Vergas clarified, "but ultimately you would find yourself arriving at Adelante Space Port. However, *this* is what I wanted you to see." He pointed to my left, and the image of the pod we sat in detached from the elevator and coasted silently toward a shiny set of objects.

Drawing closer, I looked out at a series of segmented spacecraft in various states of construction. Thousands of water and oxygen tanks hung in space, along with vehicle tires and airplane parts.

Supplies, tools, and cargo containers marked with medical symbols waiting to be loaded were strapped to thick cables, and enormous earthmovers were tethered to cargo bays. Most notable were thousands of small coffin-shaped cells stacked like a honeycomb that lined the inside of one of the ships. I counted fifteen of these vessels. Despite having no connection to this time or place, I knew these efforts represented a massive undertaking.

Walter Vergas looked at me squarely. "Those are stasis chambers, Martin, and there are fifty-four thousand of them. This is the Renascentia project, and the reason we woke you. It represents my life work and the only remaining hope for humanity. We are leaving, Martin, and we need your help."

The image of the Renascentia ships vanished, and we were once again sitting in a quiet, windowless room. Both Anisa and Walter Vergas stared at me intently. Regular humans had to be truly terrified of what Conference would do to the world, would do to them. Whether those fears were legitimate or not, I was not in a position to say, but I couldn't imagine so many resources being pumped into such an endeavor without some strong evidence that the human race was on the verge of extinction. But what I could do for them was still a mystery.

"Listen, Mr. Vergas. I appreciate the light show and the million-dollar love doll you've set me up with, and believe me when I say I am impressed with what you have going on here. But it seems you have everything you need. These stasis chambers, I am guessing, keep people asleep for the long voyage; you have the likes of Anisa to pilot the ships. What can I do that Anisa here can't?"

Walter Vergas waved his hand dismissively. "This isn't the Shenzhou 75 mission, and we don't need you to pilot anything. Our stasis technology will keep a man alive for only eight years, which is far too short for the forty years it will take to get to Alpha Centauri. We might make a breakthrough in fifteen years or so, but we don't have fifteen years. Conference is sweeping the world. We don't just need the

Remedium drug. We need all the Millennial drugs, and we need them now."

"Hate to say it, but you've got the wrong man."

"No, we have the right man. We have Dr. Bruchmuller."

It couldn't be. I sat there as mute as a manatee, wondering if I'd misunderstood the man.

"You heard me correctly. We have him, Martin. He's in a room right down the hall."

All the festering hate I cultivated in my gut suddenly bubbled up. Nothing would have pleased me more at that point than to kill Dieterich slowly and painfully. My mind spun into overdrive as I envisioned murdering the son of a bitch who destroyed my life.

I couldn't say anything. My hope for a life with my family had been destroyed, but I still might have a chance at revenge. Yes, it was a terrible reason to live, but it was the only reason I had left, and I would take it. I just needed to be in the same room with him.

"While you were with Anisa, I was overseeing Dr. Bruchmuller's synchronization. It took a little longer than we expected, but his condition seems to be identical to yours." Walter sensed my ruminations and took a stern tone. "Martin, I know you must have extreme animosity for this man, but there is something you should know."

"What is that?"

"When we brought the doctor here, he made a single request in exchange for his cooperation. He wants to speak with you face-to-face. You see, Dr. Bruchmuller is the reason we sought you out in the first place."

One enigma had replaced another. I now knew why I had been brought to Panama, but I couldn't comprehend a reason for Bruchmuller ever wanting to speak to me. The man I desperately wanted to throttle was the only one who could answer my questions. Was this a game? Was it a way of torturing me further?

W Lawrence

Walter Vergas polished off his drink and set the empty glass aside. "You see, Martin, our prisoner was most disoriented when he first synchronized, much as you were, but we spent a considerable amount of effort to bring him up to speed. The first day, my colleagues explained to Dr. Bruchmuller that—while we disagreed on methods—our program recognized the foresight of the Millennial group to see the dangers of Singularity. Most of us predicted that Dr. Bruchmuller would aid us in our endeavors, but he offered nothing."

Vergas was troubled as he stood and walked in a tight circle around the table. Anisa sat there with her perfect posture in eerie silence, motionless, listening.

Walter shook his head in confusion and put out his hands. "Well, that was last year. Six months ago we synchronized the doctor again, and this time I met with him myself. I spoke to him for hours about our plans for the Renascentia project. I did my best to bring up points of commonality between our worldviews. I informed him of the dangers presented by Conference and how our timeline was reaching a critical point. Then he spoke, but instead of engaging me about his more ideological concerns, he asked about his grandson. We researched to the best of our abilities but found no record of him. He had been reported missing nearly eighty years ago. After that he asked me about you, if you were still alive."

"What did he say?" I stammered.

"He simply asked, 'Is Martin H. James still alive?' To which I replied that you were. He said, 'You will arrange for me to speak to him face-to-face, and then I will cooperate fully.'"

"He didn't say anything after that?"

"Yes. He told me you would want to speak with him, although he did not elaborate. Now, Martin, do you have any idea why he would want to speak to you?"

I frowned. "I don't have a clue in the world."

Chapter 53

The three of us had left the room where we dined and did our holographic tour and were now walking slowly down the hall. Anisa paced in front of us while Walter Vergas walked at my left shoulder. Two Hispanic gentlemen with young faces, sharp uniforms, and holstered sidearms trailed behind us at a comfortable distance. "So this is why you lied to my grandson about being close to a cure," I blurted out.

Vergas sighed. "Martin, we did not lie to Jacob Heffley."

"Oh really? Where is my cure? Where is the research team?" I did nothing to hide my anger.

"We are as close to a cure as anyone has ever come, Martin. We know Millennial has an antidote that they use to wake themselves. We know they redose themselves once they reenter their hiding places, only to reemerge years later. You and I both believe Bruchmuller developed the Millennial drug himself, and now we have that man in custody. The doctor might be willing to tell us everything he knows, and the only thing he has asked in return is to talk with you. Tell me, can you think of a single instance in the last one hundred years when you had a better chance to get your old life back?"

"You took me out of my home," I said.

"That wasn't a home, Martin; that was a tomb. Jacob told us to wake you if there was a cure. This is as good as it gets."

"You don't get it! I never expected to be woken up, Mr. Vergas," I said. "I never *wanted* to be woken up."

Walter looked at me with sympathetic eyes. "I'm very sorry, Martin. Anisa informed me of the incident at the cliff steps, but at the time we spoke with Jacob Heffley we did not know you wished to end your life—I promise you that."

"If you had known, would you have woken me anyway?" A sting of accusation poisoned my shameful question.

"Yes," Walter Vergas answered reluctantly. "Yes, we probably would have."

"Then I'm a prisoner—no better in your eyes than that murdering bastard Bruchmuller."

Walter stopped in front of a closed door guarded by two more uniformed men. He grabbed me by the shoulders with both powerful hands, and for a split second I thought he was going to rattle me something hard.

"No, that isn't true. We're desperate, Martin. Desperate! If you had any concept of the type of man I am, you would understand I do not use that word lightly. If there was any other way, we would be taking it. Right now our entire project hinges on Dr. Bruchmuller giving us what he and Millennial have kept secret for a hundred years. If death is what you seek, we will grant you your wish, but only after the doctor gives up the Millennial drugs."

I was surrounded by four armed men, an android, and a genetically modified man who could rip my head clean off with his bare hands. It wasn't exactly the ideal time to tell Walter Vergas no, even if I did want to die. Surely there were cleaner ways to go.

I bowed my head slightly in resignation and told him to get on with it. Deep breath. Exhale. One man opened the door for me, and I stepped through to see Dieterich Bruchmuller for the first time in a hundred years.

The German-born doctor lounged comfortably on a plush settee, reading a news article on a holo-display that was projected an arm's length in front of him. His accommodations were nowhere close to penal; in fact, they seemed far better than most of the places I had lived. The room itself was an ovoid shape with a rim around the edge that went from the closed balcony doors to the bay window to an open kitchen to a bedroom nestled in the corner. Steps descended at various places into the center of the room, where the sofa and entertainment station sat. A triad of skylights bathed the room in light.

Syncing Forward

Two security officers already stood guard in the room, both armed with some type of gun that strapped to their wrists. Dieterich Bruchmuller paid little attention to my entrance at first, choosing to concentrate on his reading. Once we made eye contact, he jumped up from the little sofa and stared at me in amazement. Maybe it was me being out of practice or the distance between us, but I dare say Dieterich looked happy to see me.

"Doctor, we have some guests for you," one of the security officers called out in a thick Spanish accent. "We're not going to have any problems, okay?"

Bruchmuller stepped down reticently into the living area and gestured toward us. "No, no, you won't have any problems from me, I can assure you."

The detail remained by the main door while I stepped down into the living room as well. "Hello, Dr. Bruchmuller," I greeted him coldly.

"Martin *Horatio* James," he spoke slowly and approachably, "welcome to my gilded cage. Can I offer you a drink? Perhaps one of those enzyme-laced sandwiches they are fond of feeding us?"

"No," I answered coldly. I was seriously debating whether I could kill Bruchmuller before the guards could stop me. Of course I wasn't sure I could do it with them *out* of the room either; my last encounter with this man had me on the tail end of an ass-whooping. *Maybe I could get hold of a fork or a knife in the kitchen that I could jam into his throat?* A dozen vindictive plots rolled about in my head like marbles. "What do you want, Dr. Bruchmuller?"

"Ah, down to business, it seems. Please sit, as there is something very important I must discuss with you."

I stood there defiantly. "Say what you need to say so I can get out of here."

"It is vital that you listen to me and listen carefully. Indulge me, please, and sit down."

445

I relented but was none too pleased about it. "Fine, I'm sitting. Now what is so important to the mass murderer?"

He wagged his finger at me. "Careful, careful! What you call murder, I call the preservation of our species. And a century later, it appears that history has proven me correct. 'There are more things in heaven and earth, Horatio, than are dreamt of in your philosophy,'" Bruchmuller recited. I knew that quote well; teachers and students alike had tormented me with it all throughout high school.

I said nothing back. I couldn't stand the sound of my middle name, and I hated it worse when this man said it. I recalled his unusual fascination with knowing my middle name back in 2021, and now he continued to play with it for some unknown reason. To rile me up? Elevate himself? I didn't know, and I didn't care. I sat there wordlessly, waiting for Bruchmuller to say what he had to say. From the corner of my eye I saw Vergas circling the room anxiously while Anisa approached us and sat behind me and to the right.

Dr. Bruchmuller didn't hide his admiration for the android's form, and I knew he had no idea Anisa wasn't really alive. "And who is this lovely lady?" he asked.

"I am Anisa. It is a pleasure to meet you, Doctor," the companion said pleasantly, extending an arm to shake hands with Bruchmuller. "I work for Chief Walter Vergas."

"It is a pleasure to meet you," he responded politely, but I caught him ogling its body several times. It was weird, but I almost felt a little jealous.

After the distraction of Anisa's pleasing form passed, the doctor looked at me and began. "Mr. James, there is a crypt in Charleston, West Virginia, located in the Sunset View Cemetery. It is programmed to open to your touch. Within the crypt should be several doses of Tardus, Somnus, and Remedium. These are the drugs Millennial uses to slow our bodies, to sleep, and to awaken. I will draw out the exact location and specification for opening it if our guests permit me."

Syncing Forward

I stared at him hard in the face, trying to figure out what game he was playing. He didn't seem to be lying, but it was getting real easy to second-guess myself these days.

"Doctor, even if I believed that you could somehow finagle this crypt of yours to open to my touch, it wouldn't make any sense. What would be the point? You didn't even know I was alive up until recently."

"I can assure you I am telling the truth. I am unfamiliar with the technology available to our hosts, Mr. James, but I can promise you that the readers on the crypts are extremely touchy. Any attempt to circumvent the security system, or break in, or enact any activity other than what I explicitly instruct, and there will be a catastrophic loss. It must be you who opens that crypt. You are a professional interviewer, Mr. James. Tell them if I am lying. Go on."

I glanced over at Walter Vergas, who shot me a look that said, "Well?"

"He's telling the truth. I don't know how or why, but he is." I looked back at Dr. Bruchmuller and frowned. "Why? Why give up all your secrets after so long?"

"Because of the Renascentia project Mr. Vergas told me about, of course. He has agreed to give Millennial asylum, and that is something we cannot turn down given the state of affairs in the world."

One glance at Vergas told me the deal was sincere. This independent sheng ji may have been an imposing man, but his embarrassment made him appear a foot shorter. Turning my attention back to Bruchmuller, I addressed the deception that showed all over his face. "Our hosts may buy that line of bull crap, but I don't," I snapped. "If you are so moved to cooperate with these people, why not go and open the crypt yourself? Why have me do it?"

The doctor folded his hands neatly on his lap. His proud German chin sank a bit, and his voice dropped. "I told you, the crypt is keyed to open to your touch. I couldn't open it if I wanted to. But there is more to it than that. There is a debt I need to pay, Mr. James. A debt I hope to make good on."

"What does that even mean?"

He said nothing.

We locked gazes, and for the life of me I couldn't figure out what his game was. "So that's it then?"

"I'm giving you the Remedium. I'm handing over everything. What else do you want from me, Mr. James?"

"What do I want? What do I want?!" I screamed. "You son of a bitch, you assaulted me! You blew up my company, killed my coworkers, ruined my marriage! You stole my life! You murdered my daughter!"

"I most certainly did not murder your daughter," he said, stiffening his back.

"No, but your terrorist friends did! This is your fault! Yours!" I reached out for his throat, but my fingers wrapped around Bruchmuller's shirt. As I stood up, I whipped a haymaker at his face, only to have it stopped solidly by Anisa's freakishly strong hands. Bruchmuller was trying to dislodge my grip from his chest, but it took two guards and "my" companion to separate us.

"You murdering bastard! You-you— Let go of me! Let go!" I pulled and yanked and stretched outward to get at him, only to find Bruchmuller's form slowly receding. While the guards were holding the doctor fast, Anisa was single-handedly dragging me backward toward the room's entrance, and in a matter of seconds I was staring at a closed, locked door. I pulled on the handle and beat the metal frame fruitlessly till my fist was sore.

Syncing Forward

Chapter 54

I sat at the beach, the sun setting behind me, its rays warming the back of my neck while I drew random shapes in the sand with my finger. Anisa waited a comfortable distance off, standing there like a sentry after I banished it. I sifted the warm grains through my fingers, thinking that I never got a chance to take Amara and Bella to the beach. We lived in New Jersey for years, and not once did we make it to the shore. I was always too busy or the weather was too hot or the parkway had too much traffic. So many plans that never happened.

I heard somebody cutting across the beach and turned to see Walter Vergas coming toward me, shoes in his hands and a grim look on his face. He sat down in the sand next to me and said nothing, just stared forward at the Atlantic Ocean waves.

I didn't want to talk with him, but I figured I didn't have much of a choice. I was a prisoner here every bit as much as Bruchmuller. I had food and a lovely beach to walk on and a pretty face to stare at, but I was still a prisoner.

"The doctor reneged on his promise to help, didn't he?" I asked.

"No, surprisingly," Walter answered. "Bruchmuller did exactly as he promised; he mapped out the cemetery and precise instructions on how to open the crypt. He didn't say much else, other than to iterate his warning not to have anyone else open the crypt. He also suggested that you be synchronized when you open the crypt, otherwise it may detonate. That puts this mission off another six months. No more, no less."

I nodded. I didn't mean these people any harm, and I didn't want their mission to fail, but I also couldn't look Walter Vergas in the face. I kept wishing him away with no success.

"We analyzed his biometric readings from your meeting and—for what it is worth—we believe he is telling the truth about everything. Of course, you already knew that, didn't you, Martin?"

"Yeah, I reckon I did." I turned to face Walter. "So why the long face then? You should be happy."

Chief Vergas shook his head. "The location of the crypt is deep inside the Eastern United States Province. You wouldn't know this, but the US government collapsed decades ago. After disease and riots swept through the East Coast, the sheng ji began to take over major cities like Boston, New York, Atlanta, and Miami, bringing their own form of order. There is still a massive military-run government that struggles to control everything from Maine to Florida, though. The only powers keeping the sheng ji from sweeping the whole continent are the bloodthirsty generals in the Pentagon and your noble American Governance, and neither will last for very long. Somehow we need to get in and out of there safely, which will not be an easy task."

"It sounds like chaos."

"It is. Charleston, West Virginia, is a hotly contested area. Conference controls half that city, but the US Army is scanning the citizens at checkpoints and executing on the spot anyone with a genetic modification, which means killing many of its own citizens."

"Is Conference at war with the SNC as well?" I asked.

"Conference isn't at war with anyone, Martin, any more than a man is at war with a spider. The problem we face is that we have no idea what they will do. If we send a small contingent, they may not even care that we flew into their territory, but they would overwhelm us easily. If we send a sizable force, we will undoubtedly attract Conference attention, and we may provoke them to action. So far, they have been relatively hands-off of our plans to make exodus from the planet. We'd like to keep it that way. But undoubtedly the Pentagon generals will capture and torture any unauthorized visitors."

"So what are you going to do?"

Syncing Forward

"I haven't the faintest." He sighed. "I have suggestions, but the military will make the decisions, not me. My primary task is to make sure that you continue to help us. Will you, Martin?"

I didn't want to help them. I just wanted to die. I knew at that moment that death was the only path for me. How pathetic I had become. Mine was a conflicting, damnable predicament to be in. My self-loathing turned to antagonism as I glared at Walter. "For almost a hundred years, I've done nothing but hate the man you have sequestered in that cushy room up there. He and his buddies killed thousands, and now you sit there and have the stones to ask me to help you just so that you can grant them all asylum? Frankly, I don't know who I despise more right now—Dr. Bruchmuller or you. I'll help you, but don't ever expect me to agree with you."

I stood, and Walter stood with me. He put his hands out wide, gesturing for me to stop. "Martin, they were trying to prevent what is happening now. You can't blame—"

I interrupted him. "Oh yes, I can blame them. There had to be another way, Walter! They murdered people!"

"The politics of the time didn't recognize what Singularity would do to the world."

"My family is dead! DEAD!" I shouted as I walked down the beach toward Anisa, turning around just long to shout, "Those are my politics! And you can go screw yourself, Walter! I'm going to walk away now before I change my mind, and you'd best leave me alone."

The android stood up to meet me as I stormed past it, following on my heels as I climbed the staircase to the facility's entrance. "Martin, where are you going?" Anisa asked.

"Away from Chief Vergas. Away from everybody."

It wasn't lost on me how unreasonable I was being. I knew full well that the right thing to do was make sure the Renascentia project succeeded. I remembered the hurt Bella carried with her when Victoria left, how each new mod my granddaughter received seemed to distance her from the rest of the family, how she looked down upon Jacob and his polio affliction. The sheng ji were the new masters of the planet, and every human being left was bound to die of AVIDS or worse. Billions of people dying the same terrible death as my Baby Bella.

    I suppose I could have bargained for my great-grandchildren to be on the Renascentia ships, to leave with the lucky few who would be colonizing these new worlds. Of course, there was no telling if they would even keep such a bargain. The truth was, I had lost everything in the world I cared about, and my desire to die gnawed at my soul. My priest had told me that no man is given more than he can endure, so had I truly reached the end?

    I slumped down in a reclining chair in the quarters the SNC had provided me with, staring at a 2D projection that seemed to appear from nowhere. It had been two hours since I had studied the instructions Bruchmuller provided for the crypt, neatly typed and organized with satellite recon pictures included. We were looking for a crypt surrounded by tombs. Just dandy.

    I closed my eyes, wondering, hoping maybe, that this would be my final task.

Syncing Forward

Chapter 55

We were far, far away from Panama.

I synced up once again, this time at Missouri airbase in the American Governance, then climbed onto a small military airplane in the middle of the night. Four angled wings and a long tail made it look more like a camouflaged dragonfly than an airplane. It had a large engine in the nose and several smaller ones along the body, with only a handful of windows on its side. Anisa appeared long enough to strap me in and ask how I was feeling. Its blond hair was now displayed shorter, and its skin-tight white outfit had been replaced with the same mud-colored armored uniform the others were wearing. The android looked at me quickly before disappearing back into the cockpit.

"You have a communicator in both ears," Anisa pointed out. "You will be able to talk with all of us once on the ground. For now, you and I are the only ones on this frequency."

Anisa walked away quickly and disappeared into the cockpit, leaving me with nothing but suspicious glances from the others. Six male and female soldiers were strapped in on either side of the hull. They all wore a mud-colored field uniform that looked to be made out of a dull flexible plastic, and flag patches on the sides of their wrists— the flag of the Southern Consolidated Nations. I wore an identical outfit, minus any marks of rank, of course. The soldiers avoided eye contact with me, choosing to keep to themselves.

The plane's engines screamed, and the hull shook. I felt the craft lift off vertically and then speed forward so quickly that my body strained against the safety straps. I must have looked green, but everyone else handled the flight like cool cats.

"Martin, can you hear me?" Anisa's voice chimed in my ears.

I answered awkwardly, "Yeah, clear as a bell." A few heads turned my direction but then turned back.

"Good. We need to review the intelligence from the doctor." Anisa went over the sequence of the buttons Bruchmuller had spelled out, the panel on which my hand would rest, the length of time it would take for the crypt's security to determine whether it would open or detonate, how to find and remove the drugs in the crypt, and the signal that had to be broadcast before doing anything to prevent us from becoming a half-dozen hunks of charred hamburger.

Two hours in, and the night was cracking dawn. One look out the window made my stomach churn. We were flying perhaps twenty feet off the treetops, surrounded by smaller flying disks no wider than three feet across that matched our airspeed and maneuvers flawlessly. Some were at a distance of a quarter-mile, while others flew less than a yard off the wings of our aircraft. Two other large flying machines that looked like helicopters with no crew compartment were out there as well, occasionally coming into view. Anisa explained over the communicator that these were semiautonomous drones that performed a variety of functions.

"This is a C-872J Salus transport," the soldier sitting across from me said over the noise of the engines. He had light skin and dark eyes and appeared to be of mixed background. It was the first time any of them offered to talk to me, and as much as I hated being here, the conversation was admittedly a relief. "I'm Teniente Coronel Nilio Colochi of the Naciones Consolidado. This man on my right is Sargento Primero Flores."

A lieutenant colonel and a first sergeant, I translated in my head. "Nice to meet you both. I'm Martin James."

"We don't know what you are, but we know who you are, Mr. James. Along with your companion, the eight of us here are tasked explicitly with protecting you by any means necessary. However, it seems that, beyond a set of coordinates, we don't have a clue as to why we're out here. You mind filling us in on who you work for and what we are doing before we get our asses shot off?"

Syncing Forward

I looked over at the cockpit and Anisa who returned to view. Before I could speak, Anisa strode evenly to the colonel and interjected, *"Coronel Colochi, sabes perfectamente que no podemos decir que lo que estamos haciendo aquí. Por favor asista a sus deberes."* It generally translated into telling the colonel to mind his own business.

He ignored Anisa's comments, shaking his head with a frustrated smile and focusing on me. "The men have a running bet that you are some type of sheng ji. That those goggles you wore on the transport up from Panama were to hide some kind of reptilian appendage or laser eyes or some shit like—"

"Aviones enemigos entrantes!" a voice called over the communicator. Enemy aircraft were coming. I looked out the window; our drones swarmed about the Salus like insects. Occasionally a pack of them would fly off, but a few less would return. The chatter in the plane switched into rapid Spanish, and I felt as if I were back at my in-laws, barely able to keep up. The colonel rushed to the cockpit and barked at the pilots, but what he said, I could not tell. An explosion off the left side of the transport shook us so badly that I gripped the harness as if it were the only thing keeping me alive.

"Anisa, what's happening?" I whispered. I knew it would hear me.

My companion looked busy with another soldier as they secured some equipment that had shaken loose in the explosion, but my intercom noise lowered and I heard Anisa speaking clear as day to me. "Martin. There are three transports, seventy-eight drones, and six battlecopters on this mission, and we are split into three teams. Team 2 is under attack and is not expected to remain airborne. I received information from Drone-6AR2L that their Salus transport has lost two engines and is lining up for a crash landing. Team 3 and our team are still on mission. Our—"

"No, Anisa! What is happening? Who is shooting at us?"

"United States FR-320 Diamondback midrange interceptors. Stand by—the two closest interceptors have been destroyed. There are no other aircraft in range, but we are off course and slowing. I will identify the cause of the error and update you."

Anisa took her concerns to the colonel, asking him what was happening. As it spoke, the Salus banked sharply to the right, and I watched one of the drones that hovered close by explode in blue electric flame. The skin of the transport pinged with shrapnel as we nosed down and spun sharply left.

Colonel Colochi stood nose to nose with Anisa and boomed. "Listen, *Mecánica,* my job is to get Mr. James to the coordinates, and that's what I am doing. I don't have time to explain my tactics to you. Now sit down!" He shoved his head back into the cockpit, gripping the hatchway tightly, and yelled to the pilot, "*Quite la alimentación al motor principal, lento a trescientos kilometros por hora! Vuelven a coordenadas originales!*"

The transport lurched and banked again and leveled off. Several seconds passed before I took a deep breath at the calm that had returned to our tiny aircraft. The Salus seemed to be yawing back and forth from time to time, but we were still in the air.

Anisa spoke over the intercom to me. "I don't understand. The Salus is not damaged, but the pilot is making unnecessary rudder controls."

I looked at Sergeant Flores, and he gave me a wink—I had figured it out. "I think I understand what is going on here. Anisa, tell me what is going on with the last team."

"They are being pursued by six interceptors. The pilot appears to be heading toward Washington, DC."

"It's a ruse, Anisa," I explained. "Colonel Colochi is pretending to our aircraft is damaged and unable to go on. So he doglegged us off course on purpose, then turned to make it look like we were leaving. Pretty damn clever. I'm glad he is on our side."

"As am I," Anisa replied, and I'd be damned if it didn't look surprised to boot.

Syncing Forward

I looked out the right window as we leveled off and watched as three drones let loose a volley of machine-gun fire into the forest below, cutting branches from the trees. Whatever lay below the tree line fired back at the drones, and two disintegrated into powder along with the treetops themselves. The sound from the weapon was like a foghorn, and it shook the Salus violently just by its proximity.

"Martin, it's an acoustic cannon. Your ear units should protect your eardrums from close shots, but we need to avoid a direct shot at all costs." Anisa took my hand and gently cupped it. "Martin, we are almost there. It seems likely we will make it to the landing site. We are twelve kilometers out."

The Salus transport slowed and dropped below the treetops and into a clearing. The doors opened up, and the men and women soldiers dropped into position below, fanning out to secure the landing zone while Anisa unfastened me and took me by the arm. I was a bit wobbly on my legs still since it was my first time walking since being synced in the airplane after the air acrobatics, but I let my pride push her hand away as I avoided the curious gazes of Sergeant Flores and the others.

"We're clear," Anisa announced as we stepped off the transport and into the middle of the cemetery.

The acoustic cannon Anisa had referred to earlier fired again, and the soldiers chattered over the communicators about how we were down to ten drones. I looked about; we had landed in a roundabout where hearses would unload their coffins and funeral processions would drop off their passengers. The asphalt was cracked and pocked with weeds, shadowed by an abandoned chapel to the west. Three pathways diverged from the roundabout and disappeared into a forest of tombstones.

Sergeant Flores approached quickly and pressured me for a direction. "Come on, Señor James. We need to do this quick, okay?"

"It's this way." Anisa pointed to the path on the left. "SAT images confirm the structures are configured as we were told."

W Lawrence

Our drones whipped overhead, scouting for us, or maybe drawing fire. In a flash, all but two zoomed off toward the south, and Flores barked at the Salus pilot to be ready for extraction.

With the exception of twigs and leaves crunching underfoot, the cemetery was eerily silent. We double-timed it for about a quarter-mile up a hill and down the other side, where the mausoleums came into view. Hundreds of stone structures lay huddled beneath the trees, each one built to memorialize some lost love one or grand patriarch of a family. Long abandoned, the grounds were overgrown, and branches and leaves from the woods were draped over every resting place in sight. However, one structure stood taller than the rest of the mausoleums. A mansard stone roof held aloft by eight columns was crumbling on one side, as two of the columns had fallen, bringing part of the roof with it.

"That is where we are headed," Anisa pointed, gesturing to the giant tomb. As we approached, I noticed the crumbling stone all about the base. Nonetheless, the gate was intact and clear of debris. Wrought-iron bars were twisted into a rose pattern in the center and then spread back out to meet the hinges on either side.

"We have incoming!" one of the women called over the intercom. Anisa immediately grabbed me by my scruff and pushed me behind a holding tomb we had just passed.

The foghorn sounded again, breaking the quiet. Everywhere around me trees splintered and stone crumbled. The left side of the mausoleum blasted apart in shards of stone that sliced through a soldier's calf muscle and blasted apart another drone.

My face got shoved into the dirt as Anisa shielded me, but even on the ground and encased in full armor, I felt my body vibrating from the acoustic shot. After seeing what the mobile cannon could do to wood and stone, I was terrified at what it could possibly do to my bones. Would it rip me limb from limb? Turn my bones to powder? The shot it had delivered must have been a glancing blow. A direct hit would level everything around us.

Syncing Forward

A tracked vehicle rumbled through the trees, entering a small clearing, its barrel swiveling toward our position. The wounded soldier was still screaming on the ground, gripping his bleeding leg as a second soldier tended to his comrade.

"Come on!" Anisa yelled, yanking me out of the composting leaves around the tomb. "The gun is charging! We have to run, now!"

I didn't need to be told twice. Even at a full sprint Anisa still outpaced me. Anisa gripping my sleeve tightly, I nearly lost my balance a dozen times in six seconds as my companion dragged me through the cemetery. It practically threw me into a small depression in the ground filled with dried leaves and took off running back to where we had left the soldiers. Its legs and arms were a blur. Running a serpentine pattern, it reached the wounded soldier, picked him up, and carried him at such speed that I thought for a moment I was out of synchronization and feeling the effects of the Millennial drug again. He was screaming in pain, but the android dropped him in the leaf pile, leaving to rescue the next soldier.

Flores was bringing the other four soldiers to our position, hoping the sloping terrain would shield us from the painful death that would certainly follow being struck. There was a high-pitched sound—the cannon was on the verge of discharging again. I covered my ears and buried my head in the decaying leaves, convinced that this blast would be the end of me.

Two of our battlecopters darted overhead, on a beeline for the tracked cannon. One dove down directly and collided with the barrel of the gun. It sent fire and fiberglass fragments scattering across the hillside and bent the cannon into a state of disrepair. The second battlecopter rotated its own machine gun straight down and fired at the already damaged section.

Lead clinked against the metal tank at a blistering rate, drilling a white-hot hole in the very top and surely killing anyone who was unfortunate enough to be driving the machine. Seconds later, smoke rose from the wreckage.

Colonel Colochi stepped out from a covered position. "Intel says we're clear for the time being. There are no assets near this position—for now. Mr. James, let's get this over with so we don't get shipped home in a dustpan, no?"

The sound of rending metal made us all turn to look at the wreckage of the acoustic gun. A hole had been carved by the battle-copter in the front of the turret—a hole made larger by bare hands as a figure climbed topside from the smoking ruins, its cotton pullover shirt ripped and bloody. It was a teenager, maybe a tweenager, a boy with pale skin and almost female facial features.

"Sheng ji!" Sergeant Flores cried out. The boy barely looked at us. He went into a sprint toward the road, toward the transport, as Flores and three of the others gave chase. The closest soldier—Juanito, I thought I heard Flores call him—was so close that that he couldn't get his rifle up in time, but instead he swung the rifle butt down as this teenager ran toward him.

The fight seemed downright unfair as the six-foot-two-inch brute directed all that weight and power toward the kid's skull . . until the boy pivoted underneath the soldier and drove his hand right under the man's armor. The small, pale hand disappeared into Juanito's armpit and reappeared a split second later, bloodied and holding a rib. Juanito's body fell to the ground, and the teenager spun to face us.

The sheng ji opened his mouth wide. A swarm of blackness flew out from his mouth and nostrils. The terrifying scene only grew worse as the swarm coalesced and snaked through the air toward me. The boy never stopped moving, leaving behind the black cloud that was now only thirty or so feet away and closing fast.

Anisa was pulling me backward once more. The sergeant screamed out "Impulso!" and one of the soldiers leveled a thick white rifle at the swarm and pulled the trigger. There was a sound of glass exploding as an invisible wave struck the black swarm and caused the center to turn into an even finer dust that fell to the ground. The soldier pulled the trigger over and over. Each time, more of the swarm vanished into powder until it was completely gone.

Syncing Forward

A scream erupted from our left, and another soldier ran futilely as a dark cloud surrounded him. Worse—it was penetrating him. The female soldier with the strange rifle fired directly at her compatriot, but the shots had a ghastly side effect. The skin on his face and hands exploded like boils along with the cloud around him. The injured man begged her to stop, but she kept firing until he hit the ground, leaves sticking to his bloody body.

I ran to interfere, but Anisa held me fast. "Jesus, Anisa, what is she doing? Make her stop!"

"She can't," Anisa answered levelly. "That's an EMP rifle, and those are drillers. They will work through his bloodstream and rip the blood vessels open in his brain if she doesn't destroy them now." Each trigger pull detonated the tiny flying wafers, microscopic explosions of glass and skin making a grisly mess of the man. I wrestled hopelessly against the android's grip, watching in horror as the man's uniform soaked with blood.

He jerked and spasmed and then went still. The swarms were gone, and the female soldier with the EMP rifle—who moments ago was blowing holes in her friend's flesh—stooped to bandage him. The drones swooped through the trees as Colonel Colochi screamed for the pilot to take off before the sheng ji boy arrived. The drones and soldiers put the sheng ji into a crossfire from above and behind, and I watched his thin crimson-stained body collapse in the dead leaves. The sheng ji looked so innocent and helpless. My mind raced to process how one teenage sheng ji had managed to put our entire group in peril.

Flores confirmed that Juanito was dead, cursing while another SNC soldier harnessed the body and dragged it back toward the transport. The man who had been swarmed was being carried back toward the landing site by his bloodied arms and legs. The master sergeant cursed aloud, furious about his injured and dead, as everyone else tended to their relatively minor wounds. Not like I was thrilled about it either—in fact, I was downright mortified.

"How are we going to get in now?" one of the female soldiers asked, thumbing the remains of the giant mausoleum. *"No hay nada más!"*

The magnificent structure had been turned into two mounds of rubble covered by a dust cloud. The iron gate was embedded in a tree eighty feet away. The columns had vanished in a single shot from the acoustic cannon. I trotted over to the remains and looked about, frantic that what I needed might have been destroyed.

"Señor James, it is gone, man. Sorry, but we need to fly!" Flores said.

"No!" I hollered back. "We don't need the mausoleum."

Anisa clarified. "First Sergeant, we kept it classified until now, but we need the tomb near the mausoleum with the metal doors. Over here."

"Not cool, Mecánica." Flores shook his head. "This is why the men don't trust your kind."

Anisa ignored the sergeant's commentary. It had no ego to defend, no reason to comment back that it was only following orders. To be honest, the conversation was barely registering with me as I looked down at the ground and my eyes widened. We'd found it. Anisa wasn't even looking at me, but I heard it in my earpiece speaking to me alone: "The signal is being broadcast. Proceed."

Thank God the acoustic cannon shot hadn't set off the crypt or everything would truly have been for nothing. With the medic and the injured soldier back in the Salus, only six of us now stared down at a pair of metal doors. Everybody was waiting on me.

I tried pulling them open but found the hinges stuck with age and rust and dirt. Anisa stepped in and pulled them open with ease, revealing a set of roughly hewn stone stairs that led to a decorated bricked wall.

In the old days, they would keep coffins in holding tombs during the winter months, waiting for the ground to thaw enough for shovels to break ground. Most cemeteries still built them, although

Syncing Forward

they were primarily used for the storage of tools instead of bodies. This one held far more.

Flores shone a light down on the wall, and I traced my finger just above the decorations. Bruchmüller had warned us to touch nothing until I found the buttons built into the design. A set of birds. A sun rising over a flat horizon made of ten squares. I prayed quickly to not screw this up, knowing there would be no second chance.

My fingertips pressed against the birds, and what seemed to be a flap gave way, allowing my hand to slide in up to the wrist. There was no light, no whirling sound, nothing to indicate that this was electronic in nature at all. I felt my index finger make contact with a needle prick, and instead of drawing my hand away, I pressed down hard. I heard a snap, and some type of C-clamp within the hole fastened onto my wrist and finger.

"Qué pasa?" one of the male soldiers whispered, only to be hushed by another.

The stone squares under the sunrise popped out about a quarter-inch and I panicked, forgetting the combination Bruchmuller had provided. The pain in my punctured finger was nothing compared to my heart beating so hard that I thought it might thump itself right through my rib cage.

"Are you okay, Mr. James?" the colonel asked from behind.

"The far block on the right," Anisa reminded me with a whisper. The fear abated slightly; the instructions were coming back to me. "I— I'm fine. I just needed a second."

The android gripped a thick strap that wound around my back and braced its legs on the steps. Even though it was under orders to let me be the one to disarm the tomb, it was still poised to protect me. I believed it might be fast enough to save me too—just maybe.

The block furthest to the right slid into the brick and made a mechanical noise. I pressed the next block in. Then the next block. After four from the right were depressed, I selected the second from the left, the first from the left, and the fifth from the left. I went back to the first square and pressed it again, pushing it deeper into the wall, my finger disappearing almost up to my knuckle. It clicked.

There was a sound of escaping gas as the faux-brick wall slipped to the side and opened up to a near-dustless chamber that was not much bigger than a large walk-in closet. LED lights silently came to life, pushing out the darkness and illuminating the Millennial crypt in a sickly light. Fiber-optic cables and electrical tubing fed from the walls to the metal sarcophagus in the center of the room. There was little space to walk around it, but I managed to squeeze into the room and toward the head of the clear plastic chamber. Colonel Colochi followed, along with Anisa and Sergeant Flores.

Bruchmuller mentioned that a self-loading rack containing the three drugs was mounted on the upper-left-hand side of the sarcophagus. Even within the sealed environment, a fine layer of dust obscured the plastic window, and I automatically wiped away the film and peered inside. What I saw made me do a double take and rub at the window frantically.

My skin crawled, my jaw dropped, and tunnel vision set in as I stared into the sarcophagus.

"Mr. James, what's wrong? What do you have there?"

I frantically searched for clamps or buttons or anything that would open the see-through shielding. I sliced my finger on a sharp edge but ignored the streaking blood as I tore at the chamber in frustration.

"Help me! Help me open this damned thing!"

"Calm down, Martin." Anisa grabbed for my hand.

The voices became indistinguishable as I began weeping and sobbing like a child.

"Mira aquí!"

"Hay una mujer dentro . . ."

Lying there in the Millennial sarcophagus, her eyes closed, was Amara.

Chapter 56

April 19, 2126. One hundred four years after I was injected by Dr. Bruchmuller with the Tardus drug, I stood over the still form of my older daughter, Amara, as she lay sleeping. When we found her in the crypt, I begged them to wake her. Colonel Colochi, Sergeant Flores, even Anisa all ignored my pleading.

They dragged me clawing and screaming from the hole in the ground as Anisa removed the rectangular rack from the crypt's machinery. She opened the metal box, quickly inspected the rows of thin metal vials within, then closed it back up. Once Anisa was finished with her task, the soldiers helped me remove my daughter and bring her to the transport.

"Anisa, give me the Remedium," I commanded.

"I am sorry, Martin, but I have strict instructions to protect the Millennial drugs at all costs. Nothing is to be touched until all three drugs are synthesized effectively."

"There are handfuls of vials in there!" I shouted. "Give me one of them!"

Colonel Colochi put his hand on my shoulder. "Mr. James, we need you to sit down. It's going to be a bumpy—"

"Give it to me! That's for my daughter!" I grabbed at Anisa, who held the box fast against its side. Even without the colonel and two other soldiers yanking me in the opposite direction, I could tell it was futile to fight with Anisa. It didn't care.

The Salus launched into the air, skimming the trees as we made our way back to the Governance. I watched Anisa stuff the precious drugs into a backpack and strap it to its back. Damned machine.

Amara was secured on a litter near the nose of the plane, and it was there that I knelt for hours, holding her cold, lifeless hand. Thoughts reeled as I tried to come up with any explanation as to why

W Lawrence

Amara would be there, but the only ones that made sense were too painful to consider, so I waited.

Syncing Forward

Chapter 57

That was six months ago—or a couple of hours ago. One of us awake, the other asleep, both of us syncing forward. Always sinking, always sinking. Back in Panama, nobody was giving me the answers I needed about the Remedium drug, about when it would be available. I needed to interact like a normal human being, to get answers from Vergas, to get answers from Bruchmuller. I struggled to leave Amara's side for my dosage of radiation, afraid that when I returned she would be gone. My child was alive, but how, I didn't know. Hesitantly I requested the Accelerate treatment and waited.

Anisa and four armed security men brought me back to see Dieterich Bruchmuller's quarters, and once again the two of us met in the short window provided by our simultaneous synchronizations. The man was expecting me, as he had set out tea and two chairs on opposite sides of the table.

"Welcome back, Mr. James. The sentiment may be one-sided, but I am happy to see you alive. Please sit. I am sure you have many questions." Bruchmuller gestured to the empty chair.

"You son of a bitch, what did you do to my daughter?" I hissed, stepping forward.

One of the security officers got between us and held up his hand, pleading in broken English, "*Por favor*, Señor James, no start a fight." I looked and saw that another security officer had his hand on his sidearm. Anisa stood close by at attention in a rigid, artificial manner. No doubt it could pounce on either of us before the guards could even react to anything me or Bruchmuller could try on each other. Oh, how desperately I wanted to throttle this monster, but it quickly dawned on me that my usefulness to the SNC, to the Renascentia program, had drawn to a close. With the Millennial drugs safely in their possession, I had nothing left to give these people. Neither did my sleeping daughter.

I sat carefully in the chair and looked squarely at Bruchmuller through the wisps of steam in the teacups. I repeated, "What did you do to Amara?"

"I saved her," he answered. "I saved her from certain death."

"You're lying. You kidnapped her."

"Is that your professional opinion, Mr. James, or are you just lashing out at me?" He took a sip of his tea and set it down. "I was captured by the Department of Homeland Security shortly after we destroyed Innovo, but not before I was able to dose myself with the last vials of Tardus and Somnus in my possession, knowing full well they would never be able to draw them out of my system before they were absorbed. My body slowed, and I went to sleep. I was hoping that I would be rescued from the morgue and found by one of the other members in our cell. But that didn't happen. After injecting you, the secret was out.

"I awoke in a dark room, who knew for how long, kept away from any sunlight, clocks, or calendars. Homeland Security interrogated me at length, but I found out quickly they only had the ability to—synchronize, I believe you call it—to synchronize me for short periods of time. Outlasting them was easy to do.

"But then I met a young DHS agent by the name of Amara James. The face, the name, the mannerisms—I knew who she was from the outset. She was part of the interrogation team, but it was she who broke me out of Walter Reed's secret underground facility. I made a deal with her: help my grandson get to his crypt and get me out of Walter Reed, and I would give her the Remedium drug."

It couldn't be true, and I told Bruchmuller as much. "Even if Amara could have pulled off something like that, she would have told me."

"Well, I'm sorry to be the one to say this, Mr. James, but she was afraid to tell you. She was afraid to tell anyone except me and my colleagues."

Syncing Forward

"The news said Amara died in an explosion. There was a funeral—"

"Closed casket, no doubt," Bruchmuller surmised.

"There was a body! Bella had to go to the morgue."

"Let me guess. Burned? Undoubtedly one of the pursuing agents."

"No. I refuse to believe it. Amara wouldn't have turned her back on her family. She never would have put Bella and me through hell like that."

"To obtain the Remedium? To synchronize you permanently? To save her father from a life of torment?" Bruchmuller leaned over the table and enunciated each word perfectly. "She was willing to do anything. A dedicated child is nothing to be ashamed of. I'm surprised at your reaction, Mr. James."

A memory of my last meeting with Amara came rushing to the surface of my consciousness. Amara was on the phone out by the lab in Pennsylvania, talking to some unknown person.

"Yes, I told you I would be there by tonight. Yes, alone! Just relax. Listen, I need to go."

Dear God, she hadn't been planning just some meeting with the Millennial terrorists but with Bruchmuller's grandson. Was that why she was furious with Bella for synchronizing me at the time? The puzzle pieces started to fit together quickly: the call from Amara's partner, her insight into the Millennial group, the closed casket, the letter left for Ivan. Every little phrase she had uttered streamed into my brain.

"I am the number-one expert on Millennial in the United States..."

"I've turned down three promotions to keep my field investigation going..."

"Mods are deadly..."

"There are far worse things than Millennial out there..."

I dropped my face into my hands, my heart aching, the shock setting in. It was true—all of it. "My daughter is not a terrorist!" I growled.

"Neither are we," Bruchmuller countered. "We are just men and women who dared to do the right thing when nobody else would. Just like Amara."

My thoughts ran wild. I did this to her. I had pressed her to find the Remedium. I encouraged her. Amara told Bernard that Millennial was responsible for who she became, but it wasn't true. It was me. I destroyed her life.

But there was one mystery that I couldn't get my head wrapped around, one thing that made no sense to me even if Amara had joined Millennial. I straightened myself up and looked at Bruchmuller, whose visage was strangely compassionate. "Doctor," I asked, "if this is true, why did Amara stay in the crypt? Why was it me who had to open it?"

"It was keyed to your daughter's blood, and by design it was keyed to yours," Bruchmuller corrected. "You can disagree with our methods, and you can hate me for what I've done, but trust me when I say Millennial has always been focused on the preservation of the family. Even our crypts were keyed to be opened by immediate family members."

"Why didn't you just tell me? Send me a message? Anything?"

"And risk the message being intercepted? Amara and I were on the run, Mr. James. We went to the cemetery to get the Remedium drug, but your daughter knew we were being pursued by her former colleagues. It was her plan to hide in the crypts—not mine—and to wait several months so that everyone stopped looking for us in Charleston. They would think they lost our trail. I showed her what to do, how to set the calendar so that she would wake her at a specific date, but we were hurried, and she must have made an error. Or maybe the autodosing machine wasn't functioning properly. It's possible, I suppose. I set out for the next crypt in the next town over, but was recaptured before I could reach it."

Syncing Forward

Bruchmuller finished explaining how nobody knew what he and Amara had planned besides him. Homeland Defense had placed him in a detention facility for years following his recapture, and there was no getting the message out. Innovo never shared the Accelerate technology with the government, and they didn't dare use the Pause again. He remained in the custody of the United States government till it collapsed and was eventually traded to the Chinese in exchange for technology to fight Conference.

"So you see, Mr. James, you helped Millennial save humanity," he summarized. "You and your daughter. It appears you have lived up to your name. Be proud of yourself that there is hope for us yet."

This final revelation was a gut punch, and I felt a panicky need to escape from Dieterich Bruchmuller's presence. I finally took a gulp of the tea in front of me to wet my dried-out throat. It was tepid and bitter. After setting it down, I stood and walked uneasily toward the door. Anisa shadowed me, and I heard it politely excuse itself from Dieterich Bruchmuller's presence. Both security officers stepped out of the way, and one opened the door with the touch of his palm.

"Mr. James," Bruchmuller called after me before I left, "can you do one thing for me?"

I stopped and waited, listening, my back turned to the doctor.

"Your daughter rescued my grandson and rescued me, but I feel as if I failed her in some respects. Please tell her I tried, and that I am sorry."

I walked out the door and heard it shut behind me, Anisa's footsteps padding lightly behind me as I went.

Chapter 58

Amara's room was on the far end of the Atlantic Cargo Ground Control facility, but I remembered how to get there. Besides, it wasn't like Anisa was going to let me wander. The companion increased its pace so that it could walk beside me, but when it tried to hold my hand, I pulled away.

"Martin, are you not happy with what Dr. Bruchmuller has told you?"

"No."

"But your daughter is alive. And the doctor is right in that your efforts have made the Renascentia mission possible."

I didn't want to admit any part in Bruchmuller's vindication. Instead, I informed Anisa that I wanted lunch in Amara's room.

"You are aware that Amara will not receive a dose of Remedium before you sync forward again, yes?"

"I'm aware," I answered coldly. "I still don't understand why. There should be plenty."

Anisa held a door open for me as we stepped outside to follow the railing to the next building up. "Doctor Huang believes that we should hold on to the largest sample possible until they go into full production. He posted an update twenty-six minutes ago saying that the second trial shows promise. If all goes well, we should have conclusive answers within the next four to six months. If they take Dr. Bruchmuller's offer to assist, we could be looking at a faster turnaround still. Of course there are security concerns, but Chief Vergas believes we can mitigate those."

We passed a group of agitated Chinese men and women who were chattering about who knew what as we went to the building where Amara was kept. I looked at them inquisitively, and curiosity got the better of me. "Okay, what were they yipping about?"

Syncing Forward

"A new intelligence report that shows Conference has converted approximately one-fifth of all life-forms on earth down to the genetic level. Finding unmodified genetic samples for the Renascentia ships is becoming increasingly difficult. Last week they found tainted soil samples in a shipment bound for Adelante Space Port. They believe that the nanos found in the soil were part of an elaborate self-replicating surveillance system. It appears that Conference may not be as neutral about our launching as originally thought."

"Dandy," I mumbled. I thought of the sheng ji boy in Charleston ripping the rib from the soldier's chest the way a child might pull a string of licorice from a candy bag. Then I thought of Victoria. I wondered if she was still alive, if she would recognize me, if she would even care who I was or that her aunt was alive, or if she would pull me apart like a plastic doll. Amara never got to meet Victoria, never knew her when she just a brilliant, loving child learning about the world. I think she would have been a good aunt to her. If she had not disappeared, maybe things would have been different. Maybe.

We made it to the guest facility, a sunbathed room with a large balcony that overlooked a stunning scenic view of palm trees and white sand beaches. It was the kind of place that you would vacation in just to stand there and enjoy the warm breeze blowing in from the ocean while you gazed at the endless horizon. My gaze was fixed on my daughter, lying on a bed in the center of the room, her eyes closed and her hands at her sides. While she looked dead, I knew that she was merely sleeping through the years, her cells slowed to a fraction of their normal cycle while the rest of the world moved on.

I sat in a solid white chair at her bedside with my right hand on Amara's cold arm. Anisa sat next to me and tried to hold my hand again. I didn't push the android away this time. The warmth of Anisa's touch was so strange. How could somebody who was alive feel so dead, while a machine could feel so human?

Anisa scanned my face with her eyes. "You appear worried to me, Martin."

"I have a lot to worry about."

"Are you concerned that they won't be able to duplicate the antidote for you and Amara?"

"Yes. But there's more to it than that. Let's say Dr. Huang and his team are successful, and they make swimming pools full of these drugs. What then? What happens to my daughter? To me? I highly doubt they'll save seats on the Renascentia ships for us."

"Chief Vergas made it very clear that you and Amara are welcome on the mission, provided we can launch in time, of course."

"Yeah, we'll see."

I pondered how the chain of events that had led us to this time and place might have been the single factor that allowed the Renascentia Project to succeed. Would they have developed the chemo-preservation technology on their own? Or convinced Millennial to assist them? Neither solution seemed likely, and, in all probability, they would have failed in the looming shadow of Conference. As the world's population died by the billions, the new dominant force would have simply overwhelmed the rest of humanity.

I remembered Father Gutierrez reassuring me when we went to visit Bella's gravestone. *"Of this I have no doubt, however: there is a plan for your life. God doesn't make mistakes."* Was all of this Providence? My pushing the Bruchmuller interview too far, Amara's obsession with curing me, Bruchmuller's remorse—was it all meant to be? Was I going to be a proud figure in humanity's future history, selflessly sacrificing his life for the perpetuation of our species?

I sat quietly for a long time before I spoke again. "I'm ashamed, Anisa."

"Ashamed of what, Martin?"

"Ashamed of the actions that brought me to this place. Ashamed that I wasn't a good enough father, a good enough son. Ashamed that I drove my daughter to destroy her life with the small hope that she could save me. And now . . I don't know what to say when she wakes up."

Syncing Forward

Its machine mind did everything it could to comprehend how to react to my sadness while looking sympathetic. "Your daughter is alive. If all goes well with the drug synthesis, you will finally have what you have been searching for all these years. I don't understand your reaction."

"Nah, I didn't think you would." The sun beamed warm and comforting on my skin through the skylight.

Anisa posed a pleasant smile. "Would you care for a walk on the beach?"

"I'm inclined just sit and wait here, if it's all the same to you."

There was no profound response, no deep truth to stir my soul. Anisa simply said, "I will wait with you, Martin."

And so I sit here, waiting for the seconds and years to tick by, wondering if there would be anything left for my daughter to wake up to, wondering if she will awaken on a whole new world, or in the depths of space, or to her own world transformed by its new masters. Perhaps Amara will never wake, slumbering through the centuries quietly, motionless, as I watch over her.

Epilogue

Was I awake? The nightmares finally stopped at least. All over, my body tingled with pins and needles. Yes, I had to be awake. I could hear the fan humming in this godforsaken crypt, but it somehow sounded deeper, fainter, further away. It was cold now too. Very different from how the Tardus and Somnus drugs made me feel when they first coursed through my veins.

The tightness in my chest was still there from the body blow I took in Charleston. The son of a bitch probably broke a rib or two, although I busted both his knees and left him wailing in the alley, so I guess he came out on the worse end of that deal. Truth was, I wished I could have avoided that fight. I wished I could have avoided a lot of things. I burned every bridge, lied to every friend, hid every detail from my family.

The Millennial crypt's timer must have dosed me with the Remedium drug. When I tried to look around, I found my eyelids were dry and heavy, as if I had fallen asleep with four days' worth of eye shadow on. When they finally opened, I could barely see anything except a wall of black and a host of twinkling lights. Why were there lights in the crypt?

I wasn't in the crypt. There was no plastic sarcophagus surrounding me. Instead, there was a giant window above me and on the other side a curtain of night decorated by thousands of flashing stars. Warmth pressed against my left palm, and I realized somebody was holding my hand. The touch was accompanied by a soft, masculine, familiar voice.

"Shhh, you're okay. You're okay."

My instinct was to bend that hand forward ninety degrees before applying pressure to the first and second metacarpals, immobilizing the wrist and opening the body and throat to follow-up blows. In fact, I gripped his hand firmly and used it as an anchor to sit

Syncing Forward

up in a flash, but that voice was comforting and reminded me of when I was a kid.

It wasn't Bruchmuller or the agents or anyone who would harm me. Even through blurry vision I could make out his face, the face that hadn't changed in twenty years. He wrapped his other arm around me and held me like the child I was inside.

"Daddy?" I whispered. My voice would do nothing more.

"You're okay now. I've got you," he said, comforting me.

My eyes were too dry to shed tears, my throat to dry to sob. All I could manage was to grab him around the neck and hold my father. How had he found me? Where was I? What happened to the Millennial drugs I secured? Did he have them?

I tried to speak, but all that escaped was a parched cough.

"Drink this. You've been asleep for a long time."

He gave me a bottle with a straw, and I gulped down the oily liquid till I felt my voice might return. Trying once again I asked, "Where is the Remedium?"

"We got it, Amara. Don't worry. You did it, kiddo." My father pushed a smile through his grieving expression.

I exhaled and shivered. Gripping his hand in mine, I nodded and felt the tiny bit of strength my body still contained disappear. I nuzzled my head into his shoulder and shuddered as it dawned on me my plan had actually worked. The wait was finally over. I may have booked a one-way ticket to hell to do it, but I saved my father. Maybe now he could salvage a normal life. Bella too. Maybe all of us could.

When I looked up from his comforting hug, my glances tried to lock in on anything that might be familiar. Nothing was. The room was oddly shaped. The computer strange. The hum I heard when I first woke was coming from all around us. "Where are we?" I asked.

My father brushed the hair out of my eyes and back behind my ear. "We're going home."

W Lawrence

Acknowledgments

A huge thank you to C. S. Lakin (author of *A Thin Film of Lies* and *Intended for Harm*) and Rachel Starr Thomson (author of *The Seventh World Trilogy* and *The Thirteenth* series) for editing my book and never falling into the trap of telling me what I wanted to hear.

A special thanks to Lasse Perälä, who painted the cover for *Syncing Forward*.

Many kind regards to Richard Zacks (author of *Pirate Hunter*), Steven R. Boyett (author of *Mortality Bridge*), Jeff Towson (author of *What Would Ben Graham Do Now?*), and Brian Niskala (author of *Rhinehoth*) who gave me invaluable advice and encouragement.

My gratitude to friends Brad E., Dave S., Erik M., Jessica T., Jose P., Jyoti S., Matt B., and Ron S. for helping me along the way . . . even when they didn't know they were helping.

Thanks to my dad, who gave me a love of reading. Thanks to my mom, who encouraged my writing before I knew I enjoyed it. Most of all, thanks to my wife, who is not only my biggest champion, but who didn't smother me in my sleep after I failed to clean anything in the house for the past two years.

Contact

I hope you enjoyed reading *Syncing Forward*. Sadly, the dystopian world within these pages is not only possible but, in my opinion, represents a best-case scenario for humanity. Regardless of how outlandish the geopolitical conditions or technology may sound, most are based on real research, demographics, and actual historical trends. I described the world how I believe it could be if more of us don't start asking "Have we gone too far?"

Comments? Questions? I would love to hear from you. Please e-mail me at syncingforward@gmail.com. You can also find *Syncing Forward* on Facebook, Twitter, or on the web at:

http://syncingforward.com.

The world is what we make of it.

W. Lawrence

Printed in Great Britain
by Amazon.co.uk, Ltd.,
Marston Gate.